Through the Aftermath

A Post-Apocalyptic Anthology

Edited by Shawn Schuster

This book is a work of fiction. Any references to historical events, real people, or real places are used fictitiously. Other names, characters, places, and events are products of the author's imagination, and any resemblance to actual events, places, names, or persons, is entirely coincidental.

Text copyright © 2022 by Shawn Schuster

All rights reserved. For information regarding reproduction in total or in part, contact the editor at shawn@shawnschuster.com

Cover illustration by Shawn Schuster

ISBN: 978-1-7777252-3-5

BISAC:

FIC003000   **FICTION** / Anthologies (multiple authors)

FIC028040   **FICTION** / Science Fiction / Collections & Anthologies

FIC028070   **FICTION** / Science Fiction / Apocalyptic & Post-Apocalyptic)

ACKNOWLEDGMENT IS MADE FOR permission to print the following material:

"Atomic Death and Taxes" © 2022 by M.P. Fitzgerald

"A Father's Love" © 2022 by Scott M. Baker

"Fear in a Handful of Dust" © 2022 by T.S. Beier

"Lost Souls" © 2021 by Stefan de Koster

"Shade" © 2022 by Shawn Schuster

"A Very Zombie Thanksgiving" © 2022 by K.E. Radke

"Beyond the Walls" © 2022 by Maira Dawn

"The Memory Store" © 2021 by Mandy Shunnarah

"Therion" © 2022 by Cassandra Stevenson

"Raiding the Broken World" © 2021 by Koen ter Horst

"Going Silent" © 2021 by Jeremy Zentner

"Winds of Change" © 2022 by David A. Simpson

"Life (Love?) in the Time of Crazy" © 2021 by I.M. Captive

"Eve" © 2021 by P.S. Shuller

"Not a Raccoon Stealing Doritos in the Basement" © 2022 by E.A. Field

"Firestorms" © 2022 by V.J. Dunn

"Spaceman" © 2021 by James Shortridge

"Tanner's Apocalypse" © 2022 by Cal Brett

"Edge of Survival" © 2021 by Kyla Stone, Originally published in Origins of Honor. Reprinted by permission of the author.

Contents

Introduction	IX
1. Atomic Death and Taxes	1
2. A Father's Love	12
3. Fear in a Handful of Dust	29
4. Lost Souls	41
5. Shade	58
6. A Very Zombie Thanksgiving	70
7. Beyond the Walls	86
8. The Memory Store	105
9. Therion	118
10. Raiding the Broken World	124
11. Going Silent	140
12. Winds of Change	161
13. Life (Love?) in The Time of Crazy	175
14. Eve	197
15. Not a Raccoon Stealing Doritos in the Basement	214
16. Firestorms	228
17. Spaceman	245

18.	Tanner's Apocalypse	264
19.	Edge of Survival	280

Dedicated to the Memory of Peter Meredith

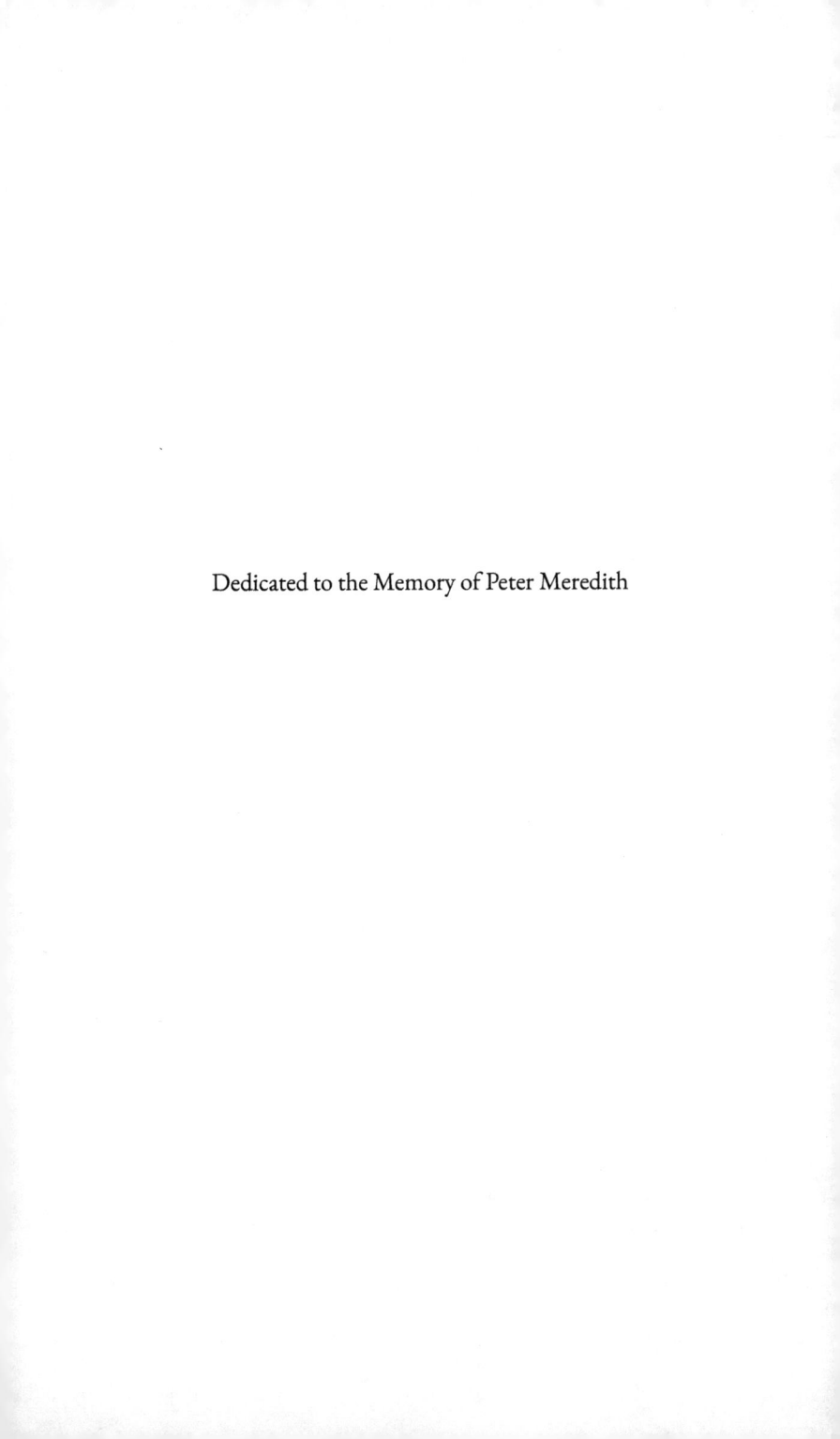

Introduction

There's just something about the wasteland.

Post-apocalyptic stories are like nothing else. We're drawn to them for reasons we can't quite explain. Whether it's the guzzoline-thirsty wasteland of The Road Warrior, the robot-infested bleak future of Terminator, or Fallout's dark-humored charm of a destroyed 1950's world-of-tomorrow, we just can't get enough. I've heard people theorize that we love these stories because they're indicative of "survival against-all-odds" or because we're drawn to the concept of a world "devoid of the laws and structure of our modern day-to-day lives." Honestly, I think it's because these kinds of stories, when written WELL, are just freakin' AWESOME and linger in our imaginations in a way most stories don't. It can take all the best elements of fiction, horror, and sci-fi, and wrap them into a wonderful deck of cards that are very much stacked against you. It's survival at survival's best. Again, we just can't get enough, can we?

Well, if you're reading this right now, I'm guessing you can't. And that definitely makes you one of us. So welcome, my friend. You're in good company. And you're about to take your first step into a new set of post-apocalyptic worlds we just know you'll enjoy.

If I were to tell you this book you're now reading was 15 years in the making, it would definitely be the truth. I met Shawn back in 2007, when he and I were both doing MMORPG podcasts. We immediately recognized we both had a passion for post-apocalyptic... well, EVERYTHING. It only made sense to combine efforts, and thus the "Through the Aftermath" podcast was born. 15 years and nearly 70 podcast episodes later, we've continued this passion project and have become friends with a wonderful world of post-apocalyptic listeners and fans, all with the same passion for these stories as we have. It only made sense that it would evolve into other things. In particular, Shawn has always had a specific love for post-apocalyptic short stories, and always dreamed of putting together an anthology of some great ones.

This book you're now reading is the culmination of that dream.

Shawn has pooled together some incredibly talented post-apocalyptic writers and put together an anthology of stories that we know you'll absolutely *devour*. (And was that a deliberate zombie pun? Why, yes. Yes it was.)

And these stories are not just your run-of-the-mill post-apocalyptic stories—these are incredibly unique ones at that. Oh yes. We think you're going to enjoy these.

So, dear Survivor, sit back and enjoy. Keep your seat belts buckled and your hands in the vehicle at all times. And never mind the raiders on our left. Shawn's driving this bus and he'll keep you safe. And you're about to see some scenery that you won't believe.

In the meantime, "Stay alive out there."

- Jonathan Morris
Co-host, Through the Aftermath Podcast

Atomic Death and Taxes

Written by M.P. Fitzgerald

M.P. FITZGERALD IS AN author who does not think you have the gumption to read a post-apocalyptic parody where the IRS survives nuclear Armageddon. In fact, he dares you to head over to https://mpfitzgerald.art where you can grab his novel, *A Happy Bureaucracy*, for free. Don't be a coward, and eat irradiated SPAM.

If he could read, which he couldn't, he would see that the ancient can of food that he had opened was called Vienna Sausages. Oh, there was a picture of the meat on the can; he knew what he was getting into. But to appreciate the full effect of the false promise that was on the label was to at least have the semi-pretentious name of the product in mind when you opened it. The decades-old meat that he now looked at was not like the carefully cut pieces of hot dog that lay delicately under the yellowed text of the label. No, what Spider was greeted with was a pink, uniform sludge. What he was about to eat was an affront to the word "food."

Spider was hiding. Though most people in the United Wastes were hiding most of the time, this particular detail was important because it meant that he could light no fires. The offensive, decades-old sludge in front of him could not be cooked. The smoke would be seen from miles away; the light of the fire would alert others to his presence. If his pursuers were not nearby, if he had actually escaped them for the last time, there was still the ever-present threat of slavers, raiders, and the high-octane-fueled nightmares of land pirates. The unfortunate truth of the apocalypse was that everyone was out to get you. That, and the fact that being a "foodie" was a terribly misaligned hobby.

He sighed deeply, feeling the dead dust of the abandoned bank that he was squatting in cake the inside of his nostrils. He had to let it go. Even if he could light a fire, there was no amount of cooking, no amount of uplifting that would make the pink sludge any better. He pinched his nose, closed his eyes, and downed the can of "meat" like it was an especially hateful shot of whiskey. A vague and menacing taste of chicken and burnt tin assaulted his senses. He had been shot, stabbed, burnt, and beaten in his life. He had lost his ring finger to an especially salty ex, and he had once nearly bled out under an uncaring sun. Spider had been through some shit, but these Vienna Sausages were top of the list for unpleasant torture.

The can of food was surprisingly filling.

It had to be. It was his last.

With the deed—no, the *sin*—complete, Spider leaned against the concrete wall and sat down. There was time to sleep, hell, there was always time to sleep in the post-nuclear holocaust of the United Wastes... but could he risk it? He had only a single bullet left. The Enforcer he had killed did not go down easily. He had emptied most of his revolver before the bastard finally went down. If his agent was still alive, if she was still out there, would one be enough? Did a single bullet matter if she got the jump on him while he slept? There were no good answers.

Spider was always in trouble. This did not make him special, but selling drugs in the United Wastes presented its own special kind of trouble. Deals went sour, junkies robbed him at gunpoint, and rival dealers were always trying to off him. These were troubles that he was at least used to. Now he was being pursued by the largest, most well-equipped gang in the land: the IRS.

He did not know how they found him, he did not know how they knew that he was "self-employed," but it did not matter. They, just like all of the other rival gangs, wanted a cut of his business. And just like everyone else, they came armed.

He was able to escape them unharmed. Once the Enforcer was dead, the Auditor fled. But there was no telling when she would come back or who was going to be with her when she did. So Spider sought refuge. Spider hid. He holed up in the first ruined building in the irradiated city that he could find. If he knew how to read he would know that he had picked an old bank. He had no context for the paper money covered in dust that surrounded him. He had only ever used the stuff as toilet paper. In the United Wastes, you got paid with bullets or canned food, which meant that poor Spider was now dirt poor.

He fought off the creeping allure of slumber and ignored the rest that his full belly demanded from him. Still, it was a losing battle, and the moment he decided to give in, she announced herself.

"Hello?!" she said before she saw him. "This is the IRS!"

Fuck.

Spider reached for his revolver.

The woman turned the corner, leading her movements with her fallen Enforcer's shotgun. Their eyes met. Neither moved.

She was not tall. She was not menacing. There was little about her that suggested that she had been living in the same apocalypse. While Spider was decked out in coyote leathers and armor made of car tires—while he was caked in dirt, dust, and dried blood—she was clean. Glasses lay unbroken on her sharp nose, and a collared shirt and tie reflected light off of its stark white surface. Spider, he wore mismatched boots and scavenged pants from a victim of the nuclear war. This woman wore black ironed slacks and flats. To Spider, the stark contrast of the dusty and mostly destroyed bank that surrounded them to her clean and professional appearance was not just unsettling, but bat-shit insane and terrifying. And though her narrow shoulders would not carry the kick of the massive shotgun well, the short distance between them meant that she would get a kill.

He kept his finger on the trigger and his eyes on hers.

"We sent you several notices about your unpaid taxes," the woman said. "You have had plenty of time to take care of them. How do you plan on paying them?" Business was not just how she dressed, apparently.

"W-what?" said Spider not eloquently.

The woman's shoulders fell. She sighed audibly. "Your *taxes*. How are you paying them?"

"What notices? I ain't met ya before today!"

"Fuck you Spider. We sent them by priority mail through the postal service months ago. Stop playing dumb. *How are you going to pay your taxes?*"

Spider blinked. Hard. He did what no one in the United Wastes should, he took his eyes off of his enemy and looked around him. Half of the bank was in rubble. There were more irradiated skeletons on the earth than living people to meet. The world had ended, and what replaced it was savage, brutal, and dying.

"What the fuck is the postal service?" Spider asked.

"A place that has *seriously* dropped the ball," the woman replied. "Now, how the fuck are you paying your debts?" she continued with extra vinegar in her voice while she scratched the tip of her nose with her middle finger. The foul gesture was one he had only seen one other woman do before...

"Susan?!" said Spider as phantom pain ran down his missing finger. "Holy shit! Is that you?"

"You're kidding," the tax woman replied. "Did you seriously not recognize me?!"

He stared at the clean, professional, and beautiful woman in front of him. "Absolutely not," he said.

Susan lowered her shotgun by a few degrees, a courtesy that Spider did not mirror, especially now that he knew that she was his ex. She shifted her weight and rolled her eyes. "We spent three years selling drugs together in these wastes!" she said with a cocked eyebrow.

"Yeah," Spider replied with no charm, "but you looked like shit then."

Her shotgun was raised and pointed in an instant. "I'll take that as some sort of backward compliment," she said.

"You still look like shit," he lied.

She cocked a slug into her chamber.

Dust motes settled in the cruel light as the silence stretched thin as taffy.

Spider had taste, he could cook, if he had the right tools he could wizard a dead raccoon into pâté. But he was no educated man, and beyond cursing, his wit was as dull as a religious pot-luck. Some things just took him longer.

"You sold me out to the IRS!" he screamed, taffy silence broken.

"No shit, Spider."

"Well, you shouldn't have!"

"You left me at the altar—"

"You *still* mad 'bout that?"

She did not answer immediately. Her eyes still spoke of pain. He hated those eyes. "No," she said, her eyes disagreed. "I'm better off that you did. I want you to know that, Spider. I'm a better person without you, and the IRS is the best thing that has happened to me."

"Oh?"

"They got running water, good food, and people are decent there, Spider, something you know nothing about being." She gave him her half-smirk, just another taunt in her bottomless arsenal against him. He did not challenge her on that last point, however. She was right. She adjusted her glasses with her middle finger, sure to let it linger just so that he saw the gesture. "I didn't even know I needed these glasses until the IRS," she said, "I'm even *seeing* better since I left you Spider."

"Since I left *you*," Spider corrected. He instantly regretted doing so. Those damn eyes again. He left their gaze, better to look at her trigger finger anyway.

"They really did not have to offer me much to sell you out," she said.

"Oh? Running water, good food, and dorky glasses were enough to sell your soul, huh?"

She laughed, a sound once sonorous to his heart was now like broken glass in a blender. "You are worth so much less than the luxury of running water, Spider," she said, half-smirk wild. "They only had to offer me a *job*, said I could have it if I got a 'small business owner' like yourself to pay your dues."

"You're a bitch."

"Your cooking sucks."

Daggers! His trigger finger itched like a swarm of pissed-off bed bugs.

"Now," she said, "how are you paying your goddamn taxes?"

He never wanted to give her the satisfaction even when they were lovesick puppies selling crystal to cannibals. Now she was an ex that had gone the extra mile and betrayed him to the biggest gang in the modern Armageddon. He *absolutely* did not want to admit any of his shortcomings. But Susan had always been smarter than him. Truth be told: she kept an eye on the numbers and inventory when he made a deal. She was not just a business partner then, she was the business. She could read and she understood math beyond her fingers and toes. He would never admit it aloud, but her mind scared him more than an irradiated bear on fire. And now that mind held a shotgun and was motivated by a heart that was not merely bruised but shattered. What choice did he have?

"What uh..." he stumbled, "what *exactly* is taxes?"

"You're an idiot."

"You gonna tell me or taunt me?"

She rolled her eyes. "See all this money?" She asked pointing at what he thought was toilet paper. "Used to be that people got paid in this stuff, traded for food, drugs, you name it. Every time they made money they would give a portion of that to the government which would build things like roads." She shifted her weight once more. She knew that he wasn't getting it. "Give the IRS some of your stuff so that everyone gets nice stuff too."

"Why the fuck would I do *that?!*" Spider asked in earnest.

"Because it benefits others, Spider."

"Who cares? It benefits me not to benefit others. I earned my stuff."

"Look," Susan said, "running water, good food—I *know* you like good food, Spider—these are things we can all have after the IRS rebuilds society. They can't do that if everyone is a selfish self-aggrandizing ass like you."

Spider squinted at the woman he had scorned. There was more going on here than just her hurt eyes. She believed in what she was saying.

"You drank their Kool-Aid!" he said, his voice frayed in anger.

"Yeah, I did, they got grape and cherry flavor there, Spider. It's awesome."

"What?"

"They got real Kool-Aid in the bunker."

"I thought Kool-Aid was just a thing people said for like cults and stuff," he said. He had honestly never considered that it was an actual thing that you could drink.

Susan shook her head. "Spider, help the IRS by doing your *duty* and Kool-Aid can be a thing again."

They swallowed their breaths in arrested silence. It was dumb, but she was serious. She had every reason to kill him where he sat, but she would let him walk away alive for the *slight* chance of a civilized world.

"Fine," he said deflating his shoulders and lowering his revolver. "The IRS wants money, take all the money here," he said motioning toward the scattered bills that lay on the dusty floor of the bank. "They can have it all."

"No."

"What do you mean *no?!*" he cried in bafflement.

"You are missing the point. The money has to come from what you have *earned*, Spider. This only works if we pitch in our own stuff."

"That's bullshit!" he said, revolver back up. "You always been high on your horse with morsels!"

"*Morals*," Susan corrected. "Morals not *morsels!* God! You're such an idiot, Spider!"

"Whatever! I ain't got no money anyways and you know it!"

"I know what you got," Susan said, half-smirk ablaze. "The IRS, see, they're smart, Spider. They know that things have changed. You think I have nice glasses and bitchin' Kool-Aid because people pay in money? These things were the payments. They know we barter in calories and bullets. They wouldn't hire me if you were some deadbeat target, Spider. I told them about our canned wienie stash."

"You bitch."

She ignored the jab. "I'm not even here for my share of our profits, Spider. How's *that* for some high horse morals? You pay up a portion of those wienies for a better future for all and I let you walk. We never have to see each other again."

He lowered his revolver to his hip. He'd be hard-pressed to admit that he ever wanted to see her again before now, but somehow the prospect of this being their last meeting still hurt. He hated her. But he also hated that she hated him. Hated himself for making her. Spider never believed in anything but the bite of his bullets. He didn't think that she had either. But here she was, preaching the very basic cornerstone of society to a man who wore coyote leathers and car tires. He could not give her what she wanted. But then again, he never could in the past either.

"I can't give you the canned food," he said, his voice peppered with guilt.

The shotgun erupted violence over her head. This was no warning shot, it was an exclamation to her rage, to her frustration. "HAND OVER THE FUCKING CANNED WIENIES!" she screamed. Her hands trembled. Plaster fell from the ceiling in chunks, joining the dust on the ground. She cocked the shotgun once more and pointed it at Spider's head. "Pay your goddamn taxes, Spider."

Spider kept his revolver at his hips. They both knew that he could make the shot from his position, but he did not want to anger her anymore by raising it. "I said I *can't*, not that I *won't*," he said. "I ate the last one just before you came in. They're gone. All of them. There are no more wienies from our stash."

She laughed. The action was twice as jarring as it was the first time. "I'm actually surprised," she said and continued to laugh. "Do you know that? Shit, Spider! I did not think that you could *possibly* disappoint me anymore. You are such an asshole."

He dared not to move. She met his eyes. "Fine, it's fine," she said. "You don't have to pay in wienies. They'll take bullets too. Give me your ammo and I'll be on my way."

"That's a death sentence," Spider said simply, betraying the hurt in his heart.

"I don't care," she replied.

Their eyes locked. He once found them so comforting. So beautiful. Now, all he saw was his own sins. Now he just saw the pain that he had inflicted on the one woman he never wanted to inflict harm upon.

That hurt was there even before he left her at the altar. He did not know exactly when they were filled with hurt, but it was at least a year before she stopped looking at him with excitement. But they didn't part. He hated her for it. Hated that she was a coward for never breaking it off even when they both knew that it was not working. He hated her forcing his hand. She made him the bad guy. And Spider? Well, he could play a pretty good bad guy if he had to. In fact, it came naturally to him.

Once, she would have risked her life for his and vice versa. Now, she did not even have the decency to shoot him herself. She would rather leave him defenseless in a cruel world and never think about him again. A coward, like always. Fine. What was that last part of their vows? Till death... *fucking irony*. He could play the bad guy. They bartered in calories or bullets.

She was faster than he remembered, but Spider paid his taxes…

A Father's Love

Written by Scott M. Baker

Scott M. Baker was born and raised in Everett, Massachusetts, and spent twenty-three years in northern Virginia working for the Central Intelligence Agency. He has traveled extensively through Europe, Asia, and the Middle East, many of the locations and cultures becoming incorporated in his stories. Scott is now retired and lives outside of Concord, New Hampshire, with his wife, his stepdaughter, and two cats who treat him as their human servant.

Scott is currently writing the *Nurse Alissa vs. the Zombies* and *The Chronicles of Paul* sagas, his latest zombie apocalypse series, as well as his paranormal series.

A sharp, icy wind blew down the street. It generated tiny whirlwinds that scooped up rubbish accumulated over the months, scattering it along the deserted sidewalks and depositing it with the rest of the litter when the wind died out. The gusts picked up again a few seconds later, spewing the debris even more. Piles of it gathered in doorways, gutters, and around the occasional corpse lying in the street.

The noise created by the wind covered the footsteps coming from the north and the crunching of shards of shattered glass under heavy boots. Not that anyone was still around to hear. Few people had lived past Day One and the following weeks.

Benjamin Denning was among the handful who had made it this far, though God only knew how. And why. Surviving this nightmare didn't mean living, only existing. Barely existing. Every day was a struggle to find food, water, and a safe place to spend the night, let alone maintain one's sanity. Denning probably would have placed the barrel of his shotgun against the roof of his mouth and pulled the trigger if he didn't need to stay alive to look after his son, Timmy.

Denning paused in front of a clothing store with one of its panes still intact and stared at his reflection, amazed at how he appeared. Jeans, military-style boots, and a leather bomber jacket. A scarf wrapped around his mouth, goggles protecting his eyes, and a camouflage Boonie hat. What still shocked him were his weapons: a Vepr-12 semi-automatic shotgun, a .40 Caliber Glock resting in a holster around his hip, and a Winchester 8.5-inch Bowie knife strapped to his right leg. Not like anything he would expect from a man who seven months ago earned his living as a CPA.

I guess it's true, he thought. *People adapt and do things they never thought possible to survive.*

A noise came from the alley a few yards ahead. It sounded like a metal garbage can being knocked over. Possibly animals; either rats or raccoons foraging for what little food hadn't already been picked clean by humans. Or it could be something far more dangerous.

Crouching to present a smaller target, Denning aimed the Vepr at the alley, ready to fire if necessary. Keeping his focus on the entrance, he leaned back and placed his forefinger across his lips, warning Timmy to remain quiet.

A rustling of paper and garbage continued for a few minutes then stopped, the scavenger obviously finding nothing edible. A shadow emerged, larger than that belonging to typical vermin. Denning moved his finger from the guard onto the trigger and applied pressure, hoping he would not have to waste ammo.

A Golden Retriever stuck its head around the corner of the alley wall. On seeing Denning, it stopped and cowered. Denning relaxed.

"It's okay, boy. Come here."

The dog backed up a few inches.

"Wait."

It stopped.

Denning placed the Vepr on the ground, then slowly reached into his jacket pocket and removed a stick of moldy cheese. He held it up for the dog to see. Its ears perked up.

"You want some, boy?"

Denning broke the seal and pulled down the plastic coating. Breaking off a quarter of the stick, he gently tossed it across the street. The chunk landed a few feet from the dog. It sniffed the air and, detecting the scent of food, warily moved out of the safety of the alley. Denning felt bad for it, wondering how the poor creature had survived so long. The Retriever was emaciated, its bones pushing against the skin. More than half its fur was missing, with what remained filthy and matted.

The dog kept its eyes on Denning the entire time. It bent its head and sniffed the cheese. Realizing it was food, the dog wolfed down the chunk, barely chewing before swallowing.

Denning broke off another quarter of the cheese. He whistled to get the dog's attention and tossed the chunk into the middle of the street. The dog hesitated.

"Come on, boy. You know you want it."

The dog limped over to the cheese. It kept its left hind leg raised, the appendage having suffered either a sprain or a break. When the dog reached the cheese, it sniffed it once before gulping it down. As the hungry creature ate, Denning broke the rest of the cheese in half.

"Don't say anything to scare it," he warned Timmy.

The Retriever finished the morsel and looked at Denning, hoping for more. Denning dropped one chunk two feet in front of him.

"I promise I won't hurt you."

Keeping his gaze locked on Denning, the dog inched closer. It paused near the cheese, stretched forward, snapped up the chunk, and retreated a yard to enjoy its treat. When it finished, Denning held out his left hand, the last piece of moldy cheese in his palm.

"Come on. It's all yours."

The Retriever approached slowly, frequently pausing to scope out the human. Denning urged him on. Finally, the dog abandoned its reservations and moved up to Denning, taking the last of the cheese. Denning slowly moved his hand above the dog's head and lightly petted it. The Retriever's tail wagged.

"You're a sweet thing."

Denning brought his right hand around too quickly for the Retriever to respond, drawing the razor-sharp blade of the Bowie knife across the animal's throat, slicing it almost to the spine. It let out a yelp. As it quickly bled out, the dog stared at Denning with a look of sadness, betrayal, and pain.

He petted the Retriever, his voice filled with regret. "I'm sorry, boy. Really. But we have to eat."

People adapt and do things they never thought possible to survive.

Ninety minutes later, Denning and Timmy were set up in the rear storeroom of a local hardware center. Denning had skinned, gutted, and started to roast the dog over a fire he had made himself. If anyone had told him a year ago he would develop such skills, Denning would have called them crazy. Sadly, he had used them many times since Day One on everything from rats and squirrels to, sadly, cats and dogs. It bothered him to kill animals, especially those he considered pets, but you had to do whatever was necessary to survive, no matter how uncomfortable.

Denning tested the meat with the tip of his hunting knife, pushing the blade in two inches. Blood flowed from the wound.

"It'll be a little while before we eat," he said to his son. "You must be hungry."

Timmy didn't respond, not that Denning expected him to. Timmy had said nothing since the death of his mother and older sister three months ago. Not that he could blame his son. Their deaths were horrifying. Their demise still haunted Denning.

Everything following Day One had been horrifying. Denning was uncertain how it came about because it happened so fast. Working sixty-plus hours a week to keep food on the table and a roof over his family's head gave him little time to watch television, and when he did, he tuned in to mindless reality shows or old movies. Never the news. Maybe others knew the end was coming. Maybe the government did as well. Not that it mattered. The world Denning had known fell part on that cataclysmic day.

Billions died on Day One. They were lucky. Over the next few weeks, it seemed as though society and the government were in a race to see which could collapse first. Social services such as the police, fire departments, and hospitals were overwhelmed and ground to a halt within days. Looting became rampant, only now for essentials such as food, water, medicine, weapons, and toilet paper rather than large screen TVs and Rolex watches. Once the stores had been stripped clean, those desperate to survive began raiding their neighbors for food.

Cities around the world were wracked by endless violence. The weak, the timid, the sick, the elderly, and those who had no means to defend themselves died first. Soon, local citizens armed themselves and took to the streets to quell the gangs, rioters, and looters. Every city and town became a battlefield, only with no Geneva Convention or laws to limit the conduct of the combatants. Hundreds of millions of people died in the carnage.

If that was not bad enough, the aftereffects of that apocalyptic day ravaged the world. Many of the sick and wounded might have been saved with proper medical treatment, but that no longer existed. As the death toll mounted, society's ability to properly dispose of the bodies ceased functioning. The mounting piles of corpses led to rot and decay, further leading to disease and epidemics. Within a month, half of those who had survived Day One had joined the ranks of the deceased. The other half took their own lives rather than live through damnation.

Denning had been on the road on a business trip when the end came. Thankfully, the trip had been only a few hundred miles away, so he had taken his car. It meant he had been able to return home easily. Though easy was a relative term. The trip took him five days. During that time, he watched the complete degeneration of society and observed how, in a matter of days, civilized people devolved into fear, panic, and, ultimately, brutality. Some took advantage of the opportunity to rape, murder, and loot for sheer pleasure. Some lost all sense of humanity as they took from others what they needed to survive. Denning had his car hi-jacked on the third day by a family with two kids, the father holding him at gunpoint while the mother ushered her kids into the backseat. He had to walk the rest of the way.

When Denning arrived home, he found the neighborhood in shambles. Several homes had been vacated by their owners and looted. A few had been burned. The debris from ransacked houses littered the streets and lawns, including several abandoned vehicles and five corpses.

Those few who had stayed behind had gone into full survival mode. Everyone refused to help him out. Even Stan, his next-door neighbor, whose kids played together all the time, shoved a shotgun in his face, called him a sick son of a bitch, and threatened to shoot Denning if he didn't get off his property.

Things only got worse. Denning's family had all been sickened by the effects of the apocalypse. His wife, Catherine, and his daughter, Jessica, had it bad—Timmy not so much. Denning tried to nurse Catherine and Jessica back to health, but they were too far gone. He even walked to the nearby CVS to find antibiotics and anything else that might help his family, only to find the store being ransacked. He managed to procure what he needed, but not before shooting one man dead, crippling another in the leg, and robbing a young mother of her supplies in front of her two small children. Not that it did any good. Catherine and Jessica died within twenty-four hours of each other.

After burying the bodies in their backyard and spending the next two days drunk, Denning gathered whatever useful items from around the house he could carry. He considered putting a bullet through his head and joining Catherine and Jessica in the afterlife but could not leave Timmy alone to fend for himself. Instead, he and Timmy hit the road, hoping to find a better place to live.

None existed.

Denning quickly learned the safest way to survive was to avoid contact with others and fend for himself—especially since he had Timmy. He couldn't let anything happen to the boy. Such thinking had kept him alive these past few months. With luck, their good fortune would continue.

Denning placed the blade of the hunting knife against the meat and pushed it in again. Juices flowed out, but no blood. He sliced off a three-inch-long piece of meat and tossed it into his mouth. It tasted gamey, but it was edible. Cutting off another chunk, he reached out to give it to Timmy.

"It's pretty good. Try it."

The bell on the front door rang, and a voice called from out front.

"Is anyone in here?"

"Is anyone in here?" Josh stood inside the entrance to the hardware store. He was not surprised that no one answered.

"We're not here to cause trouble. We smelled the cooking from outside. We're hungry. We're willing to trade for some of what you're preparing."

Still no answer.

"This is not going to end well," Richard said from the street.

"I agree," said Heather. "For all we know, it could be a gang back there. I don't want to go through that again."

"Let's get out of here while we can," added Al.

"Come on, guys," argued Josh. "We haven't eaten in days. I'm starving."

"We all are," agreed Heather. "But this is stupid."

Josh ignored her and shouted again. "Dude, we're not here to hurt you. We just want to trade some of what we have for some of what you're cooking. How about it?"

Nothing.

"Now can we go?" urged Heather.

Josh thought for a moment. "You stay here. I'm going back to see if I can reason with them."

"You're nuts," said Al.

Josh yelled out onto the sidewalk. "Richard, cover our asses. I'm going to see if I can get these people to trade."

Before Richard could stop him, Josh headed down the center aisle toward the back of the store, his AR-15 slung over his right shoulder and pointing toward the ground, his hand clutching the grip.

"I'm coming back just to talk."

"I'm coming back just to talk."

Shit, thought Denning. He hoped if he stayed quiet, the intruders would go away. No such luck. He had to protect Timmy at all costs.

Reaching into his backpack, Denning pulled out his cell phone and switched it on. It only had eight percent power remaining. Enough for what had to be done. He slipped it into his back pocket, then placed the Vepr in Timmy's lap.

"Don't be afraid. I've taught you how to use this. If anyone other than me comes through that door, blast them. Got that?"

Timmy didn't respond, but somehow Denning sensed his son knew what to do. He patted Timmy on his leg.

"I'll be back. Be quiet."

Unsheathing his hunting knife, Denning made his way to the swinging double doors leading into the shop. He paused and peered through the slit between the doors' rubber padding. A lone figure slowly walked down the aisle. He couldn't make out a lot of details in the shadows, but the man looked like everyone else struggling to survive: haggard, emaciated, and with eyes that had witnessed more than any sane person should have. He seemed harmless enough. However, he had an AR-15 slung over his shoulder with his finger near the trigger, making the man a threat that had to be neutralized.

As the man got closer, he paused five feet from the doors. "Dude, give me a shout-out. Hell, tell me to fuck off. Just answer me."

Josh saw the light on the opposite side of the double doors go out. That wasn't a good sign. But he had already come this far, so Josh figured he would give it another chance.

"Dude, give me a shout-out. Hell, tell me to fuck off. Just answer me."

Nothing. The others were right. This had been an insane idea. Josh lifted his left hand to show he meant no harm and started to walk backward toward—

The double doors burst open. Someone lunged at Josh, a hunting knife clutched in their hand. He should have had enough time to raise the AR-15 and take down his target, but the shock of his attacker coming through the doors caught him by surprise. That lost moment would be fatal.

The attacker drove the hunting knife upwards beneath Josh's chin. The blade drove through his lower jaw, sliced his tongue in half, and crashed into the roof of his mouth with such force that it shattered the bone. Josh spasmed as the blade cut up into his brain at a slight angle. His right eye lost vision when the optical nerve was severed. Josh remained fully aware of what was happening, though he could not speak or function. The agony ended when the assailant twisted the knife one hundred and eighty degrees, scrambling Josh's brain and putting him out of his misery.

Denning grabbed the intruder by the front of his shirt, pulled the knife from his skull, wiped off the blood and gore on the intruder's clothes, then quietly lowered the body to the floor.

Through the last rays of sunshine outside, Denning made out three more figures standing by the entrance to the hardware store. Hopefully, they would run. If not, then he could easily take care of them.

Denning opened his cell phone, selected the music app, and scrolled to the song he wanted. Pressing the PLAY button, he placed the phone on a nearby shelf, then rushed down the aisle on the left of the store, where he hid behind a John Deere riding mower.

"I heard something," said Heather, one ear cocked toward the store.

"What?" asked Al.

"I don't know, but it didn't sound good." Heather took a step inside. "Josh, is everything alright?"

No answer.

Heather grew nervous. "Josh, please an—"

An unfamiliar voice whispered from the rear of the store followed by a scream accompanied by a blast of heavy metal music. The voice sang about being beaten and not taking much more.

Al raised his AK-47 and aimed it down the center aisle. "What the hell is that?"

Richard joined them. "Let the Bodies Hit the Floor by Drowning Pool."

Al stared at his friend. "You gotta be fucking kidding."

"No." Richard motioned toward the street. "Let's go."

"What about Josh?" asked Heather.

"He's probably dead."

"You don't know that."

Richard tried to hide his aggravation. "Come on while we have the chance."

"I'm not leaving him." Heather unholstered her .357 Magnum, raised it into the high-ready position, and moved down the aisle on the left side of the store, cautiously making her way to the back.

"Fuck," mumbled Richard. He tapped Al on the shoulder and pointed to the middle aisle. "You go that way and keep an eye on her. I'll break to the right."

The two men split and headed for the rear storage room.

Denning watched from the shadows as the woman slowly made her way down the aisle, her Magnum raised and ready to fire. She paused at each cross-aisle, checking around the corner to make certain no one waited to ambush her. Smart woman. Too bad she didn't think to check out the displays to the left.

Denning waited for the woman to pass, then emerged from behind the John Deere. As expected, she heard the noise and spun around to defend herself, but it was too late.

Denning drove the blade into the flesh between the woman's cervix. Her eyes opened wide. She let out a shocked gasp.

He leaned in close and whispered into her ear, "Next time, leave me and my son alone, bitch!" As the lyrics talked about nothing being wrong with the singer, Denning pushed the blade up, carving the woman up to her sternum as if she were a deer. Leaving the blade embedded in her chest, he stepped away. The gash widened. The intestines and internal organs slowly pushed their way through before flowing out, falling to the floor with a sickening plop, barely audible over the sound of the music. The gutted corpse swayed on its feet for a few seconds before collapsing as the chorus broke into a repetitious theme of letting bodies hit the floor.

A male voice came from the other side of the aisle. "Heather, are you okay?"

Whoever asked about the bitch started to come through the cross-aisle. Denning didn't have time to retrieve his knife, so he grabbed the closest thing nearby that could be used as a weapon—a three-foot-long crowbar. Denning swung it like a baseball bat, striking the man on the right side of the head with full force. He heard the skull crack even over the music. The body fell to the side, hit the shelves, then toppled onto its back on the floor. Denning stepped over and hovered above the stunned man.

"Don't fuck with my family."

"W-we were—"

Before the man could finish his sentence, Denning drove the pointed end of the crowbar into the front of his skull. It cut through the bone and brain, not stopping until it dug into the rear bone. The man's eyes went lifeless. Denning did not want to take any chances.

Pushing the crowbar forward, he broke the top of the skull from the rest of the body, tearing off the flesh along the front and sides of the head. The cap fell onto the floor, providing a dish for the brains to slide into.

Three down, one to go.

Richard reached the end of the aisle. Aiming his Sig Sauer in front of him, he peered around the corner. No one was there, but he did see the phone on a shelf at the end of the center aisle that played the deafening music. Stepping forward, Richard checked the center aisle. Al made his way down it. He gave his friend a thumbs up, crossed over to the double doors leading into the storage room, and peered inside.

A fire with meat cooking above it occupied one corner of the area. Behind it, a lone figure sat against the wall. A shotgun sat on his lap. Based on the figure's size, he assumed it was a child. He couldn't tell because its head was bowed with a hoodie draped over it.

Richard slid the Sig Sauer between his pants and his back, gently pushed open the doors, and stepped inside with his hands raised in front of him.

"Hey, kid. I'm not here to hurt you. See? I put my weapon away."

The child didn't even bother to look up.

Richard circled the fire, cautiously moving closer to the child. "Hey, can you hear me?"

Still no response.

How could the kid sleep through this? Shit, maybe the kid was sick, which would help explain why the father was going psycho on their asses.

Moving closer to the child, Richard reached out to shake his shoulder and see if the kid was all right.

Denning stood over the two ravaged bodies of the intruders. Puddles of blood spread out under them. He removed the Bowie knife from the woman's chest, wiped it clean on her pants, and slid it back into the sheath. *That'll teach them to fuck with me and my—*

The music suddenly cut off, and an eerie silence descended across the hardware store. *Shit, his cellphone must have run out of power. Good luck ever charging it again.*

Denning heard one of the double doors leading into the storeroom swing open and a voice say, "Hey, kid. I'm not here to hurt you. See? I put my weapon away."

Fuck, one of the bastards had snuck by him, and now Timmy was in danger.

Unholstering his Glock, Denning raced to the storeroom.

Richard shook the kid's shoulder, again not getting a response.

A crazed man burst through the storeroom doors brandishing a Glock. On spotting Richard, the man swung the weapon in his direction. Without thinking, Richard grabbed the kid by the collar and lifted him, placing the child in front of him as a shield. He immediately realized that was a bad move. The man, whom Richard assumed was the father, came toward them, the Glock aimed at Richard. Richard reached behind and withdrew his Sig Sauer, holding it at the gunman.

"I don't want any trouble," pleaded Richard.

"Too late, asshole. If you hurt my son, I'll kill you."

"I don't want to hurt your son. I just don't want you to shoot me."

"Then drop the weapon."

"Okay." Richard tossed the Sig Sauer onto the floor between himself and the gunman. "Please, just listen. My friends and I didn't come in here to hurt you. We smelled what you were cooking and only wanted to see if you would trade what we had for some food. Honest."

The gunman took a step closer, the Glock still aimed at Richard. "Let Timmy go. Now!"

The boy's name was Timmy. Good. Maybe he could reason with the kid.

"Timmy, please tell your father I meant you no harm. If I wanted to hurt you, I had plenty of time." Richard spun Timmy around to face him, hoping the boy would understand. "I only want... Jesus fucking Christ."

Richard released the boy, who fell face-first to the ground. The minute his line of fire was clear, the gunman emptied his Glock into Richard. Richard died instantly when the second bullet struck him on the side of the head.

Denning ran over to Timmy. "That was close. Are you okay?"

Denning rolled the boy over. Timmy looked none the worse for wear. Dead skin had sloughed off Timmy's face, and two of the remaining teeth had fallen onto the floor. His gaze focused on Timmy's sockets, the pupils having long since melted. He brushed the maggots from his son's face.

"You're okay. No one will hurt you so long as I'm here."

Denning propped the corpse against the wall, adjusting the body so it wouldn't fall over, then pulled the hoodie down so it partially covered the rotting face. Timmy was all he had left. Without his son, Denning would have offed himself a long time ago.

Removing the Bowie knife, Denning carved off several strips of dog meat and leaned against the wall by his son. He threw two pieces into his mouth and chewed, then slid a slice between Timmy's open jaws.

"Eat up, kid. We have a long day ahead of us tomorrow."

Fear in a Handful of Dust

Written by T.S. Beier

―⸺⁓⸺―

T.S. (Tina) Beier is the author of the post-apocalyptic novel *What Branches Grow*, which was a Top 5 Category Finalist in the 2020 Kindle Book Awards and Semi-Finalist in the 2021 SPSFC (Self-Published Science Fiction Competition). She is a writer for PostApocalypticMedia.com, a book reviewer, an editor, a co-host of the Double Spaced podcast, and co-owner of a small press in Canada. Tina is also the author of the *Burnt Ship Trilogy* space opera (*Escaping First Contact, A Threat Revealed,* and *Dead in the Water*). She has a B.A. in English, a Graduate Certificate in Creative Writing, and a Certificate in Publishing. She is obsessed with science fiction, *Fallout*, and abandoned buildings. Tina lives in Ontario, Canada, with her husband, two feral children, and a cuddly shepherd-mastiff named Ruger.

> Website: http://nostromopublications.com
> Instagram: https://www.instagram.com/tinasbeier/
> YouTube: https://www.youtube.com/c/SoundFuryBookReviews
> Twitter: https://twitter.com/TSBeier

Even grass, the most resilient of Earth's flora, couldn't grow in the Valley of Giants.

"We shouldn't be here," Stacey whispered as she followed Lara over the concrete barriers that littered their path like oversized tombstones. Unlike her friend, who planted each foot as though she were stomping a particularly offensive bug, Stacey moved gingerly. For all she knew, the ground was strewn with tripwires and snares.

Lara vaulted over a fallen barrier chunk, landing with a look back at her friend as if expecting a compliment to her skill. Instead, Stacey's chin was elevated, her gaze fixated on the looming wall of concrete beside her. Most of it, like the piece she stood on, had toppled over, the monoliths cracking when they fell and leaving slabs sticking out of the wine-dark ground like four-foot-tall ribs. Some towered still, seeming to sway in the dimness of pre-dawn.

Stacey pressed a hand to a gaping crack at eye level, as if to apply pressure to a wound. The barrier had always existed off in the distance for her, like a mountain or the sea; she'd never been so close to one before.

How had these structures been built? The barrier, less such now than a simple marker of forbidden territory, was made of concrete, a rare compound they reserved back in town for post holes to build fences for livestock. How had so much been gathered for just this one wall? The metal inside, rebar, was coveted by the town. The elders refused to allow anyone to push the monoliths over themselves, wary of the wrath of something they refused to name or explain, but every time a piece of the ancient wall toppled, the workers scrambled with makeshift sledge hammers and worn chisels to extricate the metal rods.

"If you're so worried about getting caught, maybe you shouldn't be standing on top of one of those things?" Lara called.

Stacey blinked, then jumped off. She landed awkwardly, grunting and throwing out her arms to steady herself.

"Careful there; I don't want to carry you home with a broken ankle," Lara teased.

Stacey lowered her chin, raised her eyebrows, and slightly pursed her lips in defiance, but Lara's form, now a shadow in the dim light, was already several feet away from her.

"This is stupid," Stacey said, catching up as Lara paused her trek to survey the landscape. "No one actually expects you to go through with that dare. We're twenty, not thirteen."

"Juan said no one will accept me as a periphery scout if I don't prove myself. This is the best way."

That was an excuse, not a reason.

Stacey frowned. "Then why am I here? I'm an aggy!"

"You've always wanted to know what's here, too."

While this was true in the sense that everyone under thirty wanted to know what was in the Valley that made it so forbidden, Lara was obsessed. Growing up, she always talked about what the giants were and why there was a valley of them, though never within earshot of the adults. Last night, Claire had finally dared Lara to just "fucking go, already," which was the only excuse Lara needed to make the journey.

And, of course, as usual, she dragged Stacey into it.

Stacey's head turned involuntarily south, the direction of home. She could go back, could tell her friend she was on her own. She returned her gaze north and peered into the distance—nothing moved.

Despite being happily on the agricultural track (she had some pretty strong opinions on how to reorder the okra and pepper plants on Farm F), Stacey wasn't above curiosity about the Broken World outside the barriers. They'd been told since before they could walk that they shouldn't venture past the concrete barrier to the north.

Their hamlet was protected, so the elders said, because they were on a coast. Even then, they were neither to boat out of the cove nor scale the rocky cliffs to the west. Lara wanted to be a scout because they sometimes got to travel into what the elders called the "danger zone." Stacey's grandmother always hummed a song when anyone mentioned it, a tune that never failed to elicit groans or eye rolls from the other older people.

Lara's high ponytail bobbed up and down as Stacey fought to keep up with it.

"What are you looking for?" Stacey called out. "How far do we have to go?"

Lara didn't reply at first, continuing to jog and scan the area as the sun began to poke its head over the horizon. The orb's appearance didn't change the lighting much. It was an overcast day, muggy, as usual, and Stacey's first thought was about how they needed rain by Sittingday to keep from having to use reserve water on the spinach.

"I need to find a piece of old tech," Lara said.

Stacey sighed heavily. "Old tech? Really? We could be out here for hours!" She lowered her voice. "We're already further than anyone else has ever gone—let's go back."

"What's that?" Lara replied, ignoring her friend. She took off at a gentler pace, skirting smaller pieces of concrete and jagged hunks of metal that looked like a fast ticket to lockjaw city. Why didn't the scavengers from town come here for metal? It wouldn't take much to pry it out of the earth. Oh right, forbidden. Stacey had almost forgotten they were not supposed to be here, given how peaceful and quiet it was.

Perhaps the giants had left? Or died? Whatever they were.

As Stacey made her way to Lara, she slowed to examine the objects strewn about the space. Rotten, circular, soft drums that she knew were called tires rested here and there. Shards of glass the size of her forearm lay buried under the dust. Bullet casings, hunks of scarred and charred metal, and bones filled in the rest of the gaps. Bones lay scattered everywhere. This was a graveyard.

Bile rose in her throat.

"Lara! This is unholy ground!"

Lara didn't even turn. "That's bullshit and you know it. Your Gran doesn't believe in gods and that nonsense and neither should you. You know all that is just made up by the elders to keep us in line, right?"

Stacey had heard this before, but unlike the nights when they had a few beers behind Thomas' barn, she was too nervous to argue theology. Lara grabbed something from the ground. She held it up. It looked like a pinecone.

"What is that?" Stacey asked.

"See this pack?" Lara said, pointing at a bag lying beside an intact skeleton. "In scout training, they tell us if we come across a dead body we should search for useful or identifying items. I found this thing just outside it. See how heavy it is?" She passed it over. "Think it counts as old tech? I'm not sure. For all I know, it could be a cleaning tool."

In Stacey's mind, a handful of dust would have counted as old tech just to get them the fuck out of here. Still, she examined it, running her fingers gently over the conical object. Just like a true pinecone's seeds, this item had ridges along its body, but they didn't come off when she flicked them—they were etched in, though, unlike a carving or engraving, this had to have been made in what Gran called a factory, as it was too precise for hand-made.

It had a circle at the top, similar but not identical to those on the tin cans the scavengers often brought back. Stacey peered closer—she'd been warned her whole life by her Gran about how touching old tech required delicacy—and saw the circle was connected to a hole in the neck. She pulled gently at it. It started to give. She pushed it back down quickly before it could fully engage the mechanism inside, unsure what it did. She glanced at the skeleton who had presumably owned it. The bones were charred as if the person had died from flame. A helmet, cracked, lay beside them. Boots, burnt, still held the feet bones. She shuddered.

"Let's keep looking. You can hold that," Lara said. Stacey imagined pulling her arm back as far as her scapula would allow her and heaving the pinecone away, but nodded. If she pushed Lara too hard, she'd only keep going. Best to agree with her and get this over with.

They pushed further north for another twenty minutes, Lara pausing often to look at things but not finding anything of value. Stacey ran her fingers over the pinecone idly as she walked. It fit perfectly in her palm. What was it? What was it for? A soldier had it, given the helmet and boots, so maybe it was a weapon? It was old tech, but it wasn't that high-tech. It wouldn't be a communication device, would it? She held it up to her ear and shook it. Nothing rattled. She slipped the ring over her middle finger, pretending it was a bauble like the one widowed Mayor Jessica wore and liked to brag about her wife purchasing for her back before the world broke.

"Got something!" Lara exclaimed. "Look at this shit."

Stacey closed her other fingers over the pinecone and went to see if "this shit" was what allowed them to finally go home. She was going to owe Mahmoud lunch for a week if he had to cover for her lateness today. Then again, maybe she could turn it into taking him out for lunch?

Her attention snapped back to Lara when the other young woman grunted. Lara pulled at a yellow stick encased in the ground. No, it wasn't a stick; it was metal, Stacey realized upon closer inspection. Lara pulled with all her might and the stick made a loud ratcheting noise, then slammed into the ground an inch from Lara's toes.

The Grim Reaper ran a finger from Stacey's lumbar to her occipital bone. She started to back away as a sharp hiss made her wince and six plumes of dust burst into the air like mini geysers.

A three-by-three-foot square slab of metal rose in the air and then fell backwards with a dull thud. It reminded Stacey of the hatch in Gran's house that led to her cold cellar. But Gran's cellar didn't open with hydraulics.

Lara finally realized she'd fucked up and started moving backwards, slowly. A shape the size of a border collie leapt into the air, spider-like, from its housing underground. Aside from the size, it was nothing like a dog. It was like nothing either young woman had ever seen.

Lara, breathing hard, and Stacey, eyes wide, stared at the moving old tech.

"Calibrating," it said, causing Lara to gasp.

"Run," Stacey whispered.

"It might be friendly," Lara replied, though she kept her voice low.

"It might not be!" Stacey hissed.

"Commencing search," the thing said. With its spindly legs and squat torso, it resembled an insect. On its back rested a series of cylindrical tubes, one of which emitted a small but bright red light that was painful to look at. The red light moved across the ground, a single ant searching for food, until it climbed up Lara's leg and stopped at her chest.

"Organic," it said. Was it talking to them? "Hostile," it said as Stacey shoved her friend to the side. The bullet whizzed over Stacey's outstretched right arm, where Lara's chest would have been. A half-inch furrow sliced into her umber skin.

Stacey shrieked even as the animal instinct part of her took over, forcing her to run. Lara followed suit and the young women dove behind an old vehicle. A bus, Stacey's brain somehow dredged up. Bullets struck the ground beside them and riddled the bus like a sieve. They screamed and ducked low, using the large bumper as cover.

Lara took Stacey's left wrist and pointed. Twenty feet away lay a concrete slab, as big as the bus. Bullets hit the window above them, spraying the girls with glass shards. Lara furrowed her brow, somehow angry rather than pissing-her-pants scared like Stacey. She picked up a rock. She launched it underhand behind her, over the bus, striking something to the north with a dull clang. The bullets stopped and the area became still once more.

A gentle mechanical whirring indicated that the thing was leaving to investigate the thrown rock, or at least that's what Stacey hoped. Lara took a deep breath, then took Stacey's hand and ran. As they did so, the little red light appeared to their left on the ground. Stacey let go of Lara and jumped to the right, head turned to watch the light. She began an erratic zigzag, stopping only when she reached the concrete block. Lara joined her, breathing steadily but her face was red.

"We have to kill it," Stacey said. She refused to look at her arm, as if examining it would make it worse.

"Kill it?" Lara exclaimed.

"If we don't, it'll head to town! You heard it was commencing a search and when it found us 'organics,' it tried to kill us! Who do you think killed all these people?" She gestured to the bones.

"Time for us to avenge them, then," Lara snarled. She picked up a nearby skull by the eye sockets and popped her head over the edge of the concrete. She launched the cranium at the metal being, striking it on the back. The skull shattered to pieces and the thing only began searching again, unperturbed. Lara dropped down. Stacey gritted her teeth. The mechanical monster's gyros whirled as it walked.

"It can't find us," Stacey whispered after a moment.

Lara nodded. "It's strong but stupid. I'll sneak around that way. I'll grab that piece of metal there," she said, pointing, "and smash it."

It was the only plan they had. Neither had brought guns, as they weren't allowed to use one unless they were scouts, guards, or hunters. And even then, they were locked up unless the person was on duty.

As Lara left, ducking low, Stacey finally looked at her right arm. It was bleeding, but not profusely. She was too scared or excited—adrenaline, her brain reminded her—to feel anything but a dull pain.

"Searching," the thing said in its eerie, masculine monotone. Were these things what killed not just these soldiers, but all people? Had it and its siblings killed Gran's husband, Stacey's parents, the mayor's wife? Everyone's parents? Was this why the town was only made up of grandparents and grandchildren, and why everyone under thirty was an orphan? If so, why was the barrier wall so large? And yes, this metallic creature could easily kill Stacey, but soldiers in the past, as she had read in some of Gran's hidden books, had far more powerful guns than the hunting rifles and shotguns they had in town. There was no way these small things killed everyone and broke the world.

Speculation died with Lara's roar. Stacey popped up from behind the barrier, pinecone still gripped in her fist, to see Lara land a massive slam onto the thing's back with a piece of metal. The blow would have knocked the average person down for the count, but the thing simply side-stepped with its grasshopper-like legs until it was facing

Lara. She struck again with the piece of metal, striking its front leg. It buckled, but its red light returned. Lara dove to the right, scrabbling in the dirt to get up to her feet, as bullets fired. The thing righted itself, and this time the red light splayed out like birdshot, encompassing a wider range than the pinpoint from its previous targeting parameters. It resumed its attack. One of the bullets struck home.

Lara and Stacey both screamed as Lara fell to the ground, her seeping blood deepening the red of the wine-dark dirt. The mechanical monster stopped firing and emitted strange ratcheting noises.

"Piece of shit!" Stacey exclaimed, standing. She assumed the jerk-face motherfucker... was reloading its weapon from whatever compartment inside it stored ammunition. She had to get it away from Lara. Her friend was still breathing, struggling to get up, but Stacey knew she couldn't reach her in time.

If she lured it over here, though...

"Here!" she yelled. She stupidly hadn't grabbed anything to throw before standing. If she ducked now, it would turn back to Lara, finish her off if she wasn't already dying. The pinecone. She didn't hesitate. "Here, shithead!" she called and let it fly.

Something stayed in her hand. The ring. Her fingers clasped around it. The pinecone missed its mark, landing just in front of the thing. It sprayed out its red sweeper light again, blanketing Lara in several dots. Stacey prepared to yell, to run to that pile of tires, then—

The explosion sent her stumbling backwards, more so in shock than from the blast itself. She landed hard on her ass, and she gritted her teeth when dirt peppered the wound in her arm.

She scrambled to her feet, determined to find a rock, something, to finish it off before it let loose another concussive blast. How did such a little thing have such power?

"It's dead, Estacia!" Lara's voice was laced with pain.

The dust cleared. Shock and relief were so overpowering that Stacey didn't even bother correcting the use of her hated full name.

"How?" Stacey asked. Lara didn't explain, just lay back in the dust.

The thing, the metal monster, was gone. Stacey frowned, glancing around to make sure it hadn't jumped onto a plinth somewhere. No, there was one of its unmistakable, grasshopper-like legs over by a pile of barbed wire. She picked it up, examining its gyros and components.

"Is this a good amount of proof?" she asked Lara, unable to keep the scorn from her voice. Lara had managed to stand, leaning heavily on her right leg. Blood stained her pant leg, but it was more of a blossom than a widening puddle. Lara's hand clasped her hip.

"Can you walk?" Stacey asked.

Lara nodded. "If you'll help me?" Her voice carried notes of contrition. Stacey glanced down at the metal leg in her hand. Now, even more than Lara, she needed to know. She spotted a backpack a few feet away. She picked it up and slid the leg into it.

As she approached Lara to offer her an arm, Stacey paused.

"Just a second," she said. Lara didn't complain. Whether it was due to the pain or her guilt over dragging them into this mess, Stacey didn't care. She approached one of the monoliths, staring up at it. A faint breeze teased her curly black hair.

Ignoring the throbbing in her arm, she climbed protruding pieces of foot-thick rebar until she was thirty feet up. From this vantage point, she could see much larger versions of the metal thing's components—legs and chassis—cluttering the landscape as far as she could see. Now she understood why the elders called it the Valley of Giants. Compared to the others, that thing had been an insect. The implications stung worse than sand in the eyes.

"It's their graveyard, too," she whispered.

She and Lara did not talk as they made their way through the pock-marked Valley of Giants. They didn't talk as Stacey helped Lara over the barriers and onto the gravel pathway leading to town. They didn't talk until Peter, the guard on duty, whom they'd circumvented that morning, came running to them, his face a mask of distress.

"We live surrounded by the bones of our self-made killers," Gran said as she poured Stacey a cup of tea and set it before her. Gran slid into her chair, studying Stacey for a moment, then stared down at the metal leg on the kitchen table. She interlaced her fingers, then unlaced them again, pressing them flat on the scarred wooden table.

Estacia leaned back, arms crossed, her tea untouched. She was due for a lecture, but rather than one given to a misbehaving child, it would be an explanation to an adult of what had come before and, perhaps, what was yet to come.

Lost Souls

Written by Stefan de Koster

Stefan de Koster was born in Eindhoven and raised in Rotterdam, the Netherlands. He has always been obsessed with high and dark fantasy, as well as language construction—hobbies that got out of hand when he started playing tabletop role-playing games. He ended up with a post-apocalyptic fantasy setting—complete with rudimentary versions of entire made-up language families—that just didn't work for his games. With half a mind to scuttle the project, he let himself be persuaded to try his hand at writing a story in the setting—his first serious one ever—and Lost Souls is the result!

This story won first place in the 2021 Post-Apocalyptic Media Short Story Contest.

Rain pummeled Ánne's body as he crested the dune. The ocean entering his vision was a murky, seething mass occasionally lit by flashes of lightning. He was glad for his sealskin coat; the towering beachgrass offered little shelter from the torrential downpour. In the dying light,

Ánne could hardly make out the short silhouette of his guide. Minute by minute, he regretted embarking on this madman's trip more.

"How much further?" he called out over the noise. His guide paused for a moment and yelled something inaudible. Ánne swore. His coat kept out the rain but could do little to ease the cold. He thumbed his only heat stone. He might need it later; probably best to not tap into it right now. Grumbling, he gritted his teeth and broke into a jog. How could such a tiny woman—no, a girl still—keep up such a killing pace?

Syluw finally came to a stop near a crumbling brick wall. The girl looked hesitant. Ánne caught up with her, panting. "Where to now, Miss Necromancer?"

The corner of her mouth twitched. "I prefer the term medium," she replied curtly. "I rarely work with actual corpses."

They stood in awkward silence for about ten seconds, and then Ánne gave in. He was cold, tired, and not in the mood for arguing with a teenager again. "Alright, Miss Medium then! I'm sorry, OK? Just... where do we go next?"

Syluw pouted and muttered something. "What was that?" Ánne demanded. She shot him a furious look. "I lost it, alright? Tracking a rogue spirit is actually quite hard. Not that I'd expect a brawn-for-brain soldier like you to understand."

Ánne hit the wall in frustration. He had to calm down. This girl was not his daughter, and he needed her. Probably. If she wasn't making everything up. He was half praying she was.

Ánne sat down on a brick poking out of the sand and stared at the wall. It looked oddly familiar. Suddenly, he realized it wasn't straight, but curved round. He knew exactly where they were. "Executive decision," he said, standing up. "We make camp here. This is the Titankeep, or what's left of it. We weather the storm here, and try to pick up the trail tomorrow." She was about to protest, but Ánne cut her off.

"Listen, it's dark, the storm's about to hit its peak, we have lost the trail, and the nearest homestead is at least two hours away from here. You needed a bodyguard to keep you safe, and I'm doing just that. We camp here, and that's final."

Syluw's shoulders sagged in defeat.

Rivulets cascaded over the weathered rim of the Titankeep. Ánne had managed to build a relatively dry shelter on the lee side of the ruins; his sealskin coat acting as a canopy for the both of them. The girl sat demonstratively as far away from him as the little shelter allowed, with her back against a toppled brick. She was chewing on some kind of dried fruit. "Listen, girl," Ánne tried, " I'm not asking you to huddle together, but you'll catch pneumonia if you don't at least use my sheepskin blanket. I have a heat stone, so I'll survive."

"I told you I'm fine," she bit back. "Why can't you get it into that thick skull of yours? I don't need a fucking chaperone to wipe my ass. Just keep the wildlife away from me, like I asked you to. And stop calling me 'girl' all the time. I passed sixteen a winter ago."

Ánne sighed. Almost exactly Cíutu's age. Perhaps he should give up; she was an adult, and she certainly looked like she was in a better state than he was, physically at least. He knew nothing about the powers of a medium; perhaps she did have some way of staying warm and staving off fatigue?

"Very well then," he said, "I apologize for patronizing you." Then he added a bit wryly, "I sometimes forget that I don't have to be a father anymore."

She looked up. "You have a family?"

"A wife and a daughter. Your age," he added. "Although it's just me and my wife now. My daughter went her own way."

"Too much patronizing?" the girl volunteered with a smirk.

"Could be part of it," Ánne admitted, "but more importantly, I disapproved of her partner. A peddler, and bloody Norfolk to boot. No future there. Still, she ran off with him before last winter, and not a word since."

"Sounds like she did love him," the girl replied. "Maybe you should have supported her."

"She'd still have left us," he said bitterly, then added: "but maybe on better terms."

Ánne turned to Syluw. "So what about you then? Even for a traveling medium, you are quite far away from home. Your name isn't exactly common in these parts." He tried it: "It's pronounced 'Seelew,' right?"

Syluw chuckled. "That's pretty close for a Merfolk, actually." She stared at her feet in silence for a minute or two, then started talking.

"I was born in Ensy. Sunwards and Dawnwards from here—I'm Hillfolk," she added in response to Ánne's nonplussed stare. "Anyway, I was raised in an orphanage. Worked in the marl quarries to repay the debt. When it got out I was Gifted, a wandering Artificer took me under his wing. Been traveling with him since. We got separated," she replied before Ánne could ask the question. "Look, I think I've had enough talk for tonight. Let's rest up and try to pick up the trail tomorrow."

Ánne nodded. "You sleep. I'll keep watch. It's too late to wake me up once we're being attacked."

The young woman gave him a nod, then curled up in her cloak. She drifted off in minutes. Maybe she was a mortal after all. Ánne wrapped himself in his sheepskin blanket and focused on his heat stone. He found its thermal energy reservoir and gave it a light mental Push. In response, it instantly gave off a gentle warmth. He tucked it under his tunic, feeling better already. Then he loaded his shotpipe and balanced it between his knees. The steel tube—as long as his legs—was heavy, but it greatly improved his accuracy. Better fulfill his role as a bodyguard properly.

Ánne woke up being stared down by a curious herring gull. He slowly raised his shotpipe. When the gull saw him move, it bounded forward, opening its beak. Without hesitation, Ánne rose. He rammed the shotpipe into the gull's gaping gullet and Pushed. The lead rod in the chamber jerked forward. Ánne could feel it nick the barrel as it shot out, burying itself into the gull's gut and ripping open the bird's abdomen on its way out. Ánne had seen enough fighting to know it was lethal. The gull rolled backward in a cacophony of screams.

Syluw jerked awake, pulling out a dagger with unnatural speed. "What was that?" she demanded. Then her eye fell on the huge flailing bird. "By the Creation! Did you do that?" Her face was a mixture of respect and disgust.

"Young herring gull. Must've thought we were an easy snack. We need to move—the storm has passed, and there will be more birds in the sky. More dangerous ones as well."

Ánne left out that he had dozed off near dawn. Damn it all. Five years ago, he wouldn't have fallen asleep on watch. He skirted the wretched bird and picked up his lead rod. It was mangled, and not just from the impact. He must have accelerated it too quickly. Well fuck. He was really losing his touch. The rod was useless to him now.

He turned to the bird. It had managed to work its way to the edge of the wall, but it wouldn't even last until noon. Probably a kindness to finish it off now. He tested the rod's kinetic energy reserve. Satisfied, he tossed it toward the bird and Pushed full power. The rod crumpled as it struggled against its inertia. Then, it smashed into the gull's skull, coating the wall in gore. Grimacing, Ánne checked his shotpipe. Its muzzle was cracked, but it would still be usable.

He untied his sealskin coat, shook off the moisture, and donned it in one fluid motion. "Have you picked up our target's trail yet?"

His voice snapped Syluw out of her daze. "Possibly. I may have found a fresh victim. It could still be close."

"Works for me. And you may want to put that dagger away for now."

Blushing, she sheathed the blue blade. He knew the dull, flexible material well. Titancraft. It made him uncomfortable. It wasn't a weapon for killing wildlife, but for killing people. Gifted people. Where did she get it?

"Good," he said, "now let's get out of here. You go in front, and we stick together. That should discourage most gulls. Provided they have any sense."

The watery autumn sun failed to alleviate the chill of morning. As the pair trudged along a damp sheep trail on the inland side of the dunes, Ánne scanned the horizon. No seagulls. That was a good start, but he wasn't particularly worried about just gulls.

Syluw's mood appeared to have improved significantly overnight. Immediately upon picking up the scent, her step had become energetic again. However, this time she made sure Ánne could keep up. Suddenly, she turned around and kept on walking backward with unnatural finesse. "So, I guess One-Shot Ánne lives up to his reputation then?"

Ánne sighed. "Rumors breed myths. I was just a fairly competent shooter in the right place at the right time. I shot thousands of bullets during the Norfolk war. One of them just happened to end it."

He stared over the grassy plain. "And now I mostly guard sheepherders. I settled. Let the youngsters talk of sailing upriver and raiding and looting. I have done my part and am glad it's behind me. Meanwhile, the old folk in town teach their children I'm some kind of bullet juggler. All the town kids want to see me do is trick shots."

Syluw tilted her head. "Tricks? Like what?"

Ánne huffed. "Hitting the same mark a dozen times in a row, shooting shells out of the sky. Bouncing bullets. Cheap tricks that are worth shit when you're staring down a Norfolk soldier.

Or a ghost," he added, hoping she would change the topic.

Oblivious to his hint, Syluw continued. "Bouncing bullets? Like, actually hitting your own shots?"

"I'm not going to give a demonstration if that's what you want. My shots are too precious to waste on party tricks. It takes me ages to charge them, and lead and steel ain't cheap either."

"Party pooper." Syluw winked. She seemed a lot more talkative than yesterday. Ánne figured he could hazard a question in return. It would probably be good to know more about her powers. Then again, something else bothered him as well...

"So, about that dagger of yours..." Syluw stiffened. "It's my mentor's," she said curtly. Then she relaxed a bit. "He sometimes needs it for exorcisms. Titancraft affects the spirit, so it works pretty well on lost souls. I borrowed it."

"Your mentor must be a pretty influential person if he got his hands on a Titancraft blade."

Syluw turned away from him. "He is," she muttered. Then she chuckled. "He's a traveling academic. Intelligent, but couldn't cook if his life depended on it. I've been taking more care of him than he has of me."

"You sound very fond of him."

She turned to him. Her eyes were slightly wet. "I am. He's...like the father I never had."

"Are you ok?"

She wiped away her tears. "Yup. All good. It's just, we got separated when we landed here on Téser. But he always said job first, so here I am."

"That why you asked for my help?"

"Well, even if I weren't solo, we always try to pick up a local guide or bodyguard. Neither of us are fighters. But I guess I got lucky to land a mythical warrior on my first solo job?" Her smirk was back.

Ánne harrumphed, looking away over the plain. Then he overtook her in one swift step and tried to press her head down to the ground. Halfway down, it felt like he hit a solid barrier, and she wouldn't budge.

"What do you think you're doing?" she demanded indignantly as Ánne lay down flat on his belly.

"Buzzard," he grunted. "Get down, if you value your life." With quick but meticulous motions, he loaded his shotpipe with a gravel bag. If that monster swooped down, grapeshot might be his only option.

The bird soared overhead, heading Evenlightwards. As it disappeared over the horizon, Ánne relaxed. "You could have just told me to get down before trying to grab me," she said as she brushed herself off.

"If you spot a buzzard, you can be sure it spotted you a hundred times over. We should be glad it wasn't interested in us." He hesitated, then added: "Next time I'll shout. Just make sure you lie down right away."

He was a strong man. How had she stayed upright?

They continued their trek without encountering any large beasts other than a single startled mouse. As the sun approached its zenith, they reached the crumbling remains of a titan village. Ánne called for a break, and they sat down in the shadow of a clump of sorrel poking out of the concrete foundations.

Ánne cut off a young leaf and took a few bites to make his oatcakes a bit less bland. Syluw stuck with her dried fruits. "You sure burn a lot of sugar," he noted.

"I need to be constantly switched on for tracking," Syluw said, "so I need the energy. It's not too bad, but you don't want to know what it does to my digestive system."

"True, I don't." Ánne got up. He drank a few gulps of water to wash away the sourness in his mouth. "You ready to move on?"

Syluw bounded up. "I wasn't the one who wanted a rest. We're almost there, too." She pointed towards a small copse of trees about a quarter of an hour ahead. "Should be over there."

Ánne frowned. "You sure?"

"Wellllll... no," Syluw said. "Just that something big died there recently. Violently."

"Rogue spirits do that, don't they?" he said unconvinced.

She turned and looked into his eyes. "Some do, Ánne."

"Alright, alright," he said, "the treeline it is. Stick close to me. Trees obscure my line of sight. Don't want to be caught off-guard by another buzzard."

It took them almost half of an uneventful hour to clear the distance. As they drew close to the forest's edge, Syluw changed course slightly. "It's this way. We're really close now!" She trotted off towards an opening in the foliage.

Ánne was about to tell her off when he saw a gray shape detach itself from a tree to the left.

His heart froze.

"Goshawk! Run, run, run!" he yelled as he brought up his shotpipe.

Syluw tore into a dash, but the goshawk was closing in fast. By the time Ánne had the raptor in his sight, Syluw was in his line of fire. Fuck. "Duck!" It took all his self-restraint to accelerate his shot slow enough to let it maintain its integrity. Helplessly, he watched as the projectile was still picking up speed as it left the barrel. There was no way it would make it in time.

Ánne yelled as the goshawk bore down on Syluw, and a flurry of feathers obscured her from his view as the goshawk was pelted by gravel. Ánne sank to his knees. He had failed; the shot had definitely connected too late.

Then Syluw rolled into his view and broke into a mad dash for the treeline as the bird recovered and gave chase. Ánne's heart kicked back into action.

"Over here!" Ánne shouted. "Lure it away from the trees!"

Syluw changed directions with the agility of a hare and nearly matched one in speed as well. The goshawk gave chase on foot, keeping up with a series of fast strides.

Ánne reached for one of the remaining lead rods on his belt. No time for the shotpipe; he would have to shoot without assistance. Syluw veered left and right with uncanny speed, just managing to keep the goshawk out of reach. Ánne tried to aim, but could hardly keep up with the pair. This was not going to be an easy shot.

The goshawk swiped a talon at Syluw. As she dodged, there was a slight pause in the bird's movements. Ánne threw his rod like a spear and Pushed. The projectile picked up speed and tore through the goshawk's back feathers. Cursing, Ánne grabbed his last rod, but the goshawk was on the move again. "Tag with me!" he shouted at Syluw.

She dashed towards him and barely dodged the accelerating missile. The rod nicked the goshawk's chest and drew blood, but the angle was off. That would be nowhere near enough to stop it. And now the bird was coming for him.

Ánne gritted his teeth. No other option now.

With all his strength, he Pushed on his gravel shot. As the goshawk went in for the kill, Ánne rolled to the side. Dozens of tiny rocks dug into the bird's back, and this close, Ánne could keep pushing. For just a short moment, the goshawk was pinned to the ground. Then the grapeshot ran out of energy. Triumphantly, the goshawk reared up and opened its beak for the kill. Ánne heard Syluw scream. He groaned from the effort as the twisted tangle of lead rods he had been Pushing finally returned and nailed the monster's neck to the ground. The bird went silent.

Ánne leaned against a tree. He was exhausted. Syluw sat next to him. She had finished looking after his wounds and was now bandaging herself. Every exposed part of her body was covered in scratches and bruises, and she had a long cut across her back. Still, it didn't seem like any of it was too serious.

"That," she said, "was a pretty amazing last shot. I couldn't even sense when you brought back that second rod."

"Didn't. I used the first bar to change its course."

"You bounced it?" She grinned.

"Gave you a demonstration after all, huh?" He grimaced. "By the Creation, we got off lucky," he grunted.

Syluw looked at him incredulously. "You call this lucky?" She showed him the cut on her back. "If I had been a heartbeat later, I would have had a talon between my ribs!"

"That's why we're lucky, Syluw. No offense meant, but by all means, you should have been dead. No one dodges a goshawk like you did today. No one normal at least. I won't pry, but, well... I'm glad you're still alive."

"Thanks," she said. "I may know a bit more than just communing with the dead. I also have the Gift of Artifice, but please keep that quiet. It's pretty rare to have two, according to my mentor."

"My lips are sealed. And I don't understand enough about the Gift anyway." He rose and extended his hand to help her up. "After all, I'm just a brawn-for-brain soldier." She grinned back at him and took his hand.

"Let's see if we can end this adventure and get back to civilization. If you Merfolk even know what that means. My present companion isn't making a very convincing case." She winked.

Ánne laughed. "Well, guess I'll disprove that. You're welcome to stay with me and the missus for a start. Then, we can look for that mentor of yours. I have old war buddies in almost every town on Téser; we'll have found the guy in days."

She turned away from him and started walking. "That would be lovely," she muttered.

The carcass leaning against the tree was still fresh. The sheep's head had been torn off, and its guts spilled out of a hole in its belly. Its body had been raked by claws, and the air was filled with the smell of sheep dung. "A ghost did this?" Ánne asked incredulously.

"I told you," Syluw said, wrinkling her nose. "Restless spirits can do that. What do these claw marks look like to you?"

"Dog, if I had to guess," Ánne said. "No wolves on Téser. But I've never seen a shepherd's dog do this to one of the flock."

"That doesn't matter. A rogue spirit takes control, and if the host's mind is weak, it is consumed within days. This dog is just an incarnation of hatred now. The spirit will keep killing until its host's body gives out. That is the sad nature of all undead."

"A wild dog," Ánne grimaced. "That is bad news. If this thing entered a town..."

"It would massacre the place."

Ánne whistled. "You weren't kidding when you told me this might concern the safety of the entire island."

"I didn't know it was a dog when I recruited you. But I'll admit this is worse than I imagined. We'll have to exorcize it as soon as possible."

"So, any new leads now that we're here?"

"That's the strange thing," Syluw said. "Usually, restless spirits have their own... wavelength that I can detect. But I just put the sheep's spirit to rest, and there's just no other..." She went quiet. Ánne could hear a growl coming from the bushes.

"Looks like it was here all along," he said as he placed himself between the noise and Syluw. She stared in shock.

"Impossible! There's no way I would have missed a signature this big. Not unless—but ghosts don't know Nullification..."

As the beast emerged from the undergrowth, it took Ánne a few moments to recognize it as a dog. It was the standard black-and-white shepherd's dog favored on Téser because of their gentleness. However, slavering, snarling, and covered in blood, it was a nightmare incarnate. The monster stared him down with bloodshot eyes.

"So, Ms. Medium, what's the plan?" Ánne said, never looking away from the beast.

"We," Syluw hesitated, "we normally subdue it. Then I can exorcize the spirit. But it's too late for the dog, so you don't have to hold back. You can kill it." She looked uncertain.

"I honestly wonder if I can." Ánne slowly took four grapnel shots from his pack. "This ain't a frail bird. Shotspikes and rods are useless against a mammal that big. I'll try to get it tangled up. You do your thing once I restrain it.

"Right." Syluw sounded tense.

He swallowed hard. "No promises though. If I die, you run, hear me? Get away from here with that insane speed of yours and never look back."

She bit her lip. "I can't abandon you."

"Don't be ridiculous. No use doubling the victim count. Go Evenlightwards until you hit the coast, then follow it Sunwards. You'll stumble upon a village called Ráca in two days. You could probably do it in one. They're good people. They will help you find that mentor of yours." He paused. "And tell my wife I love her."

"Don't count yourself dead yet. We'll beat this thing together. And you'll need me. This thing isn't natural, even for an undead."

Ánne handed her two thin, spider silk ropes. "Tie this to the brambles over there, and put the grapnels somewhere clear. We'll want to slow that thing down as soon as possible."

She looked grim. "Let's go."

As if on cue, the dog shot forward, like it had been held by an invisible lease that had snapped. Its frothing mouth opened wide to reveal a set of teeth larger than Ánne's fingers.

Ánne veered to the left as Syluw backed off to the brambles. Then he fired his first grapnel into the beast's flank. He let go of the rope for now; the beast would just drag him along.

Unfazed, it closed the distance and snapped at Ánne. He threw himself backward and hit the forest floor hard. The beast's maw shut an arm's length away from him. Its breath reeked of rotting meat. Swallowing back bile, Ánne pulled a bronze knife from his belt and thrust, tapping its small kinetic energy reserve. The knife buried itself into the dog's nose. It didn't even seem to faze the monster. Ánne yanked the knife back with a Push to roll out of the way of its fangs.

As Ánne got up, a paw caught his ammunition belt. He slashed the straps to free himself. Turning around, he aimed his last grapnel. This time, he embedded it in the beast's neck. Ánne dashed underneath its belly and looped the rope around its back leg.

The dog tried to lunge for him but staggered due to the rope. Ánne used the moment of respite to unhook his last grapeshot from his discarded belt. It was better than nothing. He grabbed the trailing rope of his first grapnel with one hand, then raised the grapeshot with the other. The dog turned and bared its fangs. Its fetid maw was only a pace away from him. As the beast opened it, he heard Syluw yell his name. Ignoring his fear, he jumped and Pushed as fast as he dared on his grapeshot. It shot up, dragging him along into the air. The dog's maw snapped shut, and he could feel its fangs close around his right foot. He screamed as it was torn off at its ankle, but he didn't stop Pushing until the grapeshot was depleted, and he landed in a slow arc on the dog's back. Panting and cursing, he tossed the useless bag of gravel.

The furious dog twisted and bucked, trying to throw him off. Ánne did not have the energy to stay on its back, and he let himself slide down to the other side, still clutching the rope. He ended up dangling helplessly just two paces above the ground. If only he could reach the monster's legs, he could restrain it! The beast opened its maw again, ready to finish the job...

Something streaked past him and hit the dog square in its jaws. The two grapnels Syluw held dug deeply into its flesh. Ánne let go of the rope and hit the leafy floor hard. He groaned. "Last rope. Tie this fucker down."

Without pausing, Syluw leapt for the last rope and swung around the beast's legs. She rammed Ánne's dropped dagger into its leg to secure the knot.

The monster struggled and twisted, entangling itself until it finally toppled. Its mouth frothed and its eyes darted around madly. As Syluw took out her Titancraft dagger to finish the job, Ánne's consciousness faded.

A painful throbbing woke Ánne up. His foot hurt. He opened his eyes and grasped at it, but found only a bandaged stump. He slumped back and felt bark pressing against his back. So it hadn't been a dream after all. Bloody mongrel.

He scanned his surroundings but didn't recognize them. It was the same copse of trees, but a different section. He tried to call for Syluw, but his throat was parched. All he managed was a croak.

Looks like they had survived somehow. As he eased himself against the tree, he gasped from pain. Syluw would probably have to carry him out of here. And then he wouldn't touch that bloody shotpipe ever again. He'd had enough. After helping Syluw find her mentor, he should get a prosthetic foot done. Some of his buddies were worse off. And then he could do something different with his life. Maybe... he could go find his daughter? Would she still hate him?

He was disturbed from his musings by a loud conversation. "... a huge disappointment. Can hardly believe I fell for the rumors."

The voices moved closer. One of them was masculine, but the other sounded like Syluw.

"That is hardly my fault. Anyway, I held up my end of the bargain. Now, release him. You gave me your word!"

Ánne could detect some glee in the male voice. "I said I would release him if the marksman passed. He didn't. He lost his bloody foot! What am I supposed to do with a footless body when I have a perfectly serviceable one right here?"

"You were going to... possess him as well?"

"Quite so. This mentor of yours isn't all too powerful. I would love to add a strong Artificer to my arsenal... but alas, this one was a disappointment. I will have to dispose of him later."

"Unnecessary. He's already dead. Blood loss. But that's not the issue here! You swore by the Creation." She sounded desperate. "And what is this about passing? Were you just testing him?"

"Not just him, my dear," the man said with malice. "The marksman was a failure. But you. You passed with flying colors."

"What are you..." Syluw cut off, and Ánne heard her retch. Still in a daze, he tried to move, to help her. His body refused to listen to his pleas. He heard something heavy fall down on the leaves and the rustling of approaching footsteps. Then Syluw came into view.

She was alright! Relief flooded over him as he attempted to croak her name. Then he stopped. Her face was contorted in an evil grin. "Well," she said mockingly, "looks like she did grow soft in the end. And she even bandaged you!" Syluw approached, her stare as cold as ice. "How futile."

Ánne felt a sharp pain between his ribs and was faintly aware of a warm sensation spreading over his abdomen. "No loose ends," Syluw said. Then, Ánne slumped down and his world went black.

Shade

Written by Shawn Schuster

―ℓℓ―

SHAWN HAS BEEN A writer and editor for various publications since 2007. He's traveled the world as a gaming journalist, played drums in a thrash metal band, attended a law enforcement academy, bred and raised cattle, and has homeschooled his two youngest children for the last five years. He currently lives on a mountain in the middle of nowhere with his wife, three cats named after Tolkien characters, a zoo of various farm animals, and his (mostly) wonderful children.

―ℓℓ―

Ruth picked at the cotton sleeve that kept her arm from burning. The sun was high in the sky, past the point where the young girl should be heading to shelter, but Papa's bicentennial present wasn't going to deliver itself. She had to get home soon.

The wasteland before her was flat and barren with no shade in sight. The sun could burn exposed skin in minutes and she knew better than to travel at this time of day.

According to Papa, a person could reach out and grab an entire ear of corn from anywhere in these fields before the war. He loved to tell stories of his youth, running through the unending maze of stalks with no direction in mind. He talked about that corn almost as lovingly as he talked about his memory of trees. Papa loved trees.

Ruth shared her father's love for trees. She wanted nothing more than to bask in natural shade with leaves and bark and flowers and fruit, not those horrifying wooden skeletons that haunt her small town now.

A playful meow rose from Ruth's shoulder bag as if Ash could sense that the girl was thinking of loving something other than him. The small kitten pushed his head through the flap and stared at Ruth expectantly. Ruth gave him a few reassuring strokes on his fluffy gray head and nudged him back into the bag for his own protection.

Traveling with a little furball in this heat was a challenge, but Ash was well cared-for. He knew to stay shaded during the day while his nocturnal instincts went into overdrive in the cool night air catching a variety of rodents and other small creatures for the next morning's breakfast.

Ash had been Ruth's traveling companion for about four months now, ever since Papa rescued him as a tiny malnourished kitten. Papa suggested the name to pay tribute to the animal's gray-mottled fur, but also because he found him in the wreckage of a burned-out barn. Ruth thought the name was too perfect for a third reason: Ash is also the name of a tree.

The cat circled around inside the large bag a few times before finding the perfect spot next to Papa's gift to rest. He was content (for the moment) that Ruth was safe and his nap could continue.

The young girl clutched her satchel tightly and imagined the look of surprise on Papa's face when she pulled out that gift.

So what would you get the man who already has everything, anyway? What would you get the man who has surrounded himself in a stronghold of solitude made of apocalyptic scrap metal treasures? It was a difficult choice but she was confident that he would love what she chose. Papa loved his country and this bicentennial celebration was not only a proud moment for the nation but also for him as a war veteran. It didn't hurt that the festivities fell on his birthday, too.

Along her path home, Ruth spotted the bones of a two-story farmhouse. She decided it would be a good place to rest until the sun sets and her travel could continue through the night.

The girl searched the structure just as Papa had shown her. "Slice the pie," he'd say while demonstrating how to strategically look around blind corners. He learned his techniques in the jungle villages of Vietnam, but they applied just as well in the ruins of central Indiana.

She settled down in the only room of the house with a remaining roof and pulled off her bag to review the week's findings and let Ash stretch his legs. He scurried over to a corner, chasing some real or imaginary gremlin.

This was always her favorite part. Papa taught her how to find the most value from the old pre-war scrap, and she enjoyed sorting through the different colored metals, glass, and plastic.

Of course, she always saved the shiniest bits of plastic for Ash to play with.

Tomorrow would mark one week until the big bicentennial celebration in town. Two hundred years was a chunk of time that Ruth couldn't imagine, having only lived eleven of those herself. But she knew that this was a big deal for a country left in ruins.

The survivors of the Great War of 1969 were determined to show that they still believed in the United States, despite how it all ended. While most of America's military was stuck fighting a losing war in Vietnam, the Soviet Union surprised everyone by hosting a nuclear pissing contest with China that resulted in the annihilation of most of

Asia's population. But no one was prepared for the fallout and sickness that would eventually kill the rest of the world over the next seven years.

And that's why this bicentennial celebration was so important. North America didn't suffer the casualty numbers of Asia and Europe, but its infrastructure still crumbled. Once society fell apart, every single survivor felt the effects.

Here in 1976, the citizens had a chance to use an important milestone to show the world that they had not given up. They were determined to prove that America will rise again with the help of small-town patriotism and determination. The Spirit of '76 was alive and well in Sheridan, Indiana.

Of course, Papa scoffed at all of this. The self-appointed town council was made up of the same bureaucrats who ruined it in the first place, so he would have no part of it. He kept to himself just on the outskirts of town, safely secured in his castle of burned-out cars and other remnants of society that could stack high enough to block the world out.

And then there was Ruth and her unrivaled sense of optimism about the future. She may not remember life before the war, but she was completely mesmerized by the romantic vision of it all: Superstores, fresh food markets, entire buildings full of books, and trees!

A sudden thump woke Ruth from her daydream. Something was prowling around outside the farmhouse. Ash stared at the wall to their left, slowly lowering his body into a stealthy hunter position. Ruth held her breath and listened.

The sun slapped a warning on her face as she peeked outside. She pulled her hood up and dared to creep out further away from the safety of her shelter.

As she inched around the rear corner of the building, someone grabbed her from behind and yanked her straight back and off the ground.

Ruth struggled to escape from her captor's grasp, but the grip only tightened. Her arms were held behind her and a hairy face planted itself against her cheek. Papa prepared her for this exact situation, but every drop of her training evaporated in the heat of panic.

"I will rip your throat out if you make another sound, do you hear me?" The voice hissed as the man's stubble cut into her neck and his sour stench cut into her nostrils.

"Yes," the girl managed to croak. The training part of her brain was starting to return. Stay calm, Ruth. Assess the threat.

The man handled her like a ragdoll, twisting her body around to face him. He was a giant compared to her. Not a literal giant, like she'd read about in her Bible stories with David and Goliath, but he was much larger than Papa.

It was his eyes that affected her the most. Sunken deep into his face, those eyes were wild and angry. They were both experienced and naive. Ruth could tell by those eyes that the man was also in the advanced stages of dehydration. He might not be as much of a challenge as she thought.

"Give me your water!" He motioned toward her canteen. This was the first time Ruth realized that his right hand held a gun. Now *there* was the real threat.

The girl inched down steadily to gather her canteen, but the impatient man reached out to grab it first. His hand caught the strap that held the bag on her shoulder, and it snapped. Ruth stumbled backward, dropping the bag to the dirt. He snatched it up and bolted into the open wasteland.

Ruth pushed herself back up to her feet, swinging blindly in front of her, but the man was gone. Ash trotted back over to make sure she was OK. Only a few pieces of scrap wire and plastic lie where her bag fell. Her canteen was gone. Her canned food was gone. *Papa's present was gone.*

She shielded her eyes to scan the horizon.

The sun was too bright to see clearly, but Ruth could make out a figure moving off to the west. She took off immediately, determined to catch up to the man before he got too far, but the toe of her boot caught on something hard and she tumbled to the ground.

The girl looked back to see what tripped her, hoping by some miracle that Papa's gift had fallen from the bag.

It was a gun. The man dropped his pistol.

She plucked the gun from the dirt and ran as fast as she could toward the man just as his shape disappeared into a barn on the horizon.

When Ruth reached the building, she ducked down within the shadow of a grain silo to plan her next move and catch her breath in the cooler air. Ash caught up and nuzzled her elbow.

The gun was heavy in her hand and its corroded metal made her realize that it might not even work. It might not even be loaded. She wasn't sure how to check but she knew that her finger went on the curved metal trigger part.

A small hole in the barn's rusted siding allowed a peek inside, but it was too dark to make out anything except old tractor parts and dirt. She lurked around to the front of the building where the large doors once stood and let her eyes adjust to the dark clutter as she crept inside.

That's when she saw it: a raggedy boot shuffled behind some boxes in the hay loft above her. She wasn't sure if she'd get a chance for a clear shot, so she decided to sneak to a closer angle. She lowered her body down to the dirt floor, crawling on her elbows and knees, gun carelessly cradled in her hand, pointed upward and—

BAM!

The gun's explosion was much louder than Ruth imagined. She didn't understand that the gun would go off so easily and so powerfully, and now it wasn't even in her hand anymore. Where did it go?

The ringing in her ears was excruciating, but she knew she had to get that gun back. She glanced up and noticed that the boot was gone, too. She couldn't hear anything but that horrible ringing.

On her hands and knees, she felt around in the dirt and behind crates. The gun was nowhere to be found. Ruth's whimpering sounded strange to her own ears.

The man was suddenly down on the ground floor now, shouting at Ruth, but she couldn't understand his muffled words. One hand was pressing on a bloody spot on his left leg and he looked ready to collapse. He lunged at the girl with everything he had, awkwardly tackling her to the ground.

Ruth lie flat on her stomach, gasping for breath with her face in the dirt. The man's body weight held her down as one of his forearms pressed hard against the back of her head in an attempt to smother her. Ruth was in a position that Papa had always warned her about. She was helpless.

The only thing she could do at this point was to kick her legs backward as hard and as fast as she could. Luckily, she connected a few good shots to his kidneys with her boot heels.

The man readjusted himself to hold down her legs, but that gave just enough freedom for Ruth to squirm away from under him. She tucked her arms and rolled her body until she hit a wall and curled up into a sitting position behind a crate. Her eyes burned and she coughed debris from her throat. She had no idea where the man was;

she couldn't see, could barely breathe, and the ringing still dominated her ears.

A cackle erupted from in front of her as she wiped the dust from her eyes. The man's blurry silhouette towered over her. He must've found the gun because he now held it directly at Ruth's temple. Without so much as a parting word, he jerked the trigger once, then twice. Ruth winced but there was no loud bang this time, only clicks. The gun was jammed. Maybe it was Ruth's limp-grip firing or maybe it was all the dirt, but something caused the handgun to malfunction.

This was the girl's only chance for escape, but instead of bolting out the door to safety, she ran for the ladder and climbed up to the loft in search of her bag. Ruth figured the man probably couldn't climb with his injured leg, so she used the loft to her advantage.

Aside from a few open cans of her food strewn about, it looked like everything else was still in the bag, including Papa's gift. She grabbed the satchel and peeked back over the edge.

The man's shouts were becoming clearer as her hearing was beginning to return.

"You have nowhere to go now!" he croaked from below.

Ruth searched the second-story walls for another way out, but the hay door was blocked with junk. The loft's floor shook as the troll of a man lumbered up the ladder. He was pulling himself up with his arms and his one good leg on every step. A slow process, but it appeared to be working. She was trapped and absolutely terrified. Stay calm, Ruth.

Just as he peeked over the top of the ladder, Ruth surprised him with one good kick to his temple. It was a solid kick, just as she'd done hundreds of times with the soccer ball Papa gave her last year for her birthday.

The man lost his balance and fell to the ground with a thud. Ruth watched his body for a few moments, not daring to make a sound. He didn't move at all, not even to writhe in pain from the fall. She didn't think he could be dead, but she wasn't going to stick around to find out what a ten-foot fall could do to a man in his weakened condition.

Ruth clutched her bag tightly and leapt off the ladder to the floor in a puff of dust, inches away from the man's body. She had a sudden vision of his hand clamping onto her leg as she passed, but he didn't budge. She scampered toward the exit with every single ounce of her remaining energy, snatched Ash up from the shadowy corner near the door, and headed home.

The junk fortress was a welcome sight. The watchtowers clipped over the horizon first, beautifully backlit by the setting sun. Every battered street sign and random piece of scrap metal that made up the bulwark brought back so many memories of scavenging trips through Indianapolis with Papa.

Ruth broke into a sob when she was close enough to smell the familiar stale gasoline and sun-baked rust.

"Please, Papa, open the door," she moaned as her elbow thudded against the security gate over and over again. Ash let out an accompanying meow.

Her scavenging trip had lasted almost a week more than they had planned. Papa was probably worried sick but she hoped he wasn't out looking for her. His gift was special, and he'd see that it was worth the wait.

Ruth pulled herself back up to her feet and headed to the side entrance that Papa had made especially for her and Ash. It was too small for most full-grown adults to fit through, and Ruth knew exactly how to avoid the traps.

Once inside, Ruth searched room by room for Papa, calling out his name. Each call added a bit more desperation to her voice until they turned into near screams.

"Papa! I'm here! Please come out," she cried. "I"m sorry I was gone for so long but I have a surprise for you. I have your present right here!"

Only the wind answered her back, blowing dirt and sand through windows that Papa had been promising to fix for months.

"Papa! I don't want to ruin the surprise but if you want me to give you a hint, I—"

Ruth's plea caught in her throat.

She glimpsed Papa's boot lying on the kitchen floor. As she crept around the corner, the dim orange light revealed the rest of Papa sprawled on his back. His favorite stool was tipped on its side and flies buzzed everywhere.

"Daddy?" Ruth whispered the word that she hadn't used in years. The word that she only used when she wanted a favor. Right now the favor she wanted was for him to get up.

His body was stiff and white. She couldn't deny that familiar bomb sickness in his distant eyes.

Ruth and Ash spent the night lying near her father's body. She didn't sleep, but she did dream. She dreamed of Papa's voice and his hugs and his brown-eyed stare. She dreamed of his wise advice and the way he laughed through his nose when she said something funny.

The girl pulled the gift out of her bag and laid it next to Papa. Despite what the sickness had done to him, she could still see his face the way it was before.

"Look, Papa. I got this for you." Her voice shook with her hands.

―⁓⁓―

Papa's funeral was too crowded; he would've hated it. Everyone from town was there—even the ones who thought Papa was a troublemaker.

After the dirt was piled over his casket and the last people had given Ruth their condolences, she sat by her father's grave and prayed.

She prayed for guidance and wisdom. She prayed for peace and safety. Mostly she prayed that she would see her father again one day in the Heaven he taught her so much about. She hoped God was listening.

Ruth gathered up a shovel from the shed and a bucket of water from the storage barrels. Papa's gift was carefully wrapped in canvas and burlap to help preserve the moisture inside. The girl removed the bundle and set it on the ground. She was nervous that the trip may have killed it. She couldn't deal with losing this life, too.

Ruth soaked the sapling's young roots, going against her usual instinct to preserve every drop of water. She pushed the tiny tree into the loose dirt of Papa's grave, poured the rest of the water on top, and prayed again.

―⁓⁓―

A young girl picked at the cotton sleeve that kept her arm from burning. Her mother stepped forward, guiding her under the tree's narrow shadow. An old gray cat napped at the base.

"Happy Birthday, Papa," Ruth whispered, holding her young daughter tight. "Enjoy your shade."

The tree had grown substantially with Ruth's careful attention over the years. Now it was time to show her daughter how to care for Papa's gift.

A Very Zombie Thanksgiving

Written by K.E. Radke

—ele—

When K.E. Radke isn't killing helpless victims in her zombie books, she's writing in another genre—Urban Fantasy and Romance—where people live wonderful, fulfilled lives... sometimes. She currently resides in Las Vegas with her family, two corgis, and a Yorkie, where she's forced to be a chauffeur and watch UFC with all her boys, which might be why she writes angry, bitter characters so darn well.

—ele—

There's no place for me in this family. I stare over the balustrade at my uncles almost huddled on top of each other watching the football game and the pack of women surrounding the kitchen island with wine in their hands.

My cousins are behind me, playing on my PlayStation 5. And I have to sit here and pretend I want to share gaming time with them. Because of the holidays. What a crock of crap.

And the worst part is everyone is on a health kick and it was a unanimous family decision to try out plant-based meat.

Now when I say unanimous, I really mean my mom—who holds every holiday dinner at our house—made a health-conscious choice, and everyone went along with it because she cooks everything.

You don't get a vote if you depend on someone else to provide the food, which is why I bought a bunch of snacks yesterday and snuck them up to my room. I've been living off cheese puffs, pretzels, popcorn, and beef jerky.

To tell the truth, my mom's health kick has been going on for too long, and she finally got tired of making double breakfasts, lunches, and dinners, and now everyone has to suffer because she's on a diet. It was the longest argument known to man because no one agreed with her. You would think four against one had good odds to win this war for our tastebuds—my dad, sister, brother, and me against her.

But she knew the power she held over us.

I'll never forget what she said next. If you don't like it, cook your own food. Knowing damn well she doesn't allow us in her kitchen because every time we attempt to make something, we ruin her pots.

We thought we could change her mind because Thanksgiving dinner isn't a Thanksgiving dinner without real turkey and ham.

I think she took our argument as a personal challenge.

It was the first time my brother and sister and I were on the same team... since forever.

The garbage bin is a smorgasbord of empty takeout and pizza boxes. It's an unspoken agreement between us to keep my mom away from the refuse so she doesn't find out.

My dad sends us each a twenty-dollar weekly bribe under the codeword: Lab Dues.

The house doesn't even smell like Thanksgiving.

We're secretly hoping dinner is a disaster and Christmas will put everything back in its rightful place on our table. This plant-based meat crap will be a distant memory and something we laugh over for years to come.

Until she comes to her senses, my siblings and I pooled our bribe money together and bought a small fridge for dorms. We agreed to hide it in my closet because I'm the oldest. I've learned my mom doesn't come into my room if it's cleaned up and I do my own laundry. She thinks I'm maturing, but the truth is I don't want to starve on leaves and fake meat.

Fruits and vegetables are great, but sometimes I need a greasy, cheese-filled, meaty calzone. Or actual pasta. A guy can only have so much spaghetti squash and zucchini noodles before he's forced to steal from the grocery store.

Which I'm not proud to say I've done.

"Guess what the turkey is made out of." My sister, Clara, leans on the railing next to me.

"Spinach and kale?" I guess.

"Tofu."

I grimace. "That's not even plant-based meat. That's—." I don't even have a word for it.

"Cruel and unusual punishment," she finishes for me.

Our younger brother, Philip, slides in between us. "Maggie says she'll order us a pizza if we cover for her when the delivery guy gets here."

"Who's paying for the pizza?" I ask.

"No one, her boyfriend is the delivery guy and aunt Geraldine doesn't want him around," Phillip explains. "It's going to fall off the truck."

"Between the three of us, Maggie will never be missed," Clara says.

We all nod in agreement.

"Spartacus," my mom shouts at me from the kitchen. "Tell everyone it's time to eat."

Everyone thinks I'm joking when I tell them my name. My mom blames herself. It was the first and last time my dad got to pick out the first name for his offspring. Clara's middle name is Achillia and Phillip's is Tetraites. He's a huge fan of Roman gladiators.

Pushing away from the banister, I turn around and yell, "Time to eat!"

All my cousins completely ignore my announcement. There are seven of them standing right in front of the big screen attached to the wall. I have to squeeze between them and the TV, and even then, they all stretch their necks to look beyond me.

"Go downstairs to eat," I say, waving my arms in front of them so they can't see the screen.

"Get out of the way!"

"I'm dying!"

"He's going to die!"

"Hitman702 knows where you are!"

The TV turns black and there's a huge intake of breath.

Clara has the plug to the TV in her hand. She holds it up. "The faster you eat, the faster we can come back up here and play."

They all groan, but head for the stairs.

"Savage," Philip murmurs under his breath as we follow our cousins to the living room.

"Do we have a deal?" Maggie asks, staring at her phone when we hit the first floor.

"As long as you go ask your mom something right before you leave, we got you covered," Phillip says.

My brother is a planner, which is why I know we can get away with this. And we've had a lot of practice lying to adults recently.

Some of our aunts and uncles fill the open dining area, picking a chair to sit on. There are never enough seats at the long table, and a lot of the men end up back in front of the TV watching football. Usually, the kids are forced to eat at the breakfast table and the kitchen bar top—anywhere with a surface to catch the food falling off our plates or out of our mouths.

But this year, when I squeeze into the dining room behind my siblings for our family's tradition to watch my mom make the first cut of the turkey, there are empty seats.

I'm sure some of them ate before they got here. There was a rumor that Aunt Kimberly ordered an entire turkey dinner from Popeyes. I should probably find out if they ate before they got here, or if they plan to eat once they get home.

Two turkeys are in front of my mother. They both look identical on the outside, but when she cuts into the first one, the insides are white. My dad claps and stares at me and my siblings to join him.

We're still clapping when she cuts the second turkey that looks like meat, but it's an imposter. It fools the people sitting at the table and our cousins. When my mother looks up, the huge smile on her face falters at the number of people in the room. The table that can accommodate sixteen people is half full.

"Spartacus, Clara, Phillip, eat in here with us. Kids grab a chair," she encourages everyone in the room. Our uncles and aunts are served first. They all choose the imposter turkey over the tofu one.

My mom puts a slice of tofu turkey on their plate anyway.

The adults are passing the side dishes around as all the kids get in line to get a plate of imposter turkey. I watch my uncle Omar cut through the imposter turkey with his fork and read the question forming in his head from his facial expression—why is it so easy to cut this meat with a fork—and shove it in his mouth. He immediately stops chewing and stares down at the meat. With his mouth full, he says, "What kind of turkey is this?"

Aunt Avery slides her fork out of her mouth and slowly chews until she's able to swallow the piece of imposter turkey. The full wine glass next to her is emptied before she pushes the imposter meat aside and eats the mashed potatoes.

The next victim is Aunt Jaime. She actually spits out the meat in a napkin and then swishes soda in her mouth to remove the taste.

My siblings and I grab an empty plate and sit at the table, passing the side dishes to each other. Our dad catches our eyes, and he silently communicates to get in line for turkey at the same time my mom proudly announces, "That's the last piece of this turkey."

She acts like people had a choice over her plant-based meat and real turkey. All that's left is the tofu turkey, and he doesn't have the heart to force us to eat that.

My dad takes his place next to my mom and eats every bite of the imposter turkey on his plate. He can't shove it down his throat fast enough to get it over with. The glass next to him is emptied, and he refills it with wine before he scarfs down the tofu turkey slice.

Mom doesn't even grimace while eating the plant-based meat, but I notice her topping the imposter turkey with the healthy plant-based mac and cheese or mashed potatoes before putting it in her mouth.

Polite conversation is interrupted by my dad toppling over his glass of wine. His hands clutch the table and he spasms, pulling the tablecloth toward him and moving everyone's plate.

"Bradley?" My mom sits upright in her chair and slams her hand against my dad's back because a choking noise is coming out of him. His face is beet red, like he can't breathe.

Uncle Raymond also hits my dad's back to unclog his throat.

I'm on my feet with everyone else the second my dad collapses out of his chair and falls onto the floor.

"Call an ambulance!" several people shout at the same time.

All the adults are lifting the massive table to move it out of the way, plates of food forgotten. On the floor, my dad is turning purple and Uncle Omar is lifting him up to give him the Heimlich.

After a minute of Uncle Omar squeezing my father's stomach, Uncle Raymond takes over until my dad falls forward in his arms. My aunts move forward to help lie my dad on the floor.

"I—wh—Brad—is he—." My mom can't put a sentence together. She falls to the ground next to my father and places her head against his chest, listening for a heartbeat.

Clara, Phillip, and I meet each other's eyes, and their tears mirror my own.

"An ambulance is on the way," someone calls out.

My mom's face is buried in my dad's chest, and she's clutching his shirt, bawling her eyes out. I move forward, pushing my relatives out of the way to get to her.

Aunt Jaime puts a hand on my mom's back and rubs it with tiny circular movements. "Oh honey, come here." She tries to pull my mom away from my dad, but my mom tightens her grip on his shirt.

I kneel beside my mom before anyone can stop me and put my hand on her shoulder. "Mom." Her face whips around and red, puffy eyes meet mine. Black lines run down her face and her lipstick is smudged around her mouth. I put my arms around her and she falls against me, crying harder.

Beside me I hear whispers, "Someone get the children out of here."

There's movement behind me, but all I can stare at is my dad's purple, oxygen-deprived face. Eyes bulging out of their sockets. His mouth slack.

I hang onto my mom, needing her as much as she needs me.

And then my dad's eyelid twitches. His irises change from hazel to a milky gray and he's no longer a bluish hue. My arms tighten around my mom and then his eyelid twitches again. "Mom." The breathless word is barely audible, but she hears me, making me let her go in order to cup my face with her hands. My eyes don't sway from my dad and she follows my gaze. His eyelid twitches again and a low moan escapes from his mouth.

"Bradley?" She hovers over him as another groan vibrates his chest. Looking down into his eyes, her tears drop onto his face. "The ambulance is coming."

My dad lifts his arm to my mom's head and pulls her toward his face.

"Save your breath. Don't speak. Everything will be okay," she says and tries to pull back. His hand doesn't allow her to, and he opens his mouth and snaps down on her face. Teeth pierce her skin and a shattering scream explodes out of her. Fear roils through me, and I'm grabbing my dad's wrist to get her out of his grip.

Hair unravels from my mom's perfect bun, and I can't untangle my dad's fingers from her long tresses. Someone wrenches me out of the way and I'm against the wall as Uncle Raymond, Grady, and Omar hold my dad against the ground while Aunt Jaime helps my mom escape.

Blood is smeared across my dad's mouth, and his snapping jaws catch Uncle Raymond's arm near his shoulder. Flesh rips open and white bone is visible. The flap of skin hangs out of my dad's mouth and I feel everything in my stomach racing up my throat.

"What's wrong with him?" I ask no one and flatten myself against the wall. I can't find the courage to get to my mom. Half her face is gone, and the dark wooden floor is slick with blood. Her body is limp in Aunt Jaime's arms as Aunt Avery uses napkins to stop the bleeding on the open wound.

Shouts turn to static and all I can hear is a pulsing beat in my ears. My brain doesn't understand what my eyes are witnessing and my breaths turn short and sharp, making me woozy. Or maybe it's all the blood.

Towels and bowls of water are set on the table. More aunts and uncles flood the dining room to help. A hand wraps around my leg and I scream. Attached to the hand is Phillip. He's hiding under the table. I get a glimpse of Clara before Aunt Edith is in front of me. Her mouth is moving, but I can't hear anything except static.

She's leading me away from my parents when someone's screams rip through the ringing in my ears. We both turn toward it and see Aunt Jaime holding up her hand.

Three fingers are gone. Red liquid pours down her mangled hand. Aunt Avery abruptly stands and retreats, not sure what to do. I watch in horror as my mom crawls along the floor and takes a bite out of Aunt Jaime's calf. Tendons and muscles are ripped out with teeth and Aunt Jamie's hair-raising screech has my hands covering my ears.

Uncle Raymond collapses on the ground, blood oozing from his wound, and frees my dad's left side. My dad rolls toward Uncle Omar and sinks his teeth into the arm holding him hostage. Flesh is stretched between my dad's teeth as he yanks on the skin he desperately needs to have. Blood spills down my dad's chin and Uncle Omar punches him in the face, yelling, "Back Demon! Get back!"

Pain never registers on my dad's face from the hits Omar lands. And my uncle doesn't miss. Not a single punch.

Phillip crawls out from under the table and grabs my shirt, pulling me away from our parents and bloody relatives. But I can't look away. Animalistic growls and hisses fill the room and Uncle Raymond is on his feet again, snapping his jaws. He reaches for my uncle Omar, wrapping his fingers around my uncle's shirt, joining my dad.

It's two against one.

Uncle Omar grabs the carving knife and rams it into my dad's neck. Red liquid gushes out of the wound like a geyser, spraying everyone in the vicinity.

A scream is caught in my throat and tears fill my eyes. There's no way he'll survive. And I wait for my dad to collapse to the ground.

But he doesn't.

He clamps down on his next piece of flesh and Uncle Omar is brought to the ground. The knife is left in my dad's neck as if it belongs there.

I lean over and vomit. Clara is suddenly there helping Phillip pull me away from our family members feasting on each other.

My feet scramble to catch up with the rest of my body. Our cousins, Frederick and Fiona, are peering into the dining room, sobbing for their parents. When I try to grab their arms to make them come with us—wherever we're going—they fight back, refusing to move.

My brother is pulling me up the stairs while my sister is pushing me. But I freeze halfway up and shout a warning. "Get away from them!"

Uncle Grady lurches toward Frederick, reaching for him with gray fingers. Raspy growls intertwine with chewing noises. Fiona pushes her brother out of Uncle Grady's grasp and gets herself caught instead.

I close my eyes, feeling the tears run down my face.

But I can't shut out the thundering screams her vocal cords are capable of. The sound reverberates in every bone in my body and fear gives my feet the boost they need to race up the stairs. I almost trample over my brother.

Three people are huddled in the corner of the gaming den, hidden by shadows, and I stop at the top of the stairs, on the verge of hyperventilating. My cousins don't say a word, they just stare at me, silent tears falling down their faces.

"To Spartacus's room," Phillip whispers. He's on the ground, peering downstairs.

No one argues. We go down the hall and turn into my bedroom. As soon as all six of us are inside, Clara shuts the door.

Everyone is quiet for a really long time.

"Do you think we're safe up here?" Ines breaks the silence in a wobbly whisper.

"We just have to wait for the ambulance to show up," Phillip guarantees on a sob. I recognize the tone. It's the same one he uses when he has to convince himself to do something unimaginable. "They will know what to do."

Victor nods. He's hugging his knees to his chest, rocking back and forth.

"Did anyone else see the giant carving knife in dad's neck?" Clara's face is drained of color. Her knees falter, unable to hold her up. She's on all fours, crying into the carpet.

My sister never cries.

I can't stop the tears from falling down my face and finally give up wiping them away and let them fall.

The house is full of noise. Shouts and screams and cries for help all layer on top of each other.

Pounding footsteps run up the stairs and we all stare at my door. Clara is tripping over herself to get to her feet and plasters her body against the door to hold it closed. I'm right behind her and every noise we make is blasted like an alarm to my ears.

"Hello?" the broken voice whispers. Someone sobs. The sound is muffled like they're holding their hands against their mouth.

"Vivian," my sister whispers.

And then there's a loud noise. My sister and I make eye contact.

"Vivian?" Victor lifts his head. His sister. He gets up and tries to push us out of his way. "My sister needs help!" His voice rises, and the house suddenly shakes with growls and hisses.

Phillip grabs Victor and places a hand over his mouth. "Sit down and shut up. Let me think." He slowly releases Victor's mouth and is relieved to see the boy listen to him. Our six-year-old cousin is spoiled rotten and listens to no one.

Getting on the ground, Phillip looks under the crack in the door. "It's clear. No one else has come upstairs. We can get Vivian and wait for the ambulance."

Victor is nodding. Our two other cousins say nothing. Clara can't keep her breathing under control and she's shaking her head.

"I'll get her," I volunteer. My heart drops to my stomach the moment I make the decision.

"What if she's—." Clara can't finish the sentence.

"I don't think they can talk," I say and try to sound brave. "I think they—maybe it's rabies? Or the bird flu?"

"It's not a real bird. It's tofu and plant-based meat." Phillip's voice becomes so low that we can't hear him if he's saying anything. He's still on the ground, looking through the crack under the door.

"I'm going to peek out the door, find Vivian, and bring her back here. If anything comes up the stairs, shut the door, and I'll go into whoever's room is closest. Once the ambulance gets here, they'll help us—." I don't know what they'll help us with. My dad had a carving knife in his neck and I think my mom ate my aunt Jaime.

No one bothers to force me to finish my thought, so I take a deep breath and make Clara move so I can open the door. I'm holding my breath with every turn of the doorknob as I pull on it to peek into the hallway.

It's clear, and I slide through the crack of the door. Phillip doesn't let me shut the door and whispers, "I'll hold it open for you."

The floor creaks under my foot and I speed up because I don't remember the floor ever creaking when I walked over it before.

Exiting the short hallway, I stand at the entrance and inspect the den. We turned off the lights before we went down for dinner, and the TV cord lies on the ground, unplugged by the socket. Between the bean bags and gamer chairs, there's a body lying on the floor.

There's an iron scent in the air and smacking noises. Every once in a while, something sounds like it's being moved around. I avoid the balustrade, not ready to face the aftermath below.

Carefully moving forward, I make sure nothing is coming up the stairs and hurry as quietly as possible to the body. My toe pushes the person onto their back, and I'm relieved when it is Vivian. Her eyes are closed and she doesn't react when I nudge her with my foot again.

She's only a year younger than me, so we're about the same size, and I've never been considered strong. I copy the movies and put her arm around my neck and try to lift her up. It doesn't work. Her torso is barely off the ground when I let go of her arm and her head flops back to the wooden floor with a loud thump.

I stand motionless, waiting for something to hear the noise and decide to come for me. Footsteps creep down the corridor and Phillip stands at the entrance to the hall. He waves his arms and makes the universal hurry-up gesture.

Letting out a slow breath, I kneel next to Vivian's head and scoop her up by her armpits. When I get her into a sitting position, I wrap my hands around her waist and take a step forward. Warm liquid surrounds my foot and I slip, falling hard on my butt with a loud smacking noise.

Strangled groans, one after another, rise together and Phillip stands motionless with his arms frozen at crazy angles. The only part of his body that moves is his neck. He stretches it to get a glimpse of the scene below, but I know he can't see a thing from where he's standing. We've tried spying on our parents a lot over the years and he'll have to get closer to the railing to see anything.

Breathing hard and sucking down the painful shouts I want to let loose, I manage to stay mostly quiet until the ache subsides. What did I step in?

There's a puddle near Vivian and it's so dark I can't see what it is.

Phillip tiptoes into the den and grabs Vivian by the ankles and pulls.

Why didn't I think of that?

Vivian slowly slides across the floor, and I get up to help Phillip pull her down the hallway. When we get her closer to the entrance, the light from downstairs reaches us, and Phillip gasps, staring at my legs.

I have crimson stains all over me. And then I notice the red path trailing Vivian's body. A huge chunk of skin is missing from her arm.

"We'll need towels," Clara's voice makes my brother and I jump. She hops over Vivian and stays in the shadows as she crosses the den to the other side where the bathroom is.

My cousin's mouth opens with a low groan.

"She's waking up," Phillip whispers. He's on the ground next to her. "Try not to make any noise."

Her eyes pop open at the sound of his voice and her head turns toward him. She launches at him, bright red eyes glowing in the dark, and I yank my brother out of the way just in time, ripping his shirt. Snapping jaws bounce off the wall.

"Get in the room," I say as my cousin's jerky limbs get her on her feet. I hear a door open and slam shut behind me.

Vivian croaks out a noise I'm guessing only belongs in the animal kingdom. She crouches, hunched over, getting ready to pounce, and all I can do is retreat further into the short corridor until I hit the wall.

A shadow appears behind Vivian, and a crutch hits my cousin in the head from behind. Vivian swirls around and I get a flash of Clara before she dashes across the den and trips over a beanbag.

She's crying again. Loud sobs of terror she can't muffle.

Downstairs, there's a blast of raspy hisses and groans.

Vivian sprints toward my crawling sister and I run after her, grabbing the crutch my sister dropped on the ground during her getaway. Using it as a spear, I push my cousin as hard as I can and she trips over my sister, crashing into the ground face first.

At my sister's side, I pull her up and we watch Vivian jump to her feet. She snaps her jaws, and then I notice her arm is twisted in the wrong direction. I glance around the room. We're at an equal distance from both sides of the hallways leading to our rooms.

Philip is in my room on one side and Clara and my brother's room on the other.

Clara's sharp intake of breath makes me glance at her. But she's worried about the attention we're getting below us. Up against the railing, we can see everyone downstairs. They're all soaked in blood from open wounds and biting each other. Their gray eyes are locked on us—their next victims.

Most of our family members are unrecognizable.

One body is splayed open, the ribcage on display showing it harbors no organs. I can't even identify the person by their clothing because it's ripped to shreds.

Rapid footfalls bring my attention back to Vivian as she runs straight at Clara and me. I grab my sister and hold on to her tightly.

"Duck!" Phillip's voice bellows from the hallway.

Clara and I fall to the ground and Vivian flips over the banister. We watch her plunge to the ground. Her head cracks open on impact.

Family members converge on her only to stare for a few seconds before moving away.

We run past Phillip, and when he doesn't follow, we skid to a halt.

"Sirens," he says with so much hope he breaks down in tears again.

The noise only gets louder and all three of us are at the top of the stairs, listening to doors slamming and the sound of rushed movements outside of our house.

"Help!" Clara yells. Below us, the people we no longer recognize answer her call with growls and guttural rumbles. We join her cries for help when we see bodies lining up outside the front door. Someone is trying to peer inside through the frosted glass.

We're screaming at the top of our lungs, and I watch my family members gather at the bottom of the stairs, fighting to get to us first.

The front door jamb splinters. Several of my aunts and uncles turn toward the entrance to my house.

A man crashes through the front yelling, "We've entered the home to cries of help!" He's immediately tackled and submerged by teeth. Angry shouts and agonizing screams blur together, and we fall silent upstairs, watching our family eat the medics alive.

Beyond the Walls

Written by Maira Dawn

―――♥♥―――

AN AVID READER FROM a very young age, Maira Dawn turned writer after raising her children. Although Maira enjoys time with her family, you can often find her deep in a world of her creation, typing away so she can share the story with others. Other favorite activities are hiking, photography, and oil painting.

Maira first wrote on Wattpad and quickly gathered a following. She then released her first series, *Sanctuary's Aggression*, on Amazon where it has done well. Most known for that first eight-book series, she is now writing her second series, *What Used To Be*, and has released the first book.

This short story, *Beyond the Walls*, is part of the *What Used To Be* series. Wolf and Jayden also show up in book 2, *What Used to be Arkansas*.

If you enjoyed this story and would like to read more, you can find Maira Dawn Books on Amazon.

―――♥♥―――

Chapter 1

Wolf sighed and flipped his long black hair back over his shoulder. He'd been out here for two days. That was a day too long, and he still had nothing to show for it.

He scanned the overgrown fields around him. It was lonesome out here beyond the community's walls, and the feeling didn't sit well with him. In addition, the dry summer had made the grass crunchy and the path dusty, and it was so quiet he heard every step his moccasin-encased feet made.

And something was tracking him. It moved through the tall golden grasses on his right.

Wolf's heart gave a couple of hard thumps. Now that there were fewer people, animals were more brazen. He put a hand to his crossbow and rose to his tiptoes, but couldn't see anything.

Whatever it was had stopped.

After waiting a few moments, he chuckled. It was probably just some little bunny half paralyzed with fright.

"It's your lucky day, rabbit. I ain't hunting."

The fourteen-year-old set his shoulders and continued. The little ones needed medicine. Someone had to get it, no matter what it was like out here. He could do this. He would make his little town of parentless kids proud.

Wolf stared at the intersection a few yards in front of him and trudged toward it. At the crossroads, he turned and stared off in each direction.

This is where it got tricky because this was as far as he'd wandered since The Fall. From here on out, the landscape and buildings were a mystery.

Oh, he knew what had been there, but what was there now? So here he stood, playing eeny, meeny, miny, moe to decide which direction to take.

Wolf shrugged and decided to go south. A tiny smudge on the horizon gave him the slight hope of still-standing buildings—maybe even an intact town.

After taking a few swigs from his canteen, Wolf started down the dusty road at a jog and passed a few houses with extensive fields in between. Most seemed damaged and deserted, except for one.

The beige ranch sat close to the country road. To the side of the house, a man about fifty was digging a hole and loading the dirt into a red wheelbarrow with peeling paint.

Wolf slowed and stopped. He'd hardly come across people around here. And there was no way around the man now. He eyed the rifle propped against the side of the wheelbarrow. Should he say something or skedaddle?

Before he could decide, the man glanced up. "I don't want any trouble," he warned, reaching for the gun.

Wolf raised his hands to show he didn't have any weapons besides the Bowie knife at his side and the crossbow on his back. "Neither do I, sir".

The man looked him over. "What's a boy your age doing out here?"

"I ain't that young. The way the world is now, I'm fully grown."

The corner of the man's mouth jerked up as he started to smile, then his expression saddened. "I suppose that's true."

Wolf asked the question that troubled him every time he left his safe little community. "Where's everyone at?"

"You mean since the sky fell?" The man scoffed. "Well, plenty were burned out of their places. A lot got sick from all that stuff—wasn't made to be in close quarters with humans, it seems. Others moved off to where more people are. I heard tell there are some setting themselves up as kings. People flock to them like sheep—as if they can't figure out this new life on their own."

The man eyed Wolf's buckskin shirt and pants. "Looks like you got it figured out."

The boy looked down and brushed his pant leg. "I'm trying. They're still a little stiff though."

"Keep trying. You'll get it. You seem like a determined kid." The man tapped the shovel a few times on the hard ground in front of him. "So, whatcha doing out here?"

"I need medicine. Is there a drugstore up ahead?"

The man nodded. "Yeah, there is. I haven't been that way for a while so I don't know what's left up there. There's some kind of weird... hound that way. You'd do better to turn around and search somewhere else."

Hound? "Is it rabid or something? I need to get those meds."

"I'm not sure." The man pursed his lips, then said, "Stay right there," and disappeared behind his house. After a couple of minutes, he came back walking a bicycle and waved Wolf over. "Here, take this. It's a spare, so keep it. Maybe it'll keep you ahead of that little monster."

Wolf grinned. Why hadn't he thought about this before? "Thank you, mister. I really appreciate this."

The man glanced from the town to Wolf. "You get hurt or anything, you can come back here. Ya hear?"

The boy nodded his goodbye. "I do, sir. Thanks again."

Elated, Wolf pedaled down the road, feeling as if he soared with the birds now instead of creeping along like a limping turtle. He kept his eyes on the town ahead and could soon make out buildings.

Several yards to Wolf's right, the long grasses again rustled and bent as something forced its way through them.

The boy sent darting glances that way. Was it the same animal that followed him before? Could it be the hound the man had warned him about?

Wolf pedaled faster, ready to grab his bow. He had confidence in his abilities. He'd taken down several deer and even a wild boar—all on his own. And boars were quick as all get out. If he could take out that boar, this dog was nothing. It sounded like it would be a favor to the neighborhood to get rid of the thing.

As the houses along the road got closer, the rustling in the grass ceased. Soon after that, Wolf passed a dirty sign welcoming him to Juniper Valley. Below that was a decorative sign proclaiming, "Home of the largest berry festival in Arkansas."

Wolf examined what seemed to be a ghost town. "Sorry to tell you, but not anymore, folks."

He rolled into the middle of the small downtown area. At the crossroads, gas stations sat at two of the corners and a hair salon on a third. Across from that was a mom-and-pop grocer called Tucker's, which advertised a pharmacy.

"Bingo!" Relieved, Wolf propped the bike against the nearest light pole and rushed to the front door.

The glass doors of the small building were still shut and intact—which was a good sign. People tended to smash places they looted.

As Wolf reached out to grab the door handle, a faint cough and groan came from his left.

He flattened himself against the wall beside the door, head swinging one way then another as he searched for the source of the noise. When he saw no one, he inched his way to the side wall and slipped around the corner.

Now standing between Tucker's grocery and a clothing boutique, he felt more secure. Against the store walls were two large, green dumpsters. Wolf crouched behind the closest one.

When an unpleasant aroma wafted through the alleyway, the boy held a finger to his nose. Something besides garbage was rank.

Another cough and a loud troubled moan came from beyond the alley.

Someone needed help.

Or maybe they wanted to draw him out.

Wolf stood and continued toward the back of the buildings, careful not to rustle any garbage strewn about the path.

The further down the alleyway he went, the stronger the smell. On reaching the next dumpster, he found a partially eaten wild piglet behind it. Something had gnawed on it in the last twenty-four hours.

It wasn't the first time the predator had used the gruesome makeshift den. There was a pile of broken, discolored bones beside the uneaten meat. Was it the hound? If so, it might come back soon.

A few more steps and he peeked around the back of the building. To his right was the grocery's parking lot, and beyond that, the road.

Wolf went left, creeping along the back wall of the clothing store. At the corner, he stopped and peeked around the side of it. The lot beside the store had at one time ended the commercial part of town and started a row of houses. Now the house there was no more than a pile of blackened timber, except for a front door that was leaned up against one side.

In the middle of that uncomfortable mess lay a boy around Wolf's age.

Chapter 2

Wolf gasped. The dark-skinned teen's head lolled to one side, his lips dry and cracked.

Wolf touched the canteen strapped across his body. He scanned the area—just because the boy was really in trouble didn't mean it wasn't someone else's trap.

On alert, Wolf slowly placed one foot in front of the other as he used the backside of the clothing store for partial cover. After reaching the end, he crouched and once again examined the town for any movement.

Deciding it was safe, he rushed to the woodpile and scrambled over it until he was at the teen's side.

The boy heard him coming and jerked back, eyes wide.

Wolf clamped a hand over the boy's mouth. "I'm not here to hurt you!" He looked around again. "Are you alone?"

The boy nodded his head yes, his short dreads shaking.

Reluctant but knowing he had to take the chance sometime, Wolf slowly lifted his hand from the mouth of the wounded boy, who then clamped his lips together.

"What's your name?" Wolf asked.

"Jayden." His throat was so dry he croaked the answer.

Wolf pulled the canteen over his head, popped the lid, and handed it to him. "It's water."

Jayden pushed himself up and grabbed the canteen, chugging its contents.

"Take your time," Wolf said. "You don't want to throw it up."

Jayden nodded. He dropped the canteen onto his lap and fell back onto the woodpile.

"How long have you been here?" Wolf asked as he glanced at Jayden's legs. The boy had yet to move them. Was he injured?

"Two days, almost three. I was sure I was a goner."

"Almost were. Are you from around here?"

"Yeah. My parents died during The Fall—burned with this house." Jayden banged his fist against the burnt lumber beside him. "I only survived because I was at my friend's place across the street. After a while, people started to leave, but I just couldn't go with them. My friend's family gave me their keys and waved goodbye. Mostly I'm alone, but the other day strangers came through." Jayden grimaced and pointed across the street. "I couldn't get inside the house in time to hide. Lucky me, I had something they were looking for."

Wolf raised his eyebrows. "What?"

Jayden glanced at his legs. "A wheelchair. I can't walk—never been able to."

Wolf shook his head. How could people be like that? It boggled his mind.

Jayden continued in a bitter tone. "They said they were sorry, that someone in their group needed it." He flashed Wolf an angry gaze. "I suppose you're ready to leave me here too—now you know how it is."

"What? Of course not," Wolf reassured him.

"Well, if you can just get me set up with a way to get around, I'll be fine."

"I will. Don't worry." Wolf wasn't sure how he'd do that, but he would try.

"What are you doing here, anyway?" Jayden asked as he sipped more water.

"Looking for meds—penicillin, amoxicillin, anything like that."

Jayden pointed to the grocery store. "Last time I checked, there was still some of that in there."

Wolf's spirits rose. "Awesome."

Wolf allowed Jayden a few more sips before saying, "Hey, how about we get you out of this nest of two-by-fours? It can't be comfortable."

"It isn't. But could you run into the store and get me something to eat before we go? There were still a few cans of vegetables left in there."

"Sure," Wolf replied, puzzled by Jayden's behavior. "But I'll get you out of here first."

Jayden jerked away. "No. I'll stay here until you get back."

Wolf straightened and stared at him. "What's this about?"

Jayden glanced around. "It's just—um—"

"Is this about that hound?"

The teen's eyes grew bigger. "You know about that thing?"

"A man down the road told me about him. Said he didn't come this way anymore because of it."

Jayden looked at the ground. "Smart man."

Wolf scoffed. "You live here."

"I'm usually inside. The wheelchair doesn't roll around on these bumpy roads so good anymore."

"Is that dog really that bad?" Wolf pointed to the weapon he carried on his back. "I've got my crossbow."

"Good weapon." Jayden pushed himself into a straighter sitting position. "And yes—that dog is fast and mean. And not like anything I've ever seen before."

"I take it you think this woodpile is gonna save you?" Wolf swept his hand over the pile.

"I dragged myself over here. Those idiots left me in the middle of the road. It was near night and with all the commotion, I knew that thing was coming. I curled up in this here pile and used this to whack him." He held up a two-by-four with several nails in it. "It was a fight, but in the end, he realized I wasn't gonna be the easiest meal of the day."

Jayden flexed his biceps. "Superior upper body strength."

Wolf chuckled. The boy was tough. He'd give him that. "All right, you stay here while I get you some food. Is there a wheelchair in there? Some stores had them."

"There was one. I don't know if they took that one or not."

"Okay. I'll check." Wolf gave Jayden one last glance before he took off. He hated leaving the boy. It was clear he'd suffered over the last couple of days. He doubted Jayden could fight off a flea at this point.

Leaving the side door open, Wolf rushed through the small store. It still had a lot of stuff, which told him Jayden didn't get much company. Of course, it was better he didn't if everyone was going to be like the looters who took the teen's wheelchair.

He grabbed a couple of bottles of water and the cans of vegetables Jayden mentioned. Wolf also found a can of Vienna sausages, whatever that was. It seemed to be meat and Wolf figured a little protein would do Jayden good.

What he didn't find was a wheelchair.

At the back of the store was a large sign that said "Pharmacy." It would only take a minute to look for the medication he needed.

He hadn't taken two steps when Jayden yelled out. "Get out of here! Go on, go away!"

Wolf turned and headed out the front of the store. Looking around, he rushed to Jayden's side but saw nothing. "Was it here?"

"I saw the bush in front of that line of trees moving around. I figure that's him. He stalks people like that."

Wolf remembered the tall grasses along the road moving like that. Had that been the dog? "Okay. Let's get you inside then. Which house are you staying in?"

Jayden pointed to a blue house across the street and to the left—too far for Wolf to carry a boy that was as big as he was. "No wheelchair in the store. I gotta find something to move you with."

The bushes near the trees shook again.

Jayden snapped his fingers. "There's a wheelbarrow two houses down—in the front yard. But that's toward the dog."

Wolf glanced from where Jayden pointed, to the bushes where the dog hid. The house and the dog were in the same direction, but the bushes were several backyards away and to the right. The white house was only two small front yards away and to the left.

He could do this.

Wolf made sure Jayden had his board with nails. "You good?" he asked.

"As good as I'm going to get." Jayden sat up as best he could on the pile of wood.

Wolf moved a few pieces closer to support Jayden's back. "I'm just going to get that wheelbarrow and come right back."

Jayden nodded, grasping his makeshift weapon more firmly. He glanced up at Wolf. "We got this."

Wolf grinned. "Of course we do, dude. It's just a dog."

"Uh, yeah. A kinda crazy one."

A crazy one? Wolf forgot the strange comment as he swung the crossbow off his back. At a quick walk, he crossed the open area where the animal could see him. Once Wolf was in the shadow of the first house, he quickened his pace, running toward the front yard of the second house.

He reached it without incident. And the fact that Jayden had not called out an alarm was a good sign too.

Wolf returned the crossbow to his back, grabbed the wheelbarrow, then sprinted back toward the first house.

Jayden's face lit up when he saw Wolf coming toward him. "You did it!"

Wolf parked the makeshift trolly as close to the woodpile as possible. He glanced at the brush and froze when it shook, but no animal emerged. "Okay, let's get you into this thing."

Jayden put down his two-by-four and held his hands out. "Pull me up, then turn me toward the wheelbarrow. I can do the rest."

"Will do." Wolf did as instructed.

Jayden had enough strength in his legs to hold himself in position for the few seconds it took to move from Wolf's grasp into the wheelbarrow. Once seated, he pulled his legs in and pushed with his arms until he was comfortable.

He held out a hand. "Better give me my stick—just in case."

Wolf handed Jayden his weapon. "You keep an eye on the woods, okay?"

Jayden craned his neck until they were in the shadow of the first house. He blew out a sigh. "Okay. We are doing good."

Wolf picked up speed, then scrambled when he hit a low spot in the grass and Jayden almost tumbled out. After that, Jayden laid his weapon beside him and grabbed the sides of the wheelbarrow.

The boys were almost to the road when an open area between houses gave them a full view of the trees with the brush below it.

"It's there!" Jayden said, pointing.

Wolf glanced over his shoulder at the infamous dog and froze, skidding to a halt. It was like nothing he'd ever seen before.

The nightmare animal had four legs and its head and body roughly resembled a dog—but the resemblance ended there.

It had no fur, but rather fire-red skin the color of lava, as if it had crawled up from the bowels of the earth.

"What is that?" Wolf stammered.

Jayden slapped his arm. "Go! It's fast. Very fast."

Wolf set his gaze on the blue house with the partly open white door and willed himself there as quickly as possible.

Jayden's fingers whitened as they clamped the sides of the wheelbarrow.

When they reached the other side of the road, the fire hound's panting breath was right behind them.

Jayden took one hand off the wheelbarrow to grab his weapon.

The vicious animal moved parallel to the teens.

Wolf's eyes widened as the hound's shoulders bunched to jump. "Get away!" he shouted, kicking out at it.

The animal jerked back, growled, and revealed razor-sharp teeth like a shark's. Crooked and blood-stained, they overfilled its mouth.

Short spikes lined the backbone of its skinny body.

The fire hound's black, soulless eyes stared at Wolf with emotions he'd never seen in an animal's eyes before—rage, hatred, and death.

Wolf's mouth went dry. What was this thing?

He snapped his head forward and found speed he didn't know he had. The fire hound's hot breath spurred him on.

Wolf went at the door full tilt, stopping only when the wheelbarrow crashed into the doorframe and banged into the door, shoving it wide open.

Wolf grabbed the top of the door frame and pulled himself up, distracting the fire hound so Jayden could drag himself and his weapon over the lip of the wheelbarrow and onto the floor.

The fire hound snapped at Wolf's foot, almost chomping it.

Wolf swung and kicked the animal in the face.

It jumped away and changed direction, disappearing behind the house's outside wall to the left of the door.

Wolf swung back and let go, landing inside the door right beside Jayden. Together, they shoved the wheelbarrow as hard as they could and watched it roll backward, toppling over onto the front walkway.

Wolf grabbed his crossbow from his back and aimed at the open door.

Jayden reached out and grabbed the side of the door, ready to swing it shut.

A deep, raspy growl came from just outside. The fire hound lunged from the left, landing squarely on the walkway in front of them. The skin of what should've been its ruff wrinkled and its legs became stiff. It was ready to pounce.

Inside the house, Wolf took a step forward, almost touching the hound's head with his crossbow, his finger on the trigger. He stared into the animal's glaring black eyes.

"I will kill you."

Something shifted in the fire hound's gaze—some kind of intelligence. It gave a vicious growl.

Wolf tightened his grip on the crossbow and squeezed the trigger.

Nothing. He tried again. Another misfire.

The beast lowered its head and flexed its spine as it got ready to spring.

Wolf's heart hammered. In one motion, he stepped backward into the house and he and Jayden slammed the door shut. The hound's skull thudded against it.

Wolf looked at him with raised eyebrows. "You call that a dog?"

Chapter Three

Sitting in the living room, Wolf tried to make sense out of what had just happened. He shuddered at the memory of the vile lava-colored hound.

The thing was an affront to everything natural—worse than any horrors he'd dreamed of.

"For critter's sake," he said. "We need to figure this out. We can't stay locked up in here forever."

Jayden gave him a puzzled look then laughed. "For critter's sake? No, that's not it. It's 'for—'"

Wolf raised a hand to stop him. "I'm not taking anyone's name in vain. Things are bad enough. I'm not saying anything to make anyone up there mad."

"I don't really think it's vaining anyone," Jayden said. "I mean, how is that going to make him mad?"

"I don't know, but I ain't gonna chance it. And neither should you, dude. From what I just saw, the world is more of a mess than I imagined it to be."

He ran a hand over the back of his neck. "What we need to work on is a plan for getting out of here without that thing seeing us. You can't stay here alone. I've lost people before, and I don't want to lose you too. Come with me. We have a friendly community with everything you need—except a wheelchair. We'll need to look for one on the way back."

Jayden was quiet for a moment as his gaze moved to the front window, out toward his burned-out home. "This is the only place I know."

Wolf imagined it would be hard to leave a place that had been a home with an actual mother and father.

Jayden's gaze made its way back to him. "But you're right. It's a miracle I made it this long. I'll go with you." He sighed. "And I know where a wheelchair is, but you won't like it."

An hour later, Jayden had packed a few precious items, and Wolf found himself pushing the wheelbarrow with his new friend in it down the sidewalk toward the side of town opposite where he entered.

He glanced longingly at the store with the pharmacy but knew every moment mattered. It wasn't like he could leave Jayden on the sidewalk while he went inside when that hound could be on them any second.

His loaded and cocked crossbow lay across his back—not something he normally did, but the situation demanded it—and it comforted him.

Wolf threw several glances over his shoulder, hoping they got out of town before that evil animal saw them.

The sidewalk they walked on ended at a small park. The teens looked over a couple of metal and plastic swing sets and slides. On the other side of them were a picnic and viewing area. There had been a white chest-high fence surrounding the place. Now the stakes from one section littered the ground, leaving a gaping hole with a view of the deep gorge just beyond it.

On the near lip of the sheer cliff was a wheelchair.

Wolf almost asked, but reckoned it was a story he didn't want to know. He pushed Jayden closer and stopped beside the chair.

He couldn't stop himself from peeking over to the rocky bottom of the gorge. Brightly colored clothing littered the ground far below. His heart dropped. It wasn't just clothing.

He helped Jayden get settled in the chair, then turned back to the wheelbarrow to retrieve the teen's weapon and backpack.

Jayden gasped and yelled, "It's coming!" He grabbed his backpack but fumbled his weapon.

Wolf's hands pricked with invisible needles as he swung his crossbow off his back and turned to aim. The monster looked every bit as vile as the first time he'd seen it—maybe more—because now it appeared to have the victory.

Wolf locked his jaw, grinding his teeth. That deadly monster would not win. He would not let it.

Already halfway across the small park, it sailed over a picnic table. Quickly, Wolf aimed and squeezed the trigger.

The arrow caught the fire hound along its back flank.

It jerked and let out an unearthly howl, but kept coming.

Wolf glanced at his crossbow. There was no time to load it again.

The fire hound was on him in an instant. Wolf used his crossbow to push it back, using the weapon's rough points as little daggers.

Pure muscle, the fire hound was stronger than the teen and seemed to be made for battle. It shoved him back and Wolf's feet slid closer to the edge of the cliff.

Pulling in a sharp breath, the teen stabbed the crossbow harder. He was outmatched, but Jayden's life was at stake, and perhaps others' were too. He would never give up, not while he had a breath left in his body.

Jayden wheeled up beside Wolf and slammed the fire hound with his heavy backpack over and over.

The animal backed away, grabbing for Wolf's arm but getting only a mouthful of shirtsleeve. Its shark-like teeth shredded the deerskin, showing the boy what could easily happen to him.

Desperate, Wolf looked around and spotted Jayden's weapon laying in the grass beside the wheelbarrow. He grabbed the two-by-four, making sure the end with exposed nails faced the hound, and held it like a baseball bat. He eyed the sheer drop beside him.

The fire hound again launched itself from the picnic table, triumph already in its gaze. Wolf braced himself as the enraged animal flew at him. A brief prayer flitted through his mind and he grasped the board tighter.

Sure it would succeed, the animal stretched its mouth wide.

When Wolf smelled its rancid breath, he swung. The board hit the monster in the middle of its body, propelling the animal further than he'd intended.

The fire hound soared over the gorge and dropped. An angry screech sounded farther and farther away until the animal hit the rocks below with a loud smack.

Wolf let the broken two-by-four fall to the ground and fell to his knees.

Chapter Four

Two days later, Wolf's heart soared as he turned onto the last path toward home and breathed in the familiar scent. He patted his pack which held the medicine he'd finally been successful in getting from the store in Jayden's town.

They'd also told the old man where his bike was and that the hound was gone—they'd watched over the edge for a long time to make sure the thing stayed dead.

Jayden glanced at Wolf, who pushed him over the bumpy trail. "Tell me again."

Wolf chuckled. "We have a great place—it's all kids. You and I are some of the oldest. And we are making it! We started gardens and we hunt and fish and stuff."

"I can fish!"

"Yep. We need that. We gotta feed the littles. They don't have anyone else, just us." Wolf stopped pushing and changed the subject. "Jayden, how many of those vile animals are there?"

Jayden raised his hands. "That's the only one I ever saw."

Wolf stared up the path toward his community. "We don't need to tell them then. They have enough things to deal with. They don't need to know about monsters that no longer exist."

"If you think that is best," Jayden said.

"It is," Wolf said, sounding more confident than he felt. "A wild pig got in the camp once and gave the little ones nightmares for days."

Wolf thought about his best friend, the community's leader, Axel. He had enough on his shoulders. He'd just worry over the fire hound for nothing.

He grabbed the handles of the wheelchair again and pushed, giving a hard nod. "It is," he repeated. "Now let me tell you a little more about sitting on the side of the Red River for an evening of fishing and watching the sun go down."

Jayden smiled in anticipation and said, "Tell me every awesome part of it."

The Memory Store

Written by Mandy Shunnarah

MANDY SHUNNARAH (THEY/THEM) IS an Alabama-born, Palestinian-American writer who now calls Columbus, Ohio, home. *The Memory Store* is their first sci-fi short story, but it won't be their last. The other weird things they write for the internet include essays, poetry, and short stories that have been published in *The New York Times, Electric Literature, The Rumpus*, and many more. Their first book, *Midwest Shreds: Skaters and Skateparks in Middle America*, is forthcoming from Belt Publishing. When they're not writing, they can most often be found roller skating at skateparks, being buried under their six cats, eating a shit ton of Waffle House hashbrowns (triple smothered, triple covered), and wandering around old graveyards––just not all at the same time.

Read more at mandyshunnarah.com.

This story won second place in the 2021 Post-Apocalyptic Media Short Story Contest.

Healing is hard. Forgetting is easy.

Xoey stood beneath the glowing marquee of The Memory Store. She'd passed this store many times because it was the closest one to the micro-apartment she shared with her roommate, though there were about three dozen locations throughout the city. She sighed, knowing that not going to her appointment was only delaying the inevitable.

"Welcome Xoey Appleton-Nandini-García 12," an automated voice said when she entered the store, reading her biometric data. "A Memory Specialist will be with you shortly."

The black floor lit up with a glowing arrow directing her to an all-white private room with a plush twin bed.

The concept of The Memory Store was simple supply and demand. There was high demand for good memories and low, but present, demand for bad memories. Sell your bad memories for next-to-nothing in a crowded market. Sell your best memories for a fortune in the most in-demand market in the world.

"Choose your dream theme," the voice instructed.

The options were infinite, just like memory. You could choose from a real place, historical or present, a fictional place from any immersive film or virtual reality, or nothing at all. In a world so full of stimulation and countless possibilities, the sensory deprivation dreamless sleep was rumored to be the most common choice.

Xoey chose a forest with a lush canopy of leaves, a trail weaving through the tree trunks, deer dashing through the hollows, and rabbits bouncing through the grass. It's hard to believe such things really existed.

"Now make yourself comfortable," the voice said in a subdued, calming tone and dimmed the lights.

As she waited for the Memory Specialist, Xoey thought about the people who bought bad memories. The artists who believed you had to suffer to create work that's true; the memory activists who insisted that bad memories were a normal part of the human experience and that to extricate them is to make our species subhuman, a step back in evolution. Xoey had researched all the arguments and read the studies.

Suicide was nearly nonexistent since widespread use of memory extraction!

Are mentally ill people the next endangered species?

With such little demand for antiquated mental health services like therapy and psychiatry, those who regret implanting bad memories work to fight The Memory Store's no-return policy.

There were stories of people who had their best memories extracted only to become unmoored. They fell out of love with their spouse, they swore their children had been adopted, they felt no connection to their homes, and they wondered why they ever did the hobbies that once brought them joy. They forgot connection points that made the most important people and places and things in their lives meaningful. Those who sold their best memories often did so in bouts of depression, finding a Memory Store location closer than a mental health clinic. Or they had compelling reasons to need money suddenly: to escape unhousedness, to put up the ransom for a kidnapping, to fulfill a lifelong dream of living a life of luxury on the moon colony. These were normal, happy people—until they weren't.

Then there were people who had regular appointments at The Memory Store. Disgraced politicians, celebrities who had been publicly dumped, those from all walks of life who had been publicly shamed—people who were constantly being reminded of their scandal in the media, by protesters outside their homes, by hecklers who sought to do them harm.

There were, too, victims of abuse who were unable to leave their abusers who had standing appointments at The Memory Store. They wanted only to forget.

And there were people who wanted The Memory Store to extract from them the worst things they'd ever done. Memories so vile they paid years of their salary to ensure the memories were destroyed instead of resold.

There were also the ethicists who worried over the implications of all the unsold bad memories and how they were donated to prisons... and whether bad memories might be used as biological-mental warfare.

Xoey laid back on the bed, the mattress and pillow adjusting automatically to support her head and spine in the most optimal way. The ceiling was a giant screen with animated script.

Healing is hard. Forgetting is easy.

The tagline for The Memory Store dotted every gleaming, glow-in-the-dark billboard in the city. It was on the side of every skyscraper, scrolled across the news banners on the tops of windshields on every self-driving bus and car, and in the augmented reality shown through every pair of glasses. Which is to say, The Memory Store was everywhere—a place impossible to forget, though forgetting was their specialty.

There were millennia of suppressing emotions and refusing to talk about feelings before the therapy craze of the 2000s. Suddenly it was okay to not be okay, antipsychotic medication was normalized and encouraged, and not going to talk therapy was seen as a red flag, one worthy of refusing dates, cutting off contact with family, and writing kind, but firm, emails ending years-long friendships. Those intrepid travelers, through the bureaucracy of insurance, the inertia of Congress, and the apathy of public opinion in the early 2000s, eventually won out. By the 2020s there were PSAs about mental healthcare, free helplines where you could speak to professionals, yoga in schools, endless classes on mindfulness and how to breathe properly; how to think positive thoughts, and how not to think anything at all.

And in cultivating this awareness—or consciousness, as these early pioneers in wellness preferred to call it—in mental health, the cause of widespread mental illness was revealed: America. Or perhaps, more accurately, that which America holds most dear: capitalism and its requisite productivity and wealth creation. Some in the 2020s rejected this, saying, "this is just the way things are," but eventually the mental healthcare activists' message and burgeoning socialist platform caught on. It really was ridiculous to not have universal education and expect students to go tens of thousands or hundreds of thousands of dollars into debt to get a job that would maybe, if they were lucky, allow them to pay off their student debt before they died. It was asinine to not have universal healthcare and for a sick person to lose their home just so they could recover from their illness and be forced to live on the streets. It truly was cruel and manipulative to demand a 40+ hour workweek so people would be too exhausted to consider their lot in life and lack the energy and time for organizing to do anything about it.

But—and there's always a but, isn't there? In the 70 years that followed, universal education and universal healthcare were granted, but the cost of housing and food rose so much that it hardly mattered. There were still people struggling to afford what they needed and people were depressed and anxious and burned out as a result. What America had failed to do was address the root cause of the nations' and its peoples' ills. So the market—capitalism made manifest—convinced the people their troubles may have been caused by the demands of labor in the form of long hours and low pay, but people's inability to cope was no one's fault but their own.

Capitalism was the problem, but capitalism insisted it was also the solution. The wellness industry was all too happy to capitalize on the problem. It began as social media influencers—thought leaders, as they preferred to call themselves—hawking boutique vitamins, affirmational bracelets, polished crystals with every imaginable healing power, juice cleanses, workbooks on introspection, cozy hand-knitted shawls, CBD lotion, vape pens, water bottles to remind you to drink, watches to remind you to move, anything and everything under the all-encompassing umbrella of #selfcare. This evolved into meditation apps, sleep apps, breathing exercise apps, talk therapy apps, video therapy apps, reiki apps, tarot apps, mood tracker apps, period tracker apps, daily questionnaire apps that claimed to delve deep into your psyche—anything mental, physical, or emotional that could be tracked and counted and quantified and extracted for data.

Now, in 2099, on the cusp of the new century, it's The Memory Store. Because why bother tracking your emotional and biometric data and doing talk therapy, where everything you said was repeated back to you in an affirming way without judgment when you could simply make the bad memories disappear? The Memory Store made trauma go poof! After all, healing is hard. Forgetting is easy.

"Your Memory Specialist is approaching," the automated voice warned.

A woman entered, appearing normal except for her eyes, which were milky—no pupils, no irises.

"Hello, Xoey. I'm your Memory Specialist, Xara Sánchez-Takomi-McDowell 15."

Xoey had heard of The Vacants before, but she'd never seen one in person. People who sold so many of their memories that they didn't know who they were or where they'd come from and didn't recognize anyone they knew. They were so far gone that they had no basis for creating new memories and no way to regain the memories they lost. They were often such burdens to their families that many opted to return them to The Memory Stores, having the store pay the family for the Vacants' labor in exchange for the family never suing or speaking ill of the company. When a person disappeared, one never knew if it was because they'd been kidnapped, they'd run away, or because of a memory appointment gone horribly wrong. Xoey gulped, hoping she wouldn't become a Vacant.

"I see you're nervous," Xara said. "Is this your first time?"

"Yes," Xoey replied, surprised that Xara could see at all.

"We don't see many first-timers in their forties. Most people start in their teens. But don't worry, the procedure is completely painless. There's no downtime and no medical side effects. You'll simply go to sleep and wake up without the memory like it was never there."

Xara even gave Xoey a pat on the hand, an attempt at comfort that came off stilted and forced, as though Xara wasn't her own. "Will you be selling a good memory or a bad memory today?"

"A good memory."

"How nice! We rarely get those," Xara said. "You'll leave here a rich woman, Xoey Appleton-Nandini-García 12, and you won't even know what you're missing. I'll place some nodes on your head and—"

"I have a question," Xoey gasped. "How do I know you'll only take the one memory I want to sell and not all the other memories connected to it? If I won't know what I'm missing, how will I know you didn't rip me off and take a bunch of memories when I only wanted to sell one?"

Xara chuckled. "That's a great question, Xoey, and you'd be surprised how many memory sellers wonder the same thing. Although the people selling bad memories often don't mind if you take more than they asked for, as long as you don't extract a good memory instead..." she added, grinning.

"Our system has been fully tested and government approved. The science, which is proprietary to our lab, is unparalleled. Our scientists figured out how to isolate specific memories, so we can sense the edges of each memory and know where to cut—though no actual incision is involved. Instead of thinking of memories as spaghetti, all thrown together and touching one another, our technology sees each memory as an individual item that can be cleanly separated from the rest of your mind, and it removes it non-invasively."

"I want to know that you'll only take the one memory, no more."

"Of course, like we agreed. We pride ourselves on excellent customer service," Xara smiled. Xoey wondered if Xara's own Memory Specialist had told her that before they extracted the last memory she would ever sell.

Xara placed each node on Xoey's head with precision, stopping to consult a hologram of a diagram showing the placements specifically calculated to optimize removal of Xoey's memory. Xara then pulled a panel from the wall and lowered it over Xoey's body. The panel would wirelessly read Xoey's heart rate, pulse, oxygen saturation, brain activity, and other vitals throughout the procedure.

"Would you like a few moments undisturbed to enjoy the memory one last time?" Xara asked when she completed her preparations.

She thought about the type of person who would buy this memory, who would have it permanently superimposed in their own memory as though it had been there from the start. She wondered if she would even remember having sold a memory or if The Memory Store's concierge service would ensure she woke up in her micro apartment none the wiser.

"No," Xoey said, feeling her eyes twitch with suppressed tears. "I've had it for a long time."

"Very well," said Xara, pressing a button on the panel. "You'll be asleep before you can say 'forgetting is easy.'"

"Forgetting is—"

In Xoey's mind's eye, she saw a forest, full and thriving. Not logged, not burned, not extracted of its resources. In the lab, Xara and the precision robot used to remove memories identified the one Xoey wanted to sell. Each memory The Memory Store removed was viewed by a Vacant for cataloging purposes and to ensure the robot cut the edges as far as they could go without interfering with other memories. Sometimes the robot and the Memory Specialist could see the grayed parts of the memory, things the seller didn't even realize they'd remembered; things their subconscious had pushed to the periphery.

Not that this mattered to either the robot or The Vacant. Neither could form memories themselves. The Vacant would forget everything she'd seen within a few minutes of seeing it. The robot could only store information, not react to them or attach emotional meaning to them.

The robot extracted the metadata from Xoey's memory: The year was 2076 (23 years ago) in what remained of Antarctica. The memory played as a hologram; the perspective through Xoey's eyes.

A much younger Xoey, about 17 then, with long curly brown hair tied back into a braid wearing jeans (how dated!) and a short-sleeve t-shirt (made of cotton! how retro!) and muddied boots stood with her hands in her pockets next to a woman who appeared ancient. The woman was holding a coat with a fur-lined hood in her arms. It wasn't nearly cold enough for her to need it.

The robot was able to pull more metadata as the memory progressed. According to the emotional markers attached to the memory and the parts of the Xoey's brain that lit up when this memory was prodded, the old woman is Xoey's great-great-grandmother.

"It's nothing like it used to be," Grandmother said, the many lines of her face obscuring her disappointed expression.

"Was this continent really covered in ice once?" Xoey asked, toeing at the muddy ground.

"Like you wouldn't believe. Blankets of snow as far as the eye could see. And beyond that?" Grandma paused. "The ocean... with ice shelves dozens of feet thick and strong enough to hold multiple families of polar bears with each individual weighing a ton."

Xoey looked out to the Southern Ocean now, no ice shelves or ice sheets in sight. It had been decades since Grandmother had been to Antarctica since it required a special dispensation to visit due to its fragile state. And yet, along the coast, construction crews rushed to build resorts. With the ice gone and Antarctica's temperatures becoming more moderate by the year, the continent was destined to become the world's first truly international resort, owned and operated by hospitality representatives from each of the 54 nations who agreed to the Antarctic Treaty and once, a long time ago, held it dear.

"I can't even imagine what that must have been like."

"This place was beautiful until 2031. The ice had been melting before that, but that's when things really got bad."

"That's the year California split off, right?" Xoey asked. "And all the coastlines around the world moved inland twenty miles and a bunch of people lost their homes?"

"Smart kid. You get that from me," Grandmother said, smiling and pulling Xoey into a hug.

Xoey began to cry softly. "Are you sure this is what you want?"

"I am. I've never been surer of anything in my life," Grandmother replied, pushing back to look into Xoey's eyes.

"Not even that you wanted to devote your life to climate research in the coldest place on Earth?"

Grandmother laughed, or tried to before her weary throat choked the sound. "Not even that. Now walk with me."

They trekked along the coast through the black gravel rocks and mud until the sounds of construction were far beyond them. When they arrived at an outcropping, a place only a trained eye such as Grandmother's would notice, she fell to her knees along the bank. Xoey bent to help her up, momentarily worried she was in pain, then remembered her knees were solid metal, replaced a half-century before, all feeling gone.

Along the bank, in an oblong shape roughly eight feet wide and ten feet long, was a transparent sheet of ice roughly three inches thick. From a distance, it was nearly invisible, especially without snow topping it.

Still on her knees, Grandmother said, "'Many years later, as he faced the firing squad, Colonel Aureliano Buendía was to remember that distant afternoon when his father took him to discover ice. I have taken you to discover ice and fulfilled my dying wish."

Xoey knew the quote —it was from a novel published in 1967, the year Grandmother was born, and one of her favorites. At 109, she had lived her hundred years and then some, decades of which were spent in the solitude of Antarctica.

Grandmother tugged Xoey's hand so that Xoey crouched on the ground beside her.

"Touch it," Grandmother instructed. Xoey had felt ice made from machines before, but ice made by nature was all but nonexistent. She reached out and pressed her fingers into its chill, feeling the ache in her fingertips; the tingling and burning sensation that comes before numbness.

It occurred to her: this was one of the last pieces of ice on Earth and she was one of the last people to see it.

When Xoey removed her hand from the sheet of ice, Grandmother held her. "Remember, Xoey, that when you face the firing squads of your life, that you have known ice. Never forget the inseparability of the past, present, and future. And know that in all my 109 years, you have given me the happiest day of my life."

Grandmother smiled and Xoey saw tears running like rivers through the wrinkled canyons of her face. Then Grandmother crawled onto the ice and put her jacket under her head as a pillow. Xoey shoved the ice sheet carrying her great-great-grandmother into the waters of the Southern Ocean, hard enough that the tide would carry her out to sea. At some point, the pill Grandmother had taken would slow her heart until there was no sound left. She would return to the place she loved most and devoted her life to saving, though she had known all along the forces against her were more powerful than she was. She had placed her fragile humanity before her own kind of firing squad.

But it was summer in Antarctica and the sun would not set on her great-great-grandmother until she was long gone—and there was nothing more powerful than that.

"I love you!" Xoey called when Grandmother was a hundred or so feet from shore. Grandmother didn't rise on her bed of ice or respond, at least not that Xoey could hear, but she felt loved all the same. When she could no longer see the speckle of her grandmother's floating frame, she began making the long walk back to the Divided States of America research station.

"Here. Cut here," Xara said, though the robot didn't need direction. "Oh, Xoey. You are going to be a rich woman."

For a moment, Xara considered stopping the procedure, finding the memory too beautiful to remove. Surely if it was possible to extract a memory it was possible to duplicate it. There had to be a way to let Xoey keep this memory, this beautiful memory, while also selling a copy? There had to be...

The implants behind each of Xara's eyes reset and her train of thought ended abruptly. From one moment to the next, all she knew was that her name was Xara, she was a Memory Specialist at The Memory Store location 58147, and her latest appointment had just arrived. She had better attend to the memory seller.

Xoey awoke in her micro apartment to the sound of her roommate, Xerin, jogging on her hover treadmill. She'd been dreaming about a forest. She'd been running to keep pace with a doe.

"Oh good, you're awake," Xerin said. "I have some messages for you from the Memory Store people. They said the money is in your account and that if you have any more good memories you'd like to sell to please contact them right away. They were able to sell yours almost immediately after extracting it."

Xoey sat up, hearing Xerin's words but not registering them. She didn't recall visiting The Memory Store but Xerin wouldn't lie. Still sitting on her bed, she wondered why she had four different editions of One Hundred Years of Solitude beside her bed and was so badly craving a glass of cold water. No, not cold—ice water. She went to the kitchen and tried to remember what she meant to use the money from The Memory Store on anyway.

"Forgetting is easy," she mumbled, rubbing her temples.

Therion

Written by Cassandra Stevenson

Cassandra Stevenson lives in Brisbane, Australia. The 35-year-old married mother of three school-aged children has been passionate about reading and writing since she was in high school and has written page after page of crazy worlds and adventures for pure entertainment. She hopes to continue writing words until she dies, even if nobody other than her family and friends ever reads them.

She stood there and listened, the steps getting closer. The baby in her arms was squirming and kicking and playing with her hand. She was frozen in fear, her breathing rough. She tried to calm and quieten herself by forcefully slowing her breathing. The little hitch in her chest seemed there to stay. The baby grabbed her finger and started mauling it, his slobbery gums pressing down hard into her second knuckle.

She shifted slowly, pressing her back into the wall behind her; the cold of the rusting metal seeping through her clothes and into her skin. She was under-dressed for the environment. It had been unavoidable. When she got ready this morning she hadn't been preparing to run out into this frozen wasteland. She hadn't been prepared for any of this. Tears welled in her eyes. She took a deep, shaky breath and pushed the thought away. She needed to be present and alert to get out of this. She couldn't be out here wallowing in pity or misery. This baby was counting on her.

There was a soft scrape behind her on the opposite side of the wall. Her head came up swiftly, her ears listening intently for the slightest of sounds. Her heart stopped in her chest and her breathing followed suit automatically. It was them. How they had found her didn't matter. She tried to shrink herself even further into the corner, trying to blend in with the shadows. The fading afternoon light from the jagged hole that was once a window barely illuminated her soft, golden brown hair. Her chest began to ache from the trapped air in her lungs. She slowly let the air out in a small, soundless trickle.

There was the soft rattling of the breathing equipment the hunting creatures wore. Air wooshed out gently and rattled on the intake. The brush of a coat over the dirt as they crept closer. The scrape of heavy boots on the frozen ground. She couldn't go back or she would be punished. She would be sent to the bestiary where she would be used to breed half-man, half-beast abominations, like the one hunting her, until she died. If the first one didn't kill her, it would be a torturous life. The baby definitely couldn't go back. They killed most of the boys, the ones they didn't use for slaves to work the fields or breeding. It was why she had fled.

The footsteps continued down past her rotted-out doorway. She risked a peek and caught sight of the man-beast stalking away further down the path. The rattle of its equipment got softer as it moved away; the boot scrapes became less pronounced. She sucked in a shaky lungful of cold air.

She thought she could take it when she was pregnant—that she could bear the pain of letting go of her baby if they didn't fit the criteria. There was always a 50/50 chance she'd had a boy. And an 80/20 chance they'd kill it if it was a boy. She bore it with grace and determination when her time came, hoping to impress her masters with her strong lineage. But when they shook their heads and his execution was now set, her heart had sunk. After all that work. After all that pain. She had laid him proudly in front of them on that stone altar, hopeful he would get to live. Her baby boy. They had looked over him with disdain; one shake of the old crone's head had sealed his fate.

She had gathered him up in his worn, almost-blue blanket, her back ramrod-straight, tears furiously being held in check. She had been able to flee shortly after. A momentary lapse in concentration by her guardian when another woman broke down wailing after her baby boy was also rejected and she was free. The guardian was distracted by the commotion and she had somehow skirted the gate and wall with the speed and grace of a fleeing deer. Blinded with panic, she had been free to escape, to run into the icy wasteland with nothing but the clothes on her back and a baby that was barely three months old in her arms.

Wracking her brain, she couldn't think of her next move clearly. She was frozen with indecision. To stay and do nothing would mean a slow, cold death for her and her baby. Or to be found here would mean to die a painful death of scarring rapes and horrific births. She had to leave. But where to go? She was born here. Her mother was born here. Her mother still lived here. She had known nothing else. Where could she go? She had never been into the wasteland. She didn't know of anything out here.

But there had to be people. They kept bringing them in in a slow trickle. One or two wild women every year appeared, shackled and dragged behind the caravans coming in the large front gates. She had never met any of these women; where they were kept, she had no idea.

The baby mewled softly, dragging her back to the present. Her heart fluttered, her mind almost seizing in panic. She put her hand quickly over his mouth to cut off the sound. The retreating footsteps had stopped anyway. There was a sliding sound, dirt scraping against the icy, frozen ground. The man-beast had turned around. The baby struggled against her hand, his mouth opening and shutting under her palm. He squirmed furiously. She removed her hand and squished his face into her chest, trying to stifle his little grunts as he searched for food .

The footsteps proceeded to close in on her at that same dreadfully slow pace. She swallowed thickly, gulping in the frigid air silently. She had to do something. She had to think. It was so cold. Her toes were hurting inside her thin leather boots. The soles of her shoes were as worn as the threadbare fabric on all of her layers of clothing. She looked all around searching for an escape. She slowly slid her back down the wall until her fingertips could touch the ground, hugging the baby to her chest with one arm, her hands searching in the dirt with the other. Her hand closed around a small smooth stone.

She stood up just as slowly and looked at the rock in the dull beam of light. It was gray and dull with a single fleck of sparkle. It was cold and flat and light. She faced the door-shaped hole in the wall and quickly threw the stone as far as she could. It thunked loudly off a wall and skittered off into the dense darkness in the opposite direction of where she wanted to run. The breathing of the man-beast quickened as he turned toward the sound. His footsteps hurried away, following the echoes—his large form disappearing into the darkness. She counted to one hundred in her head.

All sounds were gone except the wind whistling through the boneyard of centuries-old buildings she would never know the meaning of. She had to leave now—and quietly. She quickly ducked out of the rusty hole in the wall, scampering out into open ground. Her eyes were wide with fright, the baby clutched in her arms tightly. Anxiety gripped her every move. Her soft-soled boots helped her navigate the long winding path without noise; they weren't particularly warm though. She could feel her toes beginning to go numb from contact with the frozen ground. She silently slipped into the shadows of the buildings as she picked her way through to the edge of the old city.

After what seemed like hours, she had finally reached the end of her cover. She peered down the gentle sloped, but rocky, hillside. She crouched down to listen and watch intently. No sounds but the wind. Her arms were beginning to ache from holding the baby. She let out a breath she hadn't realized she was holding, turning the air into white clouds around her, and took the first step down. With every gentle scrunch of her feet on the rocks, her fear would kick back into overdrive. Is it far enough away? Would it hear her? She walked in a step-and-pause motion. Step, scrunch, pause, breathe. It took a long time to make it to the bottom of the hill. With every step she took, her heart raced in her chest.

She finally moved into the small copse of skeleton-like trees. The baby in her arms began to make small unhappy noises. He was about at the end of his patience. She could feel the impending meltdown on the horizon. And if he cried, that would be it for both of them. She tucked herself into the center of the trees for cover and unwound her scarf and opened her cloak. She hurriedly pulled on the ties of her shirt enough to loosen them and put the baby to her breast. She shoved her nipple straight into his mouth, quieting the cry that rose to his lips.

He sucked hungrily. She pulled the ties on her shirt tight with one hand while securing him under her shirt with the other. She pulled the cloak around them both and secured him in place with her scarf. She wound it over her shoulders, crossing it over in front to secure his head, back, and bottom before tying it off behind her to support him while he fed and slept, allowing her arms to rest. She used his blanket as a makeshift shawl to go over her head and shoulders for extra warmth. The muscles in her arms finally began to relax; she had been holding him for hours.

The wind cut through a small gap at the front of her coat and she shivered. Her hands felt like icy stumps and her feet were numb and clumsy. How was she going to survive? She had no idea. She needed shelter and warmth—and fast. She broached the edge of the small layer of trees at the bottom of the hill. The ground was flat and held no hiding spots. The moon was full and bright, illuminating the desolate land before her. She needed to get through here as fast as possible. There was no way of knowing how far it stretched. She couldn't see an end. It would mean death if the man-beast saw her. She was willing to try anything, to go anywhere, to risk everything, to be free. She put her hands into her coat pockets and stepped out into the abyss.

Raiding the Broken World

Written by Koen ter Horst

―₌₌₌―

Koen ter Horst is a resident of the Netherlands where he lives in Rotterdam. Married and a father of four, of which one by blood, he tries to find as much time and energy as he can to put into writing. He always loved being able to take others with him into worlds of make-believe. After his study in Chemistry, his fantasies became much more scientific, taking great joy out of making science fiction that is remotely possible and turning magic systems in fantasy into a science. He is currently juggling many writing projects—all within the fantasy and science fiction genre—hoping that one of them will allow him to become a full-time writer.

This story won third place in the 2021 Post-Apocalyptic Media Short Story Contest.

―₌₌₌―

The drawer fell from the cabinet and onto the floor with a loud clang. Documents and folders sailed across the concrete in every direction. Owain's hand flew to the grip of his flanged mace.

His body tensed as he held his breath and tucked his tail between his legs. He could hear no sound nor feel any vibrations except those from his pounding heart.

After a minute, he slowly exhaled, calming his nerves. Sudden noise could awaken monsters, and the fewer of those he had to fight, the better.

He knelt down and put his candle holder on the ground. Sifting through ancient documents like these was a large investment of time and rarely paid off. Still, he had plenty of rations and was not tight for Grams at the moment. He could indulge himself in his hobby.

Few raiders browsed the ancient documents and fewer still could read them. Owain could not read the documents per se—as the humans had never agreed on a single language—but he did know a few words across the tongues local to this area. Enough to pick out anything of interest. There were people at the raiders' union who could translate it for him later. In fact, he knew one who would do it for free.

He took a small blanket from his pack and made himself a comfortable area to sit in. Like the filing cabinet, the ancient chair and desk in the room could not be trusted. After organizing the documents, he sat down and took the first piece of paper.

After about two hours, Owain held a document that piqued his interest. It was a yellowed folder with a few pieces of paper in it. On the folder were bold, red letters he recognized. Information with those words on it was usually hidden away in the strangest places, but most of it was useless to him.

This document, however, had frequent uses of a word he had learned: "magie," which meant 'magic' in the local language. It was rare to find documents about magic. History lessons taught him that the humans had gone extinct when they unleashed magic.

The folder held a small painting. These tiny paintings were a miracle to Owain, as their level of detail was so precise. He had seen quite a few, but rarely one like this. It was painted to look blurred, and the painting itself depicted what looked like a drawn schematic. He could barely make out a cup-like object. Why would anybody make a painting of a drawing?

Still, the mention of magic made him curious enough that he put the folder in his backpack. He would enjoy reading a translation of this later. For now, he set aside his curiosity and continued to look through the piles of paper all around him.

Owain stepped outside four hours later. He stretched as the softest of breezes stroked his fur.

He liked exploring underground ruins, but it was always nice to be back out in the open. Above, he could see the thick layer of clouds that covered Gaia. Dark shadows on the clouds betrayed where the skylands of Aerar hung close to the low sky.

He stood in what once was a park, although the only clue of this was the large swath of dirt beneath his paws. There was no grass anymore as there was not enough air for normal vegetation. Only some species of moss managed to survive here, nestled in nooks and crannies. Around the park were spires of stone, metal, and glass. Once, they had been buildings: houses and places of work. Now, they were ruins. Most notable of the ruins was a red brick building with white trim and dark, pointed roofs. It used to be a national museum—or so he had been told—but Owain dared not enter. Large buildings with open areas like that often turned into a lair filled with scores of monsters.

Or a single terrifying one.

His ship was docked close by on a small square. He set off towards it, keeping to the edge of the park. It was safer that way. After a few steps, a figure emerged from behind a pillar a short distance away. She beckoned him to come closer.

It was a raider like him, as nobody else would venture below the clouds. Rabbitkin were generally a head shorter than wolfkin like him, but they were in no way lesser. Other raiders could be two things: helpful or trouble. On the off chance this orange rabbitkin was helpful, he walked towards her. He unslung his shield.

Once they were a few feet away from each other, which was just close enough to talk down on Gaia, she tutted.

"Taking out your shield? Such an act of hostility."

Owain glanced at her fur. The fur itself was ginger, yes, but there were bright orange swirling patterns all over it. She was a fire elementalist, then. Often temperamental and dangerous.

"You don't have to worry. It's a shield, I'm not going to slam it into your face."

She gave him a teasing smile. "So, what did you find?"

"Straight to business, I see. Admirable."

"Oh, you know. Places to be. Grams to earn."

"I found some old documents. Nothing too interesting. Certainly not worth much."

She frowned. "Nobody just collects old paper. It must be something useful. Valuable."

"Isn't a guy allowed to have a hobby?" He gave a toothy smile.

The rabbitkin made sure they stayed out of each other's reach. Considering she had magic and he did not, that was a bad sign.

"Unlikely," she said matter-of-factly.

"I suppose my word isn't going to cut it? I hoped it would. Your talent would be wasted on me."

"Look, wolf boy, just give it to me."

Owain was quite convinced that the document held little monetary value, but he did not want to give it up. It was so rare to find ancient papers he deemed worth reading, and who said she'd stop at just his document?

"Shove it, cottontail," he snarled. "Go find your own relics."

The rabbitkin was taken aback for a second, then as she gave a grunt, the marks on her body glowed with orange light. Owain dropped and slid across the floor, dodging a spray of fire and barely managing to find cover behind a crumbling pillar of a nearby building. He growled in pain as the heat slammed into his skin. If his fur had not been black already, he would see it being singed.

"Leave me alone!" he barked.

A chuckle reverberated through the ruined structure. "Of course, little wolfkin!" his assailant said. "As soon as you hand over the relic."

The document she was after was stored safely in his backpack. So far his attacker held back, but how long would it take her to figure out his pack was fireproof?

"Why do you want it so badly?" he said.

"Grams. Why else."

"There are enough relics around here," Owain said as he unclasped a small chakram. "No need to hunt me."

"Let's be honest; a kin-at-arms like you? You have no chance against an elementalist like me. This is easier for me than going out and looking for something else."

He gnashed his teeth. Why were magic wielders so arrogant? Well, he would show them what a mere kin-at-arms could do.

Owain spun a small chakram around his finger as he glanced around the pillar. He withdrew his head just as a blast of fire crashed into the stone, sending fragments of the crumbling structure flying.

Taking a deep breath, he sprinted from behind the pillar and threw the chakram in the direction from which the fire came. The orange patterns in the rabbitkin's fur glowed just as the chakram struck her in the face.

A deluge of curses crashed toward him. Blood trickled from her cheek.

"How dare you!"

"What? I'm just a kin-at-arms, aren't I?" he snapped at her.

She kept cursing as she sent burst after burst of fire at his new hiding place. An ancient painting hung nearby. After a few seconds it caught fire, and the furless pinkskin depicted on it went up in flames.

A human going up in flames, how poetic.

He grabbed another chakram but was not sure how to get a clear line of sight. The last one had not done enough damage to discourage his assailant, leaving him at the mercy of the fire-spewing maniac. He got into scraps before, but usually with the monsters that inhabited these human ruins. To be fighting another raider... it just did not feel right.

Usually, he would talk or charm his way out, but not this time. Either he had to find a way to escape or he had to take her out. If he could get close enough he could take her out with his mace.

For a second, the fire stopped coming. Owain used the reprise to dash from his hiding place. As he turned a corner and ran into a corridor, he threw the chakram just as a gout of flame blasted into him. He managed to put his shield up in time, but the power of the blast still knocked him off his paws, throwing him to the floor.

The pain was blinding and the wind was knocked out of him. He lay on the floor, clutching his shield. It took him a few heartbeats to realize that something changed.

There was no more fire.

He scrambled to get up and saw that the rabbitkin was gasping for breath, desperately searching the floor. His chakram had hit the mark. It had severed her collar holding a breathing rune. The air on Gaia was far too thin to breathe without one.

Owain ran at the rabbitkin. When he grasped her throat, she looked up, her eyes large and bloodshot. With a swift movement, he rammed his shield into her face. The elementalist went limp. He searched the floor and managed to find the collar. Grabbing a piece of string, he tied the rune to the rabbitkin's neck. At once, her wheezing eased into labored breaths. She would be knocked out for a while, but she'd live.

Looking down at her, he smirked. "Sorry, it seems that you were right to worry. I guess I did slam my shield into your face."

It took him about fifteen minutes to get to his ship. He slid down a slope of rubble, knocking loose a few stones. When he came to a stop, he could see his ship a good hundred feet away, kept out of sight by a broken floor.

His breath caught in his throat; the ship was guarded.

Owain sprinted behind cover, thanking the Winds that the air on Gaia was too thin for sound to travel far. The downside was that he could not hear what they were saying, either. He could see two other raiders. One was a moosekin and the other was a wolfkin like him. It was difficult to tell from a distance whether they had magic or not, but any raider would be dangerous.

Especially two against one.

It was likely that the rabbitkin he knocked out was a part of their group, which meant that she was hunting him specifically. There were raiders who preferred to prey on others, rather than do the leg work themselves. Just the thought made Owain grip his mace's handle so hard it hurt.

Another group of raiders meant another ship. If they were keeping his ship under guard, then he would take theirs. It was the most heinous crime a raider could do to another raider—short of murder—but there were exceptions.

A few minutes later, Owain was at what used to be the top floor of a tall building. There were barely any walls left at this height and at least half the floor had crumbled away. The roof was actually missing. It was a precarious place to be, but it gave him a good view of his surroundings. Besides, any raider worth their salt knew how to spot the safest places to put their paws.

He could barely make out his ship from here, and he could see movement around it. Raiders did not travel far from their ships, which meant that their ship had to be close by. It would be bigger than his, to account for a small team. That cut down the number of places it could be hidden. If it were him, he would hide the ship in a small square or the like, to give as much cover as possible.

Taking out a piece of paper, Owain made a rough map of such locations and decided on an order in which to search them. He had to be fast about it, as there was no telling when the rabbitkin would wake up. She might start to track him again. After all, she had found him once before.

He hurried down and darted from building to building, keeping constant vigilance. He cursed his luck for getting into such trouble. To be fair, this situation was more a result of his stubbornness than luck. If he just showed them what he found he could end this without too much trouble. However, even if they deemed his document worthless, raiders like that would take it regardless. His honor did not allow that.

So far, nobody followed him. Every time he entered a new building, he waited a few seconds, scanning his surroundings. It was tiresome.

He was used to being careful, but this prolonged paranoia drained him.

Owain leaned against an interior wall, peering out. He felt a slight tremor in the stone, but his attention was drawn by some debris falling down. It was a subtle movement, but it was where he was standing a minute ago. Was he already being followed? As he stared at the disturbance, something kept nagging at the back of his mind, screaming danger.

The realization that he felt a tremor finally sank in.

As he pushed himself off the wall, the stone burst into a spray of chunks and dust. It launched him to the ground—again—but the claw that emerged missed him by a hair. With a frustrated screech, the monster crawled from the wall. It looked like a scorpion with spines covering its body.

This was an ironclaw, the nightmare of kin-at-arms. Its exoskeleton was made of metal, which made bows, swords, and spears useless against them. As most kin-at-arms relied on those weapons to deal with the majority of the monsters and lacked the magic to deal with these creatures, they usually wound up dead. Owain scoffed. He was not like most kin-at-arms who used sharp weapons; he used a mace!

While scrambling to get up, he took out his mace and spun around. The ironclaw advanced on the wolfkin but hesitated a moment. It was used to its prey running away. After a second, it rushed forward and lashed out with its tail, holding its claws up to protect itself. The stinger slammed into Owain's shield. The blow sent a wave of pain through his arm, but the adrenaline flooding his system allowed him to swing his mace. The weapon crashed into the monster's defense, sending bits of exoskeleton flying.

The ironclaw took a step back with a shrill chirp, but Owain was not giving in now. He pressed his advantage and used his shield to bat away the monster's stinger, then struck with his mace again. He nearly lost his balance as a result of his reckless attack, but the flanged metal head connected with the monster's, and a loud crunch could be heard. The ironclaw collapsed on the ground, ooze leaking from its head.

Owain hung his mace at his hip and reached inside the monster's head. After rummaging around for a few seconds, scooping out flesh and organs, he pulled out a small, yellow crystal.

Each monster had a crystal core, which was a valuable material. So precious, in fact, that this was the currency used in Aeras, measured in Grams.

Wiping his hand on his trousers he looked around before darting to the next building.

After an hour, he found a small square where a ship was docked. The ship was about twice the size of his own and unguarded. Their crew must have only counted three. Would they be on his tail by now? Would they guess what he was about to do?

Were they secretly guarding the ship? Due to the unwritten rules, one rarely needed to guard their ship. Monsters were not interested either; they only cared about eating living flesh.

Owain picked up a small stone and threw it at the ship. It bounced off the hull, but nothing else happened. He waited a bit longer before creeping closer to the ship. Whoever piloted that ship down here was skilled. It was surrounded by tall, crumbling buildings with only a tight window to the sky above.

Once within reach, he placed his hand on the ship's hull. There were no vibrations he could feel. A good sign. Owain climbed onboard. There was nobody to be seen. For a second he relaxed and let out a breath he did not realize he had been holding. Raiding was such a tense occupation.

He climbed on board the ship and looked around. Where he had a hatch that he could open for some extra storage, this ship had an actual lower level. There would be beds there and plenty of room to store provisions and equipment for a small band of raiders.

Thinking about it, he frowned. It was the perfect hiding spot.

He held his shield in front of him and descended the stairs. When his paw hit the floorboards, a shape burst from the shadows. In reflex, he tilted the shield just as a sword slammed into it. The blow knocked both him and his assailant back.

Some said that the mousekin were handed the shortest end of the stick of all beastkin, but Owain begged to differ. What they lacked in size, they made up for in ferocity—and the ability to hit him below the shield. Owain lowered his stance to compensate as best he could. This gray-furred mousekin's ears twitched as she leered at him.

"Get off my ship," the mousekin said with a dramatic wave of her sword.

She wore a thick gambeson, metal shoulder guards, and a helmet. Well-protected against sharp weapons. Owain gripped his mace tighter.

The mousekin's eyes darted to the mace. "One of those, are you?"

Owain was taken aback. "One of those what?"

"Murderers," the mousekin hissed.

"Hey now!" Owain blustered. "I am not! And look who's talking!"

"What's that supposed to mean, doggy?"

Owain growled. Each beastkin had their own special insult the other kin liked to use.

"Listen up, pipsqueak. Don't you tell me that your mates aren't a cottontail, a wolfkin, and a deer."

The mousekin hesitated for a second. "Ah," she said with a squeak. "You have fallen victim, have you?"

"Yea, so don't you dare claim the moral high ground."

Her shoulders slumped. "I didn't want to team up with them, you know? I had no choice. I had to earn a living. It's why they don't trust me, why they left me here."

"That seems dumb," Owain said, not lowering his shield. "What's stopping you from just stealing their ship?"

The tip of her sword lowered as the pipsqueak cast her eyes down.

"No way," Owain whispered. "You can't fly a ship?"

"I'm new at this, okay!" she shouted, completely dropping her guard.

For a minute, the two stared at each other in silence.

"So, what now?" the mousekin asked.

"Your squad members are staking out my ship, so I'm taking this one."

Her little ear twitched. "What about me?"

"What about you?" Owain said.

"If I step aside, they'll leave me here!"

"Yup."

"You would have to fight me to get the ship from me."

Owain nodded.

"You might get hurt."

"True."

The mousekin stammered, "You might die."

"So could you."

"Ah, damn the Winds!" the mousekin yelled as she threw the sword onto the floor.

The noise was deafening in the tight space.

She sat down and rested her head in her hands. "I don't want to kill other people."

"Then don't," Owain said as he returned his mace to his frog. "Stick to finding relics, if you want to keep being a raider."

"I—I do, or I have to. I have no other options."

"We can take the ship back together and you can find a new group to raid with," Owain said.

"I guess so. Can't I stick to you? You seem nice enough."

Owain shrugged. "I'm not in it for the profit. I make enough to get by as a raider, but I live on my ship. I'm here for the lost human knowledge."

"I see," the mousekin said. "Until I find a more fitting squad, then? I'll carry my weight."

The wolfkin sighed. "I suppose that is fine. What's your name, anyway?"

"Gwinn!"

"I'm Owain. Let's go."

Gwinn nodded and rushed past Owain to the deck. She danced around the riggings like it was nothing.

"Well, you're not clueless about flying," Owain said, crossing his arms.

"I know how to prepare the ship; they taught me that much. I can't actually fly it, though. I think the ship doesn't like me."

He scowled. "If you're part of the crew then the ship shouldn't dislike you."

Gwinn gave him a shrug and continued with what she was doing.

Owain walked to the crystal that rested in the middle of the deck. It was surrounded by brass machinery, and inside the crystal, a cloud-like substance swirled. The air elemental.

Elementalists could communicate with it directly, others could get no more than a vague feeling from them. He placed a finger on the crystal surface and the elemental inside whirled in agitation.

"Gwinn, how did your crew get this ship?"

"Eh..." She stopped in her tracks halfway down a line of rope. "I'm not sure, but I think they stole it."

"Good, that gives us a chance, at least," he said as he placed both his hands on the crystal.

The surface felt hot and cold at the same time, sending biting pain up his arms. Owain gritted his teeth and persevered. Slowly, the sensation faded away and the shape in the crystal calmed down.

"What are you doing?" Gwinn asked. "You look like you're in pain. Are you sure you should be doing that?"

Panting slightly Owain said, "I'm showing the elemental that we are not the thieves who took it."

She scratched behind her ear. "But we are taking it, aren't we?"

As he drew back his hands he said, "An air crystal forms a bond with its pilot. Somehow your teammates managed to subdue this one to work for them, but she hated their guts."

"So I was right? It did dislike me!"

"Well, yea. Now that it has been freed from its captors, it may listen to us."

"It may?"

"Let's find out!" Owain said as he bounded to the ship's helm.

The ship's controls were simple enough, but flying was a different matter. Flying a ship involved reading the minute changes in air currents and dealing with the elemental's temperament, just to name a few difficulties. Flipping a few switches, the sails and fins adjusted and the crystal's mechanics started to spin and whir. Keeping the ship stable, he waited until the magic-powered updraft launched it into the sky. There, he steered the ship to climb as fast as possible, leaving Gaia behind him.

The flight was uneventful, thank the Winds. No pirates, no turbulence, and no magical anomalies.

"You really know how to fly!" Gwinn said.

"This was smooth sailing," Owain said. "Anybody could have done that." Seeing her expression he quickly added, "Anyone who knows how to pilot a ship, of course."

The two of them walked towards the nearest union outpost. They had landed on a fairly small skyland, one that Owain visited frequently. He liked the people who lived here.

On some skylands, the guild had massive buildings, but here they had a building the size of a small shop. Inside, the walls were plastered with posters showing what missions were available. Behind the counter was an old moosekin with one cracked antler.

"Heya Lox, how's the union?"

The cowkin perked up and grinned. "Well, well, if it isn't Owain. And a friend! That's a first."

"Temporary teammate," Owain said. "She helped me get away from Gaia."

"An alliance of need," Gwinn said. "But, who knows?"

Owain sighed. "I'm not the best to hang around if you want to earn Grams. I'd probably bore you to death."

Gwinn shook her head but kept her tongue.

"So," Lox said. "What kind of text did you find this time?"

Owain smiled and passed him the folder. "Who knows, am I right? It mentions something about magic, so that's always interesting."

"Magic, eh?" Lox said as he took out the sheets and looked them over.

"I hope your Gaian hasn't gotten rusty," Owain said.

"There is no such thing as Gaian, and no, I am not becoming rusty."

Gwinn tugged Owain's gambeson. "Shouldn't you let him do his... thing?"

"Nah." He shrugged. "Banter is what keeps that old mind of his sharp."

Lox sighed. "If your skill in fighting matched half your wits you'd be the best raider around."

"Well, I can't hog all the glory, now can I? Lox?"

The guild worker had fallen silent, squinting at the pages. Were his hands... shaking?

"Lox, buddy? Are you all right?"

When Lox tore his attention from the pages his eyes were huge.

"Owain," he said, his voice catching in his throat. "This is huge!"

"What do you mean, buddy?"

"Well, let's say you won't have to worry about Grams anytime soon."

Going Silent

Written by Jeremy Zentner

Jeremy Zentner is a librarian in central Illinois. He's been the recipient of the Lois C. Bruner award in creative nonfiction and has published short stories in science fiction and horror. When he's not spending time with his family or finding books for library patrons, he's writing novels and stories of titillating wonders.

Website: https://intergalacticpub.wordpress.com/
Twitter: @GeekArtZentner

It's the sixth month since the silence, and I pray something here works.

My hands pull the lever, and I'm relieved to hear emergency generators hum to life. The sting in my cheeks begins to fade as warm air rushes through the vents. Ceiling lights illuminate the cubicles as their work holos light up. The massive engravings of the Dawning Star logo glow with corporate pride.

The company specialized in proprietary coding and programming, from what I've gathered in my search for safer shelter. The enterprise is extremely niche, which means their mainframes are closed from outside communications. Even their internal exchanges are hard-wired as I notice the collection of cords threaded between the cubicles like a digital spider web.

No AI corruption here.

The first thing I do is take Mason off my back and sit the two of us on a floating chair in the nearest cubicle. I let my little baby drain out some of the milk from my aching chest. We spend a few moments in blissful child-rearing bonding, Mason smiling every time he sees my eyes before hastily returning attention to my nourishing breast. I'm about to switch to my right side before a bedazzling light erupts into a visual assault of news briefs and emergency announcements. Mason's eyes swell as his feeding mouth gapes open in astonishment. The initial shock of the broadcasting holo quickly subsides, and we're left watching the announcer drone on about outdated prevention methods and safety refuges. At least, that's what his lips say.

"...evacuation sites have been relocated to the historic sites in Dome Town, residents need to arrive before..."

"Ah!" I snort, feeling the warm pour of spit-up. "Come on, Masy. You can't waste all that precious food."

His eyes look amused as I switch him to the other side.

"...Broadcasts from courier ships claim that the rogue corruption wreaking havoc on Rhyolite's AI infrastructure may be alien in origin, hence why most firewalls are unable to protect against...."

When Mason is done, I wipe up the remaining spit-up before harnessing my bra strap and burp Mason, thankfully without any further regurgitation.

"Good boy..." I say, remembering that the eBooks tell me to talk to my baby for proper language and psychological development.

I turn back to the announcer on the holo, wondering if there will be any news about the power grid. Suddenly, a ray of sunlight burst through, followed by dozens more, shooting in like a cascade of yellow lasers, brightening the room with natural sunshine. Dust and plaster fill the chamber with noxious-smelling fumes as well.

I take to the ground, laying Mason ever-so-carefully onto the carpet. He starts to cry as I hastily throw on my jacket and scarf. When I'm ready, I strap Mason to my back again. Heading to the stairwell, I rush down three flights before kicking open the exit I broke into.

Outside, the air is brisk. I peer around a corner to see the military shooting into the building's upper levels. I decide to hike to the next block, vacant of people, and most importantly, gunfire. I keep to the sidewalk, and continue my journey, trying to slow the pace of my heart. Energy conservation is a struggle, but I take out my last protein bar and start eating.

Vibrations tremble the ground and there's a convoy of armored personnel carriers driving parallel to me. A lift bike pulls up ahead and the driver meets my gaze.

"Did you just leave that building?" the soldier asks.

"Yeah," I say. "No AI there."

"We registered electromagnetic radiation. Needed to take action."

I smile.

"What?" he asks.

"Plants emit electromagnetic radiation."

He rolls his eyes and then says, "We read broadcast waves and infrared."

"Just staying warm, looking for news on the holo."

"The mandate says no power generators."

"I know. Why are they still broadcasting on the emergency waves?"

"That's for…" he trails off.

"What?"

"Never mind," he says. "Find your way to Dome Town. They're taking people into orbit there."

"Are they sure the sentience can't get into a shuttle?" I ask.

"Shuttles launch on radio silence. They dock to preordained locations via visual piloting.

Starships run on silent too. It's safer than the building we just blew to hell." I nod and he rejoins the caravan.

I feel Mason's warm tears on my neck.

I'm riding my lift bike across the tower bridge.

When I approach the upper garage gate to my apartment, I slow to a stop and a scanner is telling my cerebral plant to stand by. The trim around the gate flashes an emerald light and the doors slide open, acknowledging my membership. I enter the garage and head over to my reserved parking booth. I skim through several rows of vehicles before seeing someone I've never recognized here. I make a hasty halt, taking note of the individual's long, mauve coat and knee-high boots. A rather extravagant fashion choice for a resident in New Calico City. I can only speculate where he came from, but then I turn to see a floating auto behind me.

The person in the vehicle is sticking his head out the window, his lips flapping, his skin red with a road-raged fury. I move along quickly and get to my parking booth, embarrassed and blushingly mortified.

When I get off the lift bike, the man from the floating auto is stomping toward me. His face is determined to lay down some masculine upheaval. I start making my way to the garage's elevator, but he intercepts my path. His lips are flapping again and I can tell he's yelling with all that spittle bursting from his mouth. The lips flap and pause, and flap again. They appear to be asking if I knew just how close I came to getting run over. Then with clarity, I can see him asking if I'm deaf.

"Yeah," I tell him.

He pauses and appears to ask, "What?"

"I'm deaf," I repeat.

He looks confused, "Like really deaf?"

"Can't you hear it?" I ask him. Most linguists tell me that the deaf will naturally have an accent, a testament to our inability to truly grasp voices in common language.

"I'm sorry..." his words say.

"Don't mention it. I'm sorry. You are right. I could have gotten us killed," I say before proceeding to the elevator.

The man doesn't really follow me and appears to look for another elevator.

Then I'm surprised to see my eye candy enter. The man in the mauve long coat and knee-high boots. Underneath his coat, I can see a white shirt underneath a black vest fit for a formal event. His pants are coal-black but reflective, and I'm suddenly feeling like a peeping tom.

I look up to see him looking into me. His profile has a slight scar out of the corner of his left eye. He has longer hair than most men on Rhyolite's World. At least in the city. It's shoulder length with an auburn-brown color. His chin is peppered with red. He must be from off-world.

"Was that man harassing you?" his lips ask.

I shake my head, "Just a misunderstanding."

He nods and faces parallel to me as the elevator descends to lower regions. He gets off at floor fifty-four. He turns before the door shuts and says, "Thanks for the dance."

I get off at floor fifty-two.

It was a good day.

———*ele*———

It's been six months, two weeks since going silent.

I'm somewhere in the close suburbs when an old truck heeds my thumb. The thing is so rusted and low-tech that it looks like an homage to the original landing days on Rhyolite's World. The vehicle drives on six wheels and the wind-deflector is winged over the truck and part of the trailer like a massive acrylic nail, colored in silver dots and trimmed with black. A typical design for solar cells on vintage vehicles.

The rest of the truck is white with a gray base. The paint job has been abused by years of grime and soot. It sports an exhaust stack, in spite of the panels, but having hybrid power is common on older trucks.

The driver pulls over next to a neo-Victorian home, brightly colored in neon pink, a pristine and effeminate structure contrasting with the rust-bucket on wheels.

The driver opens the door. A rather large woman sits there with goggles over her forehead and a tan contractor's coat. Her hair is a blond that merges into white, her skin fairly thick with eczema.

Her lips say, "You going to Dome Town?" I nod.

"Get in."

I catch the early train out of New Calico. There's something on the wall holo about rogue sentience in the southern provinces, which are fairly isolated in regards to trade and travel, but still a vital part of Rhyolite's economy. Unlike most settled planets, Rhyolite's World is an open state, inviting many immigrants to settle, who in turn provide a great deal of cheap labor and investment for our vast mining operations.

The southern provinces were mostly settled by Ganymede migrants decades ago. Moon dwelling folks who mustered up the funds to colonize the region, the southern provinces being much too frigid for us third- and fourth-generation Rhyolites to care about.

Some protestors on the news didn't like the Ganymedes.

My cerebral-plant syncs to the news and I scroll the closed captioning. "...Members of Native Front still hold prejudices in the southern provinces for being ground zero of the latest hacks into the financial sector, but Rhyolite authorities say that official firewalls will safeguard the world's major institutions..."

I decide to deactivate the sync after some excruciating segments.

Through the windows, I see domes of agro-bases and mining complexes. Seven hundred kilometers from New Calico is a cluster of base communities, erected during the early days of settlement. Most of the domes were designed to fend off the harsh toxicity of the world's heavy metal deposits. The radiation gets worse when metal is mined out, so the townships look like facilities on a lunar surface.

When I get to Dome Town Station, my mother's waiting for me in her all-terrain rover.

"I thought dad was picking me up," I say.

Her lips tell me that there was something he forgot to do at the farm. I nod and get in. We make our way on the hinterland highways, driving on non-magnetic roads made of concrete and gravel. We get to the family dome and Mother parks in the garage.

We leave the vehicle and Mother goes into the kitchen. I go through an airlock to see Father in the barn dome. He's trying to talk to someone on a podium holo. He says something like "never mind" and deactivates the thing. There's a trampled automaton on the ground next to his feet, lifeless against the dusted dirt. Its pallid exo-skin is grimy with months of agro-labor.

I send his cerebral plant a text, which illuminates on his wrist holo.

He looks at it and turns to me. I see his lips say, "Friggin' thing went haywire and started smashin' shit. I had to break off its battery with a crowbar."

"You should just hire some local hands," I say.

We hug and I hear his chest say something. I back up and say, "Hm?"

"Sorry, I said there's not a lot of hands to hire any more."

I smirk, "Don't be coy. You're just afraid to work with some Ganymedes."

"That too," his lips say, smiling.

"People are going to start thinking you're racist," I step towards the swine pens. Even though I'm turned away, I can imagine what he's thinking. Then he just texts it to my cerebral plant.

Wouldn't have to worry about it if you came down for the harvest.

"I'm all grown up, Dad," I say.

I then turn to see him say, "I know."

We go back into the habitation dome and head for the dining room. Mother fixed tea and crumpets for Landfall Day and I notice a great deal of extended family snuck in already. Uncle Jon, Uncle Max, Aunt Meryl, and Aunt Penelope, my brother Wes and his wife and three kids, my cousins Miles, Henriette, and Olivia, and, of course, Nana. We all exchange hug-full pleasantries and make seats around the table.

I quickly look to Mother and see the conversation start.

"So, were you able to install a new firewall?" I see Mother's lips ask Father. Others are already chattering amongst themselves as they shovel warm crumpets into their greedy mouths.

"Nah," he says. "Damned Meedics built the bots with a completely open system. Makes it impossible to install a thing without infecting the firewall itself with corruption."

"They prefer to be called Ganymedes," I say.

I think he says something, but my eyes are low.

I look up and see him say, "How do you know?"

"Because there's a lot of Ganymedes in New Calico."

He lifts his chest in a grunt-like gesture, "One more reason to stay out of the cities."

I roll my eyes.

It's been two hours since I hitched a ride on the truck.

I'm in the sleeping cabin with five other individuals. We're all jammed-pack together like one of my parents' old cattle trailers. I'm holding Mason on my shoulder as he sleeps. I sense something inquisitive. My eyes dart up and I see someone asking, "How old?"

"Six months," I say.

"Is the father in the picture?"

"He never knew."

She nods as if she respects my rights to the womb.

"I mean," I say. "I would have told him, but I never got the chance."

She nods again.

I return to my apartment building and it's already dark. Instead of going to my flat, I take the elevator to floor sixty-one, where the residence lounge is located. Inside there's a bar, a perfect place to end up after the efforts of Landfall Day.

My eyes study the bartender as I take a seat. His lips say, "What can I get you?"

"You were on the elevator with me. Last night?"

His eyes squint quizzically at me and his lips then say, "Oh, right. How are you?"

"Okay, I guess."

"Can I fix you a drink?"

"Gin and tonic?"

"Yes, ma'am," his lips say.

"Rough ... --ay?"

"I'm sorry, can you repeat that?"

"Was your Landfall Day trying?"

"Oh," I say. "It was fine. You know. Parents."

"Ah," his lips say with a smile. "The bane of my existence."

"Heh, why's that?"

"I'm probably a big disappointment. Went into surgery instead of something more respectable. Go to the teaching hospital here, at Lo'fem Medical. Moonlight at the bar to help pay school loans."

"There's something more respectable than surgery?"

He smiles, "They're pompous jerks, my parents. Administrators on Rana Terram. To them, I was supposed to work in the family practice, then join the board, then eventually become an administrator. Surgeons are centurions to my family. Needed muscle to run things, but not decision-makers. My folks are pretty much mob bosses."

I giggle a little, "What's your name?"

"Jephya Diaz. Yours?"

I smile before a series of holos illuminate. Holos are typically reserved for whirl tournaments and sting-pong highlights. I glimpse over and see a series of different anchors from a number of news waves making incoherent ramblings.

"What's happening," I ask.

"It's the briefs," his lips say, eyes fixed on the holos. "They said there's been a confirmed corruption in the city's mainframe AI. Something broke through the firewalls."

"How?"

He points to a holo. I glimpse up to see panicked people running in the streets. Men and women getting plowed over by auto-cabs and drone carriages, vehicles doing everything they possibly can to turn traffic into a gridlocked junkyard, peppered with injured, bleeding bodies.

On the sidewalks and in the streets, police officers are beating at frenzied bodies of white, yellow, blue, and red automatons, pulverizing the contraptions with their charge batons and even shooting at the mechanized mob.

"Are those machines... trying to kill people?" I ask.

"They've lost control," Jephya says.

We've been in the truck for six hours now.

The ride is getting a bit chilly without routine marching, but things are amicable enough. There's a small porthole in the cabin that passengers occasionally peer through. I stay sitting, holding Mason in my warm embrace.

I feel rumbling vibrations against the wall and deck of the cabin. The rumblings are soon coupled with a series of wave-like pings, something indicative of a lift bike or floating auto blowing dust and gravel against the cab.

The woman across from me steals a glance from the porthole and makes eyes at me.

"It's the military. Didn't think they'd come all the way—"

She quickly grabs her ears and bends over in throbbing pain. I look down and see Mason crying. I quickly grab the earbuds in my pocket and place them in his ears. He's still crying, but he's calming. I look up to see everyone hunching over.

Our world then shook as the truck came to a shattering halt.

I jolt up, tightly keeping Mason in my arms and I try to ask if the passengers are alright, but they are clenching their ears in desperation, secreting beads of sweat as their skin smolders red.

I push open the hatch and see a gridlock of tanks and lift bikes, now halted in wrecks and smoking with metallic mutilation. My eyes shift up to see a hovering drone. It maintains a saucer shape, sporting several speakers directed downward against the swarm of people on the ground, like a prison suppression unit screeching to subdue a riot in one of the prison mines up north. The soldiers around me are screaming for mercy, begging for whatever noise that blared out of the hovering contraption to stop.

It's the corrupted AI's weapon of choice these days. Noise.

I step out of the truck and trudge forward, hoping to flee the tumultuous racket. I swerve between the vehicles, threading past the screaming men and women, their weapons useless against the agony they exhibit.

A sudden impact quakes the ground and I turn to see a blossoming fire rage from the drone as broken debris rains down. A manned attack craft soars overhead, having eliminated the corrupted drone, freeing the soldiers from their anguished, bleeding ears.

I turn back to the road and continue to step my way through the caravan.

There's a silhouette of a town ahead on the horizon. Dome Town.

There's a notification in my cerebral plant that tells me to work from home today. We all have a meeting at ten.

Jephya is still snoring next to me, his naked body slack and useless against my gentle taps. I decide to kiss those lips of his and his eyes manage to peel open, seeing me smile.

"I have to work soon. You can stay in the living room if you like, but I have a meeting on my holo," I tell him.

He mumbles something that I can't quite see.

"What?" I say.

"I need to go to work, too."

"Well, maybe I'll see you soon?" I say.

"Sure," he says, smiling. "You should deactivate your cerebral plant though. There's not a lot known on what a corrupted sentience could do to a brain plant."

"Well, how will I get in touch?"

"I'll stop by in a couple of days. The bar's closing due to a power restriction. Only the habitation units will be open."

"Alright. A couple of days then."

He smiles and gets dressed before leaving.

I activate a CGI suit on my conference holo and turn on the closed captioning.

The conference call has a group of my colleagues and bosses all discussing the recent AI uprising and the company's responsibility during these troubling times.

"So," the VP went on, "The Board Association of New Calico Infrastructure, in conjunction with city and provincial authorities, has recommended that all non-essential employees move to a remote status. In this way, we can limit power usage in the city and safeguard company mainframes from AI corruption."

The old man is a robust silver fox, I always thought. Now he speaks like a comforting presidential figure.

"There's a variety of measures that can be taken while we weather this storm," he goes on. "Most importantly, we must remain calm. The sentient is most detrimental when anarchy ensues. The reports we've received indicate that these rogue AI burst across the southern provinces where they don't have modern infrastructure and firewalls. Our tech professionals cannot hope to deal with potential corruption if order breaks down. That's why it's our civic duty to remain in, to stay out of the way, and report on any automatons or other bots prowling the streets or halls."

"Yeah, I had a question about that," one of my colleagues asks. This other man is a bit of a large individual, who sports a six-inch beard, but closely cropped hair. "Are they going to shut down the entire electric grid to wipe out the corruption?"

"Not at all," the VP reassures. "And even if they did in some minor cases, it would most likely be a temporary outage for the authorities to locate the rogue AI and eradicate it from the mainframes. Most of the drones and automatons have been temporarily decommissioned and their battery cells removed, so there shouldn't be any more violent outbursts like the other night."

"Yeah, did anyone die from that... robot riot by the way?" someone asks.

"I really haven't kept a tally on that," the VP says.

I decide to chime in, "The briefs say three thousand people were killed in drone acci—, traffic crashes. Another five thousand injured. Not sure if individual automatons killed anyone, but they're not exactly too deadly if you find a good pipe to bash them with."

"Ah," the VP says. "At least the automatons don't have the nuclear codes."

"Can we get your word on that?" my colleague asks.

We all have a chuckle before I see them cringe. Their profiles showcase a collage of crouching, screaming individuals, trembling in pain.

"What's going on?" I ask.

They can hardly do much of anything to communicate, their agony is so great.

Eventually, the closed captioning reads, "That noise..."

It's been six months, two weeks, and half a day since going silent.

There's a leaflet on the door that reads sentient corruption.

My eyes are wide and my palms are wet. The door is ajar so we walk in, Mason and I. There is clutter everywhere as if the home had been plundered by countless scavengers looking for food and supplies. I see more of the bots my father had shut down. They too were cluttered throughout the chambers and yards, smashed and beat up like piles from a scrap yard. On the living room's coffee table is a new vase I've never seen.

I decide to go down to the cellar and dial the unlocking code for their antique gun locker. Protection would be nice to have around these days.

Their old rail rifles are still inside, a folded note taped to one of them. I pick it up.

"If you get this, then I'm glad. You can take these guns for protection. After trying to hold out, we finally had to leave on one of the shuttles. You see, Wes and his family came over to help out. But one of the machines, the tractor, it got to him. Ran him over dead. We didn't even know those vehicles were connected to the grid. Your father got hurt trying to help him and for all the trouble it did, his injury put us on a priority flight. Have to fly up with Meedics if you can believe it. I don't think things will ever be the same. I love you."

"No..." I shake my head. "No, no, no..."

I return to the living room upstairs and approach the vase I'm starting to realize is an urn. My feet shuffle closer and I take off the lid. My eyes hover over the opening, peering at the horror inside.

"This isn't real," I say. "This isn't real," I screech. My lungs are bursting, frightening Mason into a cry. I wish Jephya was around.

I get a text that reads, *Meet me in the lounge.*

I thought it was closed, I text back.

Found a way to override it. Need a drink. And deactivate your implants already!

I smile and take the elevator up to meet Jephya in the lounge. He's behind the bar table fixing me a gin and tonic. He already has a beer opened.

He hands me the glass and we toast before taking a sip. Jephya takes more than a sip, though—a rather large gulp. Not too typical for him, at least as far as I can tell from the last three weeks we've seen each other.

"Listen," he starts. "I'm leaving Rhyolite on a chartered shuttle in a couple of days."

"Oh," I say. "Um... okay. This is new..."

"Yeah," he says. "My folks got me priority passage on a starship to Ganymede. They say there's a surgeon ward I can manage there."

My eyes are a little warm, but I suppress the feeling. "Oh, I see."

"I'm sorry, but this may be my only chance. Word is, they'll have to shut down the entire grid at any moment, and once they do that, I won't have a hospital to practice at."

"That would make sense, I guess."

"Yeah."

"Ganymede? I thought your parents were from Rana Terram?"

"My parents, yes. But I technically have in-laws on Ganymede."

"In-laws?"

"Yeah..."

"What the hell?" I blurt out, knowing full well that I'm slurring my words.

"It wasn't really my choice. I had a betrothed marriage, but my wife and I have an open relationship."

"An open marriage?"

"Yeah, it's not like we're in love or anything. But we have to be married to merge the companies so whatever kids we have can run things in the future."

"Kids?"

"I mean, eventually. Not now, obviously."

"Oh, obviously!" I mock.

"I'm sorry. I really liked you. But I have to go back to my family."

"On Ganymede."

"Yeah."

It's been six months, two weeks, and a full day since going silent.

I wipe away my tears and search around, trying to make sense of everything and nothing. My attention is pulled towards an automated tractor laying on its side outside. The power cells are stripped, the wheels scavenged, and Rhyolite crows pick at the cabling, making nests on the contraption. I lift the back door open and make my way toward the machine.

Yellow letters against the side paneling, now facing towards the sky, named the brand of the farming equipment. Beneath that brand are the words "Made in the Southern Provinces."

"Bastards," I say. My hand turns into a fist and I pound at the underbelly tanks of the tractor. "Damned Meedic bastards!"

I swing again and again at the vehicle, my hand throbbing with pain as I unsuccessfully pulverize the already decommissioned machine.

"Bastard..."

I'm in a maternity room, and it's sometime between midnight and dusk. A resident enters the room. Someone who doesn't look old enough to drink.

"Ma'am," she says. "Hi, um. So, unfortunately, Dr. Rao will not be able to make it."

"What?" I ask. "What's going on? He's my doctor, he promised to be here."

"It's the power grid," she says. "The government said it's about to go silent. To eradicate the corruption. Dr. Rao lives twenty minutes away by rail. It would take him six hours to walk all the way here and no one is allowed to drive the roads right now."

"Oh," I say.

"Don't worry," she says. "The maternity nurses here are quite good at their job. They're more than capable of delivering your baby."

"Yes," I say. "So, I've been told."

"Do you want me to get someone? The father perhaps?"

"There is no father."

It's been six months and four weeks since going silent.

My eyes open to an earthquake.

I'm in my parents' old bed as I grab for Mason, who's lying next to me. I stand up and head towards the window. It's still pretty early out, but there's a bright sunrise burning in the distance. Not the actual star Rhyolite's World orbits, but a new sun that flies overhead.

A new shuttle.

Grabbing for my things, I dress both Mason and myself, and we make our way outdoors, marching towards the public landing pad the town shares. All along the way, hoping, pleading with forces more powerful than I, that we can get aboard.

We trudge for several minutes, the shuttle's lights and afterburners having dimmed for quite some time now. I see several other stragglers and hopeful survivors trying to make their way to the craft. I have a rail gun in my hands just in case anyone tries anything unbecoming.

When I get to the transport, there are a couple of lengthy people ushering everyone in a mannerly fashion. I toss the gun to the side, not wishing to arouse suspicion. When it's my turn, I approach a very tall, pale skin man. He brings a lamp close to me and looks over my back.

He speaks a language I don't have much practice in lip-reading.

Ganymedic.

"I'm sorry, I'm deaf," I say.

He places the lamp down and then signs in perfect inter-world sign.

"Just you and the baby?"

"Yes," I sign back.

"Welcome aboard."

Winds of Change

Written by David A. Simpson

DAVID A. SIMPSON IS an International Best-Selling Author of the *Zombie Road* and *Feral Children* series. He has sold hundreds of thousands of copies and has been translated into three languages. His books have won numerous awards and have spent weeks in the number one slot for apocalyptic fiction on the Amazon charts.

His *Zombie Road* series has been optioned and is currently in development for television.

He lives in the north Georgia mountains, forty-five minutes from the nearest blacktop road—unless his wife is driving. Then it's more like twenty. They have a very spoiled pug, a very weird cat, and a bear that they can't seem to get rid of that thinks everything they plant in the garden is for him.

To learn more and see what he is currently working on, please visit him at the David Simpson Fan Club on Facebook or check out his website at davidasimpson.com

Billy, along with billions of others, was worried. The reports from the experts tried to explain the phenomenon but it seemed like none of them could agree. One scientist blamed global warming and the shifting sea levels. The next guest insisted it was a passing solar gust, which would dissipate in a few weeks. Preachers declared it a judgment of the gods and that the angels of the heavens had stopped restraining the four winds. Government officials issued decrees and gave speeches stating the winds would lessen and things could get back to normal shortly. The airwaves were rife with rumors, crackpot ideas, and conspiracy theories about weather modification gone wrong or the super colliders opening black holes and infinity dimensions.

Billy didn't know about all that. He just knew the roof of his shed had been ripped off and the building collapsed not long after, the torn and broken tin flying off towards the woods to wrap around wind-bent trees. He wondered if the insurance company would cover it or if it would even be in business when this all blew over. They would have so many claims they would probably be bankrupt. He had boarded up the west windows on his house. He wasn't concerned about them getting broken, but there were a few good-sized trees in his yard that would smash right through the roof if the wind picked up. It was nearly noon but with all the dirt and dust in the air, it seemed like twilight. They lost power yesterday and it would be a long time before the company could repair it. The winds had to die down first.

Billy had moved his family far away from his job. It was a long commute every day but it was worth it for a place to call their own out in the country near the Valley of Heroes. The roof on the manufactured stone house was only a few years old and it was supposed to withstand the gusts of gale force winds that sometimes roared out of the valley. The problem was the winds weren't gusts, they were constant. They were strong and steady; they were building up speed and they never let up.

Their house sat atop a small rise above the creek. Once it had been the perfect location with a lovely view of the meandering brook below. Now it was being buffeted nonstop. If only they would have built below the ridge on the downslope. He wished for the hundredth time they had put it below the crest, it wouldn't be taking such a pounding. The issue wasn't so much the winds themselves, the house was squat, rounded, and solidly built. It was all the debris they carried.

Dirt, sand, leaves from the stripped trees, shopping bags, and other trash constantly bombarded the house. They wore it down like a sandblaster. The winds howled and dust made its way inside, forced in through the tiniest cracks and up through the eves. A lawn chair tumbled and spun across the backyard, bounced off a tree, and disappeared in the gloom.

The breezes had started two weeks earlier. The forecasters called it a perfect storm. An unusual series of events loosely related, in a cause-and-effect chain reaction that should have blown itself out. Except it didn't.

An underwater volcano in the equatorial sea blew its massive top. The superheated ocean spewed millions of tons of volcanic ash into the air and caused other dormant volcanoes to come to life, adding their own lava and cinders to the atmosphere. Hundreds died from suffocation, and the tsunami hit the coastal towns with giant waves killing tens of thousands more. The cleanup would take years and the cost would be high. There was worry of global cooling and food shortages from all the ash and debris in the air but fears were calmed.

Soothing voices on the video made assurances. Crop loss in one part of the world could easily be made up elsewhere, the officials declared. Yes, fruits and vegetables might cost a little more, but there wouldn't be worldwide famines. There was no truth to the misleading rumors. The world economy wasn't fragile, they insisted. The winds created by the eruptions were "actually good" they said, helping spread the ash and dust over a greater area lessening the impact.

But the winds didn't end.

The breezes weren't bad at first, just steady. Days passed before anyone noticed, other than a few weather professionals whose anemometers never stopped spinning. At the air shuttle pads, the wind socks spun in constant motion but nothing to cause alarm. When the meteorologists started mentioning it on the nightly newscasts, the winds had blown for a week and were steadily picking up speed. Only a little. Only a bit faster each day but they didn't die down or gust and puff. They remained steady, persistent, and constant. The wind carried gray smoke and fine red dust. Forest floors were swept clean of last year's leaves and they tumbled, broke up, and added to the tiny blowing particles. The experts tried to explain the phenomenon with charts and graphs, indicating the volcanoes caused unusually warm oceans and the resulting atmospheric pressure differences created the winds but things would calm down when the cooler waters from the northern seas arrived.

But it didn't.

The winds blew steadily for nearly two weeks and Billy had been without power for over a day when he stared out of the window at the tumbling lawn chair. He sipped his cold morning brew which was much better when it was hot. He couldn't even get a fire going in the wood burner. The winds whistled down the chimney and blew ash everywhere when he opened the door to try.

"We need to get into town." He told his wife, finally reaching a decision. "We need to get a bunch of food before it's all gone, before everybody realizes how bad it's going to get."

"You don't think it's going to stop?" she asked, casting a worried glance at their two children eating morning cereal and trying to keep the dust out of their bowls.

"Even if it stopped right now," he said, "there won't be any crops this year. Maybe not next year either. This is stripping the good soil and dumping it out into the oceans. It's worldwide according to the news people."

She nodded. "Okay. You think they'll get much stronger? You think the house will hold together?"

Billy took a long moment to answer. He felt scared. From some of the stories he read on the feeds before they lost power, he didn't think their house would. There had been a few scientists with a detailed graph showing why the winds kept getting stronger and stronger. He didn't understand all the science behind it, as he was a laborer, but he understood the theory.

It took a massive, almost unheard-of amount of energy to get a worldwide straight-line wind blowing. Once accomplished though: once the head of the breeze caught up with the tail after it circled the planet, it fed into itself. It shoved the breeze a little quicker, picked up speed, and pushed a little harder. The graphs showed the planet as basically the eye of the hurricane. The winds would continue to grow in strength, speed, and power. They didn't have any idea if or when it would stop. It might become a storm like the one on neighboring Jupiter, which raged on the gas giant for as long as anyone knew. First spotted hundreds of years ago, it reached sustained wind speeds capable of destroying anything in its path. Five times the size of their planet, it might churn on for another thousand years. The Planetary

Storm, as the news readers called it, may turn out to be the same. It was easy to be fearful at night, to believe in all sorts of strangeness but it was midday and he still felt deeply afraid, believing the worst.

"I think we need to gather as much gear as we can and head down to the caves in the Valley." He finally said, "Before it gets any worse."

He turned to her as the winds buffeted their house, howled in the eves, and branches of the trees all danced in the same direction. He wasn't prone to hasty decisions. He was a plotter and a planner who only wanted to keep his family safe. He wouldn't suggest such a thing unless he was certain. The winds weren't natural. They grew in intensity and he could think of only one protected place.

"Get the kids ready." He said. "I'll start packing up the truck with some essentials. We'll go into town, get as much food as we can and take it to the caves."

She nodded and set down the dusty cup of cold morning brew.

High above the turbulent surface, the pride of the planet orbited, and the twelve crew members stared in disbelief at what was happening below. They were aboard the space station, the first of its kind. They were nearly through their month-long mission of experiments and clear telescopic photography of the neighboring planets from high above the cloud cover.

Commander Adams was lost as to what to do; nothing like this was in any of the training protocols. The planet below appeared savage. The usual white clouds that hung low and serene above the greenish oceans were whipped around and torn apart, replaced by heavy brown, gray and red angry maelstroms. When they trained the telescopes on the surface, they could pick out vehicles and trees that sometimes surfaced above it, tumbled by the swirling storms before disappearing again. The only thing, rising above the clouds of dust, were the mountain peaks and the head of the great statue in the Valley of Heroes.

The crew had no contact with the surface. None of the communications systems worked, and fear hung heavy among the astronauts. They waited and watched. The clock ticked away the days, and their food supplies dwindled.

Billy drove slowly towards the markets. Visibility was bad, like in a heavy fog, and the windshield already possessed thousands of little nicks in it from debris. He'd tried the wipers once. They flapped so hard, he was afraid they would be torn off. Tumbling garbage cans and plastic toys went flying by them in the dirty air. He could see well enough when they were driving with the wind at their back but when they turned into it, it took them both staring hard at the road to keep them out of the ditches.

The parking lot of the nearest community's market was chaos. Panic had set in, driving everyone to act in ways they never would have thought themselves capable of a few weeks ago.

Billy couldn't imagine how bad the cities were. People probably killed each other over food instead of just the fast and desperate fights he saw when he ran through the broken door. Everyone grabbed whatever they could and tried to reach their vehicle without losing anything to the winds or someone else.

He'd left Karla and the kids in the truck not wanting to risk losing them in the confusion after he saw a small riot. He dashed inside, bent nearly double against the wind with one hand holding his goggles in place, the other batting away flying papers and other debris. He grabbed a cart and ran towards the canned goods and saw that everyone else had the same idea. It was gridlocked with carts and shouting and the shelves were almost bare. A lot of them were fighting over water but Billy thought he'd be okay drinking from the creek that flowed through the bottom part of the cave. Most of these people would be dead soon, he thought. If he was right and the winds kept getting stronger, within a week there wouldn't be any structures left standing. He zig-zagged his way through the maddened shoppers, amazed that some were in the electronics section gathering up useless gizmos.

Maybe they thought the winds would die down soon.

Maybe they knew something he didn't.

Maybe they were stupid.

The sporting goods section was almost deserted. Bigger than most shops in the area, this was the last stop many travelers made on their way to the natural springs or the Valley of Heroes. This was where they would grab last-minute packages of bread, gear they'd forgotten, maybe an inexpensive floater or fishing pole, and, of course, enough distilled spirits to last all weekend.

Billy started shoveling case after case of freeze-dried food into his cart. He filled it and plenty more remained on the shelves. He grabbed a sleeping blanket, heaved it out of the bag, and used it to cover his stash, hiding it from view. If the other panicked shoppers saw what he had, they'd empty the shelves before he could return for another load. He ran for the door and back out into the wind. He trudged beside the cart, pressing his weight against it to keep it from toppling over and spilling everything. He let it slam against the truck—parking lot dings didn't matter anymore—and dropped the rear hatch.

He tossed everything in, yelled that he was going back for more, and ran towards the store, struggling to keep the cart with him. An overloaded one came rolling by at an alarming speed, hit a bump, and tumbled off across the parking lot, bouncing high in the wind. Hundreds of cans were scattered, a few flying away, but most rolled madly on the asphalt. Someone's hard-fought prize was lost in the gloom, biting winds, and flying dust. He watched the cans scatter and knew the ones that weren't whipped away would wind up against the short stone wall at the end of the parking lot. He bet hundreds of cans were stacked up against it. He'd get down there and collect it all as soon as he made one more run at the freeze-dried foods. Once they were in the caves, they wouldn't be coming out for a while, and when they did, there wouldn't be much left on the surface.

Billy struggled back through the broken market doors, getting out of the harsh, driving winds and catching his breath. Breathing through the cloth tied around his face was hard because it was caked with dust. It was better than breathing it all into his lungs, though. He yanked it down, sucked in air then hurried back to the sports section. The groaning of the building became louder than the constant howling and he saw one corner lifting off, murky daylight and wind-driven debris forced inside.

He remembered how his shed collapsed moments after it lost its roof and tried to shout for everyone to get out. No one could hear him above the din, they ignored his warnings. He abandoned his cart and ran as the ceiling peeled slowly at first. The beams and plaster broke, cracking it open like a can of vegetables. The wind whistled then roared. Once it found a grip, the roof ripped free, tumbling into the next building. A chain reaction of collapsing structures followed.

Billy threw himself back into the outside havoc as the walls folded in on themselves. Blinded by the grit, he barely avoided a dumpster that skidded across the parking lot. Papers and branches slapped at him, rubble bit into his clothes and stung his skin. He bounced against his truck and wrenched at the door, trying to open it against the wind.

When she saw him struggling, his wife put her feet to the door and shoved. Between them, he managed to slip in and the door slammed shut behind him. The front of the truck was hammered by another cart bouncing off the grill.

The kids both cried and his wife's face was a mask of barely contained terror.

"We'll be okay." He said, breathing hard. "We'll be safe in the caves, and the tombs are carved from solid rock, they'll be safe, too."

"It's forbidden to enter them." She said by rote, a lifetime of instilled teachings deeply ingrained. She touched her fingers to her forehead out of habit, not even realizing she did.

Billy didn't argue. She was a whole lot more religious than he was but if the caves started flooding, he'd convince her to go into the catacombs below the statues. She'd do it for the kids, even if she thought she'd be doomed herself.

He hit the accelerator and turned away from the driving wind, putting the back of his truck against it. He wiped at the grit in his eyes, tried to control his fear, and hoped it wasn't too late to make it to the Valley of Heroes.

Commander Adams rested his head against the window of the space station, the telescope pushed aside. The head of the Warrior King statue slipped from view. It was the last of the creations formed from their ancestors' hands. It had been built on a leveled mountaintop and towered over the valley for thousands of years. Nothing else, no buildings, no trees, no bridge was higher than the Warrior King. It had always been there and always would. He was a constant in an ever-changing world. Only the mountains stood taller than him. Now dirt and flotsam filled the winds and the statue disappeared, lost in the blowing red cloud that destroyed everything. It stripped the land bare of any soil. It left no leaf on any branch. It filled in ponds, lakes, and oceans with tumbling trees, broken bits of buildings, and uncountable tons of dirt and sand. He and his crew were lost. Doomed to orbit their planet forever with no way to drop back down to the surface without being destroyed and nowhere to go even if they could.

———ele———

Billy's heavy truck was low to the ground. Even still, they felt like they were on the edge of being lifted from the road and tossed into the raging storm winds. He went as fast as he dared, now regretting the choice to come in for supplies. The winds increased in speed and intensity. They were heavy with water sucked from the lakes and he barely saw the road. A massive tree slowly tipped over in front of them and he couldn't risk accelerating under it, the heavy limbs would crush them. They watched as it crashed down across both lanes, its giant root ball stripped bare of all the dirt clinging to it within seconds. The roots were bare and whipping frantically in the gusts as the great tree slowly started to roll, the winds pushing it across the bare ground.

When the path was wide enough, Billy accelerated past it, the branches slapping at their truck. They barely noticed the sounds, the screaming of the winds drowned out everything else. The truck lifted and settled, again and again, each time Billy gripped the wheel tighter and thought it would be the last. *This time,* he thought. *This time it will start tumbling, the windows will shatter and we'll all be sucked out to ride the winds as broken corpses.* When they finally reached the entrance to the valley and slid between the sheer rock walls, the driving force of the wind that had nearly forced them off the road died down.

They were still being battered by the blowing dirt and debris as it scoured the paint and sandblasted the windshield, but, in the channel, he didn't have to worry about being sent tumbling across the barren lands or smashed by a flying house.

"Can we stay here a while?" Karla asked, grateful for the pause in the merciless pounding and rocking they had been taking.

"It's only going to get worse," Billy said. "If we stop now, we might not make it. We're close. Just around the curve are the hot springs and I can get really close with the truck. We can crawl to the caves from there."

They neared the end of the canyon and the fierce winds created a wall of air filled with rocks and sand and water from the oceans. Usually, this was a breathtaking view into the Cydon Valley. A visitor could see the steam rising from the hot springs, the pyramids of the ancients, and the Warrior King statue that towered over everything with his calm and wise face.

Billy reached over and took his wife's hand as they started into the brutal, howling pandemonium. The wind snatched the truck from the road and spun them into the air. Their screams were drowned out by the wail of the vortex. For a few seconds, they had a view of the ancient statue as it toppled, the body crumbling into chunks of stone. Its outstretched arm wielding the sword shattered and was carried away, the head landed and rolled a few times to stop facing up into the winds. The planet wobbled slightly as earthquakes tore holes in the surface and volcanoes ejected more ash into the air. Once green and blue and teeming with life, it was completely enveloped in swirling red dust. Continents shifted positions and mountains crumbled. Oceans were emptied and then filled with sand.

―⁓―

"We all agree? One hundred percent?" The commander asked for the final time.

Each crew member nodded their head. It had to be done. It was a hard thing but there wasn't a choice. Their planet was dead but there was hope they could maybe, possibly travel to their neighbor. They knew it held life, the long-distance probes they had sent over the years proved that and their telescopes showed it was mostly covered in water. They were certain they would find the air breathable. There had been manned missions planned sometime in the future when their space program grew more ambitious and there had been excited talk of colonization.

Although it wasn't designed for it, the calculations showed the space station could make it by riding the solar winds. Once they arrived, they could slow their descent with the parasails and land on one of the vast green continents. They had done the math, the odds were in their favor. It *could* be done. The only problem was there wasn't enough food. There wasn't enough for another week, let alone enough to feed twelve for the year it would take.

"We offer our bodies so our people may live," Joseph said and the others agreed.

They said their goodbyes to one another, tethered themselves firmly with the cables, and stepped into the airlock. They held hands and the tears froze on their faces as the outside hatch was cracked open. The warm air hissed out and the icy cold vacuum of space replaced it. They died almost instantly and within minutes were frozen solid.

Ten of them.

The two crew members remaining stared through the porthole at the stiff, floating bodies of their friends. If they ate sparingly, there would be enough protein to keep them alive until they made it to the blue planet.

"Eve," Commander Adams said as they turned away from the airlock. "Open the solar sails and let's ride the light to our new home."

Life (Love?) in The Time of Crazy

Written by I.M. Captive

―ellє―

I. M. Captive is the nom de plume of a Clinical Psychologist who retired in 2014 after working for thirty-one years as a supervising psychologist in a foster care agency. He remains in private practice in Nassau County.

He has a lovely wife and two wonderful sons, none of whom find anything he writes even slightly amusing. (sigh)

―ellє―

A Diary by I.M. Captive
for Joan, friend and inspiration

East Meadow, Nassau County, New York Spring 2020.

Day 1 of lockdown 3/23/20
Have decided to attempt a diary.

My words for my entertainment and self-discovery. Honest. Liberating.

Will anyone else ever read them? Don't know. Don't care.

Will I write every day? Hell no!

I'm not that interesting. You're not that interesting. Go away.

When I feel like it, I'll write. Or not.

Took inventory.

Feel as safe as anybody can in *The Time of Crazy*.

Tell myself I have *enough*.

Sure, missed the initial rush on toilet paper. Didn't see that one coming. Should have.

But...

Have cornered the market on merlot. The liquor stores are empty. East Meadow is dry.

You can wash your tush with water; try drinking toilet paper.

Grabbed the last 4-pack of 2-ply at the local CVS from the old lady who was holding it. But she's old and probably wasn't going to make it anyway.

And if she dies with a dirty butt? We all do.

My soon-to-be-ex-wife once accused me of being selfish.

'Selfish'? Moi?

2

People?

Don't like 'em. Don't trust 'em. Don't need 'em. Don't want 'em. Have no reason to.

Mistreated all my life.

Now rid of them.

If they want to bury themselves in their own garbage? Drown in their melting glaciers? Choke on their own pollution and wash it down with their own filth?

What's it to me? Nothing.

Free of their toxicity, I embrace my solitary damaged self within the tranquility of *The Crazy*.

Now I can redefine myself, and whom I shall reemerge as into a brighter, brave new, unknown, vastly different world.

I'm in here somewhere. I just gotta find me.

On the other hand, the corona captivity will not be completely unproductive. The birth rate, divorce rate, suicide, homicide and domestic violence rates, alcoholism and drug abuse rates will soar.

Almost makes me feel sorry for them.

3

Rediscovering the joys of literature and music.

Working my way through Shakespeare from his first play, Henry VI Part 1, through his last, Two Noble Kinsman (a collaboration).

Rereading authors I first read years ago.

With some, "OK. Now I remember why I didn't like you the first time."

Others, like Dr. Seuss, I now find delightful.

Tolkien? Tolkien got me through my time in the Army.

Reacquainting myself with forgotten masters.

P.G. Wodehouse. Damon Runyon. O. Henry. Dorothy Parker. Thoreau. Ibsen. Jonathan Swift.

And the neglected glorious.

Hemingway. Fitzgerald. Steinbeck. Faulkner. Robert Louis Stevenson. The wolves, Virginia and Thomas. Lewis Carroll.

Moliere? Tolstoy? George Elliot? O'Neil? Aristophanes? Who?

Shame on those who don't know them.

These are the drinking buddies with whom I share my merlot.

I am never alone when I have a book.

Who reads these days? They're all on their cell phones, iPods etc., butchering the English language and communication in general (most certainly communication as an art) with *txtg*. The laziest and most intentionally self-limiting language on this planet.

Binge-watching bad TV. Science fiction stuff like *Attack of the Killer Gerbil from Mars* and *Amazon Women Versus the Radioactive Eggplant*.

Have grown fond of Yugoslavian soap operas, which is strange since I don't speak Yugoslavian.

Considering most soap opera dialogue, that's probably for the best.

And music.

Asked once by a co-worker what music made me feel 'happy'?

'Happy'? Now there's an alien concept.

"Joplin," I said.

"Wow!" she said. "I love Janis!"

Wanted to bite her nose off. I meant Scott.

Now my home ripples with ragtime.

Apart from my DVR-ed favorite shows, I avoid TV. Which channel would I watch?

Eschew *news*, 'fake' or otherwise. Depresses and horrifies me.

Damn it! Have resolved to write a poem! Stand back!

4

>a pleased necrophiliac Fred
>remarked to his late wife in bed,
>"You know it's a given
>I wish you were livin',
>but sex has improved since you're dead!"

Not bad, huh?

5

Personal hygiene has suffered.
Let's just say I no longer look like my passport picture.
Deodorant? Who am I out to impress?

Have come to appreciate the manipulative chasm between the Philosophical and Commercial.
Philosophical: Why don't they make brown underpants?
Commercial: They want you to be embarrassed and buy more.
Hah! I have defied them!

6

Have given up.

Time to bathe and do laundry. Underwear crackles when I walk. At one level, the sound is comforting. Reassures me I'm alive and mobile. But the odor has become distracting.

Once upon a time, deluded myself I'd bathe when it got to the point where I was scraping my butt along the sidewalk.

Alas. As Shaw wrote, "Middle-class morality claims its victim."

7

Apparently, have gotten a reputation on the local internet. And a nickname.

Bacchus. The god of wine. How'd they find me?

Was contacted by East Meadow's most famous (infamous?) marijuana dealer. (He got great reviews on the *East Meadow Captive Couples* website.)

He wanted to barter an ounce of pot for a quart of merlot. Let him squirm.

Got him to throw in a chicken. Cooked.

He dropped the deal when I demanded a roll of toilet paper.

Conceded.

Left the quart in the alcove; he left the ounce. And the chicken.

8

Bad move.

Awoke this morning to find something in my toilet unlike anything I have ever seen in my life. Am only glad I flushed it before it leaped out at me. And how did it get there? Did elves (Or pixies? Or Scientologists?) come in the middle of the night and leave it for me as a gift? Perhaps even as a companion?

If so, would they have tested positive? Or it?
Gave the dealer a very bad review on yelp.
In retrospect, maybe I was hallucinating.
Anyway, it's gone.
Kept the chicken.

9

Continually discovering the infinite and myriad joys of pornography.

The internet offers a hitherto unknown galaxy of sexual niches.

Can choose how many legs each participant has.

Amazingly, the coronavirus has created its own porn niches.

Contagious Cuties Homebound Hotties Quarantined Queens

Would not have thought it possible to look sexy in a ventilator.

Most corona-era porn is as erotic as a block of ice. You cannot give a satisfactory blowjob through a facemask.

Alas have had to reconcile myself with a sad truth: There is only so often you can masturbate. After a while, it becomes unproductive. Even painful. Luckily, sometimes I'm laughing so hard, I just can't.

But I try. Trying counts. Must be careful.

Pornography is adicktive.

10

Briefly glimpsed the news.

New York, where hundreds are dying daily, is locked tighter than a clam's sphincter, while elsewhere people are protesting (in large infectious groups) to reopen themselves to the virus.

And the South?
Why do all the assholes sink to the bottom of this country?

The best and worst part of democracy: Even the assholes get to vote.

Common sense is an oxymoron.

11

Not particularly religious, but...
Missed not having a family Seder.
Considered having a Seder by myself.
The world's lamest Seder.
Asking myself the Four Questions. (Knowing the answers.) Hiding the Affikomen. (Knowing where to look.)
Oy.
Not for nothing, Pope Francis didn't bring in much of a crowd for Easter at the Vatican either.
Next year in Jerusalem!

12

Halfway through Macbeth, the phone rang.
As Dorothy Parker said, "What fresh hell is this?"
Occurred to me that nobody had called since I'd entered seclusion.
Is it partly because I'm an obnoxious son-of-a-bitch?

No.

It's completely because I'm an obnoxious son-of-a-bitch.

Do I miss people?

Hmmm?

Not as much as toilet paper.

"Hello?" Said none too kindly.

"Hi." My soon-to-be-ex. "We need to talk."

Just what I needed.

So why, despite my every instinct, was I pleased?

She'd moved back in with her parents when we broke up. Now they were happily(?) quarantined separately together.

Imagine the nice things they were saying about me?

"We can't divorce," she said. "Nassau County Divorce Courts are all completely screwed up with the virus."

"Hmmm? So now what?"

"We have several options."

Always the better organized of the two of us. She paid the bills. I wasn't sure where the checkbook was.

Whatever else can be said about our soon-to-be-late marriage, neither of us had ever screwed the other out of a dime. Or cheated. I give her that.

"We can negotiate the terms of our divorce ourselves or feed the lawyers."

"Hmmm? Let me think about this. I'll get back to you."

She hesitated.

"How are you?" she asked.

"I'm thinking about getting a pet."

"Are you crazy?"

"I figure a Great Dane will feed me for two weeks, properly refrigerated. And those drumsticks? Definitely not a Shih Tzu."

"Ewww"

"How are you?" I asked. Hopefully sounding as indifferent as I wanted to pretend to be.

"My mother is driving me nuts!" she hissed with an intensity that melted my ear wax.

"Sweetheart, did you say something?" my soon-to-be-ex-mother-in-law asked distantly.

Teeth gnashing. Hers.

"No, Mom, it's OK."

"Her hearing's still good?" I enquired, not so innocently.

The acuity of my soon-to-be-ex-mother-in-law's hearing is the stuff of legend, as is her lack of boundaries.

"My mother can hear me menstruate."

"Through a tampon?"

I heard her nod.

"That *is* good hearing."

I heard her shudder.

"I'm sleeping in the bedroom where I lived when I was thirteen. It's wall-to-wall unicorns!"

"Tres Freudian," I suggested.

"What was I thinking? If I never see another pony, it'll be too soon. Get back to me. Stay safe and well. And smart!" A resounding exclamation point.

She was gone.

She has always been problematic for me.

My next wife will beg me for anal sex and have tits the size of my head.

13

Have tried to shake off her call. Can't.

Wounded.

Thought I was rid of people.

And now her?

Good. Kind. Loving. Lovely. Generous. Protective. Supportive. Gorgeous. Wonderful. *Her.*

She is both all people and the exception to all people.

Part of me loved (loves?) her for that; part of me hated (hates?) her for that.

If I've broken her heart, so—in different but no less agonizing ways—has she mine.

My dilemma. My humanity hook.

Her.

I can survive the virus. Can I survive her?

Just what I need.

An existential crisis in the middle of a pandemic.

14

Why did (do?) I love her? Had to.

She's just too good not to love.

I may be crazy. I may be an asshole.

Wait? What's the next line?

Oh yeah.

But I am not so crazy or stupid not to vibrate with how deserving of love she is.

Me?

The *loved* cannot understand the terrifying burden of being *loved*. Love is so simple and benevolent for them.

And, for them, it is.

But for *us*? The disliked and abused? Love has blades.

Love. Seek it; shun it; you will still ache.

How do you cope with the agonizing suspense of waiting for the one you've risked loving—whose love both thrills and terrifies you—to realize how unworthy you are? And flee. Leaving you with your guts hanging out. Yet again, confirming you're unlovable and hope shameful and self-deluding.

Kinder for her (safer for me) to preemptively end it.

I thought I had driven her out. But, now, here she was.

So I hang, skewered upon her love.

15

It's on me to call her.

Cowardly silence or terrifying talk? Offering what? Fear? Insecurity? The tattered armor that leaves me vulnerable? The panic that makes me fly before her inevitable (self-imagined?) slap?

Too late. I let her in. The only ones who can hurt you are the ones let in.

16

I called.

"Hello," she said.

"Are you wearing panties?"

"I'll get my daughter; shall I?" my soon-to-be-ex-mother-in-law asked, in a voice colder than Frosty the Snowman's testicles. (snowballs?)

Shit!

"It's him!" She snarled the pronoun. She could only have meant me.

A pause, then my soon-to-be-ex asked, "What did you say to my mother?"

I told her.

"Hah!" she guffawed. "I give you credit; you've never hidden what a complete asshole you are."

"That's the nicest thing you've ever said to me."

"Why did you call the house phone?" she asked, not unreasonably. "Why didn't you call my cell?"

"Tell me again, what's your cell number?"

Through gritted teeth, she recited yet again the number I've written on several walls.

We *skyped*.

Another 21st Century noun/verb blazing into existence within the ascending tail of our technological rocket. Linguistically, this is going to be one hell of a century. (If we survive.)

Webster, stick that in your lexicon!

"Jeez, you look like shit," she opined.

"Missed you too. It's been nice talking with me. *Click*," I said, impersonating a telephone being hung up.

Who hangs up a telephone anymore? What sound does a cell phone make?

"How are you doing?" I asked.

"I'm bored. Confined. Controlled. Disrespected. It's almost like being with you. I'm too old to be living with my parents. Let alone quarantined with them. Ugh! If I had it to do over again, I'd make *you* move in with my parents and *I'd* stay home."

"As if," I said.

"Fine, I'll join a convent. Are there Jewish nuns?"

"Not many," I conjectured.

"I'll start one. *Our Lady of Mah Jong*."

"Her eavesdropping?" I asked, not so innocently.

"I never know when she's listening."

"Let's try an experiment," I suggested. "In your clearest what-should-be-private voice repeat after me: Yes. Yes. Yes. I know how much you love and respect my mother, despite how she treats you. I'm sorry, Even if she doesn't appreciate you, I'm grateful."

I heard her silent giggle.

She recited this script quietly and exactly and we both listened. We both heard the distant, "Awww."

"She's good, your mother," I whispered. She groaned.

"How can I get her to stop?"

"You wanna fight back? For the next hour-and-a-half describe to me in a voice one decibel lower than she-should-be-listening-to how much you crave anal sex with me in exquisitely graphic and extended detail."

She chortled. Perhaps it was a snicker.

"You and your anal sex," she said, unquestionably shaking her head.

"Yeah. Yea and verily, I enjoy anal sex. I refuse to be embarrassed or apologetic about the fact that I enjoy anal sex."

"Damn it!" she whispered. "I agreed to anal sex! On your birthdays."

"No, damn it! You're missing the point. If I can accept that anal sex is not your cup of tea..."

"Nor much of the planet's!" she countered.

"If I don't expect it of you... If I don't resent your refusal... Why do you resent my watching somebody else do it online?"

"Sweetheart?" my soon-to-be-ex-mother-in-law said distantly, "Did I hear you say, 'Anal sex'?"

"No, Mom," said loudly. "Kill me." Sotto voce.

She began.

When she wants to, my soon-to-be-ex can talk *schmutz*.

When she reemerged, sweating, breathless and exultant, after twenty-seven minutes of incredibly graphic, excruciatingly vivid—abrasive (literally and figuratively)—details, I knew two things: (1) Her mother (if she were still eavesdropping, and she probably was) would never see her daughter the same way again; and (2) I could have driven nails.

They were, perhaps, the happiest twenty-seven minutes of my life.

Would her mother ever eavesdrop on any of our conversations again? To be determined.

I knew my baby can talk *schmutz*. But this *schmuztig*?

If I'd known that, we might still be together.

"Hah!" I whispered. "That's my warrior baby! I'm beginning to remember why I married you."

I heard her smile.

"I miss you," she said, driving a spike through my heart, and hung up.

So I writhe upon her love.

17

Watching wildly divergent and insane predictions and rancorous debates about what our children's education will look like in September.

It's all bullshit!

You can open any classroom, any class—half-a-class—a half-day class—an alternate Thursday class—any time you want.

And, when the first—kid—teacher—bus driver—lunchroom worker—crossing guard—janitor—tests positive, then what? That school's gonna close down tighter than... I'm out of metaphors.

Why do fools keep making plans, debating policies, and pretending control and predictability exist, when a careless family barbeque in Georgia can ultimately close schools in California? Or New York?

None of the models and predictions mean shit!

I won't believe anything until I see it—two months after it happens!

Classroom vs. homeschooling?

At best, there are profound differences between competent, respectable homeschooling and the traditional classroom.

Now? In most cases, *homeschooling* is yet *more* bullshit! Nobody takes it seriously.

Presuming the parents want to be bothered forcing their children to learn. "Suzie, stop playing video games and learn the multiplication table."

As if.

How many parents want to be bothered coping with the grief they'll get from their children? Or are they even any good at teaching them? Even when they're not working to support the family. (Presuming they have jobs.)

And the worst?
"What is two plus two?"
A timorous, "Three?"
Smack!
"Four! I keep telling you it's four!"

Better and far easier to let Suzie play her addictive video games. Especially, since we all know—in most cases—she can't be as effectively educated at home anyway.

In an actual school... There is an imposed structure. An unrelated adult demands your attention and cooperation. And there is a manifestly consensual, recognized agreement that this is the place you learn. That's why you're here. *To learn.*

Education is so important that you have to go *there* to do it. And we, your parents, demand that of you.

That is a school!

And the teachers? How many terrified teachers do you know? I know a bunch.

Classrooms are Petri dishes. Kids cough and sneeze all over each other, infecting everybody.

Feel sorry for the kids.
They're being cheated out of an education.
I blame the virus for disrupting our children's education. I blame us for not having created an effective alternative. But we have had so many failures.

And beyond *mere* education?
Not only can't they be effectively educated, they can't even socialize with other children. Just as important, perhaps even more so.

More victims of *The Time of Crazy*.

18

Phone rang.
"Hello?"
"Why don't you love me?"
She was drunk and tearful. She doesn't do drunk well. She weeps or sleeps. Fortunately, she's not a puker.

Vodka—like fire—is a good servant, but a bad master.

"It's not you; it's me I don't like."

"No kiddin'? You think I don' know how damaged you are? *They* did this to you! The ones who hurt you. The ones who made you hate them. And yourself. They did their best to destroy you."

"Butcha wanna know what?" she asked, drunkenly concentrating on every syllable. "You won, you dumb bastard! You defeated them! An' you got the scars to prove it. They're gone an' you're still standin'! Now it's jus' you hurtin' you. How friggin' sad."

She's the only person I know who can say 'friggin' and not sound ridiculous.

"Listen, you asshole, if you lose me, they win. I'm the best thing thas ever happen' to you!"

Vain, perhaps, but no less true.

"Andja wanna know the crazeest part? I believe you *do* love me."

"I do," I roared within my skull. But aloud?

"Whydya think I stayed this long? But you were killin' me. I'm the one who's screamin', 'I love you!'"

Small sob.

"I tried lovin' you; you threw it away. You threw me away. I couldn' waste the only life I'll ever have waitin' for you to make me feel loved?

"But now? Everything's crazy! Hundreds of thousands of people are dyin' ev'ry day. Nobody knows wha's gonna happen next. And I'm livin' with my parents. And the friggin' unicorns!"

She made a sound that was either a semi-stifled belch or a failed puke attempt.

"So, I'm gonna give you one las' chance."

And I knew I wanted her.

She was too good not to love.

"I love you," I said aloud.

Did she hear me?

She sighed.

She heard me.

"So don' let them—or you—kill *us*. Fight for me! Fight with me. Jus' fight for us! Will you do that? Because I will. I'm not gonna let them—or you—kill *us*. Whatever you are. Whoever you are, you wonderful wounded man. You make my heart laugh. Is that enough to save a marriage? I don' know. But it ain't a bad start."

She laughed.

" Besides, who else am I gonna date?"

She made that stifled belch/insufficient puke sound again.

This one was *not* a belch.

"Gotta go," she retched.

Her first gag began before she hung up.

Hoped she made it to the toilet.

19

O frabjous day! Callooh! Callay!

Favorite Chinese take-out place has reopened! East Meadow grapevine is ablaze. Dancing in the street (in facemasks)!

Po Sing has reopened!

A vastly better omen than the first robin of spring.

Forget about the first robin of spring!

This is chicken and broccoli!

20

Phone rang.

"I've got the virus," she said.

My gut convulsed.

"I feel like shit."

"Come home," I said.

"What about my parents? I can't leave them. They probably have it too. Or will."

"Fine," I said. "I'm coming."

"Are you safe?"

"Where have I been? For the past three months, I've seen less daylight than a vampire."

She hesitated.

"If you're coming, do me a favor?"

"Sure. What?"

"Open all windows and load the dishwasher. Burn whatever you've been wearing for God-knows-how-many weeks. Flush all toilets. And bathe. A shave would be appreciated."

Not unreasonable requests.

"That's five favors. Pick one."

"The toilet! Flush the toilet! Flush it repeatedly! I'll burn whatever you're wearing. With you in it!"

"OK. I'll even run off the dishwasher and vacuum."

"Wow! And if that isn't love...?" said impulsively, perhaps instinctively. She'd heard herself say the word. We both had.

Said is done. She had reintroduced the word *love* into our relationship.

21

We sleep in the bed where she slept at thirteen. Surrounded by unicorns.

And we talk. Deep talk. Honest talk. Challenging talk. Appreciative talk. Insights gained. Misunderstandings resolved. Apologies made. Obstacles defined that may never be overcome. Promises made. Hopefully kept.

Wonderful conversations.

Words that will either join us or separate us forever.

Sex? It ain't easy under the gazes of so many fascinated, amazed, delighted, horrified, aroused(?) unicorns (and her mother's hearing), but we try.

Enthusiastically, silently.

What next?

Damned if I know.

How will this end?

Damned if I know.

When/If we remerge into the *Post Corona* world, what will it look like?

Damned if I know.

But we have plenty of company. Ask any sane, intelligent, realistic, honest human being on this planet, "What will happen next?"

And, if they are sane, intelligent and realistic, and honest, they will answer, "Damned if I know."

And if we reemerge together?

It will be Day 1. Hopefully the best Day 1 of the rest of our lives.

Damned if I know.

Eve

Written by P.S. Shuller

―――ele―――

P.S. Shuller (she/they) is an autistic, asexual, queer, poet, and writer. Shuller believes deeply in the importance of being both a neurodiverse and gender non-conforming writer. Shuller's primary inspiration for their stories comes from her own life, namely, her husband, dog, and newborn. Though, it is their primary belief that, through literature, we come to better understand the overarching human experience in all of its forms. Literature, be it in a game, novel, or any other form, should speak to each person's heart regardless of gore or genre. It is for this reason that Shuller lists Joel, from *The Last of Us*, as one of their top 10 most compelling literary protagonists.

Professionally, Shuller's poetry has been published in Lavender Lime's second Volume. She has also performed her poetry in Milwaukee at Poets' Monday. Find them on Twitter @p_s_shuller. Follow their blog: The Eclectic Dumpsterfire on BlogSpot.com.

―――ele―――

His white fur tangles around mud and several burrs. He tries to bite my hands as I dump splashes of water from my canteen over his irritated skin. He turns his head, trying to nibble out the burr, but after a minute, he only whines. I say nothing and pull out his grooming brush from my pack.

I brush his fur out completely before taking a pair of scissors and cutting away the burrs and mats. When I'm done with him, he stops whining and licks my face while I push us further back into the lean-to. I look through my pack to see what we have left before I go hunting again tomorrow.

This forest is good for hunting. That is why we chose to settle here back when we were together.

But I try not to think about back then much.

It was a long haul leaving our suburban home for the relative safety of the forest. Ironically, it was Sans that led us away from the pillagers. To this day, I couldn't tell you what caused the slow craze across the country. There was no great bomb, or flood, or sign from God that the world was ending.

It was a news story here that a disabled man had been shot down in his home for his existence. It was a headline there that police had shot another Black man for walking home after dark. It was another bloated body of an old veteran dragged out of the gutter. The final news story was simply a headline that read: "Warning—government experiment gone wrong. Soldier PTSD treatment prevention causes aggression and a lack of empathy. Reports of cannibalism on the rise in Mississippi. More at 10."

The vets had told us this sort of thing was coming when the world finally made peace.

Then, one day, white men dressed in camo uniforms began shooting up our neighbors' homes. We'd heard about this happening in other states, but we never thought it would find us.

Wisconsin is too quiet for this sort of thing.

Yet, on that day, you could hear the mothers and daughters shrieking as these men pulled them into the street. The pained wails of the fathers of each household blared in our ears. We heard the door clicking, and we scrambled to grab as many supplies as we could. I pulled Sans' brush into my backpack. I carried as much formula and baby food as I could into my ratty old Vera Bradley duffle bag that I'd kept since college. I ransacked every canned good, all of our peanut butter, honey, and other non-perishable items, and slammed them into the bag as well.

Gunshots.

Screaming.

Leaving the well-paved roads for thick leaves and wet grass of the Northern Highland American Legion State Forest.

That's all I really remember, now.

It feels like a long time ago, even if it has only been five years.

I had always been told in my childhood that this sort of thing was only done in the "bad neighborhoods." This was the sort of thing that happened on the Northside of Milwaukee, but I always knew people who said that sort of thing were wrong. For, it seems that white folks always wear rose-tinted glasses when it comes to our own crimes: past, present, and future.

But, hindsight, they say, is always twenty-twenty.

I look back down at the ball of fur in my lap. A smile plays at the corner of my lips, and I feel each muscle lift separately. Sans' chest rises and falls in a steady rhythm. Sometimes, it seems like Sans is completely oblivious to the pains of this world.

But I know he's not.

He still looks for them sometimes. He waits by the door searching for two bodies that will never push open that door again. I usually call him back to my side, but I sometimes let him wait.

On bad days, I sit there and wait, too.

I think about how wrong we were, in a certain sense, about Sans. For, before the end of our world as we knew it, we often joked that Sans earned the "Most Useless Member of Our Household" award.

He doted on all of us, sure.

He was a Bichon Frise that we bought from a breeder in the first few years of our marriage. He had just really matured into himself by the time the world collapsed. When our world ended, Sans was just a lap dog with an occasional rowdy streak. He lived for one thing: to warm our laps and hands in the lavish court of our living room. I can still remember the blue rug on our living room carpet with the frays that Sans played with...

I blink myself back to reality knowing that dwelling on that past isn't going to help anyone.

I focus myself on thinking about Sans; if only, because he's all I have left.

How old is Sans anyway?

Sans is old—for a dog.

I think?

We got Sans the year we were married. Pete was born a year later. Pete was about two when this all started. It's been five years since then. So, I guess, Sans is actually somewhere between eight and nine.

Oh Pete, your hair was always so frizzy in rainy fall weather, like mine. Your eyes were so blue and clear ... like your father's. A sharp contrast to my own dark black green ones.

I cannot help but watch the siren song of those two pairs of blue eyes draw me closer. The shared look of mischief as their slightly tanned fingers find the triggers of Nerf guns. I reach out to grab my own Nerf gun for self-defense, but the only thing my fingers find at my hip is the icy cold metal of my own very real Glock 19.

The shock of steely cold shoots up my fingers, and I pull my hand away from it. I'm sort of glad my hand found it. It's been too easy to get sucked into those memories lately. It doesn't matter how many days, or weeks, or years have gone past.

Has it even been years, yet?

I just can't forget them. Their memories stalk me like ghosts in this haunted house. Their whispers lure me in at the worst times. Their reminders are everywhere in this makeshift house like some kind of phantom willow o' the wisps leading me into the forests of insanity.

I literally do not even remember where we got the damn thing—the Glock—from. It was maybe our second or third week on the road that we took it off a dead body with some ammo. We found an old hunting rifle abandoned in the shack where we attached our lean-to. No one has ever come to claim the shelter, and so no one ever really seemed to miss the old thing. It worked well enough for a while, and it had set us up.

We had a rule that the Glock was for shooting Cannibals, and the rifle was for deer and other food.

No animal has ever attacked me to date, and so, the Glock was never necessary for killing any animal. I refuse to stoop to the level of the Cannibals and hunt humans for sport.

So, I've never needed to use the rifle on a person.

I flick on the old radio in the lean-to as I carry Sans to bed with me. The static sounds from the radio as the station tries to play some unintelligible song. The quality of the sound on the radio has gone downhill in the last week.

I worry that the batteries are dying.

I only have two left that are fresh. Once those go, I have no more connection to the outside world.

I lie down on my side flicking through stations until I find one that is mostly clear.

It's the station they call "FM 91.7—Rhinelander's Random Station." Basically, the host is never the same person anytime you listen. There's no real schedule or anything. Most hosts set playlists to shuffle and let it rip.

But, there are exceptions.

One ninety-year-old guy came on once and played an entire opera for three hours. Then there was this middle-aged dude who acted the entirety of The Merry Wives of Windsor by himself, with voices, for an entire afternoon. There was another night when this country singer, originally from Nashville, took over the station and covered a bunch of Dolly Parton songs.

Then there was this couple who aspired to make it big on Broadway. They covered a bunch of famous duets, I think, yesterday? I remember they were both from a small town near Rhinelander, and they were childhood sweethearts. They never got to leave their town.

I danced with myself in the middle of the lean-to as my and my husband's first dance song was sung by this young couple. The static blips were the only things that kept me tethered to the reality that I was, or rather am, facing.

As their voices rose, I swore I could feel the fabric of my twenty-pound dress and the sweaty palms of my husband as he spun me gently in his fingers. I saw his eyes shimmering behind his glasses, and I melted under them. My own fingers grasped fruitlessly at the fabric of his black tuxedo as a pebble of static splashed into the mirage and sent it away in ripples. The black fabric slipped through my fingers like water.

After that, it was like trying to dance with a watercolor painting.

Tonight, I think the opera guy is back on. It's either him or someone like him. The music is instrumental, but it's not Tchaikovsky or any classical composer that I recognize.

A stunning instrumental guitar plucks a simple melody as a fiddle of some sort creates dissonant harmonies that seem perfect for this sort of evening. It captures the very essence of my melancholy musings while also inspiring a sense of the hunt that Sans and I are attempting to sleep off.

We managed to catch a few rabbits that I'm slow-cooking in my pit out back.

They will be ready in the morning.

"And that was the theme of my favorite video game, The Last of Us, music written by Gustavo Santaolalla, for the game of the same title. And damn if that sucker doesn't feel oddly appropriate tonight."

Oh. It's the video game kid. That makes sense. I must be knackered if I didn't recognize that song.

"It's on my agenda tonight to blast a very special message to the folks listening. My cousins and I have an initiative we call Project Oasis. Project Oasis is inviting folks to the abandoned Walmart. The address is 2121 Lincoln St, Rhinelander, WI 54501. We've been holed up in the Walmart there. I'm not allowed to give the address of the radio tower. But! But, don't fear lovely ladies, it's not too far from where we're living. Please stay tuned, more on Project Oasis after this song." The raspy radio voice crackles.

I bolt upright and Sans startles. I pet him to calm him down. My mind races as Jareth, the video game kid, plays another song from a game I don't recognize. We could make it there in a day. If I carry Sans in my pack and book it, we can do it.

It took my family two days, with an infant, from McNaughton.

Sans and I can easily make it in a day.

I make a mental list of things that we'll need. We'll need the sleeping bag. I need the radio and my batteries. I have plenty of food and I can easily hunt more on the way. I still have quite a few matches from the ones I raided a few weeks ago from an abandoned Cannibal camp near my hideout. I need the map that we managed to bring with us, find, or something. We might have raided that too? I can't remember anymore.

I pause my thoughts for a minute.

For the first time in years, I feel a sense of purpose. This radio message cut deep into some sort of fog that I didn't even know was clouding me. I finally have reason to believe that there's some hope. We might finally get a chance at a new life. I grab an old piece of notebook paper and begin frantically scribbling as Jareth gives information.

"Thanks for listening to that song. That was Gris, Pt. 2 by Berlinist from the game Gris. I feel like that was an appropriate song as I prepare to explain the goals for Project Oasis. My cousins Bethesda, Blaise, Dexter, Ender, Felicity, Guinevere, and I have all been plotting a way to return to civilization. That's right folks! You thought this radio station that we hijacked was dope, but you're about to get more bang for your buck! We're hoping to see all of our featured presenters here at 2121 Lincoln Street. It's been an honor sharing the air with you guys. But, anyway, Project Oasis is seeking folks who want to see the return of some normalcy here in Northern Wisconsin. Our goal is to recreate a democracy that will hopefully inspire those left at the Capitol. Which, as you know, fell last month after expending military force to try and quell the rebellions across the fifty states. We've lost most contact with any folks out there, but we'll give it our best. That's all I've got for now, friends. Thanks so much for listening, but I've gotta return home. That address again is 2121 Lincoln St, Rhinelander, WI 54501. It's the Walmart off of Lincoln Street. Turn up Eisenhower Parkway, and look for us behind the Taco Bell. You should see us from Lincoln St, but when you see the Taco Johns, the BP, and the Hardees you're almost there. If you see St. Mary's Urgent Care on the right, you've gone too far. We hope to see you there. This is Jareth signing off." The radio clicks and hits dead air.

I stare up at the ceiling with the paper plastered to my chest. Eventually, I fall into a fitful sleep.

The next morning, as I wake up, I hear something scratching at the pit out back. I sit up slowly trying to see if Sans is outside trying to eat the rabbit. But he's not. He's still resting on my lap. I grab the Glock from my bedside table and slowly stalk outside.

As I push open the door, I hear scrambling and muffled voices. I poke my head out, and I see two vaguely child-shaped figures trying to run as they grab some of the cooked rabbit.

Something inside my heart breaks as I look at their dirty and worn faces.

"Please don't hurt us, Miss!" The boy shouts, looking at my gun. "We heard you walking the last few days, and we were hungry. We hoped you'd ..."

"It's alright. I don't mind. Come inside." I usher them in.

After we eat and I write out my route on our map, I turn to them and ask, "I am going to find Project Oasis. Are you familiar with FM 97.1 Rhinelander's Random Station?"

"Yes," the boy grins and looks at me relieved. "We were spying and heard something muffled coming from your house. I poked in your window while you were laying on your bed. I heard you listening and I knew you were a safe person."

I eye him carefully before giving him a smile and a small nod.

"Our parents used to play that station, too," the boy says. "Every night."

As we pack up, I begin to wonder about these two little ones who stole into my camp. I find out that the boy's name is Xavier, and the girl is Jessica. Despite the fact that they stole from me, and that they're dirty as hell, I can't find it in myself to hate them. I want to love them. I discover as I watch them, a growing fiery warmth inside myself that I thought I had abandoned when I lost Pete. I realize the tingling sensation that I feel—that primal longing to smother them in hugs and read them stories—is love.

I haven't felt love in a long time, but I've chased her shadow every day.

It's not long before we pack the last of the food, put Sans in my backpack, and finally leave this place.

I don't stop in the yard at the two rounded domes that poke out of the earth.

I don't have anything more to hear ... or to say.

"Where are your parents?" I ask them while I place Sans in my backpack. "Do you think they're looking for you or the Oasis?"

"They're gone. We lost them in the forest about two days ago." The girl's voice is feather light and raspy.

I nod. "I'll help you find them, but you'll have to keep up with me. We'll take today slowly. We're just going to my old house in McNaughton. Tomorrow we'll have to keep a quick pace. It's about a three-hour walk today with no breaks and a four-hour walk tomorrow with no breaks."

The kids wince and look up at me.

"Don't worry, we'll take stops. I promise. If I were going it alone, I wouldn't risk them. But with you," I sigh, "I'll make an exception."

We finish packing the rest of my things and head out the "front door" of the lean-to into the crisp air of the forest.

Surprisingly, I think I will miss this place. I befriended the trees with their old knotted bark that I pretended were faces. I dreamed, sometimes, that the trees spoke to me and gave me counsel. I wave goodbye to squirrels and deer who seemed so graceful in, what was at first, a terrifying place. As we walk towards the parking lot at the entrance, I see trees that I marked as ones that were good for climbing for vantage points. I notice the scuff marks of boots, maybe my own boots, along the tree trunks. Nature has given us so much. For now, though, her beauty earns my thanks more than her function. Some days, I thought I could survive on the beauty of nature alone.

Even today is a crisp fall day. The leaves turn the sky red with their fire as I trace the bumpy trunks with my fingers willing myself to remember the way back to McNaughton. The fire-leaves blaze up against a background of pure evergreen and baby blue as white custard color clouds float in the sky. It's moments like these that make me understand how Tolkien wrote all of the imagery into The Lord of the Rings.

It surprises me that none of these trees awaken to remind me not to be hasty.

I risk a final glance up at the sky only to see a large falcon eclipse the sun. It circles me high overhead and calls to me.

I take it as a sign that this is the right thing.

Pete always loved falcons.

Slowly, after a few hours of hiking, our small party leaves the relative safety of the wooded lands as we cross the Northern Highland American Legion State Forest parking lot. We scurry as fast as we can across the lot and towards our next tree-covered area.

As we walk toward McNaughton, I try to keep us in wooded areas—when I can, that is. Northern Wisconsin is mostly woods. So keeping us in them isn't too difficult, but occasionally I have to risk roads. We travel into McNaughton, and I realize we've made good time.

I turn us down Fawn Lake Road.

Unsurprisingly, Sans knows this place and starts squirming in my pack.

"Calm down, doof, I know you know where we are," I admonish. "It was my home, too."

I hear the two children giggle behind me, and I find myself smiling, too.

We round one of the first bends in Fawn Lake Road, and I see my old house.

I push open one of the doors that is nearly knocked from its hinges. The children follow after me.

Despite being only four or five o'clock at night, we are all exhausted. I survey my old living room while the two children and Sans immediately pass out together on our couch.

I don't look there long.

I turn from our living room to face our kitchen. Someone pulled the TV off the desk in the kitchen and took most of the knickknacks. As I move closer, I can see shattered dishes on the floor. There are old dried bloodstains on the tile.

There must have been a fight over our valuables here.

You know where that blood really came from. You just won't admit it. You know there's only one mound behind that lean-to. You know what really happened here. Admit it.

The sob that breaks out of my throat is primal and guttural. It's the kind of cry that makes your face look like a prune, and your vocal cords shrivel up twice as much as your face. I look down at the caked blood and lie down. I gather up the few crusted, blackened, crimson flakes as they peel off the floor. I refuse to lose any of them. I see more of them attached to my clothes. I watch how the blood returns to something resembling a liquid as I sob into it. However, most of it just remains caked to the floor.

"I'm sorry. I'm sorry. I tried to save him. I did everything I could. One day he just wouldn't eat. Then, he just shook for hours in my arms. I did everything I could. I tried to raid medicines. There were no doctors. Lord knows I was never going to be one. If you had been there, you would have known what to do. I was always so useless without you." I beat the floor with my fists.

Suddenly, I feel four points of pressure at the small of my back before a soft weight settles itself down the base of my spine. I turn over and pick Sans up. I hold him to my chest and cry more. He buries his face in my shoulder. I release him to my lap, and he sniffs the blood tracks. Then he lays down on my lap with his paws beneath his chin, like he knows whose blood this is.

Actually, Sans probably knows this is my husband's blood more than I do.

"Oh, Sans, what are we gonna do?" I ask him, not for the first time in these long years.

He looks up at me with his huge, glassy, coal-black eyes. He puts his paws up on my chest, and he buries his face in my shoulder again.

I finger the small cross around my neck for a minute while I brace Sans with my other hand. I have to believe that there is something after this horrible existence. I desperately cling to the idea that some good exists after this world if there can't be any good in it now. I imagine my husband's face and my son's face. There is a bright white light behind them as they hold their hands out to me.

Here, I am forgiven for all of my transgressions. In this place, they know, and I know they know, that I tried everything.

I feel my husband's strong and warm hands around me as he pulls me in tightly. They always say that in Heaven you won't know who your loved ones are because it won't matter. But, right now, I am still of this Earth enough that I need to believe that he'll see me, know me, and hold me like he once did.

It's the only thing that's keeping me going because I know if I don't try to survive this, if I despair, I will not find Heaven.

I wake up the next morning on the tile floor of my kitchen with Sans curled into my side. The light of dawn is just poking its nose up into the window.

The warm glow spreads over me, at first slowly, and then all at once.

I stretch wide and my right shoulder pops itself back into place just like it does every morning.

I walk into the living room and wake Xavier and Jessica. The sun has risen just enough that we all walk the trails easily. Sans licks the sweat off of the back of my neck as we press on into the afternoon.

Honestly, I am surprised we didn't run into any Cannibals yesterday and I'm flabbergasted that we haven't found any today.

I risk breaking the silence as I look to my charges. "So you lost your parents in the woods?"

"Yes." Xavier says, catching up to my stride and looking up at me. "Do you think they'll be at the Oasis?"

I look up and I think long and hard for a moment. "I think it's possible. You said they listened to the station a lot. So it's definitely possible. They might be waiting for you there to see if you might have heard about it too."

Xavier nods. "I hope they're there. I know they would be the first ones to bring us if we were still together."

I smile. "Then I am glad that I was around to bring you to them."

"They'll like you. You can stay with us and be happy. You can be like our auntie." Jessica ventures with a little more strength to her tone than the only time she has ever spoken to me.

"I could." I reach to take her hand. "I suppose I could."

"Your family died didn't they?" She asks, cocking her head to the side to look at the side of my face. "I saw the mound outside your house."

"Yes. They did." I steady my voice by clearing my throat.

We fall into a reflective silence before Xavier breaks it. "Do you think about them a lot?"

"I do." My voice is so small.

"What happens if our parents are dead?" Xavier asks.

"Then we keep trying to make a better world for their memory. You... you keep trying to live even when each breath is the most painful one you've ever taken. You... I guess, you just try to make the world better because there's no real use in causing people more pain just 'cause you feel it." I shrug, still holding Jessica's hand.

Xavier nods. "I can try that."

"Good. Now we've got to be quiet. We're approaching the city and we have to use Phillips Street to cross the Wisconsin River. I don't feel like it's safe to walk across. The current is too fast for you to keep your feet, and I don't feel like taking Sans swimming," I say to them as we pass over the bridge.

Sans gives an indignant growl, and I receive two twin smiles from my charges.

As we leave the bridge, I chamber a round in my Glock. This road is too quiet, and the sun sets in my eyes. We're easy targets.

Suddenly, I hear shuffling as we turn onto Thayett Street. Then gunfire pops just like it did years ago.

I risk turning around to see a band of Cannibals pouring out of the Moonlighting bar.

I look at Xavier and Jessica, who both freeze, staring at the group of men and women who charge us.

I throw us inside the Dinky Diner and bar the door with a table. I hand my backpack to Xavier and my Glock to Jessica. I put a hand on Xavier's shoulder.

I need to make my instructions clear and fast because time is running out.

"Xavier, in that pack are Sans and the rifle. Use it when you need to. Keep running down this street. Thayett Street becomes Courtney Street which becomes Lincoln Street. All you need to do is follow this road. Shoot anyone who attacks you." I place my hand on his shoulder and squeeze.

"But, what about..."

"Don't worry about me. Take care of Sans for me. Get to the Oasis. I'll do my best to meet you there." I turn to look at Sans.

I hear the Cannibals getting closer.

"Jessica, if anyone gets close enough to you or your brother, use the gun to shoot them. That's an order." I don't look at her.

"O-okay. I'll try." Her voice waivers.

I suppose it should. She can't be more than six years old.

"You take care of them. Keep them safe. I love you." I place a kiss on Sans' head. "Try not to get too dirty. They won't be as good at grooming you as I am."

He whines and paws at me, but I don't listen.

The sun sets completely as I run out the door. I scream as loud as I can. Out of the corner of my eye, I can see Xavier and Jessica running the other way down the street.

With that done, I turn my attention towards the Cannibals. I see the bloodlust in their eyes as I approach. Their gaze hardens on me and their eyes are sharp. They know what they're doing, and they enjoy it.

I hold my ground.

I am a woman who is not strong physically.

I know what is going to happen.

But, I'll do it anyway.

"Come and get me, cowards."

Not a Raccoon Stealing Doritos in the Basement

Written by E.A. Field

E.A. FIELD IS AN adopted Korean American with a passion for all things science fiction and fantasy, rescue animals, cosplay, baking, and gaming (not necessarily in that order). E.A. has been previously published, under pen name Anne Bourne, with *Blue Moon* (Simon and Schuster, 2012) and *IRL: In Real Life* forthcoming from Rising Action Publishing Collective in 2023.

The steel box rattled as Damian set it on the counter. Why had Brad, his roommate, put it in the ceiling? Workers had discovered it upon opening the kitchen ceiling. He lit the gas fireplace by inserting the metal key, then dropped it into a bowl on the side table by the couch. The furniture had been moved to accommodate his chair, the kitchen remodeled so he could reach pots and pans. Damian checked his phone. No texts or calls from Brad, which wasn't unusual. Brad was what most people labeled as "wayward." He'd been in Sagnot Bay for two years now and wouldn't really say where he'd lived before that—just that he'd traveled a lot. He was the quintessential eligible bachelor playboy and had the bright, charming looks to back it up.

"Would it kill him to put away his shit?" Damian muttered as he rolled across the kitchen and grabbed a wrench and set of ratchets.

He placed the tools on the garage workbench, wheeled himself back inside, and shut and locked the door. He couldn't reach where the wrench went so he figured Brad could put it away when he got back. Brad paid a low rent after much debate—Damian had been reluctant to have his co-worker friend live with him. He didn't relish the idea of a parade of women through the house, beer bottles all over, and general small talk fuckery that went along with being Brad's friend. That was before his accident. After it, Brad insisted on paying rent and helping him.

They had met at A&M Auto Center, where they were mechanics. The irony of Damian being T-boned by the same vehicles he worked on was not lost on him. The T-9 vertebrae injury a year ago had left him paraplegic. The male driver of the blue Toyota Tundra was serving twelve years for the DUI, and it did little to make Damian feel better.

Now, Damian was fairly self-sufficient and it was just a matter of how to tell Brad that he wanted to live alone again. Damian had grown tired of Brad's leering at women, bravado-infused tales, and sometimes just plain bipolar-like behavior.

The box called to him. Always inquisitive, Damian couldn't help but glance at it, as if it held the secrets of the universe. It wasn't new or super beat up. Maybe Brad had forgotten it or maybe it wasn't his at all. Was it something his parents had left behind? Damian shrugged. He wheeled back to the garage again and got out a bolt cutter. After two snips the lock popped off.

Damian stared down at the contents with a furrowed brow. His parents certainly wouldn't have left this stuff. What the hell was it?

Inside the small box was a ring with an emerald surrounded by diamonds; a pair of socks with puppies; a silver spoon; a patch with a skull and torch; a torn page from a book; moonstone earrings; a nurse's badge with the picture scratched out; and a bangle with stars, moons, and the initials A.H.

Must be Brad's, he thought with a disgruntled shrug. In the back of his mind, something tickled. He dismissed it as another of Brad's eccentric behaviors and left the box on the counter.

Damian rolled to his main floor room. All his clothes were organized on a rack and his shoes off the ground, leaving the walk-in closet empty. He reached around to gather the catheter line to empty the bag as he glided into the bathroom. While he enjoyed the extra time not spent in the bathroom, he'd rather have the use of his legs again. Thank God he didn't have to use the enema system for a bowel movement yet. And maybe it was a blessing Sharon had left him five months after his accident—she was never much help to him with "delicate" matters such as bathroom habits. Damian checked his phone reflexively thinking of her. No calls, texts, or emails in ten months. It was like she'd moved out of the state. But he'd seen her around Sagnot at their coffee shop, in the grocery store, and getting her car serviced at a different mechanic shop.

The mirror caught his reflection and the tattoos on his arms and upper neck. Damian couldn't stand to look at himself for long. He rolled to the gaming computer at his desk and put the headset on. In the fantasy world of *Pirate Scourge*, he could forget his injury, the painful recovery, and the hopelessness that he'd ever walk again.

Damian clicked to shoot when a crash in real life jolted him from the game. He lifted his headset off to better listen.

Another Crash. It sounded like cans thumping down the basement stairs.

He logged out of the game. Was Brad home? Why would he go through the basement? Damian sighed as he left his room. There was no electric lift to the basement yet, so he had to content himself with opening the door a crack. In all reality, he should sell his parents' house and move to a one-floor. But Damian couldn't part with it. The only other family he had was a brother who lived in Australia.

"Brad?" he called down and flicked the light on. The old fluorescent lights flickered for a few seconds.

The crash came again, followed by a guttural grunt. Damian frowned as he tilted his head. A trapped animal?

"Fucker, enjoy my Doritos." Damian shook his head. A skunk or raccoon was likely wreaking havoc on the extra stash of food down there.

A shadow preceded the very human figure that staggered to the bottom of the stairs. Damian clenched the doorknob. The young woman's dirty blonde hair hung in ropey vines, her clothes torn, revealing a decaying torso and red oozing wounds that ravaged her forearms. Her throat had clearly been slit—sagging skin and a gaping dark slash smiled across her neck. Her mouth hung open and fangs protruded like a demented vampire.

"H ... hey—"

Damian was cut off when she hissed, and her tongue flicked out like a snake. Blood dripped off her clawed fingernails. The stench of iron and decay assaulted his nose.

Damian shoved back and slammed the door shut. He twisted the lock on the handle as he stared at the door in shock. What the fuck was that? There was no talking to that ... her. He enjoyed a good game of *Dungeons & Dragons* as much as the next nerd, but in reality, there were no real monsters, right? Either that or this woman's cosplay was next level.

Footsteps pounded up the stairs and hammering fists shook the door. Damian rolled away into the kitchen. He fumbled for the phone and dialed 911, putting it on speaker. As it rang, he grabbed the large butcher knife from the block on the counter.

"911—how may—what's your emergency?" the dispatcher answered. Her tone was rushed, distracted.

"I've had a break-in at 1436 Greenwood Lane. Someone's in my basement." Damian wheeled as fast as he could toward his room, where he kept a mid-sized gun safe. And then he remembered Brad had moved his Glock 17 and SIG P226 upstairs to clean for him. It was highly likely Brad had not returned the two guns back to the safe. He hoped the Beretta 1301 was still in there.

"All right, please move outside if you can or is there a safe room where you can wait? Police responders should be en route, but I can't guarantee that. How many intruders are there?"

Damian had thought responders were supposed to be calm, but this woman seemed on the verge of panic. Her words were slurred as if she had more pressing matters on her mind.

"One. But she's ... wrong. Bleeding everywhere, fangs," he said in a matter-of-fact tone. He didn't care if she thought he was a loon. It was the truth.

The responder was silent for too long. "Ma'am?"

"I'm sorry, what's your location?"

Damian repeated his address and the line cut off. Thrashing continued at the basement door. In a 911 call situation he was supposed to stay on the line, so was help coming or not? He cursed as he opened the safe and where three guns should have been, there were empty spaces.

He glanced at the stair lift chair.

The door splintered.

Damian spun around and headed for the lift. "Vampire strength, eh? I get it."

He side-eyed the door as he went past. The woman on the other side punched it like she was a pro wrestler. Or a rabid dog.

Damian understood the logistics of using the chair lift, but it was newly installed. He hoped the workers had done it correctly. The other problem was his catheter. Easy enough to unhook and refasten. However, once he got up there he'd have no wheelchair. *Fuck it, I have to get something other than a knife. Before the accident, he wouldn't have needed to rely on a gun so much.* Damian took a deep breath. Then he unhooked the catheter, made sure the cap was on tight, gathered the bag so it hung over his shoulder—very little piss in it, thank God—and hoisted himself out of the chair. He scrambled into the electric lift and punched the knob for up.

The lift started slowly. Achingly slowly. The fists banging on the door stopped. Damian dialed 911 again. This time there was no answer, just perpetual ringing. What the hell was going on?

There was a slam, the door falling off the hinges, as the lights went out. The lift slid to a halt.

Damian held his breath and listened to the shwump-thump of uneven, barefoot steps. Was the woman attracted to sound? Could she see in the dark? Was she fast or slow? Should he turn his phone's flashlight on? Damian wasn't going to wait like a sitting duck. He grabbed the railing and flung himself out of the lift chair. Hand over hand, he dragged himself up the stairs. Wet-sounding footsteps followed him. Nails clicked on the handrail.

He glanced at the bottom of the stairs. In the dim patches of moonlight through the window, the woman stared up at him with milky white eyes. Her hands clenched and she spasmed. On her left wrist were two bangles.

One of the gold circlets dangled and clacked together—the letters A.H.

Damian's skin chilled. He'd seen that bracelet before ... in the locked box. "Do you know Brad?" He didn't think she was capable of speech, but his rational brain couldn't contend with a dead woman who has come back to life, either.

Her neck cracked as she tilted her head to see him, and a few drops of blood sprayed from her slashed throat. She screamed and started up the stairs. Nope, does not speak English. Damian's muscles burned as he climbed the stairs.

Brad's bedroom was the second on the left. Damian huffed panicked breaths as he clawed at the handle. It twisted and he fell into the room. Damian slammed the door shut. The woman pounded on the door with skull-cracking thumps.

Swearing incoherently, he fumbled his way to the desk where the guns were laid out. Thanks, Brad. Don't put them back or anything. He scrambled for his phone for light. The Beretta was the only one fully assembled so he grabbed it and the box of twelve-gauge shells next to it. With the terrifying slowness borne of stress, he loaded the shotgun and racked it.

Damian had never been happier he'd purchased the optional extended magazine so that it held six shells and one in the chamber. He fired. The door splintered and the woman or whatever-she-was behind it shrieked. The pellet spray ensured he hit something... but she didn't go down like a normal human. No, he'd only succeeded in creating a hole in the door for her. Her face appeared and her eyes bore into him as her clawed hands reached through the shards of wood. Damian reloaded and fired again. Chunks of her head hit the doorframe; blood sprayed in oddly cold droplets over his face. She went down but her body continued to twitch as if trying to stitch itself back together.

The lights flickered back on. Beeping arose from the microwave and the coffee machine.

"Damian?" Brad's alarmed shout broke through the ringing in Damian's ears.

He lowered the Beretta as his friend bolted up the stairs. Brad held a Glock 19 out in front of him.

"What the hell is happening?" Brad yelled as he took in the bloody scene. For some reason, Brad did not seem overly surprised to see the woman lying on the ground. Did he know her?

"She was in the basement," Damian said in a hollow voice. Shock sent a fine tremor down his hands, and he put the shotgun down on the floor. "Who is... was she?"

Brad rushed into the room, skidding on the blood. He ignored Damian's question in favor of other prattle.

"Hey, are you okay? There are power outages all over and people are going crazy!" Brad, still in his hunting camo, holstered his Glock and ran a hand through his brown hair. He helped Damian up into the desk chair. Damian clutched the Beretta with him and set it on the desk. He eyed his friend—Brad was almost too calm.

"I'm fine. Tried calling the cops but they hung up on me."

Damian sat silently as Brad chattered on about people looting, police opening fire on civilians, and something about people coming back from the dead. Brad got several towels from the linen closet and threw them over the still convulsing body on the floor.

"So, what do we do with this?" Damian asked with a grimace. "What is she?"

Brad cocked a brow at the woman or what was left of her head. "I don't know her. I'll move her outside and we can let the cops have her. It's gonna be hell getting blood off this floor and my sheets."

"Why was she in the basement?" Damian fidgeted with a shotgun shell. His mind had cleared enough to try rational thought. "We don't get a lot of unexpected visitors here."

Brad paused his haphazard cleaning. "Maybe she got in the back door or fell in the window well. Hang on, let me check the rest of the house and call the cops." He clomped down the stairs. "I'll be right back, dude."

Damian opened and then closed his mouth. He hated not being able to get up. He also hated being lied to. Brad wasn't telling him something—his eyes had that shifty look, and he pinched his thumb and forefinger together a lot.

Didn't serial killers keep trophies of their victims? That would explain the woman in the basement and the matching bracelets. Had Brad stashed her down there thinking Damian would never find her before he moved her, because... how could he? No stair lift, no reason for Damian to go down there. And she'd been dead. She wouldn't have made any noise. Except Brad hadn't counted on whatever the hell this was—the undead returning to life. Damian watched the clawed hands scratching at the floor and twitching under the towels.

"No..." Damian whispered. Brad could be an asshole, but he couldn't be that vile.

Footsteps. Brad was returning and it didn't sound like any police officers were with him.

Damian scrambled for a plan. His hands clutched the Beretta with shaking fingers. He channeled all the anger at his accident, the unfairness, the depression, the diagnosis he'd been unable to accept that he'd never walk again into one simple thing: survival. There were eight pieces in that box. Was that eight women Brad had killed? Who knew what he'd done before he'd killed them? Judging from the walking corpse in the basement, they didn't have pleasant deaths.

You can pretend you didn't see inside the box... oh shit. You broke the lock and left it on the counter. Fucking idiot. He's surely seen it by now. Damian's mind raced. He didn't have to stall a confrontation.

Brad's booted steps approached. Damian couldn't believe his friend and co-worker was a serial killer about as much as seeing a revived corpse of a woman in front of him. Just injure him so he can't hurt you, then get answers. If you're wrong, Brad will heal. If you're right... then that's one less killer on the loose, right? Damian's mental bravado was strong but he wasn't sure shooting his friend was the best course of action. And, of course, there was the pesky rationale that the only things he'd ever shot were in a game, not real life.

"Where did you find this?" Brad asked. In his hands lay the gray metal box. Something tingled Damian's senses. Brad jostled the box as he reached for something on his hip, under his coat. A Glock 19.

Damian pulled the trigger. The Beretta jumped in his hands and the slug shattered Brad's left leg. He screamed and toppled down the stairs. The Glock slid out of his hand—he'd been holding it under the box, hiding it.

Damian dragged himself to the chair lift and hoisted himself into the seat. He aimed the shotgun at his friend. Brad moaned and clutched the carpet, his left tibia and fibula shattered. Damian punched the button to lower the lift down the stairs. He stopped halfway, getting a decent shot on the other leg. He racked the shotgun.

"Fuck, man!" Brad screamed, tears and blood mingled on his face. He'd probably go into shock soon.

"The workers found that box. Care to explain it?"

Brad shuddered in pain. "It's just a few things from my past. My mother's jewelry."

Damian frowned. "Try again."

"Come on, call an ambulance, you fucking shitbird! I hid it because it's sentimental."

Damian ground his teeth. Did Brad really think he was that stupid?

"You killed that girl. I don't know why she's a walking corpse, but I don't room with murderers, and I draw the line at reanimated dead bodies in my basement," Damian said, sarcasm being the only thing holding him together at the moment. His arms tingled with spiked adrenaline.

Brad panted as he struggled for words through the pain. He held up a hand. "All right, I killed her. Amy. But she attacked me! Look, I have the bite to prove it." He pulled up his sleeve and his left forearm sported an oozing wound with teeth marks around it. "She was going crazy. Everyone's gone insane—something's happening out there!"

Damian forced his breath to slow; he was starting to hyperventilate.

"How long have you been killing women? Is it only women?" Damian half-shrugged. "Not that it matters. The cops certainly have more important things to worry about right now even if I called them."

"I'm done; she was the last. I'm moving on, I swear."

"Oh, so you can continue to kill more people?" Damian's brow rose along with the certainty he couldn't let Brad leave.

"I was attacked. Aren't you listening?! Something is happening out there—please, get me to a hospital and I swear I'll leave you alone," Brad said and slumped in agony. He lay on his back with pained breaths.

You're not a killer. Are you going to become what he is? Damian warred with himself. He could call the police again and try to get an ambulance. He could try to help Brad up enough to get into a car... at which point he expected that Brad would turn on him. This is survival... and maybe a little revenge. Those women, whoever they were, didn't deserve their deaths. They had families and friends who will never know what happened.

Whatever was happening outside in the world was uncontrollable. All he had was right now. If the law wanted to arrest him, fine—maybe it was safer in a prison. Although, who was he kidding, in a wheelchair his mobility was limited and that meant so was his time. No one was going to help him if they were worried about outrunning the undead.

"That's the reason you move so much. Why you wouldn't tell me about your previous jobs," Damian said.

"Listen, just let me call an ambulance, man. I'll serve time. I'll tell them what I did." Brad reached for the Glock, which had landed a few feet away.

"Pick up that gun and lose your hand." Damian pushed strands of hair out of his eyes. He was out of time. Either he let Brad live or he became something he'd never thought he'd have to be.

Brad didn't stop. He kept army-crawling towards the gun. Damian didn't hesitate and his finger moved on the trigger. The twelve-gauge shell couldn't miss the man on the ground below. Brad's head jolted back and half his right arm was destroyed; a spray of crimson dotted with white bits of bone splattered the floor and staircase.

Damian stared down at Brad. He was sure cops would burst through the door and shoot him on the spot. He waited, but there was only the buzz of the lamps and the wind against the house.

And then a hand clenched and nails scraped on the hardwood floor.

Brad's body began to move, the limbs contorting as his fingers grew claws. Maybe he had been bitten by the woman. Damian started to connect the dots. The word 'zombie' floated through his head incredulously. This was the second dead body to come back to life in almost as many hours. It wasn't possible… yet Brad's half-face turned toward him. Fangs protruded from his mouth as he snapped; milky white eyes pierced through Damian's.

Take off the head. Damian racked the gun, shot three more times, and Brad's head was almost nonexistent. The body kept moving, but without the head, it wasn't nearly as threatening. However, he had no doubt those claws could do some damage. Damian's body ached from the spikes of adrenaline and from hauling himself up the stairs. He rubbed his face with a hand. What to do now? He needed to get rid of the bodies.

A tornado siren blared. His head shot towards the window—the sky was clear, but it was a definite warning. Of what, Damian wasn't sure. He sighed. It was going to be a long night finding rope to drag Brad and the woman out of the house, dump them somewhere more able-bodied people could deal with them, and then clean up the floor and stairs. Iron and gunshot powder scalded his nose and the thought of adding bleach to that made Damian nauseous. He debated calling Henry from work for help. Henry had never gotten along with Brad. But the fewer people the better. Damian had a hard enough time thinking of himself as a murderer now as it was.

"Not murder—self-defense. That's what it was," he muttered out loud. His voice echoed too loudly in the silent house. Yet, the silence was preferable to guttural growls and the scraping of nails. If only this was a game. He could spell himself somewhere or leave the mess for someone else to deal with.

The lights flickered. The radio switched on. The news anchor talked about looting, people panicking, something about a virus or nationwide hoax. The undead walking among us. Damian let out a slow breath. So, it wasn't just a freak thing in Sagnot. What the hell was he in the middle of now?

Damian squared his tired shoulders. After this was all cleaned up, he intended to roll down to the Shell gas station and stock up on beer. Maybe he'd take up smoking again, too. There was always something threatening to undo the world, right? What made this night any different? He'd continue to survive as long as he could, and when his time came, he wasn't going down without a fight. After all, what could be worse than finding out he was harboring a serial killer and one of said killer's victims had returned from the dead in his basement?

Damian might never walk again, but the countdown was on to see how long he could survive an actual zombie apocalypse. How many people could say they were at the beginning of the end?

For more of Damian's story, check out IRL, Emily's paranormal zombie thriller, releasing in July 2023 from Rising Action Publishing.

Firestorms

Written by VJ Dunn

VJ Dunn is a Christian author living in the Southwest USA who likes to write stuff that might be a little more off-the-wall than what the average Christian reader is used to. She knows the Lord has a sense of humor and she likes to make sure she writes with it.

Her stories lean toward a PG rating, but nothing more than what you might get from a kid's cartoon these days. VJ's characters are believable people who will make you smile, cry, think, and yeah... laugh.

A bead of sweat rolled into his right eye as he squinted through the scope, stinging enough to make him curse. Clay didn't let the discomfort stop him from squeezing the trigger, though. The only thing that would and could stop him from firing round after round would be the need to reload.

Or waking up dead.

Karina grunted. "I'm out." Clay glanced at his wife, noting how pale she looked. She'd been sick for weeks, likely due to malnourishment. Or the filthy water they tried in vain to boil and filter enough to make potable. He wouldn't be surprised if she had parasites. They both probably did.

But minuscule bugs floating around their intestines were not high on the list of worries at the moment. Their immediate concern was the horde of zombies coming at them.

"They're not zombies," Karina had laughed when Clay first labeled them. "They're just desperate people trying to survive like us."

"Yeah, but not like us, they're willing to kill to get what they want," he'd argued. "If they came asking for help, you know we'd give it. But when they come wanting to steal and God knows what else... well, it's us or them."

Clay chose "us."

Karina rolled onto her back, hugging the rifle to her chest. It was the twin to his, both SPR300 Pros, one of the best non-military rifles ever made, and bought at the highest price Clay had been willing to pay—his old truck. The beast still ran, even on the homemade fuels they'd been forced to create when gas had become a commodity no one could afford. But transportation wasn't high on the list. They didn't plan to go anywhere else, since things were the same everywhere.

Horrible.

"There's another magazine in my lower right pocket," Clay told Karina as he fired off another two rounds, easily killing his targets. The horde was down from fifteen to three.

She crawled over to him, careful to keep her head below the frame of the old refrigerator he'd tipped on its side. Karina had always complained about his "hillbilly junk"—all the broken appliances, inoperable cars, and worn-out tires he'd saved over the years, but they were both glad to have the junk now. It made good barriers at least.

Despite Karina yanking on the magazine in his pocket, Clay didn't let it distract him from watching and waiting for the other three enemies to peek over the frame of the old Chevy at the east edge of the property line. They'd made the mistake of attacking in the afternoon when the sun was low on the horizon, blinding them. They could have come from any other direction and had the advantage. Fifteen to two were pretty good odds in their favor. But the zombies never seemed to have any common sense, never had a battle strategy.

Dark hair became visible over the front quarter panel of the Chevy, just an inch above. Yet another mistake. Clay quickly fired a round.

Karina snapped the magazine in place and rolled back to her knees, peering through the scope as she aimed her rifle through the crack in the refrigerator door. The ever-widening edge of the doorframe was shredded from firing through it, but it was still a very effective blind. It had come in handy a dozen or more times so far.

Clay managed to catch another attacker at the back of the car frame when he'd stupidly tried sliding out on the ground, probably hoping Clay and Karina would be looking up.

"One more," he murmured to his wife. She'd managed to kill one of the attackers, which brought her lifetime number of kills to two. Clay didn't like to think of how many he'd shot. One was too many, but when you were faced with kill or be killed...

He killed.

The last zombie must have become suicidal when she realized all the others were dead. She jumped up, screaming, as she fired shot after shot at them. The pinging of the bullets striking the refrigerator was almost deafening.

"Stupid waste of ammo," Clay grumbled as he squeezed the trigger one last time, hitting her right between the eyes. If he was going to spend the ammo, he made sure it was going to count.

Karina seemed to deflate as she turned to sit with her back against the fridge and blew out a shuddering breath still cradling the rifle. He took the weapon and carefully placed it on the ground next to his, then wrapped an arm around her shoulders as he pulled her close, resting his chin on the top of her head. When her body started to shake, he tightened his hold.

"It's okay, baby," he murmured. "We did what we had to do. They came at us guns-blazing, you know."

Karina nodded against him as she buried her face in his chest. "I know," she said, choking on a sob. "I know. It's just... I can't... I'm not a killer!"

Despite the need to comfort his wife, Clay chuckled, bouncing her head against him. "Like I am?"

He'd been a plumber before the world had taken a dump. The only weapon he'd ever handled had been a drain snake. But when the world started getting crazier and crazier, he'd gone the way of a "prepper." Learned to shoot. Bought extra propane tanks for the house and a huge generator. Stockpiled cans of food and MREs, bottles of water, first aid supplies, and boxes of ammo for guns he didn't even have at the time. He even bought a couple of crossbows and bolts for when the ammo ran out.

He frowned at that thought. It was the first thing he'd told Karina when he'd been teaching her to shoot using a BB gun. "Don't waste ammo. Wait until you have a clean shot before firing." Yet she'd managed to run out, though she'd only killed one attacker.

"It's okay," he soothed again, running his hand down her slightly greasy hair. Sponge baths had become their norm when the weather got too chilly to bathe in the creek flowing behind the house. It was nearly impossible to get fully clean. Shiny hair, clean clothes, and good-smelling armpits were a thing of the past, like everything else that had made their lives comfortable.

Clay never realized how spoiled they'd been, not until everything went south and the only thing their money was good for was lighting a fire.

At that thought, he looked to the south, toward the city. Reddened clouds rolled and churned, billowing in angry folds as they climbed into the late afternoon sky. It had been like that for nearly a month.

Clay assumed a fire large enough to light even the daytime sky would have come their way by now. At times when the wind shifted, they could smell smoke. But it wasn't a woodsy smell, like that of a forest fire. This was something else, something odd.

Karina seemed to settle and pushed herself off his chest, wiping at her cheeks with the palms of her hands. The gesture was so childlike, Clay wanted to pull her back into his arms and protect her from the evils that continued to come their way. But he couldn't coddle her; she needed to learn to survive.

"C'mon," he said as he stood, reaching out to help her up. "Now comes the fun part."

Karina squeezed her eyes shut as if it would force out the thought of the coming chore. Clay didn't let her dwell on it as he tugged on her hand. His frail, overly sensitive wife needed to toughen up.

Dragging dead bodies off for the packs of wild dogs to feast on seemed like a good way to do just that.

Wind so forceful it knocked him off his feet buffeted Clay as he tried to grasp a pole far too insubstantial for a guy his size. Wet fingers slid from the metal, clasping into a fist when he was flung farther away, tumbling like a leaf in the voracious wind.

Terror filled him, along with helplessness. This is it... shoulda told Karina I loved her one more time. And now he'd never be able to make amends with his dad.

Inexplicably, his stormy flight ended with him upright, feet-first on a bluff overlooking the valley. Though still shaken, the frightening past few moments were completely wiped from memory as he stared wide-eyed at the sight laid out before him.

Dozens of fiery tornadoes churned across the landscape.

"No way," Clay breathed. It was an impossibility, but he didn't bother rubbing his eyes to clear them. As impossible as the scene might be, he knew it was real. The evidence was undeniable—hot wind tore at his body, forcing him back a handful of feet, while sand stung his exposed skin and hot ash burned his eyes.

Reasonably, he knew the sheer number of twisters destroying the valley below was inconceivable. Just two tornadoes appearing in the same area was an anomaly. But fifty or more...

It could very well be an extinction-level event.

At least for Copper Basin, Clay thought. But something whispered the scene before him wasn't exclusive to the valley he called home, that the devastating destruction was global and catastrophic to mankind.

"Clay!"

He turned at the sound of Karina's voice, grateful his wife was still alive, yet horrified she would be a witness to the horror unfolding before them. She had never been one to cope well with crises.

Sand and smoke continued to whip around him, swirling clouds fogging his vision. Debris from the land—and from destroyed homes—flew by as well, and he dodged a rooster weathervane when it nearly impaled itself into his skull.

He put a hand to his brow in an attempt to shield his eyes. "Where are you?" he yelled, his voice stolen by the howl of the wind. "Karina! Where are you?"

"Clay!"

Spinning in a circle, he tried to find her, tried to trace the direction of her voice, but it was impossible to tell where she was. He opened his mouth once more to call out, but the ground started shaking at that moment, toppling him to his knees.

Tornadoes and now earthquakes? The end of the world had truly come. The shaking intensified and he moaned in terror.

"Clay, wake up!"

Gasping, Clay sat straight up in the bed, arms outstretched, empty hands clasping. With a confused frown, he dropped his arms, then put his face in his hands while Karina rubbed his back in soothing circles.

The dream was prophetic. Clay hadn't realized when the recurring nightmare started years before that it foretold the future, but once the economy took a dump globally and the zombies started crawling out of wherever they'd been hiding, trying their best to take over with their own brand of craziness, he'd been slapped right in the center of the forehead.

Just like in the dreams where he'd stood on a bluff helplessly watching as the spinning firestorms destroyed the earth, he was lost, powerless, unable to stop the downward spiral consuming civilization. The best he could do was pray the psychos didn't find their way to the little farm that had been in his family for generations.

But they had found their way to them.

Karina made a noise behind him, a weary, heavy sound. The bedcovers rustled. "I'll go make some tea," she murmured.

Lagos stirred from his dog bed tucked in the corner of the room. In the moonlight streaming through the basement window, Clay watched as the mutt pushed to his feet and trotted dutifully after his mistress. Despite the tension still tightening his shoulders and chest, Clay smiled. The dog was loyal to Karina, probably thanks to all the treats she shared with him.

Clay rubbed his face with shaking hands before tossing the covers aside to climb out of bed. Noises from the kitchen told him Karina was already preparing the tea, a concoction she'd promised would help him sleep. Whenever he had the tornado dream, sleep evaded him. Karina tried to help, but the nasty-tasting tea wasn't really strong enough to numb his worried mind.

A shiver ran through him when he stood, and he quickly shoved his feet into the faux fur-lined slippers he kept on his side of the bed. The chill in the air heralded the coming freeze season, though it was too early. But the creek's temperature had dropped too low for bathing weeks before, far sooner than was normal. It wasn't a good sign.

They were in for a harsh winter.

The basement steps creaked as he shuffled up to the kitchen. After things got so crazy in the world, they'd taken to sleeping in the basement where they could bolt the heavy metal door from the inside. It wasn't a perfect defense, but at least they'd hear someone before they saw them.

And Clay kept his arsenal in the basement.

He frowned when he saw the solar lamp on the counter near the window and he hurried to move it. Even though the curtains were drawn, light around the edges could be seen a long way off, especially with the world as dark as it was now. He set the lamp inside a cabinet, though he left the door open, just barely illuminating the room. Karina glanced at him.

Clay scowled at her. "Are you trying to set up a beacon for them to find us?"

His tone was far more snappish than it needed to be, but he was tired of trying to get his wife to understand how dire their situation was. Surely after all the attacks they'd had over the past few months, she'd realize that they had to be cautious, always watching and waiting for the next one to come.

But she never seemed to get it.

Karina didn't comment, though her shoulders stiffened as she lit a match. Clay's mouth turned down while she lit the stove. Despite his years of prepping, they were on their last tank of propane. He'd already started working on converting an old non-working gas stove to a wood-burning one, but that would mean even more trips to the forest to chop wood. He hated leaving their little farm and the semblance of safety it afforded.

They didn't speak as she fixed their tea. Clay scrubbed his face with his hands once again, feeling tension rising up. He told himself he was just testy because of the dream and from the earlier stress of the day. And, despite his constant reassurances to his wife that they were just protecting themselves, he didn't like killing any more than she did.

"I'm sorry," he murmured into the silence. After a lifetime of buzzing appliances, the soft drone of electronics, and the ever-present background hum of civilization moving around them, the dead silence that accompanied the world's crash had been unnerving. It was as if the entire globe had screeched to a halt.

Even the wildlife and insects had seemed to disappear.

Not the discarded pets, though. Before they'd gone to bed, Clay had heard the snarls and yips of the wild packs as they'd fought over the zombie smorgasbord they'd been handed. Like Lagos, the poor things had once been pampered and beloved pets, but after the economic crash, pet food had been a luxury no one could afford.

Some, like he and Karina, considered their pets family and did what it took to care for them, even if it meant going without themselves. Others took the hard road and put their pets down rather than watch them suffer from starvation.

And then there were those who tossed their pets out like yesterday's garbage, expecting a domestic animal to figure out how to fend for itself. Clay hoped it was some of those people who'd ended up in the pile of dog food at the north end of his farm.

Karina looked over her shoulder again, a small smile gracing her face. The muted glow from the solar lamp cast harsh shadows along her sharp cheekbones, starkly showcasing her near-starved state. They were both barely more than walking skeletons.

"It's okay. I know you're tired. Everything is... stressful."

Clay snorted at that understatement. He hadn't relaxed in nearly two years. Just the daily grind of trying to survive was bad enough. Coupled with the additional need to be constantly vigilant against the threat of attack... he was afraid his shoulders were permanently stuck under his ears.

He rolled his head, trying to loosen the tight muscles he'd just been reminded of. "Yeah," he sighed, lifting a hand to rub at soreness as Karina poured the tea into mugs, adding a pinch of precious sugar. They were down to just a small baggie of the sweetener and used it sparingly, but the bitter tea needed all the help it could get.

They each caught up in their thoughts as they sipped the brew, the silence only broken by fierce wind howling outside the window, rattling the loose siding. The old farmhouse Clay's grandfather built needed a lot of work, but when every minute of every day was spent chasing after survival, well... upkeep took a backseat.

Karina sighed again and Clay looked up, noting the weariness that seemed to hang over her like a wet blanket. She wasn't cut out for the life they'd been handed. She'd been born into a rich family, one that had pampered her like the princess her father still called her. Or he would have if he were still alive. They'd lost all contact with both their families once everything fell apart.

Despite being completely unprepared for a hard life, his wife had managed to buck up and do her best to be helpful. But Clay couldn't help the nagging feeling in the back of his mind that things would be easier if he didn't have to watch out for her.

It was the main reason he wanted her to learn to defend herself properly. The dream came back to haunt him once again.

He cleared his throat. "We need to step up your shooting." Karina tipped her head up, looking at him in question. "Training, I mean. Your aim is off. We can't afford to waste ammo."

She nodded as her lips tightened at the corners. Clay knew she wanted to argue, to say that she wasn't cut out for killing, but she also knew it wasn't a fair argument. Neither was he, but it was just the way it was now. Fight or die.

"We're almost out of milk," Karina murmured. He frowned at the abrupt change of subject but didn't comment.

Instead, he stood and went to the sink with his mug. With having to haul water from the creek, they only did dishes once a week and reused what they could. Glasses and mugs were never completely clean.

Clay glanced over his shoulder. "I'll see if the Mayfields want to trade some potatoes for milk." They were one of only three neighbors he would have anything to do with. The others who were still in the area were no better than the zombies that kept coming around. They just wanted to steal, kill, and destroy.

It reminded him of a verse from the Bible he'd learned as a teen in his church's youth group back when the "end times" were discussed like something that would happen far, far in the future. In fact, Clay remembered the pastor claiming believers wouldn't have to go through those times, that they would all somehow be taken away beforehand.

Guess he was wrong, Clay laughed to himself, though the thought wasn't amusing.

It seemed they were right in the middle of those "end times" now. The world was upside down, chaos reigned, and good people were few and far. In fact, it seemed to pay to be bad… the zombies ran in packs like rabid wolves and there were a lot more of them than there were of folks who were just trying to stay alive when everything seemed to be against them.

Clay thought how it would be so much easier if the next time the enemy attacked, he just put the rifle down and stepped out behind whatever broken-down appliance they were hiding behind and…

Karina walked up, startling him out of his thoughts. She put her mug in the sink next to his, then slid her arms around his waist. Clay stiffened for a moment, guilt over his thoughts momentarily overwhelming him, but then he pulled her close.

They stood there for a few moments, sharing body heat in the chilly kitchen with the dingy yellowing tile and peeling rose vine wallpaper, each lost in the unending silence.

A low growl sounded; a warning. They separated and looked at Lagos, who leapt to his feet, teeth bared and hackles raised as he trotted to the back door, sniffing. Clay quickly bent and turned the solar lamp off. He blinked rapidly against the sudden darkness and then felt for Karina's arm. He pulled her close.

"Go to the basement and grab the rifles," he murmured close to her ear. He sensed her nod, then she shuffled off. He cursed himself for not grabbing his weapon when he'd come upstairs, but he'd been too rattled by that dream to think clearly.

Clay didn't want to be unarmed while he waited for his wife to return. He felt around for the drawer nearest to the sink, thankful that it didn't make noise as he pulled it open. His fingers slid over the contents, grabbing one of the butcher knives, then he shuffled to the back door.

Lagos continued sniffing at the door, alert. Clay gave a short hiss through his teeth, a warning to the dog to stay quiet. He was a mutt of an indeterminate mix of breeds, but Lagos was smart enough to understand.

Clay edged toward the door, for once glad he'd had to replace the decorative glass with plywood when one of the zombies had shot it out. He might not be able to see out, but at least whoever was out there couldn't see in either.

The dog continued to sniff at the bottom edge of the door, though he shuffled to the side when Clay stepped up to put his ear to the wood. He wasn't sure he'd be able to hear anything, so was surprised to hear low murmurs.

His jaw clenched when he eased back. It was likely the rest of the horde that had made the mistake of coming to their farm earlier. The desperados always seemed to find each other, forming large groups to terrorize the people just trying to stay alive. They were despicable. And likely seeking vengeance.

Movement behind him made Clay flinch, though he knew it was Karina. Thankfully, his wife knew to be quiet when they were being invaded. But when he heard wood screech across the tile floor, he grimaced.

"Sorry," she whispered a moment later when she handed him his rifle. "Ran into a chair."

Clay hissed as he'd done with Lagos earlier, knowing his wife no doubt would have something to say about that when they were able to speak again. He pointed to the back stairs and Karina nodded, turning in that direction. Clay followed, snapping his fingers once at Lagos, who reluctantly left his post and trailed after them.

The year before, Clay had carpeted the stairs with scraps he'd found in the attic, leftovers from his mother's redecoration efforts in the seventies. Karina hadn't been thrilled with the green shag, but he'd told her it wasn't about looks; it was about stealth. His wife had laughed at his paranoia. Clay wondered if she remembered that conversation now that they were able to silently climb the stairs.

The upstairs had three bedrooms that were mostly empty, and he motioned to Karina to take the second room overlooking the garden. Most of the plants had given up their bounty weeks before and it wouldn't be long before their dead leaves were covered in snow.

They'd gone over the situation they were facing, and what to do if they were attacked while in the house. Karina knew to crack the window with the well-oiled track, then start shooting at anything that moved.

Whether she'd do it or not... well, that remained to be seen.

Clay crept to the first bedroom's window, the one close to the back door just to the east of the kitchen. The night was partly cloudy with a half moon, so light was iffy. But he could see well enough to count half a dozen bodies below, huddled together, murmuring.

A frown creased his brow; they didn't look like they were preparing to attack. In fact, they appeared to be unarmed as they argued about something. He noticed two of the figures were much smaller.

Children.

While he hated being put in the position, Clay had no problem shooting holes in those who showed up at his place looking for trouble. But he drew a hard line at killing kids, regardless of why they were there. He figured if they were up to no good, well, it was likely an adult put them up to it. Or else they were just that desperate.

Moving to the side of the window, he pushed it up an inch so he could listen. The voices were jumbled whispers, but he caught a word here and there.

"...too late."

"But I saw a light."

"Yeah, but..."

"I'm too tired to..."

"... nowhere else..."

His frown deepened. Though he couldn't hear all of it, he was sure it wasn't a conversation had between people getting ready to attack. They were people likely just needing some help.

Clay sighed; he hated the idea of sharing what precious few commodities they had. But he had made a promise to his soft-hearted wife that if people came asking for help, he'd give it. It was those who just wanted to take that he had a problem with.

He pushed the window up higher, then checked the surrounding area to make sure there weren't others out there, possibly waiting for the group by the door to set the trap. As far as Clay could tell in the low light, they were alone.

The group below still hadn't noticed him, and Clay had to wonder how they'd managed to survive at all with the way they seemed to lack any sort of self-preservation, at least by way of vigilance in checking their surroundings.

"You folks looking for something?" His voice startled them so much that one man stumbled back and almost fell on a smaller form standing behind him. Another shadowy figure stepped forward.

"Clay? That you?"

Startling at the familiar voice, Clay laughed. "Drew?" It was impossible, but there was no mistaking his high school friend and former co-worker's voice. He hadn't talked to Drew since everything had hit the fan. Last he knew, Drew was living in the city, and he wondered if they'd walked the fifty miles to reach his farm.

"Yep, me and the family. Mom and Pop too."

"We'll be right down!" Karina said from the next bedroom. Clay had nearly forgotten she was there and said a quick prayer of thanks that she hadn't started shooting like he'd told her to.

Once they settled in the kitchen and Karina busied herself with gathering something for their friends to eat, Drew told the story of what had happened and why they'd left the city.

"They're forcing everyone who'd been any type of police—even security guards—to join."

"Who?" Karina asked Drew as she placed a plate of peanut butter sandwiches on the table. Clay knew the bread was stale and the sandwiches would be bland and dry without jelly, but it was the best they could offer at the moment. From the way the newcomers shoved the meager offering down, Clay knew they were grateful for it regardless.

"New government," Doc, Drew's father answered before taking a drink of water that Clay hoped didn't make him sick too. Even boiling the creek water didn't seem to kill everything that lived in it.

"They've taken over," Drew continued. "New laws. Curfews. Can't go to the store without a voucher and to get the voucher, you gotta let them take a DNA swab so they can put you in the system."

Doc snorted. "That's 'bout when we decided to head out. Don't want no new government having my DNA. Hell, didn't want the old government to have it either."

Clay frowned. "So, what happens to the people who don't comply? They just starve?" It seemed crazy, but with the way the world was going, it wouldn't be surprising.

"Worse," Donita, Drew's wife, said in a near whisper. Clay looked at her in question, but she just stared at the table, a haunted look marring her pretty features. Drew reached out and put a hand on her shoulder.

"Yeah, worse," his friend sighed as he looked back at Clay with a stricken look. He tilted his head to the south, toward the city.

"That glow you can see for miles around?" Clay nodded, hoping to finally have the answer as to what was causing it.

"That's what they're doing with those who don't comply." Drew's face morphed into a pained grimace. "That fire is from all the bodies they're burning."

A sharp pain hit Clay in the center of his chest at Drew's terrifying words. It was an insane thought, that the people who were in charge, who were supposed to help the citizens, would be murdering them instead.

The silence stretched on between the group as they contemplated what the future held for them, the nonconformists, but Clay knew exactly what was in store.

The firestorms are coming.

Spaceman

Written by James Shortridge

―――― ell ――――

JAMES SHORTRIDGE IS A lifelong resident of Eastern Kentucky and an avid lover of all things sci-fi and fantasy. In his personal life, he's an avid gamer and moderator of several communities on Twitch, a website for livestreaming. James has told stories since childhood, starting with epic tales told in LEGO form, but now uses the written page as an adult. He firmly believes that hope can still be found in otherwise dark and helpless times, a belief further fueled by the unexpected health struggles in his life. The prevalence of hope is a common theme in the post-apocalyptic fiction James enjoys the most, and in pieces he himself writes.

―――― ell ――――

Reality came back to him in a sudden jolt, his eyes opening as a reflective glass pane hurtled toward his forehead. A harsh smack and the world blurred into a twisted, distorted shape. The dazed man blinked and pressed his hands against the now-smudged glass. The chilled air prickling his skin snapped his mind out of the fog; this was his cryogenic pod, exactly where he was supposed to be. A sleek and shining medical ward, bathed in red light, lay beyond his glass shell. A buzzing drone sounded in precise intervals, and a metallic voice spoke in tones muffled to his ears.

"Emergency. Emergency. Breach detected on starboard side. Emergency. Crew presence requested."

The man let out a gasp, his breath coming in shudders; the glass of the pod gave way, a hissing sound rising above the alarms as the door lifted. Warmer air rushed into the pod and brushed along the man's face. The lone occupant emerged in a one-piece blue uniform that

hugged his body like a second skin. His head was buzzed of all hair, but his brows were a salt-crusted black. He hurried over to the numerical pad by the door, rapidly typed in a numbered sequence, but was greeted by an angry chirp. The man let out a huff, tried the same sequence again, and another chirp sounded.

"Damn it," he whispered.

Then, shouting:

"Computer, open this damn door!"

"Please state your credentials," the computer replied.

"Second Lieutenant John McKenzie, authorization code One-Three-Alpha-Echo-Seven!" A momentary pause. John rolled his eyes.

"Confirmed," the computer replied. "Welcome, Lieutenant McKenzie! The date is the

27th of June, in the year 2300 AD; exactly 50 years to the day of our original departure!"

"Thanks for telling me, now turn off this damn alarm!"

The noise stopped and the pulsing red light blinked into white.

"Status report. What the hell happened? Did we crash?"

"Negative, Lieutenant McKenzie; we have arrived at our intended destination of O'Hare International Spaceport."

"Then what the hell hit us?"

"Unexpected debris along the runway, Lieutenant McKenzie. I've detected hull breaches along the starboard—"

"Yeah, yeah; I heard all that."

John exhaled sharply through his nose.

"They knew we were coming back, so why not clear the runway ahead of time? Why

didn't those assholes in the control tower guide us past it?"

"No transmission was received from the control tower, Lieutenant McKenzie. I took direct control of the propulsion systems, but my predictions assumed the runway was clear. I was incorrect."

A pause.

"How is that possible?" John asked. "The boys at the tower were supposed to assume remote control—guide us in that way."

"I do not detect a control tower in range."

John scoffed.

"Did the landing damage your sensors or something? If we're at O'Hare—"

"My sensors are fully operational, Lieutenant McKenzie. No remote signal came from a control tower, because there is no control tower within scanning range."

"That makes no sense, you said we're at O'Hare—"

"We arrived on Earth exactly as scheduled, at the specified coordinates for the O'Hare

International Spaceport in the city of Chicago."

"You're sure about that?"

"They have remained unchanged since their initial input into my systems on the 4th of

April, in the year 2250 AD."

"Then—" John's mouth went dry. "Something else is wrong. Are your sensors picking up anything nearby?"

"All known radio frequencies are clear, Lieutenant McKenzie. The local terrain has a large organic composition, with minimal man-made materials in immediate range. Please note that a distant electrical storm is interfering with any long-distance scanning. I have also detected an atmospheric anomaly."

"What kind of anomaly?"

"Large amounts of hydrogen and carbon, well above the last known data of Earth's atmospheric composition. It is highly advised you equip your Exo-Atmospheric Suit before exiting the craft, as the air filters are sufficient enough to protect your respiratory system from harm."

John's fingers drummed against his outer thigh; their beat was only interrupted by the nervous twitch in his hand. A thought crossed his mind, one that he mulled on for a full minute before finally speaking up.

"External temperature?"

"63 degrees Celsius."

John let out a low whistle.

"Damn Chicago," he replied. "Even for this time of year, that is just ridiculous."

"I assure you that my scans are precise, Lieutenant McKenzie."

"I think it's best if I head out and get a look myself. Your coordinates say Chicago, but your temperature readings say Satan's crack."

"Safe travels, Lieutenant McKenzie. Reminder: your Exo Atmospheric Suit filters are sufficient enough to—"

"Yeah, I know."

John grumbled as the med-bay's doors hissed open and he stepped out into the ship's main corridor.

"God, why'd they have to give me such a nag for a computer?"

The door in front of John slid open, and he stepped out into the main corridor of the ship. Loose ceiling panels hung by electrical cords overhead. Half of the lights in the hallway were functional, with the other half buzzing and flickering intermittently. John felt an unevenness in the corridor, a slight tilt to the previously level floor, and cautiously approached the sealed room at the far end. Once inside, he secured the door behind him and removed a bulky spacesuit from a sealed chamber. The moment the loose material slid over his uniform, the suit blipped and drew in like a predator's jaws to its prey. John carefully lowered his helmet and smelled metallic air as the seals in his collar locked in place.

Once his boots were secured, the lone spaceman walked to the wall-mounted lever marked AIRLOCK RELEASE and pulled it down. More thudding from inside the walls; the locks disengaged, motors whirred, and the door in front of him lowered to form a boarding ramp. Bright sunlight poured in and reflected off of the spotless interior walls of the spacecraft. The glass of his helmet dimmed, and the swelling light retracted. John's first steps down the ramp were cautious, his palms sweaty as his mind pictured the unknown landscape awaiting him beyond.

Left foot first, then right foot. Left, then right again. This pattern repeated, with John's eyes firmly locked on the edge of the ramp and the grassy damp earth beyond. His left foot moved from hard metal to soft dirt that gave under his step, and John exhaled his held breath.

Finally, he looked up and surveyed his immediate surroundings.

"Holy shit," he said, breathless. "This can't be Chicago."

The crashed spacecraft, a gleaming silver dagger shape with three rear engines, was perched crookedly on the landing gear. Underneath, previously green grass had been upturned into damp brown earth along the side of a hill. Trees jutted up from the ground in the distance, clean of leaves and pointing up at his unexpected arrival like petrified fingers.

John stepped away from the craft and continued surveying the area. The trees and vegetation continued as far as his eyes could see, stretching all the way to the horizon.

Overhead, the sun was past the midday position as afternoon faded into evening.

The screen flickered on and John saw his own exhausted image in the body-hugging uniform reflected back at him. The darkened bridge of the ship, a hexagonal room with a raised level sitting behind the forward consoles, was draped in shadow behind him. John cleared his throat, unsure of where to begin, and then spoke what first came to mind:

"This is Second Lieutenant John McKenzie of the Federal Alliance Navy, on board the spacecraft ASN Taylor. Exactly 50 years ago, on the 27th of June in the year 2250, I departed on a high-priority mission to explore a cosmic anomaly on the very edge of our galaxy. This anomaly was believed to be a potential source of energy that we'd be able to harness for use here on Earth, to possibly end the growing energy crisis."

John swallowed hard.

"I knew the risks, and they had no qualms about accepting me. My credentials were more than satisfactory, my service record with the Navy impeccable. The most important part? I was divorced, had kids that hated me, and parents that were dead."

John let out a wry laugh.

"Basically, no one to miss me for 50 years. All I had was my career, and now—"

John paused, holding in a breath, then let it out in a groan.

"I don't know what's happened. My ship has landed in wilderness that stretches for miles in all directions. There's hydrogen and carbon in the air, and an extra surprise when I returned from my initial excursion: small amounts of radiation."

John eased back in his chair, which creaked under his weight.

"Yet, the most peculiar part of all this? My ship's computer insists we're in Chicago." On cue, the metallic voice spoke:

"That is correct, Lieutenant McKenzie. Our current location is O'Hare International Spaceport, within the city of Chicago, a major population center in the North American Federation."

John rolled his eyes.

"You say one thing," he snapped. "My own eyes say another. In any case, our landing was rough but could have been far worse. Damage to the ship was mostly external, some wiring and things knocked loose inside. Power cells are intact, and there weren't any major hull breaches. At any rate, I won't be breathing in that mess from outside."

A momentary silence.

"Now, the question remains: what to do next? I burned through what precious daylight I had left examining the ship. The computer doesn't detect anything like a settlement in range, but that storm blowing our way might be interfering. Somebody had to see me, right? There's no way that anyone missed sixty-four meters and four metric tons of steel and electronics crashing to the ground."

John propped his legs up on the console in front of him.

"Environment makes me think of South America, but the foliage isn't right. Plus, there's that whole atmospheric composition. Suppose the main task for tomorrow is to properly determine my location. At first light, I'm suiting up and taking a proper trek outside."

He sat up, taking his legs off the console, and reached for the square-shaped camera in front of the monitor.

"End report for now. Here's hoping I have good news tomorrow."

John switched the camera off, and the monitor went dark.

Light shown from the screen and the lone spaceman was looking at himself once again; a towel was around his neck, still wet from the water of his anti-radiation shower.

"This is Second Lieutenant John McKenzie of the ASN Taylor. It's day two after landing in a location the computer insists is Chicago. I had a better look around outside today. You know, walking around in a mildly radiated 60 degrees Celsius really does wonders for the body, especially when you're in a heavy Exo-Atmospheric Suit."

John held up a pre-packaged pouch of water with a straw and took a long sip. "That's not even actual water, come to think of it. Made from my recycled pee."

He shrugged.

"That's the excitement you sign up for when you travel across space: piss water and nutrition bars that are good for you in a nutritional sense."

John held up a partially unwrapped, beige-colored bar of granola-like material; he bit hard on the corner and, eventually broke off a piece into his mouth. Each chew felt like concrete chunks breaking against his teeth, and the taste of flavorless grit filled his mouth.

"But that's about it," he said with a grunt. "Tasty. Just like Dad used to pour at the construction yard."

After a quick sip from his water pouch, John resumed talking.

"Working theory was that we were bumped off course and landed in South America. Possible damage suffered during re-entry would suggest why the computer thinks we're elsewhere. The abundance of fauna also supported my claim, but I've shot that all to hell with my findings today. Mostly took soil samples along with wood scrapings from the trees. Initial data indicates plant life local to the Midwest region of North America, despite the lack of leaves in summer. Topographical layout doesn't make sense for South America either; save for a few inclines and hills, this place is flat. I mean, a precise flat."

John fell silent, fingers drumming against the arm of his chair.

"Temperature isn't even this high at the Equator. I know that global warming was bad there for a while, but I can't help but think this is something else. No people coming to see the

man that fell out of the sky means no nearby settlement. No radio chatter, but someone's bound to pick up my signature. Right?"

Silence.

"As of now, the only place I can hope to find any answers is right under my feet."

The lone spaceman waggled his eyebrows.

"I think I'll play in the dirt a little more and see what comes up."

John eased himself back in the creaking seat.

"Storm clouds to the west are close. If that thing hits tomorrow, I'll be so pissed."

Once again, John saw himself on screen and crossed his eyes.

"There he is," he said. "The idiot who jinxed himself, Second Lieutenant John McKenzie of the ANS Taylor. Day three after a bumpy landing, which consisted of attempting to take soil samples and dig through entangled undergrowth in the WORST RAIN OF MY LIFE."

John flipped himself off in the camera.

"Schmuck."

The lone spaceman dropped his hand out of frame.

"My voyage to the anomaly and back both passed by in a blip for me. Yet, there was something about seeing the rain fall that felt like I was truly home. Damn near cried, and then I actually cried when I noticed the ash mixed in with it while standing knee deep in a gritty, muddy puddle."

John took the towel hanging around his neck and rubbed it harshly against his ears.

"Oh well, might have just been wasting my time with more samples anyway. Results from the ones collected yesterday matched the atmospheric anomaly. High levels of hydrogen, scant traces of nitrogen, and quite the presence of igneous rock. Between that and the ashen rain, it makes me wonder if I'm near a volcano. Surely, I would have seen it by now."

John laughed.

"That's clearly my old Geologist training coming back to me," he deadpanned, then spoke normally: "My original interest in life was rocks and stuff like that, things that held the history of our planet in every molecule. Then came the War of Secession in '14, and the Navy needed fighter pilots. I needed money because geology assistants are paid shit. Four years later, I suddenly had a new career path."

John shrugged.

"I guess I can't complain too much about that. Now, would my shipboard computer like to speak up? Has it spotted this mysterious volcano of mine, by chance?"

Silence.

"Another joke," he quipped. "I disabled the audio function. Tired of hearing I'm in Chicago when any human with a brain can clearly see we're not."

John shook his head.

"Then again, any human with a brain would have known that storm would hit today."

John positioned the muddy rock on the console and angled the camera down so that it completely filled the screen.

"Second Lieutenant John McKenzie of the ANS Taylor reporting on day five post-crash landing at God-Knows-Where. Thank you for joining us today on the Earth's favorite game show: What the Fuck is That?"

John raised the camera up, and he was in frame again.

"A little surprise washed up by the rain, which finally let up this morning. For the first time since my arrival, the temperature is below 60 Celsius. Winter's sneaking right up on us, folks."

John now held the rock in his hand.

"Let's play, shall we? Here is your first clue: no compositional match to any known type of natural rock. For 100 points: what the fuck is this?"

Cue the lone spaceman leaning in close, eyes wide. "Second clue: it's not natural."

John backed away, nodding.

"Good guesses from everyone, but no correct answers! This rock? Plain old concrete, and look here—"

He turned the rock around and held it close, revealing faint white specks along the back. "That's paint. Concrete, with white paint in a line pattern? For a chance at 50 bonus points, what the fuck does that mean?"

A momentary silence and John nodded at the camera.

"A road, and it turned up underneath all of these trees and vegetation. We didn't just land in the middle of nowhere. At one point, there was a road around here. For all I know, there was a whole damn city."

John lowered the rock out of frame.

"Now, the next question?" He hesitated.

"What happened to it?"

"Second Lieutenant John McKenzie of the ANS Taylor," he spoke in a familiar cadence. "Yada-yada, you know who I am by now. We're officially at one week since my arrival here. The road fragment I found earlier led me to unearth more, enough to determine this isn't any small-town road. My guess is that this was at least a six-lane highway, with a major traffic flow through this area. Well, not anymore, but...you get what I mean. Followed the direction of the road northwest, and made a new discovery: a river, complete with remnants of a bridge."

John winced as he recalled the river.

"Huge and polluted; full of debris and a large amount of ash. No telling how many fish skeletons were inside, or if they were all fish. A few of those bones were—"

A full-on shudder from the spaceman.

"—little too big for fish. Then, I found something jutting out from the nearby overgrowth.

Looked like an elevator shaft leading further down, into a structure buried underneath all of this foliage. Thing is, I know for a fact that I'm at ground level. So what the hell is a building with an elevator doing below me?

John then let out a sigh.

"These huge tree roots are blocking the shaft, but I think I can get through them if I repurpose the equipment from the surgical unit. Rig up a nice cutting laser and see how that works. If I can reach one of the other floors of this building, then I could possibly discover where I am. Maybe even what happened here."

John swallowed hard, looked away from the camera, then faced it once again.

"I know I'm getting close to finding out where I am, but I'm scared as shit to learn the truth. Haven't been this scared since the war. There's been an obvious answer in the back of my mind for a couple of days now, and it's getting harder to look past it. As I walk along these roads and entombed buildings, it all starts to feel so familiar. I know this place, at least I should."

Pause. An agonizing silence. John reached for the camera.

"Oh," he remembered, easing back. "One more thing to report, an interesting little footnote: I found prints other than mine near that elevator shaft. I'm not the only one around here after all. Maybe I'll find them, and they'll be nice enough to tell me where the hell I am? Save me a lot of trouble?"

John shrugged.

"Or maybe they'll eat me alive? Hard to say. Can't wait to find out."

With a trembling hand, John switched on the camera; he stared back at himself, bleary-eyed and breathing raggedly.

"Day 10," he said, voice quivering. "All my effort in getting through the tree roots with the cutting laser finally paid off today. I made it deep enough into the elevator shaft to find doors leading to another floor. Pried them open, managed to get myself level, and see what kind of place I found."

John wiped the tears out of his eyes.

"Oh God, did I find out."

He paused to collect himself.

"Made it into a room, flipped completely upside down, but regained my bearings and saw a whole bunch of computers and equipment like that along the walls. Then I found something, and the game was over. I didn't have a drill to properly remove it, so I just used the laser."

John reached below him, out of frame.

"I'll let this speak for itself."

A half-charred metallic plaque with fresh carbon scoring around the uneven edges came into view with two legible words: O'HARE SPACEPORT.

"At one time, this plaque dedicated the newly reconstructed O'Hare International Spaceport to the brave pilots that didn't return from the Secession War. Damn computer was right all along: the coordinates didn't change, but Chicago sure as hell did. So, how did a city like Chicago change so drastically in 50 years? The answer to that question came when I finally got the bright idea to check the main CPU and confirm my theory of atmospheric damage."

The lone spaceman gave a wry laugh.

"Fun fact about ships like the Taylor: there's a secondary computer on board to ensure that vital systems remain functional in the event of a main power failure. In the case of crew in cryogenic suspension, like me, a data log is recorded every hour so the rescue team can ensure those in hibernation suffered no medical emergencies. Unfortunately, the main computer and the secondary unit were never designed to function simultaneously. Should the main computer suddenly come back online, the secondary unit switches back off. Anything it recorded is inaccessible to the main computer."

John's face dropped with the weight of his discovery; every line was now visible on his face.

"According to the main computer, the ship passed through an ion storm that crossed along our projected course and knocked out main systems. The secondary unit kicked on and extended the emergency solar panels before beginning its watch. These panels are installed on any Alliance craft to allow it to recharge the power cells and automatically jumpstart the main systems. According to the main computer, this outage lasted no more than 50 minutes before that automatic jumpstart kicked in."

John then buried his face in his hands and let out a groan.

"But the secondary unit begs to differ. While the main computer has a gap of 50 minutes, the secondary unit recorded over 438,000 hourly logs on my condition. That many hours
 translate to around 18,250 days. That translates to 50 years of logs recorded between the power loss and system restoration."

He lowered his hands and glared into the camera.

"My voyage lasted twice the intended length, and the main computer had no idea. Why? Some asshole shipbuilders never anticipated a human vessel drifting that long without rescue. It's not 2300, but 2350. While I was away, something happened: an event with the intensity of a volcanic eruption, burning so hot and so fast that Chicago was damn near leveled. Then the Earth did what it does best and grew plants where there previously weren't any. A century of overgrowth and a looming storm, and the most sophisticated thing on this ship can't find what remains of the people that lived here."

John's eyes welled up again, the bright blue starkly contrasting against the bloodshot red. The lone spaceman then looked up at the ceiling of the bridge and around at the darkened consoles and empty chairs.

"If this is Chicago, then what must the rest of the world look like?"

Second Lieutenant John McKenzie stared straight into the camera with dead, vacant eyes. The skin of his face sagged with the weight of years beyond his time. As he spoke, his voice lost all luster—each word saturated in sorrow.

"I left this world a shell of a man. Failed marriage, kids that didn't want to see me, parents in their graves, and a career that vaporized while I was asleep and far away. No matter

what was happening around me, no matter how desperate things grew, I remained hopeful that there was always a way out. There was always a solution."

John raised his arms and gestured around him.

"All of that, outside? The death and destruction hidden under the dirt? That is a failure to find a solution. That is the failure of the

Federal Alliance, the end of the united human race, and the beginning of a desperate fight for survival."

The empty man gave a weak chuckle.

"A fight that ended terribly for everyone involved. Yet, the failure isn't complete. One human still remains alive on this planet. One empty, broken shell of a human."

John reached below him, out of frame, and pulled a gun-shaped device into view.

"My cutting laser," he said. "The tool that led me to the unfortunate truth."

He placed the barrel against the side of his head.

"And my salvation from it. Instant at this range. I do this, and the failure is complete. Humanity dies, snuffed out by their own hands."

John's eyes glistened with forming tears.

"Why shouldn't I? Is this not what we deserve? Is this not what I deserve, in the end? Life should have gone on. There was still a chance to reconcile with my kids, to move on from Rowena, but now there's nothing. There's n—"

John stopped, shocked at the words he nearly uttered. The desperate man glanced down, ashamed, but met the camera's gaze again.

"There's not even hope."

Suddenly, a hollow thumping noise from the background; John turned around and gasped, lowering the cutting laser out of frame.

Someone was knocking on the rear of the ship.

"What?" he asked. "What in the—?"

John turned around and switched off the camera.

When he saw his image on the screen, John cleared his throat.

"Three weeks to the day since my return to earth. I'm aware that my last entry was...well, it certainly reflected my mission status. At the very end of it, I heard a knock on the ramp of the ship and went to investigate. Much to my surprise and relief, I found a group of people outside. I mean people like—"

John gestured to himself.

"Looked just like me, talked just like me, had protective suits like mine, and were desperate...also just like me. It was unbelievable, I saw those footprints near the elevator shaft and imagined the worst: deformed humanoid beings with three eyes and a taste for flesh." He cleared his throat.

"That's not what came asking for help. The people I met were the descendants of those who made it to the shelters when my world burned away. Radiation level has dipped low enough in the last year to try and venture out onto the surface. They had witnessed my initial descent but chose to watch me from a distance. Guess it's not every day some jackass crashes into your backyard from space."

John eased back in the chair.

"A scouting party was on their way to make first contact, so to speak, when one of them lost their footing and fell into that river. Debris pierced their suit, and a choice had to be made at that point: risk crossing the water back to their shelter or continue on in the hopes that I would help them."

The lone spaceman exhaled.

"Guess I'm a nice guy after all. I treated their injured companion with meds I had on board: anti-radiation, anti-biotics, things like that. When their condition stabilized, the others formally introduced themselves. After hearing my story, they invited me back to their shelter. That's where I learned of their pressing needs. So much time underground, and the technology keeping them alive is starting to fail."

John sat up straight in the chair.

"How fortunate that a source of spare parts is now squarely within their reach. The Taylor is to be salvaged, and I'm going with whatever's taken to see that it's used correctly. Maybe I should switch careers again? Learn how to be an engineer and keep my new home running? Eventually, I might learn enough to come back to this ship and salvage the data recorders. Then when humanity dares to reach out into the stars again? We aim in the direction of that distant anomaly and pick up where we left off. I hope I live to see those days. All of this may just be wishful thinking, really. If anything, the future is more uncertain now than it's ever been…"

The lone spaceman placed his hand on top of the camera.

"But I won't have to face it alone. This is Second Lieu—" he stopped. "This is John

McKenzie, ending his final report."

He clicked the switch for the final time, and the screen went dark.

Tanner's Apocalypse

Written by Cal Brett

CAL BRETT HAS BEEN writing most of his life (novels, short stories, screenplays, and a bunch of policies and procedures) in various genres and formats. His love of horror fiction, film, and comics has always brought him back to writing about monsters and how people might relate to them. He enjoys crafting well-researched stories of how real people would likely respond to terrible situations. His most recent novels, a zombie apocalypse series called *Worse than Dead*, are available on Amazon in the usual formats. Brett is a retired Navy Chief Petty Officer who served on ships, stations, and in war zones around the world. He earned a BA from Florida State University and has almost enough credits to complete his Master's if he is ever inclined to finish it up. He, his wife, two kids, four dogs, and a bunch of fish live in the southeastern US.

They had called it the "zombie apocalypse." Tanner didn't know why. There were no zombies so far as he could tell. There were plenty of dead people. They were all over. Their bones filled all the morgues and hospitals. In the early days, that's where everyone went. Most never left, and their remains filled all the beds, couches, chairs, and even most of the floor space in every medical facility Tanner had seen.

Outside, many open areas had bodies stacked in piles where survivors had planned to burn them. They did this until they themselves had begun to die in numbers too large to worry about those who had gone before any longer. Those who went later were easy to find as well. Their bones could be found on benches looking out over scenic views, scattered under barstools, and at the bottoms of long drops.

Tanner wondered about the suicides and why someone would take their own life when they knew the end was coming soon anyway. Maybe they wanted to end things on their own terms. Maybe they lost some great love or were in a hurry to join their family in the afterlife. Perhaps they couldn't stand the anticipation and just didn't want to wait anymore. Whatever the reasons, their corpses remained where they fell and would remain so until time and the elements ground them to dust.

The undead weren't a problem, but the bugs were. The insects were small and fat like beetles with hard shells and short, stiff wings. Maybe they were beetles—some kind of mutant, flesh-eating beetles. They came out at night, swarmed up in huge clouds in search of prey. They pursued and descended on the living and the dead in droves, consuming all the soft flesh in just a few hours.

At first, there were so many recently deceased bodies around that the bugs paid no attention to the living. When night fell, they emerged to gorge themselves on the decaying flesh and organs of the accumulated dead. Tanner had watched a fog of the bugs fall on a mound of bodies under a solar-powered streetlight one evening. In the flickering light, they burrowed into the buffet, and by morning, when the bugs scattered off to the leaves and branches where they hid in the day, there was nothing left but bones. Even the gruesome oily stain of human fluids that had pooled under the bodies had been licked dry.

As horrific as these types of images had been, Tanner recalled that he was grateful at the time. With no rotting bodies, the terrible smell of decay had gone away. He could move about without covering his nose or worrying about stepping into the sunken cavities of any former inhabitants. The bugs ate everything but the bones, leaving behind only the splattered raspberry-colored spots of their own excrement dotted across the city as they buzzed back to their daytime roosts. The circle of life. Ashes to ashes and flesh to poop.

It was only later that it became a problem. By then, the damned things had multiplied into the billions. When the freshly dead were completely devoured, the bugs began to look elsewhere for their meals. Once their tiny, sharp mandibles got a taste for the living, it was game on. Nothing was safe.

All the animals that had survived the end of humans were suddenly on the menu for the bugs. Pets and domestic animals went first. Many had nowhere to hide and didn't have the instincts to defend themselves from such a threat. Wild creatures went next. The bugs got into their nests and burrowed into their holes and even scratched through drywall to get at rats hidden between the studs of buildings.

When he was ashore, Tanner had learned to hide at night. Not just hide but seal himself into the most secure places with the thickest walls he could find. Even those places often required additional fortifications. The bugs could get in through any opening. They turned air vents and open attic space into express lanes to any tasty, warm bodies hidden inside. They would squeeze through tiny cracks and under narrow doorways. If one could get in, they could all get in and the place would soon be whirring with the sound of their tiny wings beating and sharp beaks snapping.

Tanner adjusted his pack as he walked down the sidewalk. To his right, the rusting hulks of parked cars gradually sank into the blacktop. Crossing the street, he aimed for the supermarket a few blocks away. The sky was blue and quiet. No birds sang or fluttered. Although it had been years since he had seen a bird, their absence still bothered him. The world had gone silent.

The only sounds, other than his own, were those made by the elements. Wind rattled the slats of a wooden fence as he walked by the crumbling remains of a middle-class neighborhood. When it rained, he welcomed the patter of drops on the ground and the rush of thunder in the sky. Fire had a pleasant noise in its crackle and snap, even as it consumed the old things. When buildings fell to fire, Tanner smiled knowing that it probably took thousands of the bugs with it. Not that those few thousand mattered, but it was gratifying to watch them burn.

Inside the grocery, Tanner checked expiration dates on the canned foods. Many were beyond their 'best by' dates but he had found they remained edible. He didn't look forward to the day when he could no longer eat the canned food. He would have to start planting vegetables and get better at fishing.

It wouldn't be long before fish would be his only source of fresh food, he realized. He needed to get back to the boat. He had walked a long way to find supplies but was finding less and less as everything degraded. The gulf was a few days' walk, and tomorrow he would need to start back.

One of the bugs fell from the ceiling and landed on the floor nearby with a click. Tanner stepped on it and crushed it into the dusty linoleum floor with a crunch. He looked up at the carpet of bugs that had collected on the old tiles in the ceiling. None stirred at the loss of their comrade. Not during the daytime.

That afternoon he found an old school and began barricading himself in. By the light of a small lantern, he checked for gaps and holes. He filled them heavily with caulk, pushing it deep into the cracks. He used the kind with mold and insect repellent. It wouldn't stop them if they got his scent, but the bugs tended to avoid it if they had other options.

Laying back in his sleeping bag, he turned off the lantern, letting total darkness plunge in around him. He missed the night sky when he was ashore and longed to look up at the stars. The bugs wouldn't have any of that. One step outside and they would be on him, their clicking-clacking jaws biting at him by the millions. In minutes he would be dead, in hours gnawed to the bone. He slept fitfully.

In the morning, the walk south was long and arduous with no company save the hot breeze. The bugs must have turned on their own as even the usual clouds of gnats and mosquitos were absent. No cicadas or frogs sang to him as he plodded along what was left of the long, straight road. When the afternoon shadows grew long, he found himself in the remnants of a small town. The town was just a few buildings around a traffic light, sitting on the banks of a salty marsh, but it would have to do.

He approached a narrow brick post office that looked to be sturdy and solidly built. Through the fogged window, he could see rows of brass mailboxes lining its walls, and the counter was made of solid wood. These old buildings held better than newer ones. New construction was all lightweight aluminum framing, rolled-out insulation, and thin drywall. Bugs could claw their way through it quickly if they got on a scent.

These older structures were built sturdy with thick plaster and concrete block. They had gaps and cracks, sure, but those could be filled temporarily. So long as none of the bugs smelled you—or whatever they did to track down prey—it could be safe. The front door was wedged tightly on rusted hinges but unlocked. Tanner pried it open, slipped inside, and closed it behind. Finding no bodies or bugs inside, he slipped into a small storage room and began closing himself in for the night.

He slid into his sleeping bag down between the tall metal shelves and stared up at the concrete ceiling. Outside in the lobby, there were drop ceilings with walls decorated by wood paneling from the 1970s. In the storage room, out of the public eye, it was bare walls and exposed concrete block slathered in multiple coats of off-white latex paint. The heavy wooden door had dragged tightly across the floor for so long it had left an arcing skid mark back to the wall. The gaps around the door were tight but he had caulked them anyway.

When he turned out the light, he lay listening to the mostly quiet evening. The insulation of the building and inner room blocked most sounds from outside. In the absolute silence, he mostly heard his own breathing and still air as it played about in his ear canals. But he had learned to listen beyond that first layer of noise.

He listened for the bugs. With no other sounds to compete, he could sometimes hear them scratching and scuttling as they hunted around for food. There was never just one of them, so the clicking of their shells and hard claws would magnify as they herded about in their packs. He faded off to sleep in the quiet.

A snap woke him sometime later. Pushing the button on his illuminated watch he saw it was two in the morning. He lay still, listening, hoping it was just the old building settling. He heard it again, in the corner this time. Something small moving among the stone walls.

Quickly relighting the lantern, he crawled over to investigate. Where the walls met, a small hole appeared near the floor. Tiny mandibles poked through and chewed at the syrupy paint. Tanner cursed under his breath, not wanting to create any vibration to excite the things. He had no idea if this was just a foraging party out exploring, or if the local insect colony had found him and was burrowing in from all sides.

Tanner backed up and scanned the shelves until he found a dusty ream of printer paper. Grabbing it, he knelt and pressed it over the hole. He spun and hefted a full box of the paper from the shelf and slid it against the ream to hold it in place. He held his breath and stared at the box in the flickering lamp light. The scratching continued for a few moments, then grew hesitant—then stopped.

He stood still and hoped the things determined that they had simply reached the end of the tunnel they were exploring—a dead end. He willed them to turn around and go back and report to their bug tribe that there was nothing of interest in that dark passage. For several long seconds, he wished that whatever parts of their bug brains made such decisions would do so and compel them elsewhere.

Tanner looked at his watch. It was only two-twenty in the morning, still too dark out to leave the post office. Swarms of the tiny flesh eaters would be buzzing around in the hot humid night, searching for prey. He looked around the room for any additional holes he might have missed. If the bugs wanted in, they would find a way, and he would have to fight the little fuckers off until the sun came up.

The scratching started again, and Tanner began to sweat. It started slowly, as if they were testing the barrier. Gradually the tempo increased until it sounded like they had brought in reinforcements. Tanner wondered how many of the things could squeeze into the small space and get the claws slicing at the ream of paper. How long would it take them to tear through it?

The things could get through it. Tanner knew that. But how long? The ream of paper was wrapped in a thin plastic cover, which wouldn't be easy for them. Then they would have to burrow through the paper itself. That was two inches thick—then the box of paper behind it. That was if they went straight ahead. If they decided to dig out from the sides, they would have a much shorter trip.

The scratching became more aggressive. Tanner thought he could hear scampering deep in the walls. He knew the tiny efficient horrors would be shuttling away the torn paper waste to keep their tunnel clear. They would be cramming inside to get as many diggers to the front as possible.

The plastic cover began to shift slightly as if being pulled and stretched from below. Tanner sat down and pressed his boots against the box, holding it in place. He looked at his watch again and saw it was two forty-five. In the flickering lantern light, every shadow seemed to move and jump with life. Resting his chin on his knees, he tried to stay calm, knowing there was little else he could do.

At three o'clock he began to feel a vibration through the hard rubber soles of his shoes. The motion of the bugs tunneling into the paper rumbled outward through the box, tickling his feet as it grew in intensity. Just sitting there was almost worse than being trapped. His legs and butt began to ache from being stationary. It didn't take much pressure to hold the box in place, but the muscles in his calves and thighs began to ache at being in use for so long.

Amidst the shadows dancing over the walls, he looked for tiny movement—anything that might be creeping from some other gap he hadn't noticed. Then, there it was: an oval shape with shiny black wings reflecting the lamp light. It sat still on the wall, almost as if it didn't want to be noticed.

Tanner quickly scanned the room for more but saw none. Did it come alone? Was it through the original hole first and now waited for the others to join him before it tried to feast? It was too far away to kill, so Tanner just watched it. For all he knew it was watching him, maybe radioing back to the others with its stalk-like antennae to hurry up and get through. There was a big fat meal just a few inches away.

In the silence of the room, Tanner could hear the bugs chewing at the paper. It made a snapping, crackling sound like rice cereal in milk. Spiney legs attached to beak-like mouths tore and ripped at the thin pulpy strips. Their sharp teeth ripped it down into confetti-sized bits as they moved forward like a battering ram, sheet by sheet.

The bugs outside must have become aware of what was going on because the building itself had begun to vibrate from the flapping of their stiff wings and the chewing of their teeth against mortar. Tanner wondered how many it would take to make the entire building shake. If they kept it up, he feared the old post office might not make it until morning. His legs aching and ears humming, Tanner lay back on the cold floor and did all he could do. He waited.

In the bouncing light, he lost track of time and drifted into an exhausted trance until a sharp pain made him jump. Tanner shook his fingers sending a light spray of his blood against the white walls. Looking down he followed the source to a gash in the meaty side of his palm.

"Agh!" He spat, cradling his hand.

Quickly scanning the wall, he saw that the bug was not where it had been when he closed his eyes. He located the thing down on the floor near where his hand must have rested. It was bowed-up on its haunches with its tiny mandibles stretched out menacingly as if it planned to attack alone.

"Fucker!" Tanner snapped as he crushed the bug under the sole of his boot. When he lifted the heavy shoe, what was left of the thing had been pressed into a dark purple ooze amidst the broken and fragmented remains of its spiked legs and hard-shell casing. "Fucker!" Tanner repeated as he rubbed at his bloody hand.

Time? What time was it? Tanner suddenly wondered. How long had he been zoned out? Before he looked at his watch, he scanned the walls but didn't see any more of the deadly bugs. The box and ream of paper remained firmly pressed against the wall.

Five thirty, the numbers on the watch glowed when he pressed the button.

"Shit," Tanner sighed. Thirty minutes, at least, until sunrise. The building still hummed with the buzzing and flapping of millions of insects that must be covering every inch of its exterior walls and roof. Inside too, he surmised. No way they hadn't gotten into the main lobby and any exposed ductwork. Even if he made it to daybreak, he would have to sprint through an ocean of the things to get out. The damned things would stay active until the sunlight hit their obsidian shells.

He started counting the minutes. He could hear the things in the walls, behind the concrete blocks, scouring the cavities for a way into the room. There were several gray electrical pipes running across the ceiling to the old fluorescent light fixture. He had filled in and around the holes with the insect repellent caulk, but he didn't trust that the creatures wouldn't just push one another through if they thought it was a way in.

Five forty. Opening his bag, he removed his rubberized rain hoodie and pulled it on. It was thick and hot so he seldom wore it on land, but it would provide some protection if he had to run through a swarm of them. He tightened the straps around his face and waist before pulling on his gloves. He considered putting on the Halloween mask with the clear plastic eye covers. No, he determined. If any got behind it, (and they would) they could dig into the skin of his face before he could shake them off. Better to run open-faced and brush them off as they struck him.

Five forty-five. Movement. Not a trick of the flickering lantern. The rubbery caulk around the electrical pipe began breathing in and out. The things were kneading at it from behind. Testing it.

"Damn it," Tanner cursed.

A pair of shiny black pincers pushed through the gummy caulk and disappeared back inside. A moment later, several thin antennae shoved through and whipped back and forth, taking in the vibrations of the room. They would know he was there for sure now.

Five fifty. He left the box of paper, grabbed his caulk gun, stepped up on a box, and jammed the nozzle into the tiny hole. As he squeezed the trigger, he could feel the things attacking the plastic tip that must have crushed some of them as it entered. A blob of caulk lurched from the spout and into the gap. As he pressed the trigger, white silicone spilled out and dropped to the floor in long ribbons.

Even as Tanner dropped back to the floor, the wet caulk bubbled and bowed with the bugs pushing through the uncured sealant. The insect repellent would not deter the creatures once they were in a blood-lust frenzy. A sound behind made him turn in time to see several of the bugs shuffle up from a gap between the wall and the box. Then more—dozens of the vile things began to scramble up, fanning out over the far wall.

Five fifty-five. Sunrise was still a few minutes away but Tanner knew he couldn't wait any longer. Strapping on his pack and grabbing his lantern, he put a hand on the doorknob and took a deep breath. Overhead, the bugs were coming through again near the pipe. Behind, he could hear the click-click of the matchbox-sized insects quickly covering the walls and ceiling as they charged into the room by the hundreds.

Flinging open the door, he put his arm over his face and ran. He felt the things hitting him as he charged through a fog of the bugs. His entrance sent them into a frenzy where they all seemed to take off at once, bouncing against the rubbery jacket with slap, slap, slapping sounds. One hit his cheek and dug in its mandibles before Tanner could fling it off with a gloved hand.

It was only a few paces to the door, but he could feel the weight of the bugs that had attached themselves to his clothing and were desperately trying to find a way to burrow into the fresh meat below. Given enough time, they would tear away the rubber coating, but he had no intention of giving them the time. He hit the glass front door at full speed with as much force as he could muster.

The impact knocked off many of the deadly beetles that had affixed themselves to his clothes. It also bounced Tanner away and flat on his back in a sea of scrambling insects. Though stunned, he jumped back to his feet and ran for the door while batting at the bugs running all over him. Two pinched into his right cheek while another pierced into his left eyebrow.

He felt the hot blood running down his face as he hit the front door again. This time he slowed and pushed it hard, causing the rusty hinges to squeal as he drove it open. Squeezing through, he sprinted out into the dusky morning. As he ran, millions of the bugs swirled around him in tightly packed schools. They crashed into him like kamikazes, gripped whatever they hit, and began slashing down.

He ran blindly out into the road, praying for sunlight to break the horizon. The deadly beetles pinched, pierced, and bit at him as he stumbled forward. He could feel them ripping holes in his jeans and beginning to gouge through into his flesh below. Swinging wildly at the swarm swirling around him, Tanner turned east and ran as fast as he could move.

He ran along the old road, keeping his arm over his face, only daring to look down to ensure he stayed over the cracking yellow center line. He ran on as the bugs began pushing under his poncho straps and pulling at the elastic holding the hood tightly around his face. Little pinchers began jabbing at his waist and hips through the thin t-shirt he wore underneath. He felt the temperature increase, hotter than the moist heat of the night, before he saw its source.

The first rays of the morning sun washed over the road and bounced down the overgrown main street of the crumbling town. With this, the orbiting swarm began to scatter into the shadows. Tanner fell to his knees in the sunlight, swiping and kicking at the bugs still crawling all over his body. Most slowly dispersed, but those that had already attached themselves remained in a blood frenzy.

Tanner jumped and stomped as he shook off the things. He slapped at himself to dislodge the ones that had clasped on to fabric and skin. Then, he stripped as quickly as he could manage, beating and slapping his infested clothing on the ground. The biting beetles were flung away. Those that fell close quickly met the bottom of Tanner's boot as he jumped up and down on them in the middle of the road.

"Fuckers!" Tanner screamed as he crushed the tiny scurrying bugs into purple and black mush. Cuts and slices marked his body while blood ran down his pale skin. "Fuckers!"

A few minutes later, the bugs were all crushed or had scampered away into the overgrowth beside the road. Tanner angrily re-dressed in an extra set of jeans and a t-shirt from his bag. Still bleeding, he gave the fluttering things under the tree branches his middle finger as he marched out of town. "Fuckers!"

Another day walking under the hot sun brought Tanner to the little fishing town where he had moored his sailboat, the *Carol Anne*. It sat waiting at the end of a twisted and bleached-out pier. The forty-foot cutter allowed him to spend nights at sea and skip along the coast during the day for supplies. Small solar panels ran a few appliances and charged the electric trolling motor. Tanner didn't consider himself a great sailor, but the boat was easy to handle and gave him a way to escape the bugs and all the decay.

With the sun sinking low he knew it would be cutting it close, but he didn't want to stay a second longer on land. He cast off, started the electric motor, and slowly slipped out into the channel. Open water glistened out beyond the marsh, but it was several miles and a winding channel away. Sweat ran down his neck and soaked his shirt as he drove the slow-moving vessel between the rusting buoys.

Tanner watched the bugs begin to flutter as the sky darkened. They bounced about under trees and within clusters of shrubs along the shoreline. They had a short flying range and usually didn't venture out far over water unless they were in pursuit of something. Here in the salt marshes, they might range further because they could land among the tall swamp grasses and hide from sunlight under their twisted leaves.

As the shadows lengthened, the bugs began to swarm up from their daytime lairs in the marshes on either side. The things would launch up in great numbers and swirl around in what might have been choreographed flight. Then they would return to the surface for a few seconds and go again, making different patterns in the air. It would have been beautiful if they weren't so deadly.

With the sun a smudge of melting orange on the horizon, he began to hear the things tipping at the rigging. Small groups buzzed overhead as they hopped between the tall grasses and shore. They clumsily collided with the lines and masts, tumbling down to the water and scattering over the white fiberglass decking with flailing legs and pincers.

He had begun to flick them off his clothing as he reached the end of the channel and spotted the widening bay. They attached to the fabric and pulled themselves about seeking a way into the flesh they somehow sensed was just beyond. Tanner pulled up his collar and slapped at their rigid shells as more of the things found him.

"No, no, no, no, no," Tanner cried as more of the things came. He willed the boat to move faster. The channel markers seemed to actually be passing more slowly as the craft began to push against the rising swells of the bay. He thought of raising the sails but there was no wind and he'd never be able to work the winches with all the bugs now fluttering around the boat.

The best he could do was point straight out to sea, running the little electric motor as hard as it would go. As he began to put the marshland behind him, a red light on the helm lit up, indicating battery power was almost exhausted. "Come on, come on," he chanted. "Just a little further."

He could hear the blender-like propeller begin to grind as if mixing heavier and heavier ingredients until it finally whined to a stop. The *Carol Anne* continued forward, still cutting into the waves but with less and less momentum. When it began to rock up and down on the waves, Tanner pounded the helm in frustration, uselessly pushing the power button, praying the motor would restart. The propeller ignored his gyrations. The only sounds were the buzzing swarm and the lapping waves.

"Bastards!" He howled in frustration, rolling on the deck to shake them off and crush as many as he could. Coming to his knees, covered in the biting beasts, he glanced up to see the shore in the distance. He might even be able to swim there, but why? The bugs would chew into him along the way and consume him as soon as he emerged. That was if his blood in the water didn't bring every shark in the bay before he got there. Death from above and death from below.

The boat was quickly overrun by the buzzing murder beetles. The squirming bugs blackened the deck and piled up on his shoulders. He swatted uselessly at the things, but they held tight, and more came. Blood soaked into his sweat-stained clothes as scalpel-like pinchers sliced into his skin.

Grabbing the anchor chain, he swung it ineffectually into the air and then crashed down again, pressing his face against the fiberglass deck. At the edge, he chanced a look down at the cold dark water. No bugs down there. Covered in the crawling snapping insects, he wrapped himself in the chain and surged for the cold depths below. The damned bugs could have the world, he thought, as he followed the anchor downward.

Edge of Survival

Written by Kyla Stone

KYLA STONE SPENDS HER days writing apocalyptic and dystopian fiction novels. Because what's more fun than imagining the end of the world from the comfort of your couch?

She loves writing stories exploring how ordinary people cope with extraordinary circumstances, especially situations where the normal comforts, conveniences, and rules are stripped away.

Kyla's favorite stories to read and write deal with characters struggling with inner demons who learn to face and overcome their fears, launching their transformation into the strong, brave warrior they were meant to become.

When she's not writing, you can find her practicing at the range with her Springfield XDS or shopping for cool new gear for her bug-out bag. You may find Kyla hiking to a waterfall in the Smokies, traveling to far-flung locations, or jumping out of a plane (parachute included).

Edge of Survival is a short story that was later turned into a full novel in Kyla's *Edge of Collapse* series.

Find out more about this USA Today best-selling author at her website: www.kylastone.com.

Chapter One

Liam Coleman studied the man through the ACOG scope of his M4. At first glance, he did not appear to be a threat. Liam never took anything at first glance.

The man was old, in his mid-seventies, his weathered face a network of wrinkles, his blue eyes rheumy, bald scalp shiny in the sun. He wore scuffed work boots and worn jeans beneath a heavy brown overcoat.

He was also a vandal. The old man held a half-empty bottle of whiskey by the neck in one liver-spotted hand; in the other, he gripped a can of red spray paint.

He was busy scrawling choice words across the side of a two-story gray colonial with an iron turkey weathervane set atop the roof. A double-barrel shotgun leaned against the wall beside him.

Glass from the house's broken windows peppered the front porch and glinted in the matted grass. Trash and detritus scattered across the patchy, overgrown front lawn. Almost every square inch of scuffed, peeling siding was defaced with graffiti.

The whole house seemed to sag, defeated and desolate.

It was a microcosm of the rest of the town. Mounds of trash bags piled outside of buildings. Some of the bags had burst open and refuse skittered across the streets and sidewalks and accumulated in the storm drains.

The boutique storefronts and businesses along the main street boasted shattered windows and busted front doors. Several had been burned to the ground.

No movement anywhere. No signs of life but for several rats darting in and out of a gas station with windows like blank black eyes.

The town was deserted. Utterly empty.

The old man was the first living human Liam had seen all day.

Liam moved slightly, flexing his sore shoulders. The M4 was stabilized on a flat rock in front of him. He lay on his stomach on the hard ground atop the hill overlooking the town of Tuscola, Illinois. He barely felt the pebbles and twigs beneath him.

Over his BDUs, he wore an improvised ghillie suit made from jute netting woven with grass, shrubbery, and twigs. Camo netting wound around the body and barrel of the M4 to camouflage it.

The disguise blurred the human form and blended him perfectly with his surroundings. Anyone from town who happened to glance up the hill wouldn't see anything but trees, bushes, and rocks.

The grass was matted and brown and smothered in dead leaves. A few patches of melting snow still dotted the ground here and there. The air was sharp and chilly; the rapidly setting sun did nothing to warm him.

The old man took a drink of his whiskey, wiped his mouth with the back of his arm, and went back to work spraying a new insult in colorful language.

Liam needed to talk to the old man. He needed information.

Liam had been watching the town since dawn. The evening sun hovered just above the tree line, the sky burnished in golds, oranges, and reds. He'd shifted positions several times, studying the main street, a few neighborhoods, and now the northern outskirts, the main road heading north toward more farmland.

Tuscola was a small, rural town located in the heart of Illinois' Amish and farming country off Interstate 57. The town was surrounded by hundreds of acres of growing crops.

It surprised Liam. Most of the farms he'd come across before now were dead.

The EMP attack had taken care of that.

On Christmas Eve, the world had been irrevocably changed forever. A series of simultaneous, high-altitude nuclear detonations had caused a massive electromagnetic pulse that destroyed the power grid across most of the continental United States.

It had fried the electronic systems in vehicles, aircraft, laptops and phones, even many generators—basically anything with a computer chip larger than an Apple watch. In an instant, the United States had been dragged back to the 18th century, with most people lacking the knowledge or preparation to survive.

The day of the EMP became known as Black Christmas. Hundreds of thousands died the first day. Hundreds of planes dropped from the sky like bombs. The cities were deluged with fires, explosions, and car accidents that first responders couldn't reach with their dead ambulances and fire trucks. The staggering loss of the medically fragile who depended on machines—pacemakers, oxygen tanks, dialysis—and critical medication to keep them alive.

The terrible weeks that followed were called the Black Winter. From the rumors spreading like wildfire from all areas of the country, the brutal winter had killed millions with hypothermia, starvation, and disease from poor sanitation and unclean water consumption.

And the violence. People murdering each other for a can of beans or bottle of antibiotics. Gangs and cartels fighting for supremacy in the power vacuum left by crumbling local and state governments.

The federal government remained stubbornly tight-lipped. Official reports minimized death tolls and encouraged citizens to seek shelter in the "temporary" FEMA camps that everyone knew weren't temporary.

Once the grocery shelves went bare, and the generators and heaters that survived the EMP ran out of fuel, people flocked by the millions to the overcrowded FEMA camps. Those who refused to be herded like cattle were left to survive on their own.

Since that day, every week that passed felt like a year. Every month like a decade.

Liam scanned one last time for possible sniper positions. The tops of the buildings were empty. He saw no movement, nothing out of place, no light reflections off scopes.

He'd already decided upon the route that provided him the best cover and concealment. As soon as it was dark, he would enter the town.

He inched backward, shuffling on his belly with the M4 still in his hands until he'd slid far enough down the hill that he could stand without being spotted behind the screen of tree cover. Birds twittered. A soft breeze rustled the branches of the oak, maple, and pine trees surrounding him. A chipmunk scuttled through the dead leaves a few meters southwest of him.

He took it all in. Saw everything. Heard everything. Every sense on alert.

He was used to the lack of mechanical sounds. Few planes flew overhead unless they were military. Few cars on the roads anymore, either. Most vehicles built after the early 1980s had broken down the day of the EMP. The rest had run out of gas in the following weeks.

He'd carefully rationed his fuel and had driven here in a blue 1978 Dodge D150 he'd stashed in an abandoned barn off an isolated dirt road a half mile south.

He'd been attacked on the road two times and avoided at least twice that number of ambushes. The term "highway robbery" was becoming literal again.

Liam moved stealthily to a tree about five meters down the hill and removed his ghillie suit. He folded it and placed it in the pack that he'd hidden beneath several pine boughs.

He shouldered the pack—which contained several days of food and water, a water filter, first aid kit, more ammo, and other survival supplies—and did a quick weapons check.

His Gerber MK II tactical knife was sheathed at his hip along with his Glock 19. He wore BDUs, a plate carrier, and chest rig with three preloaded magazines for the sidearm and four for the carbine. He'd also obtained night vision goggles and a few flash bangs and frag grenades from the militia.

He put on his NVGs, adjusted his grip on the carbine, keeping it in the low ready position, and began his descent down the hill. His spine twinged in discomfort. He kept going, not letting the pain slow him.

Liam had served eight years as a Delta Special Forces Operator before being medically discharged for a back injury. Five crushed discs from jumping from choppers and airplanes while with Special Forces.

He kept himself strong and fit with regular training, but he'd slowed a few steps. He couldn't run as fast or as far as he used to. The pain in his spine was a constant dull ache unless he did something to exacerbate it—and then it was like an electric shock shooting up his spinal cord.

He'd done some good during his years of service, but he'd seen too much. The worst humanity had to offer.

Like so many of his brothers in arms, the nightmares never went away. He'd learned to live with them.

He didn't have much use for humanity. There were a few people who made the whole thing worth it. And for those people, he would willingly sacrifice everything he had, including his own life.

Which was why he was here in Tuscola, two hundred and twenty miles south of Fall Creek, Michigan.

He was here to make right what he could make right.

Liam was searching for his nephew—a baby being raised by his brother's in-laws. His goal was to find them and make sure they were safe. If they weren't safe, he planned to bring them back to Fall Creek with him.

Judging by the eerie, deserted town, they were definitely not safe. He needed to find them as quickly as possible. If it wasn't already too late.

Darkness fell. Night sounds filled the air—crickets chirping, cicadas whirring, nocturnal creatures creeping through the underbrush, the hoot of an owl.

His heart rate quickened. On high alert, every sense straining for any threat, Liam exited the trees at the base of the woods. He used the terrain to his advantage, moving from tree to tree until he reached a long, deep ditch.

He followed the ditch until it came out behind a row of houses. From there, he skirted a backyard and came out on the road.

He took a knee behind a Chevy Impala parked along the curb. It was covered in dead leaves and withered pine needles. He slowed his heart rate, breathing steadily, and listened carefully. Nothing out of the ordinary. No signs of a threat.

He carefully made his way along the road, leapfrogging from car to car, from building to building, and crossed the street. He constantly scanned windows and rooftops, searching for movement.

He cut the corners, leading with his weapon in a firing position until he reached the weathered gray house with the turkey weathervane.

Keeping his back against the siding, he checked the rear window and opposite side windows for others inside the house. A darkened living room, an empty bedroom, a kitchen. A camp stove on the counter, a few clean dishes stacked beside it. Neater inside than the trashed exterior.

He crouched at the eastern corner of the house, listening. No noise but for the labored breathing of the old man and the shake and spray of the paint can. The old man was still hard at work. By the sound of it, he'd moved to the front of the house, next to the porch. The light from a lantern—kerosene, most likely—glowed softly.

Liam exhaled, steadied himself, and burst into action. He swung around the side of the porch and aimed the M4 at the old man. "Hands up! Now!"

Chapter Two

The old man turned slowly and blinked his rheumy eyes several times, startled but seemingly unsurprised. He raised both arms up high. He dropped the spray can but not the bottle, the whiskey sloshing.

"I'll do whatcha ask," he said in a creaky voice. "Just don't make me drop my booze. It's all I got left in the world."

Liam circled the porch, eyes never leaving the old man. He came in close and kicked the shotgun out of the way, almost knocking over the kerosene lantern next to the man's feet.

"Keep your hands up where I can see them," Liam said.

The old man trembled, more from age than fear. His eyes were steady. "You don't gotta kill me for the booze. I'll give it to you, though it'll break my heart to do it."

"Keep the whiskey." Liam patted him down. He was armed with a Sig Sauer P365 holstered at his hip and a folded tactical knife in his right pocket. Liam confiscated them both. He tucked the pistol into his belt and the knife into his pocket. "Whose house is this?"

"My own."

Liam raised his brows.

The old man gestured at the houses across the street. "It's camouflage, ain't it? Gotta blend in these days. If my house looked all clean and kept, it'd draw attention. And that's the last thing I'm aiming to do." He grimaced. "It's also good therapy."

It made sense. Liam gestured with the M4. "Inside."

The old man narrowed his eyes. "What for? I told ya, I got nothing."

"Not planning to hurt you, but I'm not going to wait around out here for a sniper to take me out, either. Inside, now."

"Makes sense. If there were any snipers out here." The man grunted. "Someone after you?"

"I'm the one who gets to ask the questions, not you."

"I suppose that carbine says you're right. Let's go, then."

The old man picked up the lantern but left the spray can in the front yard. Liam retrieved the shotgun and followed him up the porch steps and inside the house, weapon pointed at his back. The man shuffled slowly, his shoulders bent with age.

Liam scanned the living room—two floral couches, an oak coffee table strewn with photography books, lamps that didn't work standing in the corners. On the wall, dusty photos of grown kids and a handful of grandkids.

The old man saw him looking. "They're all gone now. All of 'em."

Liam shut the door behind them. He set the shotgun in the far corner out of easy reach. He prodded the man into the kitchen, sat him down in a kitchen chair, and directed him to set the alcohol on the table. He secured the man's hands behind his back with zip ties from his pack.

The old man wiggled his arms but didn't try to fight him. "You don't have to do that."

"I'm clearing the house."

"Fine by me. You won't find anybody but ghosts, I'm afraid."

Liam checked the house, room by room. It felt cold and unused. After he was satisfied that it was indeed empty, ghosts excluded, he moved back to the kitchen.

"Could you be so kind as to free me now? These old arms are going numb."

Liam checked beneath the table and inside the cabinets for hidden weapons. Finding nothing, he cut the zip ties with his Gerber.

The man let out a groan, stretched, and rubbed his wrists. He rested his elbows on the table and clasped his hands around the whiskey bottle. "The name's Rob McPherson. Since you're a guest in my house and all, seems we should introduce ourselves."

"Liam Coleman." Liam angled himself so he could see out the kitchen window without exposing himself while also keeping an eye on the old man.

He wished his NVGs had infrared capability. The back yard glowed green—overgrown grass, sagging fence, and patio furniture filmed in dead leaves and detritus. Several houses stood behind the fence, their windows like broken teeth.

McPherson stared at him. Not indignant, and not afraid. "You a soldier? A real one?"

"There are fake soldiers around here?"

"You could say that. Which kind are you?"

Liam was a soldier. Didn't matter whether he was still in the service or not. His years of training were embedded in his bones, in every move he made, in his every thought. In the way he looked at everything as a potential threat, always assessing exit strategies and countermoves. It was as natural as breathing.

"You look like a soldier, is all I'm saying," the old man said. "A real one."

In his mid-thirties, Liam was rugged and lean, with broad shoulders, short chestnut hair, and gray-blue eyes. He was a loner. Reserved, quiet. A recluse, his brother Lincoln used to call him. Not good with people.

A man haunted by his past, by memories of his years overseas, but also everything that had happened since the EMP—the things he'd had to do, the choices he'd been forced to make.

He closed his eyes for the briefest moment and saw it all again. The plummeting plane, the careening wreckage, the dead bodies everywhere. His brother lying in the street, unmoving.

Jessa on the bed, blood staining her legs, her chest, the sheets beneath her.

Save him, Liam. Save my baby...

He forced his eyes open and cleared his throat. "I served my country. Always will, if that's what you're after."

"It is."

"I just want to ask you a few questions."

McPherson took a swig and wiped his mouth. "Ask them, so you can be on your way, and I can get back to my drinking." He narrowed his eyes. "Alone."

"Where is everyone? What happened to this town?"

"Same thing that's happened to every town hereabouts."

"And that is?"

"You looking for someone in particular?" McPherson asked instead of answering.

Liam hesitated. "The Brooks family. Evelyn and Travis Brooks. They have an infant with them. A little boy. They were staying with Jasmine Brooks, Travis's aunt."

McPherson rubbed his grizzled jaw and nodded. "I do know them. Arrived a few months ago. Good people."

Something released in Liam's chest. "They made it."

"They did." McPherson's mouth thinned. "Did you visit the farm?"

"I went there first."

That day he'd left Chicago, Liam had asked Evelyn Brooks to give him the address of their destination. He wanted to know where his nephew was—even if he never saw him again. He'd needed to know.

When he'd arrived in Tuscola yesterday morning, Liam had gone straight to the farm. Located on ten acres a few miles south of the town limits, the large rambling farmhouse had once been yellow and white with a big wrap-around porch. It had once been warm and homey and welcoming.

It was no longer any of those things.

The house had burned to the ground. So had the barn, a few sheds, and the chicken coup. Most of the fence was still standing upright, bright white against the blackened remains of the fire. Whatever animals had once grazed within that fence—horses, cows, pigs—were long gone.

Liam had walked the property for an hour. The charred bones of the structure no longer smoldered. He picked his way through the burnt remains of a home, the detritus of a life. Walls half-collapsed. A scorched couch with cushions melted to the frame. Furniture—credenzas, bookcases, dining room table, coffee table—reduced to charcoal. Bits of blackened curtain fluttered softly in the breeze. Everything filmed in a thick layer of soot.

The scene had been exposed to the elements for weeks. There were no footprints remaining. No vehicle tracks to follow. No clues other than destruction.

Liam's chest had gone tight, anger thrumming through him. A bright splinter of rage lodged in his heart. If someone had hurt them...if anyone had dared to lay a finger on his nephew...

He would find them, and he would kill them.

That he didn't find any burned skeletons was his only solace. It meant they hadn't died here.

Didn't mean they weren't dead somewhere else.

He'd retreated to Tuscola in search of information. A full day of recon had brought him to the defaced gray house with the weathervane, to Rob McPherson, his penchant for vandalism, and his fast-dwindling bottle of whiskey.

"Do you know what happened to them?" Liam asked flatly. "Who burned it down?"

"Not in particular," McPherson said. "But in general—the same thing happened to them that happened to everyone else here."

Liam checked the windows, looking for threats. Nothing. There was no one out there. No one at all. "Tell me."

The old man took a long swig of whiskey. He set the bottle down in front of him and stared at it for a minute before exhaling slowly, like he had to work himself up to tell the tale.

"When it first happened, the government came after a couple of weeks. They said they were making a big shelter for all the nearby towns south of Champaign and east of Decatur. It's a huge FEMA camp—more like a city, you ask me. No idea how many people, but a lot.

"They promised electricity, food and water, and medications for those that needed them to stay alive. Everyone was cold and hungry, and lots of people had already died by then. Most folks went willingly. No one was forced to go, but FEMA wasn't supplying food drop-offs or anything. If you wanted food, you went to the camp. That was it.

"Then after a month, FEMA pulled a bunch of our National Guard boys who were keeping order. Needed 'em more somewhere else, I guess. Probably to try and hold back the tide of chaos in Chicago. A losing battle, if you ask me. Anyway, a few weeks after that, the camp was overrun."

"Overrun? By whom?"

"They call themselves the Syndicate. I guess it's a riff off the National Crime Syndicate, that multi-ethnic confederation of organized crime and mafia bosses from the 1930s and 40s. These newer gangs out of Chicago are highly organized, powerful, and violent, like the cartels in Mexico or the old mob.

"They think they're wannabe soldiers or something. Must have robbed a National Guard armory because their weapons are military-grade, and they march around in uniforms. Their head guy, Alexander Poe, even fancies himself a commander. He's brutal and merciless. They all are."

"What happened?"

"These guys came in one fell swoop like an enemy invasion—hundreds of them. They have a few armored trucks and lots of automatic weapons. They took over the camp, killed everyone that resisted, and rounded up the town so we couldn't fight back or go for help. Took everybody who didn't manage to hide in time and forced them into the camp. They burned houses and businesses. They killed good people."

McPherson wiped at his eyes with the back of his arm. "They came through like locusts and confiscated everything—food, supplies, cows, and horses—and consolidated them at a few nearby Amish farms. Commander Poe put some of his own people with the Amish to guard them. They go and take whatever they want, whenever they want. And not just animals and supplies, either.

"They're using citizens at the FEMA camp as slave labor for the local farms. It's a hub for human trafficking—selling women and slaves. And they're using the Amish farms for food since they're completely operational without electricity."

Liam clenched his jaw. He wasn't surprised. The Syndicate were opportunists. They'd want FEMA camps—this one in particular—because they were soft targets rich in resources and women.

People like Poe were greedy for power and control and willing to subjugate anyone to get it. They were everywhere. But now, little was stopping these thugs and tyrants from destroying everything they touched.

FEMA and the rest of the government were completely overwhelmed by the needs of hundreds of millions of people scattered across the country. With the lack of communication, limited transportation, and rapidly declining resources, many rural communities were overlooked, understaffed, and forgotten.

It made them easy pickings for gangs, militia, or whoever had the most guns.

"Now everyone's just...gone," the old man said. "The Syndicate doesn't know I'm here. I keep the outside of the housing looking as trashed and abandoned as all the others. For the first week, they sent patrols to pick up any stragglers or anyone still hiding from them. Now, they don't come. Maybe they don't care anymore. What am I going to do to them? Nothing."

He shook his head wearily. "Never seen anything like that here. Never thought I would. I love my country, Mr. Coleman. I fought in 'Nam." McPherson paused and stared forlornly at his whiskey, now almost empty. "Is that how it is everywhere now?"

"No," Liam said. "It's not like this everywhere. Things aren't good. Plenty of evil thriving. But not like this. The National Guard would never allow this."

McPherson pursed his lips. "Now there are no watch dogs. No one left to protect the flock."

"There are a few," Liam said gruffly.

McPherson drank the last of the whiskey, tilting the bottle back to make sure he got every drop. He licked his lips and sighed. "You going to get your people out of there?"

"I am."

The old man nodded, satisfied. "They killed my neighbors. They were my friends. Any damage you need to do to get the job done, don't feel bad about it."

"I'll take that into consideration."

"And be careful. They're the shoot-first, ask-questions-never type."

"I can handle myself."

"I don't doubt it."

Liam removed the man's Sig Sauer from his waistband and set it on the counter. He placed the tactical knife beside it and moved to the back door. He scanned the backyard through the window in the door before turning back to McPherson. "Anything you need?"

"You got an MRE by chance? Never thought I'd say this in a million years, but I'd love one. Whatever flavor you got."

Liam smiled a little. "I do."

Chapter Three

It didn't take Liam long to find FEMA Shelter #209. It took far longer to find the people he was searching for.

He'd spent the last two days reconning the camp. Staying inside the tree line, ghillie suit in place, glassing the area constantly. Climbing trees before dawn to get enough elevation to see clearly. Moving positions every few hours to get eyes on a different section of the camp. Tracking patrols. Security shifts. Stationary positions. The movement and daily schedule of the civilians.

The old man was right. FEMA Shelter #209 was as large as a city. Dozens of huge white tents plus hundreds—thousands—of small modular buildings like single-wide trailers set in a grid pattern, all surrounded by a tall chain link fence lined with concertina wire.

The Syndicate thugs carried long guns and were dressed in BDUs, the name tapes and patches removed from their uniforms. They looked like soldiers, purposefully preying upon a civilian's natural inclination to respect and obey American armed forces.

Guards patrolled the perimeter on an hourly circuit. Two sentries were posted in static positions every five hundred meters. Dozens more maintained order within the fence.

They were well-armed and organized but lacked the rigorous discipline of the military. Liam would need to find a way to exploit that.

The civilians looked tired, weakened, and worn out. They edged out of the way when a guard stomped past, many flinching. They feared them.

He witnessed several of them verbally berating civilians. Two others knocked a tray from a woman's hands and laughed when she knelt to pick the food off the ground. More than once, leering guards harassed women and young teenage girls.

Every hour that he watched, Liam's anger grew, a simmering rage seething just beneath the surface of his tightly controlled demeanor. If he'd had his Spec Op team with him, he'd already be storming the camp, putting an end to this brutality.

He forced himself to focus on his mission. He took breaks only to answer the call of nature and snack on a protein bar or open a can of beans and inhale the contents cold. He'd refilled his water bottles at McPherson's house from a handpump attached to his well.

He'd left the man two MREs. The rest he needed for himself. It was a good thing he'd brought supplies for several days. He was willing to wait as long as it took.

Mid-morning on the third day, he finally found them.

He was tucked in the fork of two thick oak branches about twenty-five feet off the ground, glassing another section of the endless grid. He'd rewoven his ghillie suit to include leaves and branches.

He froze mid-scan down a wide row between the tents which led to a section of showers and bathrooms. A woman strode along the path. Slim build, warm brown skin, short black hair streaked with gray.

Pulse thudding in his throat, he followed her with the binoculars until he was certain.

The last time Liam had seen Mrs. Brooks was the day of the EMP, when he came to deliver her grandson. She'd been smartly dressed, her graying hair stylishly bobbed, her makeup perfect.

Now, she wore oversized sweatpants beneath a tan jacket. Her hair was mussed and ragged. Dark shadows rimmed her eyes, her face worn with exhaustion and stress.

She held a small child dressed in a little blue coat and a long-sleeved onesie printed with blue airplanes. His nephew.

Liam's heart clenched like a fist. Memories of that day seared through his mind. Everything he'd lost. His twin brother, Lincoln. Lincoln's wife, Jessa.

That terrible day, Liam had brought Lincoln and Jessa's child to the Brooks—Jessa's parents—in Chicago, and instructed them to flee the city before the rioting and chaos took over.

Giving his nephew up felt like a giant hand had reached in and torn a wide-open hole where his heart had resided.

It had been the right thing to do to bring the baby to his grandparents. But Liam should have gone with them, should have escorted them to Tuscola himself and made sure they were safe.

His heart had been shattered into a million pieces of grief, loss, and regret, and he'd made a foolish decision. He'd allowed them to leave Chicago on their own.

He had made many mistakes in his life. He regretted each one.

His courage had never failed him in a moment of combat. Not once. He was the first to surge into battle, the first to put himself in the line of fire for his fellow soldiers and brothers in arms. He did not hesitate to fight, to eliminate a threat if that's what it took.

But when it came to emotions, to people and relationships and their messy complexity—he was not brave. He'd allowed that fear—that grief—to sever his connection with his nephew, whom he'd loved the instant he was born with a fierceness Liam couldn't name or quantify.

It was far easier to remain isolated and alone.

No longer. He'd learned differently.

He couldn't do anything to change the past. He'd lost what he'd lost, and they weren't ever coming back. But he was determined to make this right. He was here to atone.

Liam followed Mrs. Brooks with the binoculars and memorized the location of the modular building she entered. A pole with a sign scrawled with "Quadrant 4: Zone C: Row 15" helped orient him. The Brooks' trailer was located three buildings directly south of the pole.

He waited and watched a while longer. At 1900 hours, both Mr. and Mrs. Brooks emerged from their trailer. Mr. Brooks carried the baby in a sling, facing inward. Liam couldn't get a good glimpse of the baby's face before they disappeared between the buildings.

He'd seen enough. He had the information he needed. What he needed now was a few hours of rest. Lights out was at 2200 hours.

He retreated until he'd put a good half-mile between himself and the camp before unzipping his pack again and pulling out a tarp. He spread it on the ground beneath a tree and used his pack as a pillow, his M4 resting across his chest.

He didn't sleep but allowed himself to drift into a state of half-awareness, almost like meditation. He shut down every thought, stilled his body, aware only of his senses, alert only to a potential threat.

Time passed. He rested.

At 2245 hours, he sat up. Drank some water. Packed his things. Adjusted his plate carrier and did a systems check.

He was awake now, fully alert.

He would get them out of that hellhole tonight. Sneak in, grab them, and sneak out.

His pulse thudded against his skull. Adrenaline iced his veins. There were a lot of ways this could all go wrong. Too many ways to count, although he'd analyzed each one a dozen times. The stress points and weaknesses.

He'd planned for contingencies. Had backups to his backup plan. Multiple exit strategies.

He was only one man. One man with three souls to protect and defend.

He was vastly outnumbered. If the hostiles were alerted to his presence, it would be dozens to one in seconds.

He couldn't afford to make a mistake. He wouldn't make a mistake.

This time, Liam would not fail.

Chapter Four

Liam shouldered his pack and lowered his NVGs over his eyes. He made his way soundlessly through the trees. He moved slowly, mapping out his steps ahead of time, aware of twigs and crackling leaves in his path. He walked heel-to-toe and bent at the knees.

The moon was out. The night sky was cloudless, the stars sharp bright shards. A silvery glow limned the trees, the branches, and each blade of grass.

The moonlight meant he was more exposed.

He needed to be careful.

Before the edge of the tree line, he paused and checked his watch. 2258. The patrol passed by this section of fence at 2300 hours, again at 2400 hours, and every hour after that.

He took out his binoculars and glassed the area. The patrol was right on time. Two guards with M16s on slings and flashlight beams sweeping back and forth trudged along the inside perimeter of the fence.

The fence was interspersed with security floodlights powered by a generator. This section of the fence was located equidistant from the farthest lights. This area was dark.

A few hundred meters east inside the perimeter, the sentries posted at the static position leaned against the fence. One smoked a cigarette. The second one looked like he was already sleeping—his head tilted back, eyes closed.

Liam waited in complete silence, hardly breathing.

Once the patrol had passed, he examined the area one last time before moving out into the thirty meters of open space between the tree line and the fence. He kept low and moved fast, running at a crouch, his back twinging in protest but he didn't slow.

He reached the fence and squatted, dropping the M4 on its sling. He reached around in his pack and pulled out the wire cutters. He didn't usually pack tools in his go-bag, but for this trip, he'd brought several additional 'just in case' items.

He glanced toward the sentries. They weren't paying attention.

Every sense alert, he focused on a single strand of wire, since it required the fewest cuts. He snipped from the bottom up, making sure to cut a large enough hole that he could slip through quickly and easily without snagging his pack or clothes.

Mr. and Mrs. Brooks needed to be able to get through easily as well.

The trailers were packed close together with only a few feet between them. Every ten trailers deep, a wider parallel pathway lead to bathrooms, the mess hall, workstations, or wherever else the civilians needed to go.

It was imperative he eliminate the sentries on his egress route. Speed was of the essence.

He drew his Gerber tactical knife and moved east quickly and expertly, a dark form slipping from shadow to shadow, from modular building to modular building.

Sentry one, a slim black man in his thirties with a goatee, dragged on his cigarette and blew out a stream of smoke, killing his night vision. Sentry two, a larger man with a beer gut and a thick beard, continued to doze, snoring lightly, his weapon not even in his hands.

Neither of them was alert nor watchful. Neither prepared for what was coming.

Liam bent, picked up a stone, and tossed it. The first sentry turned toward the sound.

Liam slipped up behind him, placed his hand over the man's throat, and drove his knife through the base of his skull.

He dropped the hostile almost soundlessly and moved to the second one.

The dozing sentry snorted and jerked himself awake. His eyes bulged in horror as Liam slid his knife across the man's jugular. He gurgled and gasped, clutching at his throat. It took him a little longer to die. But he couldn't speak, that's what mattered.

Swiftly, Liam dragged the bodies behind the closest trailer. He wiped his knife on the thigh of sentry two and sheathed it.

He continued his mission.

The night was filled with the quiet sounds of thousands of people sleeping—heavy breathing, snoring, shifting, snorting, and a toddler crying somewhere. The air smelled faintly of plastic, burnt food, and body odor.

He found the pole with the correct designation: "Quadrant 4: Zone C: Row 15" and made his way toward it.

A door opened to his left. Liam ducked behind the side wall of the closest trailer, his heart hammering.

Footsteps thudded as a figure closed the door and walked a few steps. It was quiet for a moment, then the snap of a lighter and a cigarette being lit. Someone sighed heavily.

The smoke tickled his nostrils. He restrained a sneeze. Liam ducked low and peered around the corner, leading with the muzzle of the M4.

A woman wearing an opened coat over purple polka-dotted pajamas leaned against the trailer wall next to the door. She tilted her head back, her eyes closed, the lit cigarette tucked between two fingers. Moonlight glimmered over her dirty blonde hair and highlighted the weary lines of her face.

Not a hostile—a civilian. Threat level low, although she could alert them if she saw him. Liam made a mental note of her location as he moved along the backside of the trailer and hurried down the narrow aisle between the next several buildings.

He paused when he reached the third trailer down from the pole. The Brooks' trailer was located one layer inside the grouping, surrounded by trailers crammed in close. It wasn't as exposed as the ones located along the major pathways.

He circled it, staying alert for any passing soldiers or other sleepless citizens. He saw nothing. A generator hummed softly. The lights along the perimeter fence gave off a dull buzz in the silence. He could still smell cigarette smoke.

The windows were accessible but high. The front door was constructed of flimsy aluminum and wouldn't provide much of a hindrance.

He slipped off his pack, unzipped a compartment, and pulled out his lockpick set. It didn't take long to jimmy the lock open.

Liam stepped inside the heavily shadowed trailer and shut the door quietly behind him. The trailer was tiny and resembled a camping trailer—minuscule kitchen, with a table that folded up, so the living room also doubled as a dining room.

The narrow door to the single bedroom was open. At the foot of the bed, a makeshift bassinet made from a dresser drawer lay on the floor. His tiny nephew lay sleeping inside it.

Evelyn Brooks was sitting up in bed. A small dark shadow highlighted by the light filtering in from the bedroom window. She held a kitchen knife in one hand and pointed it at him. "Don't you dare come any closer."

Liam stopped and lifted both hands, palms out, weapon pointed away from the bed. "It's Liam Coleman."

Mrs. Brooks fumbled for a flashlight on her bedside table with her left hand and flicked it on. She pointed it at his face.

He blinked, squinting against the harsh glare, but didn't move. She needed to see that he wasn't a danger.

Her face went ashen. "It's...it's you."

Her husband rolled over in bed next to her. "Honey, what—" He caught sight of Liam and sat up quickly, instantly awake. "Liam? What are you doing here?"

"I shouldn't have left you alone in Chicago. I needed to make sure you were okay."

"In the middle of the night?" Mr. Brooks asked incredulously. He was slim, his short hair and beard mostly gray, faint wrinkles lining his eyes and mouth. Jessa had told Liam once that her father was an English professor. Or, he had been before the EMP. "How? How did you get in here?"

Mrs. Brooks shifted in the bed, swung her legs around, and sat on the edge of the bed. "They wouldn't have let him in. He must have snuck in. And if he can sneak in, he can sneak back out."

Liam's mouth twitched. Mrs. Brooks was as quick and intelligent as her daughter, Jessa, who'd been an OB-GYN—a damned good one.

"Those thugs burned our farm down," Mr. Brooks said. "They forced us here and won't let us leave."

"They act like they're soldiers, but they're not," Mrs. Brooks said.

"No, they're not," Liam said. "Not even close."

"How can this be America?" Mrs. Brooks said fiercely. "How can this have happened?"

"It's not like this everywhere," Liam said. "Mr. and Mrs. Brooks, I came to get you out of here, to take you and the baby somewhere safe."

Mrs. Brooks stared at him. "You have a plan to get us out?"

"Yes, ma'am, I do."

In the few times Liam had interacted with her, she had always seemed like an intelligent, capable, and decisive woman. She did not disappoint him now.

Mrs. Brooks sucked in a deep breath. "Let's go."

She rose to her feet, came around the bed, and gently picked up the baby. He grunted and squirmed but didn't wake up. "But you must call me Evelyn, Liam. And call my husband Travis."

She cradled the baby's sleeping head with the palm of her hand. In the dim light, he was all golden-brown skin, tiny squished features, and black curly hair. "And Little Liam."

Emotion surged in Liam's chest—gratitude, relief, love, loss, and regret. Emotions he couldn't afford to feel right now. He longed to hold his nephew again, but this was not the time. Not yet.

Liam cleared his throat. "We need to go. Get dressed and pack what the baby needs. Hurry, before the patrol returns."

"What happens if they discover us?" Evelyn's mouth tightened. "These aren't good men. They've hurt people who've tried to leave. They take people away and no one ever sees them again. Travis's aunt—she had diabetes. They wouldn't give her the proper amount of insulin. She died in here. They didn't care."

"I'll take care of them," Liam said. "Be as quiet as possible. And follow my lead."

"We will." Travis stuffed bottles and cans of baby formula and diapers, wipes, and butt cream into a backpack. "We don't want to stay here a minute longer than we have to."

Evelyn dressed the baby in a coat and hat, then tucked him into a baby carrier and wrapped the straps around her shoulders and waist.

"What if he cries?" Liam said.

Evelyn held up a pacifier. "I have this, but it's no guarantee. Babies cry."

Liam nodded tightly. He didn't know much about babies, but he knew they were unpredictable little creatures. Tension torqued through him.

Travis rested his hand on Liam's forearm. "I know how to shoot a gun. Let me help you."

Liam clenched his jaw. He didn't trust anyone but himself, but if they were discovered, he would need Travis's help.

He unholstered his Glock 19 and handed it to the man grip-first. "The magazine is fully loaded with a round already in the chamber."

"Thank you," Travis said.

Liam said, "Don't thank me yet."

Chapter Five

Travis held open the door for Evelyn and Liam. Travis went first with Evelyn and the baby in the middle, Liam taking up the rear.

The chilled night air hit them like a slap. Spring or not, the nights still dipped into the low forties.

The baby woke up. His little arms flailed on either side of the carrier. He let out an unhappy whimper. It was cold and he wasn't warm and snuggled in his bed.

"Shhhh," Evelyn whispered. He let out a few soft, gurgling whimpers.

"Hey! What are you doing?" To their right, the cigarette lady stepped out from the shadows between two trailers. Her cigarette dangled from her lips. The ember glowed like a single red eye.

Travis and Evelyn halted.

"None of your concern." Anxiety roiled in Liam's gut. He kept the muzzle of his gun lowered at a forty-five-degree angle, but the threat was clear.

He gestured at the Brooks. "We've got to go."

"You can't go anywhere." Cigarette Lady's voice rose. "It's not allowed. Who is this guy? Why does he have a gun?"

"Janet, please," Evelyn said. "We're not bothering you. Just pretend you didn't see us."

"Why would I do that?" Janet asked, her voice obstinate, resentful.

"She's going to be trouble," Evelyn said under her breath. She patted the baby's bottom and gave him his pacifier. "She doesn't like us."

Liam checked their six. "Just walk."

They kept moving. Their boots thudded across the worn dirt, dead grass, and patches of dirty half-melted snow. The lights along the perimeter fence grew brighter, the shadows between the trailers on either side of them dark and thick.

Janet followed them. Her nightgown billowed behind her, her coat flapping, her boots slapping the ground. "You're breaking the rules! You can't do that! Who is he? One of those insurgents?"

"No!" Evelyn said. "He's just a friend. One of the soldiers."

Liam reached an intersection. He swept the M4 to the left, then the right. Both worn paths were empty. Didn't mean they'd remain that way, especially with belligerent Janet trailing after them. The scent of her damn cigarette was cloying, irritating his nose, his throat.

"He's not like them. He's different." Janet scowled. She picked up her pace. "You trying to escape, is that it?"

"No!" Travis said tightly. "Please, Janet. Just go back to bed."

"Shut up!" someone shouted through the window of the trailer to their left.

Liam winced. They were making too much noise. Drawing too much attention. He scanned the area, checked behind them. Still no hostiles in sight.

"'See something, say something'" Janet quipped. "That's what they told us. We get extra rations if we report—"

Liam whirled around. He couldn't shoot an unarmed civilian. Didn't mean he wasn't tempted. Didn't mean he couldn't make her think he might do it.

He shifted the M4 and aimed it at Janet's chest.

The woman halted, startled and flustered. Her mouth opened in a big red O.

"Lady, you need to turn around right now," Liam said. "Go back to your trailer, crawl into bed, and go to sleep. This is just a nightmare. If you don't want it to become real, I suggest you obey immediately."

She took a wobbling step backward. Her cigarette slipped from her fingers and dropped to the dirt. "You can't—you have no right—"

She wasn't going to shut up. She was a threat.

It never ceased to amaze him how easily human beings could be convinced to act against their own self-interest. This woman was ready and willing to betray her fellow prisoners in order to endear herself to the tyrants who'd imprisoned her, too.

Maybe some people got so used to the walls of a prison that they didn't want anything else.

Liam reversed the M4 and gripped it by the handguard. He took two quick strides forward and struck the side of the woman's head with the buttstock. Not hard enough to truly harm her, just enough to remove her as an immediate threat. He didn't like it, but it had to be done.

She went down immediately, lights out before she hit the ground.

Travis gaped at Janet's fallen form. "Did you just—"

"She would have shouted an alarm."

Evelyn crouched awkwardly next to her, one hand steadying the baby, and felt the woman's pulse. "She's not dead. Just unconscious. She'll be fine when she wakes up."

Travis helped his wife to her feet and squeezed her hand. He gave a resigned nod. "I understand."

Liam felt no sense of relief. They weren't out of danger yet. Patrols were everywhere. He quickly dragged Janet's unconscious body behind the nearest trailer.

Evelyn stroked Little Liam's hair and patted his bottom. His lids, half-closed, grew heavy.

"The hole in the fence is already cut," Liam said. "When we get there, go through it and run into the woods. I'll lay down covering fire, then follow you. If we get separated, there's a farm one mile straight south on Ridgeline Road, which you'll hit just past this strip of woods. Sun Haven Farm. Rendezvous there. Anyone comes at you, you shoot them, Travis. Don't hesitate."

He motioned for the Brooks to keep moving. He scanned their surroundings, examining each trailer, searching the shadows for movement, checking behind them.

Rapid footsteps sounded to their right.

Adrenaline kicked his heart into high gear. Liam spun left and pushed Evelyn and Travis around the next corner. They pressed against the side of the trailer. Liam in front of them, carbine raised.

The footsteps drew closer.

A hostile rounded the corner of the row of trailers ten meters to their right. Young, Caucasian, baby-faced. The M16 in his hands carried low and not in the ready position.

The kid caught sight of them and froze. His eyes went wide as he took in the scene—Liam armed to the teeth, a woman with an infant, her husband huddled protectively beside her, also armed.

Liam's finger rested on the trigger. Ready to fire at the smallest movement, the faintest finger twitch. The guy narrowed his eyes, he was dead. He opened his mouth to shout a warning, he was dead.

Liam would not allow harm to come to his nephew or to Jessa's parents. He would die before he let that happen. And Liam would not die easily.

The hostile stared at them, startled and unsure. He didn't raise his weapon. He didn't move a muscle.

They stared back, hearts pounding. The tension stretched taut as a rubber band about to snap.

"I—I heard a baby," he stammered finally in a low whisper.

"Please," Evelyn said. "We're just trying to leave. That's all."

The young man's gaze darted to the baby. Something shifted in his face. The muzzle of the rifle lowered a few inches.

"I know it's not right," he said. "None of this is right. Go. I won't stop you."

Liam nodded. He still didn't take his finger off the trigger.

"Thank you," Evelyn whispered. "Thank you."

The hostile didn't say anything. He turned and jogged away from them, headed south. Liam watched him go, then hurried the Brooks on.

In less than a minute, they were almost to the fence.

Liam strode ahead of them and checked the last intersection. He inched out past the nearest trailer, weapon leading, and swept left, then right.

A shout sounded fifty meters to the east. Someone had discovered the bodies of the sentries.

Little Liam startled awake. He let out a wail.

Evelyn tried frantically to shush him, to no avail. It was already too late.

"Go!" Liam took up a defensive position behind a trailer. The trailer provided concealment but little cover. He couldn't get pinned down here or he was in trouble.

Evelyn and Travis ran to the fence. Evelyn knelt awkwardly and pulled the chain link apart while Travis scooted through on his hands and knees. He twisted around and held it open for her.

Little Liam's cries grew louder. Loud as trumpet blasts in the stillness, alerting everyone to their presence within a quarter-mile radius.

A flashlight beam pinned them in place.

"Hey! You there! Stop right now!" a deep voice shouted.

Chapter Six

Two hostiles ran toward them from the east. A hundred meters away, maybe less. Several more came at them from the west.

There was no time for hesitation, for indecision. Every second could mean life or death. And he and his weren't the ones who would die. Not today. Not this time.

Liam selected three round bursts and aimed at the hostiles. Exhaled. Fired.

The first man fell. Then a second and third. Several came running to take their place.

Four more hostiles appeared along the central path perpendicular to the fence. Muzzle flashes lit up the night. The rat-a-tat of automatic gunfire.

Rounds zinged past Liam's head. They punched into the trailer walls behind him with pings and thunks. A bullet struck the ground a foot from his boots. Clods of dirt sprayed his shins.

Screams and shrieks filled the air. Trailer doors flung open as people stumbled from their beds and fled in terror.

Evelyn yelped. Out of the corner of his eye, Liam glimpsed her wriggling half through the fence. Travis squatted on the other side, grabbing her arm with one hand and attempting to jerk her through. She was stuck fast.

A jagged end of chain link had hooked the shoulder strap of the baby carrier. With her arms and torso already through the hole, Evelyn couldn't reach back and untangle it. Neither could Travis. Little Liam let out several wet, hiccupping cries.

Fear pierced Liam. Arrowed straight through his heart. He did not need to think it through. It was not a choice. He'd give his life a thousand times for Lincoln and Jessa's child.

Just like he would've given himself a hundred times over if it might have prevented what happened in Chicago, if he'd been able to save his brother and the woman he'd loved.

Time slowed. Action unfolding frame by frame. Liam moved not by thought but muscle memory, his years of training taking over.

He surged out from behind the trailer, seized a frag grenade from his chest rig, and tossed it a good twenty meters in the direction of the oncoming hostiles. He leapt back behind the trailer for cover.

The explosion lit up the night. The ground shook beneath his boots. The trailer rattled against his back. More screams and shrieks of agony split the air.

Liam broke cover and moved into the wide pathway, aiming and firing short bursts. A half-dozen hostiles were already down, ripped apart by the frag. They wouldn't be getting up.

He dropped to the ground, coming to his knees in a crouch in front of Evelyn and his nephew. Shielding them with his body as he knelt, bracing the M4's stock against his shoulder, eye squinting through the optics, finger squeezing the trigger.

Rounds struck the dirt, and pinged the fence on either side of him. A bullet struck Liam's chest, knocking him back. The plate carrier protected him from penetration but not the punch of the round. It would leave an ugly bruise.

Bullets whizzed past his head. A fiery pain struck his right side just below his plate carrier. He couldn't afford to look to see how bad it was.

"We're free!" Travis shouted. "I got her free!"

"Go!" Liam shouted.

They were out of time. More hostiles were coming, running from several directions. Too many of them. They'd overwhelm him in a moment.

Liam hurled a flashbang to cover their retreat. He turned away, covering his eyes and opening his mouth. The explosive bang slammed into his eardrums, the incredibly harsh, brilliant flash still bright against his closed and covered eyelids.

The hostiles fell back, momentarily blinded, disoriented, and stunned. They stumbled around dizzily, like they were drunk, clutching at their ears and faces. One man screamed and fumbled at the flash burns on his thighs.

They'd start to "come to" in ten to fifteen seconds, though they wouldn't be able to see or hear clearly for a while. Liam let loose a barrage of firepower, mowing down any hostile in sight.

His own ears ringing, he turned and flung himself through the hole in the fence. The jagged ends of the chain link scratched his cheek and neck, scraped his clothes, and nearly snagged on his pack, but he ripped through.

He leapt to his feet and spun around. He backed away, laying down cover fire on any stragglers as the Brooks fled into the night. They raced toward the woods thirty meters away, out in the open, exposed.

Liam fired another short burst. He felt the bolt lock back and did a tactical reload. He turned and ran after the Brooks, stumbling, white-hot pain radiating from his ribs, an explosion of agony that stole his breath from his lungs.

He reached the woods just as the hostiles opened fire again. Dirt sprayed as bullets struck the ground meters to his left and right.

He pressed himself against the thick trunk of an oak tree and inhaled sharply, steadying his heart rate. He was alone. As instructed, Evelyn and Travis had gone on ahead of him.

He needed to stop their pursuers, give them time.

Blood leaked slick and wet from the hole in his side. It drenched the front of his shirt and his vest. He leaned out from the tree and swept the fence line with a barrage of firepower.

Two more hostiles went down. Then three more. Return fire ceased.

For the moment.

Time to go. Liam grabbed his IFAC and wrapped a Celox pad on the wound. It would have to do for now.

He turned and disappeared into the trees. The forest was dark and shadowed. Dead leaves crunched beneath his boots. The air smelled like damp earth and pine and sap.

Even wounded, even with his back injury, he was incredibly fit. He loped through the trees at a steady pace, his teeth gritted, his surging adrenaline blocking the worst of the pain.

When he reached the farm where he'd stashed the vehicle in the barn, Evelyn and Travis were waiting for him. Evelyn had fixed a bottle for Little Liam, who'd fallen back asleep.

"Let me drive," Travis said when he caught sight of Liam. "Liam, you take the backseat. Evelyn, take care of him."

"I'm fine," Liam insisted.

"You're hurt," Evelyn said sharply.

"I'm fi—"

"Liam Coleman, listen to me right now." Evelyn drew herself to her full height. "I might not have had the privilege of knowing you well, but I knew your brother. Lincoln was my son-in-law—don't you forget that. I know you through him. You spend your whole life taking care of people and forget you need to be taken care of yourself. You're going to let me help you."

He didn't have any fight left in him. The pain was fast sapping his stamina. The adrenaline dump left him shaky and light-headed. He didn't have much of a choice.

He tugged his keys from his pocket and tossed them to Travis. "I see where Jessa got her stubbornness."

Travis unlocked the truck. Liam winced as he clambered into the back seat. He eased off his pack and set it on the floor beside him, but he kept the M4 in his lap.

On the other side of the backseat, Evelyn strapped the baby into the car seat Liam had scavenged and installed—with help—before he'd left.

Evelyn's eyes went shiny. She cleared her throat and pointed at his pack. "You have a first aid kit in there? Let's get you fixed up."

Travis started the engine and backed out of the barn. "Where to?"

Even talking hurt. "There's a map in the glove compartment with the back roads marked. Stay off I-57. Keep alert. Head for a town in southwest Michigan called Fall Creek."

Evelyn sat sideways in the middle of the seat next to him, bracing herself awkwardly with one leg against the back of the passenger seat. Little Liam whimpered a little but quickly fell back to sleep in his car seat.

She pulled out Israeli trauma bandages and Celox blood clotting granules out of Liam's pack, along with his filled water bottle. "You're in good hands. I'm an ER nurse. Lucky for you, it's a through and through."

Darkness wavered at the corners of his vision. Fighting unconsciousness, he strained his ears for any sounds of pursuit. The growl of engines, shouting, gunfire.

But there was nothing. No one followed them as they roared onto the backroads, swerving to miss the stalled and abandoned cars still littering most roads in America.

Commander Poe's men must have lost them in the woods or else didn't have a large enough force to effectively pursue them.

"You have anyone?" Evelyn asked. "To take care of you?"

He clenched his teeth against the pain. "I do."

"That's good." Evelyn's face dimmed, her voice going distant and far away. Just before he blacked out, she said, "Because I think you're going to live."

Chapter Seven

Liam didn't know how much time had passed. He drifted in and out of consciousness, pain his only companion.

Nightmares of combat seared through his mind—the boom of machine guns and mortar fire, rounds punching past him on all sides, smoke billowing, grenades exploding, the groans of his lost teammates.

"Liam," a voice said urgently. "Liam!"

He jolted awake, his brain scrabbling through layers of darkness as he instinctively reached for his weapon. He seized his M4 from the seat beside him and struggled to sit up. Pain slashed through his ribs.

"How do you feel?" Evelyn asked.

Liam grunted as the cobwebs cleared from his head. The truck rattled over potholes, every bump in the asphalt jarring his injury.

The pain was incredible. The lower half of his shirt had been cut away. Fresh bandages wrapped his torso from his belly button to his ribs. Only a small amount of blood had leaked through. "Still alive."

Evelyn pursed her lips. "Good enough."

"What did I miss?" He gritted his teeth and quickly scanned their surroundings.

Dawn peeked over the edge of the horizon. The sky above the road was painted in shades of sherbet orange and vibrant pinks and purples.

Flat farmland pockmarked with occasional farmhouses set far off the road to both the left and right.

Not many vehicles marred the road along this stretch; most of them had made it to the shoulder. The tree line was set back several hundred meters. Few places for a good ambush. Still, he didn't relax. Couldn't relax.

"We bypassed St. Anne's just a bit ago. You've been out for about a hundred miles. We've got a roadblock. National Guard, it looks like." Travis slowed the truck to a crawl. "What do we do?"

One hundred meters ahead, concrete barriers and spools of concertina wire narrowed the road to a single lane. Several Humvees parked at 45-degree angles and a half-dozen armed soldiers dressed in BDUs were stationed at the roadblock just ahead of a blue and red sign emblazoned with the words "Welcome to Indiana: Crossroads of America."

The soldiers caught sight of them and stood at attention, rifles point their way. Liam spotted a female soldier kneeling near the left Humvee, armed with a scoped carbine, another crouched behind the right armored vehicle with an M16.

"Just drive up nice and slow. Do what they tell you."

A soft coo drew Liam's attention. The baby was awake. He twisted in his car seat, his eyes on Liam, his fat little arms reaching for the buttstock of the M4.

"That is not a chew toy," Evelyn said sternly.

Little Liam giggled and watched everything with a bright-eyed awe. He was a beautiful child. He had Jessa's honey brown skin and Lincoln's arresting gray-blue eyes. The same as Liam's own.

He was safe, now. Safe to grow up free, not in a cage. Everyone trapped at FEMA Shelter #209 deserved the same.

"What do we tell them?" Travis asked nervously.

"The truth," Liam said.

At the checkpoint, a female Chinese-American soldier in her mid-twenties approached the driver's side window and requested their licenses, registration, and destination. Her nametape read Zhang.

Three other Guardsmen listened as the Brooks told their story. They tried to keep their expressions neutral, but Liam read their surprise, anger, and then outrage as the Brooks described the atrocities they'd witnessed and endured, American citizens being held against their will.

"The lack of communication and oversight has caused a lot of problems," Zhang said. "I can't say we haven't heard rumors of organized crime taking over towns, but nothing like this." One of the Guardsmen stepped aside and spoke quietly into his radio.

"We're contacting our commanding officer," Zhang said. "I'm sure General Bryant will be informed and take decisive action. The General is a good man. The Illinois National Guard has been busting our collective butts to put this state, and this country, back together. We won't allow this to continue. Not on our watch. Not while America still has blood running through her veins. And she does, I assure you. Things are hard. They'll be hard for years. But we are still free."

"We don't give up," Evelyn said.

"Exactly." Zhang waved them forward. "I wish you well on the rest of your journey."

The last hundred miles back were uneventful. A few stragglers on the road eyed them greedily, but Liam's M4 dissuaded anyone from attacking them.

After a few hours, they wound around the last bend in the road. The bridge over Fall Creek appeared in the distance. Liam's heart swelled in his chest.

It was just a small town like any other. But here was where the people he cared about lived. And that made all the difference.

"This is it," he said, his voice choked with unexpected emotions—relief, anticipation, gratitude. And something else, something he hadn't expected to ever feel again, but knew was true with every beat of his heart. This, truly, was where he belonged. "We're home."

Special Acknowledgements

I wanted to give a special thanks to all of the authors who contributed to this anthology. Thank you for listening to and believing in this unknown guy with a vision. Of course, this entire thing wouldn't have been as great as it is without those wonderful people who believed in this project throughout the Kickstarter campaign. They are:

Trace "Ludo" Kelly
Charles Fitak
NoNameTokyo
Shawn Kelley
Eugene & Tomi Schuster
Susan R
Craig Pendan
Mashidin
Ulfsbane Farlander
8BitVal
Bill Kennedy
Apocalypse Dan
Scott "Akin" Atkins
Steven Sheeley

Makaila Fourniea

Kris S.

John Senn

Schweetz

Reality Crashes Brain

Thomas Keith Stone

Todd A Bollman

Eric Rumfelt

Randall Moore

Henry L Strong

Eddie Joo

Benjamin Smith

Michael Axe

James (Jay) Leroux

Jacob Jones

Audrey Riggs

Austin Hoffey

Scott Casey

Additional Thanks to These Kickstarter Supporters:

Moida Shirote

Liz Eddy

Dennis Robinson

Alecia

Howard Blakeslee

Laura Ruth Justice

Israel Sánchez

J Rositas

Josue Oyuela
K.C. Wiley
R. Munden
Just Peachy
Ryan Coombes
Derek & Stephanie Dwilson
Donald M.K. Avila
Colleen Feeney
Rachel Peterson
Jose Chavez
David Donatelli
Rofel Subido
SP Samedi
Abricot
Colby Rodeheaver
Risa Scranton
Honey Bunny ☐(^ ☐ ^)☐
Teddy Garrett
Drew Wheeler
Dan-o
Scott MacFarlane
Mike Galligan
E.M. Middel
Veenie
mdtommyd
Mark Clerkin
Krista Bergren-Walsh
Jordan G Ritchie
Aubrey Reese
Sam Shepherd

Caleb Knight

Lee Alexander

Doc

John Markley

Joshua Thompson

Evan Stanley

Doctor Mocker

Taengele

Kayla O'Hare

Alexander Wood

Joshua Cooper

Kathya

Elaine Tindill-Rohr

Bryant Stewart

David Wall

Vegas Morrison

Destroyer of Worlds

B. Harris

The Shunnarah-Reeds

Elfego Baca

Familie De Koster

Constantí Montsó i Cadena

Jennifer Flora Black

Trip Space-Parasite

Jonathan Mendonca

Richard O'Shea

Jacob Searcy

Eron Wyngarde

Mark Carter

Andrew Walklate

Kari-Ann Stokka
Karri Kadin
Luis Leal
Lothiat Caulderon
Liu Ellens
Joseph Cox
Shane Ede
James McGuiggan
Richard Parker
Kelly Snyder
Dione Basseri
K Stoker
Michael Mahoney
E Lynn
Melevorn
Hauke von Bremen

CPSIA information can be obtained
at www.ICGtesting.com
Printed in the USA
JSHW080442181122
33388JS00002B/4

9 781777 725235

Made in the USA
Columbia, SC
19 February 2025